CHARMING THE SERPENT

Revelation 12:7-12

[signature]

Benny:

I love you! Hope this will bring back memories.

CHARMING THE SERPENT

Patrick H. Carter

iUniverse, Inc.

New York Lincoln Shanghai

Charming the Serpent

iUniverse, Inc.

For information address:
iUniverse, Inc.
2021 Pine Lake Road, Suite 100
Lincoln, NE 68512
www.iuniverse.com

Author's Contact Information:
2002 Lakeville Drive
Kingwood, Texas 77339
Phone (281) 358-0225
path carter@aol.com

ISBN: 0-595-26966-4

Printed in the United States of America

CONTENTS

▼

CHAPTER 1

▼

ENCOUNTER!

"Oh God! Help me!"

I stamp the brake, wrench the steering wheel, and the car bounces back on the blacktop and skids sideways, tires squealing. A car speeding toward me veers away, headlights stabbing my eyes, horn blaring.

Good Lord, I almost missed the curve!

Gasping, tasting blood, I turn to the dark shadow of the man seated beside me, and stutter, "I'm…I'm sorry, I…I fell asleep!"

I'm startled to see the sharp, stark profile of the stranger splitting into a smile….

Half an hour ago I pulled into a gasoline station in Saltillo exhausted, ready for bed. Then I saw the stranger. Dressed in a dark gray pinstripe, he looked curiously out of place standing tall and erect beside a greasy Pemex gas pump. As soon as I stepped from the car the man's somber eyes locked on mine and he came forward, hand extended. "I'm Kyrus," he said, as if expecting me to recognize the name.

His voice, like a fist reaching out and clutching my shoulder, stopped me in my tracks.

"Cyrus?" I take his hand. It is cold, lifeless, all bone, no flesh.

"No, I'm Kyrus, Señor." Why does my pulse suddenly accelerate? We chatted while the attendant filled the tank.

"Bravo!" the man exclaimed when I mentioned I was on my way to Mexico City. "God sent you, Señor! My car broke down an hour ago, and I must be in Mexico City by morning."

I opened my mouth to tell the stranger I was about to check into a hotel. Instead, I heard myself saying, "Get in, Sir, I'll be honored to have your company."

Now, steering my Chevy along the winding mountain road floating like a thin, dark band of steel in shadows cast by the jagged hills, I'm wondering what has possessed me. I made a reservation at Hotel Camino Real a week ago. And besides, I never give rides to strangers!

Kah-y-rus. An uncommon name. Where is this man from? The Near East, maybe? Syria? Lebanon?

Señor Kyros has not stopped talking since he got in my car. His voice is musical, sonorous, soothing, hypnotic…a voice that almost lulled me to sleep moments ago. Hand trembling, I massage my face, my eyes, my neck.

He's lecturing me now on the ancient history of Mexico. His Spanish is polished and scholarly, reminding me of Dr. Benavides, my professor of Latinamerican History at the University of Texas. But no, Dr. Benavides was from Columbia. *Señor* Kyros must be from Spain, he just pronounced "Quetzalcóatl" with an elegant Castillian lisp.

Quetzalcóatl? Suddenly I'm wide awake. The man's talking about the Feathered Serpent, Mexico's lord of the underworld!

"…and so, his Highness, Lord Quetzalcóatl…."

My pulse pounding I turn, and Kyrus smiles at me, white teeth gleaming in the glow of the headlights.

But his eyes are not smiling.

Look out!

A monstrous eighteen-wheeler is thundering down upon us—head on!

An instant of sheer terror; the blinding glare of headlights…the blaring of a horn…the whoosh! of the big truck's airstream…the jouncing of the car as it leaves the highway….

We've stopped. I'm alive!

Sobbing, chest heaving, I reach up and pull away a splinter of glass embedded in my cheek.

"Dear God, he shattered the rearview mirror! Six inches closer and…"

I jerk erect in my seat, remembering this morning in Laredo as I was about to cross the Border…a returning tourist warning me: "Be careful. The road to Mexico City is mostly narrow blacktop, pocked with chug holes. And look out for the eighteen-wheelers; they think they own the highway. Sometimes they come straight at you, expecting you to take to the shoulder."

My passenger! I turn to apologize, but the seat beside me is empty. Of course, while I was sitting here in a stupor Señor Kyrus stepped out of the car.

I push open the door, and when my feet touch the ground, knees trembling, I stumble and almost fall. A steadying hand on the warm hood, I stagger like an old man to the front of car, then squinting against the headlights, move toward the other side, expecting to find Kyros seated on the ground, in shock from our close encounter with death.

"A-y-y-y!" I'm flat on my back, feet dangling in space, both hands clutching a prickly bush, an avalanche of rocks cascading down into a dark canyon.

Kyrus! He's lying down there in the darkness, badly hurt, maybe dying.

"Kyrus!…Kyrus." My voice echoes back, ghost-like from the vastness of the canyon.

I struggle to my feet and sobbing, moaning, stumble back to the other side of the car, colliding with the door I left open. "Got to go for help…the police!"

Abruptly, like a blow to the stomach, the truth hits me. Go for help? Don't be foolish, Kyrus didn't fall into the canyon. He couldn't have, because Kyrus is...

Go ahead, say it, Andrew: that charming fellow waiting for you at the gas station wasn't a man of flesh and blood. He was a dark spirit from another world!

Heart pounding, hands trembling, I pull myself into the car. The squeal of tires interrupts my thoughts. A car has braked on the highway and the driver is looking at me curiously.

"*Algún problema, Señor?*"

"No, thanks, I'm all right."

I start the car, make a U-turn on the narrow, rutted blacktop and head back toward Saltillo.

Twenty minutes later I see a brightly-lit sign: "Hotel El Camino Real." I shake my head. I have no recollection of passing this way.

It's a miracle I'm still alive!

CHAPTER 2

▼

AN INTRODUCTION TO THE SERPENT'S KINGDOM

"Yes, Sir, we have a suite reserved for you."

"A suite? I didn't ask for a suite!" Behind her, the bookkeeper looks up, and I realize my voice is too loud.

Her smile fades. "I know, Sir, but the Governor is hosting his Party's annual convention this week and has requisitioned every hotel room in town. The only thing we have left is the bridal suite."

"The bridal suite? You want me to stay in the bridal suite?" (Calm down, Andrew, when you get upset your Spanish is awful!)

The girl's face flushes red. "I'm sorry, Sir. I can check with another hotel if you insist, but I doubt…"

Opening my wallet, I grumble, "And how much is this going to cost me?"

"We're charging you the price of a regular room, Sir. One hundred fifty thousand pesos…fifty dollars."

The elevator door dings on the fifth floor. I hurry down the hall, the thick carpet whispering at my feet, and push open the heavy oak door, not sure how I should feel: lucky? foolish? amused? The parlor, lightly perfumed, is furnished with a pink loveseat, a 42" TV and a well-stocked bar. The bedroom has a king-size bed and a mirrored ceiling.

I smile when I see the bidet in the bathroom, remembering Chris and Tim's expressions back in April when they saw the thing for the first time in their hotel room. And here too is the wicker basket beside the commode, a reminder not to stop up the plumbing with paper.

The huge circular bathtub reminds me of how tired I am. What a day! I left Houston before dawn, drove straight through to Laredo, spent two hours clearing the Border bureaucracy, another four getting to Saltillo, then…

I shudder. What am I doing? After what happened on the highway I should be heading back to Houston. Right now! I turn.

Just a minute, Andrew! No time for a spur-of-the-moment decision—too much has happened. A good soaking in a hot tub, that's what I need!

I check the towel rack. No wash cloths. Back in April when I was in Mexico City, they didn't have them there either. And when I requested one from the cleaning lady she looked at me as if I were asking for snow from the peak of Mount Everest. I later found out the Mexicans use a rough sponge instead of a wash cloth. Ugh!

Anyway, I've brought wash cloths along this time. Going to my heavy leather bag dig through several pockets, trying to remember where I stashed them. When I lift out a pile of underwear something drops to the floor.

Mary's picture!

Picking it up I press it to my chest. A tear rolls down my cheek.

Shoulders heaving, I ease myself to the floor and sit there for a long while, propped against the bed, sobbing. I haven't cried like this since the day of the funeral!

I study the picture, a 5 X 7 in a cheap gold frame, remembering I'd dropped it into my bag a couple of days ago, when the movers were packing the things that will be in storage until I get settled in Mexico City. The man had taken the photo from a drawer and was about to wrap it when I snatched it out of his hands.

I hadn't seen the picture in years.

"Your daughter, Mr. Kelly?"

"No, my wife. Her engagement photo."

"Real pretty little lady!"

"Wasn't she, though!" I'd forgotten what an enchantress she was, this 19-year-old sophomore. She ravished my heart the first time I saw her, thumbing through the card catalog in the university library.

My eyes caress her: full mouth, petite turned-up nose, abundant wavy hair the color of an east Texas honeycomb. I feel again the stirring of the acute longing that tortured me those bittersweet months of our engagement.

Our twenty-two years together weren't free of problems, but we were happier than most couples I knew. And we fell more deeply in love as the years slipped by and our daughters Margaret and Victoria progressed from kinder, to elementary, to high school. I was a very busy psychotherapist. We bought a spacious home in Kingwood, an upscale Houston suburb nestled in an abundant oak and pine forest. Just a year ago, soon after Margaret's wedding, we packed Victoria off to Baylor, emptying the nest. At Christmas, to celebrate, I slipped Mary an envelope with our tickets for a Mediterranean cruise.

Three weeks later, our tranquil world disintegrated.

Mary climbed into her car that cold, rainy Saturday morning smiling at my worried protests: why didn't she postpone her visit with Victoria until the next weekend?

"Oh, Andrew, I couldn't disappoint her. She was so excited when she called last night."

"Then at least take the Lincoln, it'll be safer."

"No, I'd feel uncomfortable all alone in that big boat."

Will I ever forget how she smiled and waved at me as she backed her little green Mercedes convertible out of the driveway?

I was still leafing through the Houston Chronicle when the Texas State Trooper called with the devastating news: Mary'd had a head-on with a van on the rain-slick highway. They'd life-flighted her to Hermann Hospital.

She died three days later without regaining consciousness.

I groan, "Oh God, Will it ever stop hurting?"

Pulling myself to my feet I stumble into the bathroom. Splashing cold water at my tired eyes, I study my face in the mirror: dark hair and slightly tinted skin that hints at my Cajun mother...bright blue eyes and a prominent nose inherited from my Irish father...a trim mustache adds a Latin touch. When I speak Spanish to my Hispanic patients they sometimes ask where I'm from. Central America, maybe?

While the tub is filling I decide I'm in no mood to eat surrounded by babbling conventioneers. I'll call room service.

Easing myself into the bubble bath, my mind is churning. Life is strange! If Mary were alive, I wouldn't have made that trip to Mexico City six months ago. And I'd never have met Moisés Contreras, the one who is to blame for my being in this goshawful place....

The day after Mary's funeral I refer all my clients to my associates. What happened the rest of January and all of February? I can't remember, they're still a gray blotch on my calendar. I make one visit to my parents in New Orleans, but my mother's tearful sympathy does more harm than good. In March I try to take up my practice again, but after less than a week I bail out, unable to claw my way up from the black pit that's closed in on me. I'm baffled. Through the years I've helped dozens of people find a pathway out of depression, but now I'm unable to help myself; my will power seems to have shorted out.

Rejecting my partners' insistence that I check into a hospital, I spend night after dreary night hunched in my easy chair, staring at mindless movies until long after midnight. Most days I get up around noon, make myself a sandwich, then drive over to my daughter Margaret's apartment. But afternoons spent with her and my little grandson Jeff leave me tired and despondent.

One Saturday Chris and Tim take me to breakfast. They're excited about an upcoming trip to Mexico City. Chris, a dentist and Tim, a pediatrician, will be working for a week with a group of Mexican doctors in an impoverished community on the edge of the city.

"Andrew, yesterday the pastor of the Calvario Church in Mexico City called us. He and his congregation are sponsoring our mission. Guess what? When we told him about you he begged us to bring you along."

"Why? What did you tell him?"

"About the Hispanics who come to you for counseling because you speak their language."

"But on a medical mission? Where would I fit in?"

Chris lays a hand on my arm. "Man, you'd be a key player. You'd be doing something Tim and I can't do; helping people with hurting hearts and souls."

I'm skeptical, suspecting they've cooked up the invitation to "help me". I don't want to be helped!

A week later Margaret confronts me. "Daddy, yesterday I ran into Chris's wife and she asked me if you'd decided to accompany Chris and Tim to Mexico City next month. I was embarrassed. Had to admit I had no idea what she was talking about. Why haven't you told me?"

"Because I haven't the least intention of going!"

Margaret spends an hour trying to convince me, but she only makes me angry. After that, every time she brings up the trip I change the subject.

Finally, one afternoon a couple of weeks before the departure date, she tells me, her voice breaking: "Daddy, I miss Mother just as much as you do. But I've accepted the fact that I have to go on living, my husband and little boy need me. It's time you stopped feeling sorry for yourself and began thinking of others. That's why you've got to go to Mexico with Chris and Tim!"

Grimacing, I take a sip of coffee. She know she's made me angry, but she doesn't care! Picking up her cup she goes to the sink, and as she washes it, says in a quiet voice just loud enough for me to hear: "You know, it's been nice having you around so much. And you're welcome to come to my house any time, and stay as long as you wish"...she turns to face me..."after you get back from Mexico City!"

What a shock early in April, just two hours after take-off, to find myself in another world. For a moment I panic, drowning in a sea of dark faces. Then I move forward, toward the grim-looking gentleman in a green uniform waiting to check my passport.

Later, as we wait for our suitcases to appear on the belt, Chris is sweating. He's carrying in a small leather briefcase the precious tools of his profession. Will they confiscate them? And what about the antibiotics Dr. Tim persuaded us to stuff in our bags? Will they declare us smugglers and lead us away in handcuffs? When we arrive at the customs counter we do a double-take: a traffic light! The smiling young woman in a crisp gray uniform instructs us to each press a button. If the green light comes on, she tells us, we can walk right through. If the light blinks red we'll have to unzip our bags.

Green...green...green! We want to sing the Hallelujah Chorus!

Two minutes later a group of *hermanos from* the church greet us with a hearty Mexican *abrazo*: a handshake, a bear hug and three pats on the back. The *abrazo* Pastor Moisés applies to me almost cracks a rib.

A heart-stopping taxi ride to the hotel moments later: the front passenger's seat of the little red Volkswagen bug has been removed for easy access to the back seat. We three Americans, jammed together on the lumpy faded upholstery, our heads banging the ceiling, watch fearfully as the speedometer flickers between 100 and 120 kilometers, the driver constantly changing lanes, maneuvering erratically in a packed pandemonium of speeding automobiles and big noisy buses spewing black smoke.

Please forgive the typographical errors that escaped the proofreading in this first edition. A corrected edition is now in process and will be available shortly.

After the driver miraculously avoids rear-ending a huge bus suddenly pulling away from the curb I decide I'm probably not going to die on this trip after all, and might as well enjoy the ride. It turns out to be more fun than the roller coaster at Astroworld!

"Hotel del Bosque, *Señores*!" The driver wheels into the curb and brakes.

Pastor Contreras is standing on the sidewalk beside our luggage, smiling, hands on hips. We stare at him, jaws agape. We left him behind at the airport with that same pile of luggage and the promise he'd follow in another taxi with our bags.

"I was getting worried about you, brothers," he complains. "Sorry your taxi was so slow!"

The next morning we board Moisés Contreras' battered twenty-year old Ford station wagon for the trip to our mission site.

"I had to leave my car at home last night," says the pastor, pointing to a red seal on the rear window, "it doesn't circulate Mondays." He explains that every automobile in Mexico City has to "rest" one day of the week. The color of your seal determines the day your car makes its contribution to lowering the index of the city's smothering, smelly smog.

He introduces us to three smiling young people in the back of his van: Rafael, a dentist, and Carlos and Monica, medical students. They'll be our associates in this project they call a "medical brigade".

As we drive north through the heavy traffic Rafael points to a tall gray structure with shattered windows and crumbling walls, inclined precariously over the sidewalk. "It's been eight months, but they still haven't torn down most of the buildings damaged by last September's earthquake."

I've worried about being able to understand people in Mexico City. But listening to the chatter around me, I'm relieved to hear the same lyrical, gracefully phonetic Spanish I learned at the University of Texas and practiced with my Latin clients in Houston. And by the way the others smile at me when I speak I can tell they're pleased.

After an hour the pastor announces: "There it is, San Juanico." Slowing, he points to a miserable clutter of hovels perched on the side of a barren, rocky hillside. It looks like a war zone. And in a sense, it is. Five years ago ten square blocks were leveled by the explosion of a dozen huge gas storage tanks. The survivors have hammered together living space out of scraps of lumber, cardboard and tarpaper.

Pastor Contreras' church has set up a makeshift clinic in a rusty tin warehouse provided by the Salvation Army. We empty our boxes of medicine on a wobbly wooden table, and behind burlap curtains strung on haywire the doctors prepare for their patients.

They don't have to wait long. Within half an hour a line of sad-eyed visitors, most of them women and children, straggles across the bare dirt patio to the street.

Dr. Tim's first patient is a young mother in a faded red blouse and torn blue jeans nursing an abscessed lip. I shudder when she explains that a rat bit her a couple of nights ago as she slept on her straw *petate* on the dirt floor. I help her hold down her dreadfully thin, screaming four-year-old so Dr. Chris can chisel out a couple of suppurating molars frozen to the jawbone.

By the second day I'm as busy as the doctors. Word has spread among the women about the Spanish-speaking gringo willing to listen as you pour out your anger over the lazy, womanizing man you're fated to live with.

Thursday my life turns a corner. About one, after the church women have served a meal of tacos, beans and a lukewarm rice drink they called *horchata*, I head for the small room designated as my counseling office. In the narrow, dark hall I trip and almost fall on my face. I groan: the dentists have placed the compressor for their drills just outside my door. I imagine what's going to happen: every time the compressor kicks off my patient and I are going to have to yell at each other to be heard.

Waiting for me is a stout, fiftiesh woman, in a stained white apron, her face etched with sadness. At her side hunches a dark, sullen young man.

"Doctór," she says," stifling a sob, "this is my son Fernando. I told him he must come and talk with you if he wanted to continue living in my house."

The boy stares back at me, tightlipped, unsmiling.

"How can I help you, Fernando?"

He shrugs and slumps deeper into his seat. "My mother's the one with the problem."

The woman stands up and turns to face her son, wringing her hands, her voice trembling. "Tell the doctór the truth, Fernando. How you used to be hardworking and respectful to your parents. And how you've changed since you entered the university, how you yell at me, fight with your father, scream at your little brothers and sisters."

Until recently, the mother explains, they were proud of their son, willing to sacrifice for his tuition and his books.

"Then, in January, he met *Profesora* Rosa and everything changed."

"One of his professors?"

Fernando shrugs. "She teaches Biology."

"That's not all she teaches!" the mother wails.

"Why are you making such a big deal of it, *Vieja*?" He's yelling now.

"But Fernando," she sobs, grabbing him by the shoulders and shaking him, "that altar to the Feathered Serpent in your room! You're going to bring down God's curse on our house!"

I must have misunderstood her! "Did you say "feathered serpent"?

"Dr. Kelly," answers the young man, pushing away his mother's hands, his words dripping sarcasm, "being an American, you wouldn't understand. But for me, a *mexicano*, Quetzalcóatl the Feathered Serpent is the symbol of my country's noble past and our hope for the future!"

The woman brings up her hand in a resounding slap. "And he's also an angel of Satan!" she cries.

"*Madre, cállate la boca!*" her son bellows, pushing back his chair, "Your weak Jesus is for women and little children, not for me. I am a soldier of the great Lord Quetzalcóatl. Soon he will be ruling over Mexico again. You'll see!"

The voice of the youth has changed to a guttural mumble, and his lips are twisted, eyes staring.

"What's going on?" Pastor Moisés is standing in the door.

The mother falls to her knees, clutching his hands. "Padre, a demon is tormenting my boy Fernando. Help him, please!"

Her son, his face a dark storm cloud, glares at the intruder. Gripping the young man's shoulder, the pastor commands, "Vile evil spirit, I bind you by the blood of Jesus of Nazareth!"

Fernando crumbles to the floor, arms flailing.

"My son, my son, *ay, Dios mío!*" Kneeling beside her son, the mother tries to subject the hands striking her face again and gain.

Moisés pushes her aside and pulls the boy to his feet. "Fernando, say the name of Jesus!"

"Never!"

Moisés grabs him by the shoulders. "Foul demon, tell me your name!"

Fernando suddenly goes limp and Moisés eases him to the floor, where he thrashes about for a moment, then lies still.

"The spirit has left him for now," Moisés says, "but he'll be back."

Fernando stirs, sits up, and slowly rises to his feet. His mother rushes toward him, arms opened wide. He shoves her away and her back hits the wall, her knees buckling. "I'm getting out of here!" he shouts and runs from the room.

The mother follows as far as the door, then turns and shuffles slowly back to where Moses stands, lips compressed, shaking her head.

"My son, my poor son. What's going to happen to him?"

"That depends on him, *Señora*. Tell me, how did he get mixed up with evil spirits?"

She tells him about *Profesora* Rosa.

"And before the *Profesora*? Does anybody in your family practice spiritism? An aunt, maybe, or a grandmother?"

"No, Padre, nobody."

"Then he can be freed. That is, if he wants to be free. Otherwise, there's nothing I can do."

After she's left I sit staring at Moisés. Dabbing at his perspiring face with a white handkerchief, he grumbles, "Sorry to interrupt you like I did, but when I heard that boy's voice, I knew you needed help."

His somber face breaks into a grin. "Doctór, what are you thinking?"

"I don't know what to think!" So! From the beginning I've felt there was something different about this big dark Mexican with penetrating eyes and the voice of a prophet. And now....

The Pastor reaches over and touches my arm. "How about supper with me tonight? Looks like there are some things we need to talk about."

"You bet there are!" My mind is exploding with questions.

Pastor Moisés starts from the room, then turns, his face grave. "You know, I think God let this happen for a reason."

That evening I'm seated with Moisés in a quiet corner of a handsome VIPS Restaurant a block from the hotel. I look about me, impressed that the bright, spotless restaurant with cheerful orange booths and smiling waitresses in pink uniforms would fit easily into of a Kingwood shopping center.

Taking a sip of my icy *sidral* I say, "What a day! And so hot! I'm surprised, they told me Mexico City was mile high."

"April is the hottest month of the year. Come back in June, when the rainy season starts, and you'll sleep under a blanket at night."

Moisés signals the waiter, holding up his coffee cup. "Doctór, after what happened this afternoon I thought maybe we should talk."

I nod gratefully. "I've been unable to think of anything else. I'm confused. What's the difference between the Feathered Serpent and Quetzal...?"

"Quetzalcóatl. There's no difference; Quetzalcóatl means "feathered serpent" in the Nahuatl language."

"And what about that demon this afternoon? Did the Feathered Serpent have anything to do with him?"

"Of course. Demons and our ancient gods are inseparable. You need to read up on our history. You'll find it fascinating. At the same time your American Indians were wandering about hunting buffalo, our ancestors were studying the stars, writing books on philosophy and building great cities to honor their demonic gods."

"And isn't one of those ancient cities near here? The one with the pyramids?"

"Yes, it's called Teotihuacan. Saturday, if you like, I'll take you and the doctors for a visit."

"Great! I'm sure the other guys will want to go."

"You mentioned the pyramids. They're impressive. But the Temple of Quetzalcóatl is more important."

"Quetzalcóatl again?"

"Moisés shrugs. "Before the arrival of the *conquistadores* there were dozens of city-states, each with its own language and its own gods, hideous, bad-tempered and blood-thirsty, demons in disguise. They're in hiding now, but they're as dangerous as ever. And there's something you need to know: they're all Quetzalcóatl's servants!"

"Fernando called Quetzalcóatl Lord of Mexico. Why?"

"Because long ago Satan himself gave Quetzalcóatl *Me*soamerica as his own private kingdom."

I'm beginning to wonder how much of this I'm ready to believe. "Tell me Pastor Moisés, how…how did you learn such things?"

Frowning, the big man takes a long, thoughtful sip of his coffee, as if choosing carefully his next words: "When you deal with demons day after day you learn their secrets."

Moisés Contreras picks up his knife and cuts into the enchiladas *suizas* the waiter has placed before him. "Of course, if you talked with some of my brother pastors they'd tell you I'm crazy. But it's in their Bibles, if they'd just look."

"Do you have many encounters like this afternoon?"

"Quite often. It's a ministry God gave me for these last days." A shadow darkens his face.

"M-m-m-m, These enchiladas are delicious!" I study my dish: tender chicken wrapped in flour tortillas and baked in a rich white cheese sauce, with a generous helping of refried beans on the side. Why don't the Mexican restaurants in the States serve enchiladas like this?

"Say, Pastor Moisés, what do the people say about your ministry with demons? Most churches in the United States don't go in for that sort of thing."

"Nor in Mexico." Moisés smiles wryly. "But that's another problem."

Smacking his lips, Moisés puts down his fork and fixes his brooding brown eyes on me. "The doctors told you, I suppose, that I insisted they bring you along."

"Yes. And I was surprised."

"I know very little about psychology. What do you call yourself, a therapist? I understand you people deal with the dark secrets of the soul. Since you're both a man of God and a man of science, I'm hoping you might be able to appreciate my ministry. And counsel me on how to explain it to the brothers."

I stare back at the big man, surprised by the fear I feel pinching my gut. "Moisés…" I take a deep breath…"I'm open to the possibility, but…" My mind is racing. What am I getting into? "Tell you what, you're just going to have to give me time to digest all this."

I have a hard time going to sleep that night. Sometime before dawn I awake from a bad dream and fight the impulse to get up and look under the bed.

The next day I wait nervously all day for the appearance of another Fernando. When nightfall comes and it doesn't happen, I'm not sure if I'm relieved or disappointed.

CHAPTER 3

▼

TOUCHED BY THE SERPENT

Saturday morning, in less than forty-five minutes, Chris and Tim and I, accompanied by Moisés, travel from the Twentieth Century, A.D. to the Fifth Century, B.C. Picking us up at the hotel after breakfast, the Pastor expertly navigates his ancient station wagon through the light Saturday morning traffic. After half an hour we pass through a toll booth on the northern edge of the city and leave the city traffic behind. The narrow blacktop slices through barren hills sprinkled with cactus and sickly, thirsty-looking spruce.

"Look" Chris exclaims, pointing ahead. "the pyramids!"

Moisés slows. "There they are, gentlemen, wonders of ancient America, the Pyramids of the Moon and the Sun!"

Seeing them, my mind goes back to pictures I've seen of Cheops in Egypt. But these are taller! From several miles distance they dominate the horizon.

"I had no idea they were so big," Tim says. "Who built them, and how long ago?"

"We believe they were built by the Olmecs," Moisés replies, "but how long ago no one knows. When the Aztecs passed this way a thousand years ago on their way to founding Mexico City Teotihuacan was already in ruins."

As we draw nearer we can see the low, horizontal skyline of a crumbling stone city. Remembering a young man named Fernando and his altar to Quetzalcóatl, my eyes are already searching for the Feathered Serpent's temple. Surely it will be the most magnificent building in Teotihuacan.

What a disappointment! Half an hour later, when we stand at the edge of the city looking down at the Feathered Serpent's temple nestled in a shallow valley, I can't believe my eyes. The lofty Pyramid of the Sun already seems to overshadow us, even though it's half a mile away at the end of a broad esplanade. In contrast, the unremarkable pyramid of brown stones Moisés calls the Temple of Quetzalcóatl seems pedestrian and insignificant. It is maybe thirty feet tall, and some fifty feet wide at its base, with little form, no esthetic beauty. You could hardly call it a pyramid. Even the word "temple" sounds exaggerated.

"This…this is the palace of the so-called Lord of Mexico?" I ask, my shoulders sagging.

Moisés comes up to me, and placing a hand on each shoulder, says in a low voice trembling with emotion, "Doctór, it is important that you understand how the Feathered Serpent works. In the Bible Satan is called the Deceiver. *Quetzalcóatl* is his representative in Mexico, and when you're dealing with him, things are never what they seem. Yes, it's true, the Temple of Quetzalcóatl appears insignificant and harmless, but that's an illusion. Come, I'll show you what I mean."

He leads us down a flight a narrow stone steps and across a rock-strewn patio until we're standing within a dozen feet of the temple. Raising his hands he brings them together in a loud clap. A sharp, bird-like whistle echoes back from the pyramid.

The three of us cry out in surprise.

"Do it again!" Chris pleads.

Moisés complies, and again we hear a clear, melodious chirp. Our host turns to face us. "Have either of you ever seen a quetzal?" he asks.

We shake our heads.

"You've just heard his call. The quetzal is a gorgeous bird living in the jungles of Chiapas and Tabasco. He has radiant red, green and blue feathers, and often reaches a full meter in length."

"Quetzal…Quetzalcóatl. So that's where the Feathered Serpent gets his name!" I say. "Exactly. In Nahuatl, the language of our ancestors, coatl means "serpent" and quetzal is the name of the bird whose feathers encircle the serpent's throat."

"And what about the quetzal we just heard?" Chris asks, "Is he hidden there in the temple?"

I turn to see if Chris is smiling, but his face is serious. I realize that, like me, he's about convinced anything is possible in this enchanted land.

Moisés grins. "No, there's no quetzal, but in just a moment you'll meet Quetzalcóatl.

He pauses. "Now do you understand why I warned you to expect surprises when you're dealing with the Feathered Serpent? Follow me."

Taking my arm, he guides us to a spot opposite the south corner of the temple. "Wait a moment, and I'll tell you exactly where to stand."

Beginning with one heel against the temple he carefully paces off the distance: "one, two, three, four…." Stopping, he places a stone where his feet are planted.

"Come," he says, motioning toward us, "I want you to stand right here."

Striding rapidly to the north corner of the temple he paces off the same distance.

"Ready?"

"Ready!" we answer in chorus.

Dramatically he raises his hands and brings them smartly together, twice. The *quetzal* bird responds: "Chirp!" (a pause, then even louder:) "CHIRP!"

"Wow!" the three of us shout, the cry of the quetzal still ringing in our ears.

"So you heard it?" Moisés calls to us. "Know what? From here I could hear nothing."

Coming over to where we stand talking excitedly about the surprising phenomenon we'd just witnessed, he continues: "Get the picture? A worshipper comes to the temple and asks the priest's permission to visit his god. The priest claps his hands and the *quetzal* whistles a welcome. Then the priest directs the worshipper to the next position, and from across the way claps his hands again. This time only the worshipper hears the quetzal giving permission to enter into the presence of Quetzalcóatl."

Turning, he motions to us. "Well, Quetzalcóatl has invited us in. Shall we accept his invitation?"

Moisés leads us around the back of the temple to a small gray pyramid, separated from the temple by a narrow, deep rock moat. "Follow me."

Entering the moat, we walk a dozen steps until we see, jutting from the side of the pyramid—"

"The Feathered Serpent!" Tim exclaims, stopping suddenly, as if bumping into some invisible barrier.

As thick as a man's torso, feathers flaring at its throat, mouth gaping, dead eyes staring, the monument carved in dark gray volcanic rock seems to be about to break away from the pyramid and take flight.

"Hideous!" I cry, feeling I'm about to throw up my breakfast.

"Why would anyone worship something like that?" Chris exclaims, backing away.

Standing very close to the Feathered Serpent, but careful not to touch it, Moisés explains: "In the days of the Olmecs a spring flowed from where we're standing, reminding the people what the idol stood for: life-giving water. Coatl, the serpent, represented streams that flow on the earth. The Quetzal feathers represented rain that falls from the sky.

"So they were worshipping water, not the monument!" I exclaimed.

"Supposedly, Doctór, but when people come day after day to bow before an idol they end up forgetting what the image represents and worship the idol itself. You see—"

Moisés moves to one side, leaving room for two young men striding purposefully toward us. As if unaware of our presence one steps up to the serpent, encircles his grotesque neck with one arm, and then plunges a hand into the serpent's mouth! We watch, eyes wide, as he moves his lips in a hoarse mumble, then slowly withdraws his hand. His companion takes his place and repeats the ceremony.

After a moment they move away, their sandals whispering on the stone floor, eyes unfocussed, as if in a trance.

Moisés grimaces. "Come on. let's get out of here!"

He turns and hurries up the narrow stairway. Tim and Chris follow. I want to run, to put distance between myself and this evil place, but my feet seem set in concrete.

Ten steps away Moisés turns and calls, "Come, my friends, it's going to rain. We must hurry if we're going to see the rest of Teotihuacan."

I take one step, then stop, bewitched by the memory of how the faces of the two youths looked when they thrust their hands into the Serpent's mouth.

A whisper: "Do it!"

Turning suddenly, I lunge toward the idol and drive my arm into the gaping jaws.

An icy chill envelopes my hand, flows up my arm and slams into my heart. My ears roar, my eyes water, my teeth chatter.

Gasping, I stumble up the steps and overtake the other men. I'm relieved to see Moisés intent on some Spanish words Tim and Chris are trying out on him, because my body is shaking, a tornado rumbling inside of me. I don't want Moisés to guess what has just happened!

I follow them, stumbling up the grand esplanade, imagining myself a sacrificial victim being drug along in chains by priests arrayed in bright feathered headdresses, thousands standing on the tall stone walls on each side, cheering wildly.

I shake my head, trying to clear it.

"Shall we climb to the top?" Moisés stands at the foot of the pyramid, pointing upward.

"Tim cries, "Look at all the steps! How tall is this thing?"

"About ten stories."

Adjusting his backpack, he grins and yells, "Let's go!"

Dumbly I struggle up the stairs behind them. Arriving at the top, Tim and Chris run over to the remains of a sacrificial altar, talking excitedly about rivers of blood cascading down the pyramid's steps.

"Doctór, are you all right?" Moisés is standing beside me, an arm around my shoulder, studying my face.

"I'm ready to go, Moisés," I mumble.

On the way down I miss a step and pitch forward. Moisés catches my arm just in time. He refuses to let go until we reach bottom.

As soon as I feel both feet on solid ground I fall to my knees and retch convulsively, convinced I'm dying, only vaguely aware that Moisés' hands are on my head and he's rebuking the spirit oppressing me.

Afterward I lie on my back staring up at the blue sky. Tim and Chris are looking down at me, their eyes wide. I don't care, I'm just thankful to be alive.

Walking back to the car, Moisés speaks gruffly. "You put your hand into Quetzalcóatl's jaw, didn't you, Doctór?" Why did you do it? Did you forget my warning about the devil's unpleasant surprises?"

I shudder. "I must have been out of my mind!"

"I was afraid you might do something foolish. I saw how fascinated you were by those two kids.

"So that's why you were in a rush to get away from the Feathered Serpent!"

"Those guys were disciples of Quetzalcóatl. They believe they get empowerment from putting their hands into his jaws and stroking his fangs."

"Do you think they felt what I felt? It was like plunging my hand into an icy hell!"

"Probably not. Some people like to stand before the Serpent and dare one another. Usually nothing happens."

"Then why did it happen to me?" I shudder, reliving the experience. "I hope I never have a feeling like that again in my life!"

We've arrived at the car. Moisés unlocks the door on my side and taking my arm, eases me into the seat. His lips close to my ear, he whispers, "The Serpent set a trap for you. He wants to scare you away."

On the return trip little is said. I lay my head back, eyes closed, feeling drowsy, mulling over Moisés' words, vaguely aware that Chris and Tim are whispering on the back seat.

At the hotel my companions hurry into the dining room, but I'm too tired to eat. I ride the elevator up to my room, crash on the bed and fall into a troubled sleep. Two hours later I'm awakened by a pounding on my door.

"Wake up, Andrew," Chris is calling, "we'll be leaving for the airport in half an hour!"

Groaning, I pull myself from the bed and begin throwing things into my suitcase, obsessed with the urgency of getting away from this frightening place. By the time I get downstairs Chris and Tim have already checked out and Moisés is at the door gunning his motor.

Later, at the airport, boarding pass in hand, I pace back and forth, impatient with Chris and Tim, who keep thinking of new questions to ask Moisés about the Temple of Quetzalcóatl and the Pyramid of the Sun.

"Ladies and gentlemen, we will now begin boarding Continental Flight 167 at Gate 19."

I hear the announcement like a reprieve from a death sentence.

Chris and Tim give Moisés a hasty *abrazo* and head for the gate. When it's my turn Moisés refuses to release me.

"Doctór," he says, pulling me to one side, "there's something I must say to you before you leave. I've been telling myself I shouldn't, that you're not prepared to receive it. But the hand of the Lord is heavy upon me and I must!"

I stare at Moisés, afraid of what I'm about to hear, wanting to clap my hands over my ears and run for the plane. "What...what is it?"

Moisés lays a heavy hand on my shoulder. "*Hermano*, God has plans for you. Here in Mexico."

"I don't understand."

"Neither do I. I only know that the first time I heard your name on the telephone God whispered to me that he has chosen you for a mission."

"Andrew, hurry, we'll miss our plane." Chris and Tim have stopped and are looking back, their faces anxious.

I take a step away from Moisés, then turn, staring at him, my heart pounding, angry at him. Why did he have to scare me like this at the very last moment? What does he expect me to say?

He smiles at me. "Promise you'll pray about it, *hermano*."

I lift a hand in a half-hearted wave. "Adios, Moisés."

"*Hasta la vista*." ("Until we meet again.") The words chill me to the bone.

A couple of minutes into the air I look down: the lights of the city are blazing up into the dark night like the crater of an enormous volcano. I shudder; does hell look like this?

Soon the city is lost in the distance. Relief floods in. Several rows back Tim and Chris are chatting amiably. Tim looks up and smiles at me. Since that bizarre incident at Teotihuacan he and Chris have gone out of their way to assure me nothing has changed between us. It has, of course. My friends seem puzzled, sensing that I've been touched by a grotesque, sinister hand and that somehow I'm not the same person.

Well, what has happened to me? I'm not sure. Until Teotihuacan my relation with the lord of the underworld was from a distance, like a man seeing graffiti on a clean white wall and cursing the perpetrator, but having no desire to meet him face to face. Now, however, I know that something evil is still clinging to me from that encounter with the Bearded Serpent. I look at the hand I so foolishly thrust into the snake's gaping mouth, wishing I could cut it off and throw it out the window.

One thing is certain: I'll never come back to this place! Pressing my face to the window, I thank God for the thick layer of fleecy clouds reflecting the bright moonlight like a luminous wall shielding me from the darkness below.

Half an hour later Chris shakes me awake. "Time for dinner, Andrew. And guess what, we're already over the Gulf."

"Great! Texas can't be far! When the stewardess hands me my tray I devour the meal like a man just released from prison.

CHAPTER 4

▼

A DOOR OPENS

The following week I return to my office, give it a thorough dusting and announce I'm ready to go back to work. My relieved partners begin moving clients my way, and soon I have a full agenda. I feel great, the depression that has clung to me since Mary's death almost forgotten. As the weeks pass I find myself at ease with people once again, immersing myself in their problems.

In June I begin dating Katherine, an attractive 35-year-old Vice-President of a Kingwood bank. Still healing from an angry divorce, she makes it clear she's interested in a friendship, nothing more. That's fine with me. But within a month we're seeing each other several times a week and I'm spending Saturday afternoons with her and her ten-year-old daughter.

One night early in July I find myself unable to go to sleep. Katherine and I went to a movie tonight, and afterward, saying goodnight at her door, exchanged our first kiss. She clung to me for a moment, and as she pulled away I saw the questioning in her eyes.

Well, what are my intentions? Am I ready to think about remarriage? Maybe beginning a second family?

I get up, go into the kitchen and brew myself a cup of decaf. Why this restlessness? I frown at the plump little duck smiling at me from the coffee mug.

I shuffle into the living room and plop down on the sofa. Taking a sip of steaming coffee I pick up a picture of my parents and squint at it thoughtfully. They're in their seventies now, but Dad still has that cocky Irish grin and Mom's bright Cajun eyes are as alert and challenging as ever.

I smile, remembering the words of the seminary professor who led me through the therapy my counseling degree required. After dwelling at length on my family formation, my mentor remarked, "Andrew, with that French-Irish dynamite in your genes the Lord's going to have to work overtime keeping your feet on the straight-and-narrow!"

We laughed, but I knew the man was right; I seem to have a harder time stuffing my feelings than most people. Out jogging on the green-belt I get goose bumps when I come upon bright beds of smiling petunias smiling at the rising sun. I keep a silly grin for hours after joining a mockingbird in his morning concert. I treasure Cajun hugs and scream like a 12-year-old when I ride the roller coaster. Sometimes in church, when the choir hits the final triumphal notes of an anthem, I have the feeling I'm about to levitate and float through the roof.

When I'm counseling that sensitive antenna plugged into my heart is both a blessing and a problem. My clients like the way I tune into their feelings. But at least once a week I have to remind myself it's possible to empathize without ending the day emotionally drained.

Why did God give me this special awareness? I suspect there's a purpose, and that some day I'll know what it is. But sometime in the past my life slipped into a quiet, respectable ordinariness. Mary, bless her heart, considered it her sacred duty to help me curb my Irish unpredictability. So she reigned me in every time I was about to do something that might compromise my dignity or threaten our security.

She did allow me to celebrate my thirtieth birthday by running in the Boston marathon, and my fortieth doing a free-fall from ten thousand feet. But each time the opportunity came to change the course of our lives, fate seemed to intervene. At thirty-five I was offered a professorship in Denver. For a month I dreamed of weekends on the skiing slopes and big game hunting. But Victoria had developed diabetes, and Mary worried at the prospect of being more than a thousand miles away from Houston's sophisticated medical center. Three years later I was at the point of accepting an invitation to direct an inner city family counseling center in Los Angeles. But college was looming for the girls, and they convinced Mom this wasn't the time for their father to take a cut in salary....

A tear trickles down my cheek, surprising me. Hold on man, don't get sentimental! At last your life is back on track, and there are even days when you miss Mary only half the time instead of every minute.

I remember Moisés' parting words at the airport: "Doctór Andrew, God has plans for you here in Mexico." I had dismissed the strange prophecy immediately. Live in Mexico? Ridiculous!

But now...?

Pushing myself to my feet I begin pacing the room. "Come on, Andrew, use your head! Moisés is a fanatic. You know better than to take him seriously.

Then why this melancholy?

Have I been hoping unconsciously for a letter or a call from Moisés? Two months have passed, and not even a card.

Out of sight, out of mind! By now he's probably forgotten that troubling farewell at the airport.

The phone shrills. I jump, spilling what's left of my coffee. Who could be calling at this hour, a client contemplating suicide, maybe?

"Doctór Andrés?"

Moisés!

"Forgive me for calling so late, brother, but I've spent the day in prayer and a moment ago the Lord told me I must not wait another minute."

I'm too startled to answer.

"Are you there, *hermano*?"

"Yes, yes, Moisés. I was just thinking about you." (My Spanish sounds awful!)

"You have been much on my mind, Doctór. Have you prayed about my words at the airport?"

"Yes, of course." I wonder if Moisés can tell I'm lying.

"Not a day has passed without my praying for you."

"And…and I for you, Pastor Moisés." I'm feeling worse by the second.

"I've wanted to call you many times, but the Lord would not permit it. He kept telling me to wait…until I could give you a confirming word."

Fear washes over me like a cold Gulf wave. "Look, Moses, you're doing a good work. You don't need a gringo with a degree in psychology meddling in your to my surprise, he chuckles. "That's what I felt at first, Doctór. I could think of no reason why the Lord should want you down here. To be honest, I have to work at liking North Americans. But now a door has opened; a door that only you can enter."

I feel my skin prickling. "Moisés, what on earth are you talking about?"

"Several Sundays mornings ago a lady visited my church; a elegant lady, who looked out of place in our congregation. I noticed how carefully she observed everything: the singing, the sermon, prayers for the sick. Then, while I was giving the benediction, she slipped out. I was sure I'd never see her again."

He pauses, and when he speaks his voice is hoarse with emotion: "But yesterday she returned. At the end of the service she came forward for prayer. I discerned a spirit of anger in her and prayed for her and she was gloriously liberated. After the service she asked me to come to her house in Lomas de Chaapultepec and talk to her neighbors."

"And you accepted?"

"No. People there are very proud. And prejudiced. If I tried to give a talk in her home the lady's neighbors would walk out on me as soon as they heard my poor Spanish."

The phone goes silent, and I've about decided the line has been cut. Then I hear chuckle. "Doctór, I must make a confession: I'm a very stubborn man, so in spite of what I just told you, I would have gone anyway, except for what God had told me the night before as I slept. He gave me a revelation of the plan he has for you."

"Revelation?" My fingers tighten on the telephone.

"In my sleep God gave me a vision…of you walking through the front door of *Los Pinos*."

"The doors of…what? Moisés, you've lost me!"

"My brother, *Los Pinos* is Mexico's White House. Halleluja! Now I know why God wants you in Mexico City!"

My head is spinning. "Look, I—"

"Can't you see, Doctór Andrés? The Lord is going to open doors for you that I could never walk through—the doors of the rich and powerful."

I need to sit down! I ease myself onto the sofa, not knowing whether to laugh, cry or hang up.

"Moisés Contreras you are mad!"

He laughs so loud I jerk the phone away from my ear. "That's what my teachers in Seminary kept telling me! Look, Doctór, there's something you need to know about the ricos in Mexico. They have a lot of respect for Americans, especially educated, cultured Americans like yourself. When I told the lady about my good friend Doctór Andrés Kelly and assured her he would be seated in her living room next Saturday afternoon at four o'clock, she was ecstatic!"

I jump to my feet. "What? You told her what?"

"My brother, in the few years I've been serving the Lord I've learned I must respond in faith when he speaks. Immediately. And he has never let me down. You will come, won't you? The lady from Lomas de Chapultepec has already reserved you a room at the downtown María

Isabel Sheraton. And a dozen of her neighbors have agreed to attend your lecture."

I cringe, picturing myself in a luxurious living room standing before a group of sophisticated *damas y caballeros*, saying…what?

"What would I talk about? I'm no preacher!"

"Just talk about the things you deal with every day; marriage problems, the trials of men and women who live alone. Things like that."

"But look, Moisés, I have obligations here next Sunday!"

"My brother, you can take an early flight out Sunday morning and be home in a couple of hours. Of course I hope you'll stay over for our Sunday morning service. The people were disappointed last time when you and the others left Saturday night."

That was the night I vowed never to return to Mexico! I need time to think!

"Excuse me a moment, Moisés."

Going to the bathroom I turn on the faucet full force and splash my face with cold water. I'll tell Moisés I'll call him tomorrow…or the next day…or the next!…

I turn off the faucet. Why kid myself? I already know what my answer must be, this phone call was no accident!

It's after midnight when I finally cradle the phone. I sleep little that night. Next day my clients kid me about yawning…

I take an eleven A.M. flight out of Houston's Intercontinental Airport the next Saturday following Moisés' call, and land in Mexico at noon, their time. At customs, I grin when I see the "traffic light", remembering the last time.

The green light! I move ahead, my eyes already searching the waiting room for Moses' dark face and bulky frame, surprised at the pleasure of anticipation tickling my spine.

Where is the man? Did he get caught in a traffic jam? Pushing through the crowd I let my eyes wander over the room, already considering my options. Should I take a taxi to my hotel or wait a while?

I see a slim, dark-haired woman pushing through the crowd. She too seems to be looking for someone. Her husband? Lucky guy! I realize I'm staring and turn away.

"Excuse me, *Señor.*" I'm startled to see the woman standing before me.

"Would you by any chance be Doctór Andrés Kellee?"

Feeling the color rising in my face, I stutter, "Yes, I—I am."

She puts out a small, finely manicured hand. "I am Gabriela Mancini. Pastor Moisés asked me to meet you."

Taking her hand, I smile down at an exquisite porcelain face framed by ebony hair, aware that those clear, unblinking emerald eyes are inspecting me, appraising me.

Instantly I know who she must be. No wonder Moisés called her "elegant"!

"How nice of you to come on such short notice!" A tiny mole, like the period of an exclamation point, punctuates the corner of her full red lips, smiling at me now.

"Here, *muchacho*, take the gentleman's bag!" (She's small, but she speaks with authority!) A skinny kid in scuffed black pants and a dark blue Dallas Cowboys pullover comes running.

Chatting amiably, she leads me to the parking lot, and as the boy lifts my bag into the trunk of her white Gran Marquis, assures me that she and her friends are excited about having a distinguished American psychologist as their guest.

"The honor is mine, *Señorita*," I answer in my best Spanish—and mean it!

Seated, she turns to me and I'm surprised to see her eyes filling with tears. "Doctór Kellee, you're the answer to my prayers." Reaching up, she caresses a tiny gold locket at the curve of her throat, and a shadow darkens her face for an instant, then is gone. "But more about that later," she says softly, turning the key in the ignition, "I hope you're hungry, I made reservations at El Tablillo."

Half an hour later she brakes before a chic steakhouse on a wide, busy boulevard and hands her keys to a uniformed attendant. A smiling hostess leads us to a table.

She orders *vino tinto* and I a lemonade. The waiter allows us half an hour to savor our drinks, then brings a portable grill with a chunk of tender veal, wheat tortillas, onions, and tiny green chile peppers. Gabriela cuts several slices of meat and lays them on the hot grill.

By now we know a few things about each other: that I'm a widower with two grown daughters and she a divorcée with a teenage son and a daughter studying in the university. "It wasn't exactly a divorce," she says, attempting a smile. "When I explained to the archbishop the circumstances of my husband's betrayal, an annulment was granted. Since then I have—"

She swallows hard. "But this is no time to talk about my troubles. Anyway, when Pastor Moisés prayed for me last Sunday God's peace melted the knot of anger I've held in my heart so long. I've felt different ever since."

She transfers a slice of veal to my plate. "I hope you like your meat medium rare."

As we eat she talks about the meeting scheduled for that afternoon. Mostly women will attend, members of her singles group. "A lot of us need Christian counseling. You'd be shocked to hear the advice therapists here give to a single lady. Then there are the New Age seminars so in vogue these days. It's no wonder many of my friends are trapped in unhealthy relationships."

We're drinking our coffee when Gabriela sets down her cup and consults a tiny jeweled silver wrist watch. "Almost two. I'll drop you by your hotel so you can check in while I do some errands."

I reach for the check, but she lays a hand on mine. "Doctór Andrés, you are my guest."

"But I—"

"Please, you're on a professional visit, at my invitation."

The María Isabel Sheraton, a five-star hotel on handsome Avenida Reforma, has marble floors, attentive employees, and spacious, well-appointed rooms. I resist the impulse to take a second shower and opt for a quick nap. When I awake I feel refreshed. And excited.

My mind keeps returning to my hostess. "Mancini": the name sounds Italian. Combing my dark brown hair, I feel quite handsome, and wonder what she thought of me. I liked the way she called me "Kellee"!

"Whoa, Andrew," I chide himself, "you're here on business. Cool it."

She arrives at four. When she sees me discretely checking my watch she laughs. "Doctór Kellee, don't worry about the time. Here meetings always begin later than the hour announced."

She drives west on Reforma through Chapultepec Park, crosses over the Periférico, a busy loop circling the city, and continues on the graceful tree-lined boulevard until we reach a district of stately residences looming above massive stone walls.

"This is Lomas de Chapultepec I've lived here since infancy. In fact, my family has been here for three generations. When my father retired he and mother moved to a condominium and left me and my family the home I was born in."

She turns off Reforma, continues for several blocks, pulls up before a broad polished oak gate and sounds the horn. The gardener, a hoe in his big stained hands, opens the gate. Crossing the exquisitely manicured lawn I rehearse in my mind how I'm going to describe for Margaret the imposing three-story house with red slate roof. Should I call it a "villa", maybe? A uniformed maid receives us at the door.

Half an hour later the meeting begins in the spacious, richly carpeted parlor. I've decided to make my talk uncomplicated and practical, sprinkled with case histories. At first, feeling self-conscious, I stumble over my Spanish. But soon the words are flowing without conscious effort, and I can tell by the faces of the eight women and two men present that they're pleased with what they're hearing.

Later, as we munch hors-d'oeuvres, Gabriela informs me that everyone present, except for one confirmed bachelor, is either divorced or widowed. In the lively dialogue that follows I learn that most of them would like to try again, but are afraid of being hurt. Sounds familiar!

The meeting is about to break up when one of the ladies says, "Dr. Kelly, Gabriela tells us you might move to Mexico City. If you do, you can be sure many of us will want to be your clients." Everyone applauds.

Glancing at Gabriela I see her cheeks reddening. I hear myself saying, "A decision like that would require a lot of thought."

Gabriela drives me to my hotel. I'm pleased when she accepts my suggestion that she leave her car in the garage and have a last cup of coffee with me.

In the coffee shop I can tell she has something on her mind. She twists her napkin, fingers the little gold locket at her throat. At last she says, "Doctór Kellee, as you could see, we women have been gossiping about you. Please forgive us."

I smile. Does she have any idea how flattered I was that she and her friends would "gossip" about me?

I reach out, touch her arm, and quickly withdraw my hand. "No problem, *Señora* Mancini. To the contrary, I was impressed by the warmth of your friends."

She takes for my hand for a moment. "Please, Doctór, don't we know each other well enough to use first names?"

"*Con mucho gusto*, Gabriela!"

She smiles. "You can't imagine what your visit has meant to us. When we heard you were coming we were excited about having a visitor from Houston. Most of us travel to your city quite often. It's our Mecca for shopping and medical consultations. And now, having heard you speak, we feel more fortunate than ever. It took our breath away to hear a man with a Ph.D. in Psychology advocating a Christian lifestyle."

Pushing back her chair, she exclaims, "*Dios mío*, it's time for me to go. I chased my children out of the house and made them promise they wouldn't be late for supper. Now I'm the one who's going to be late!"

Rising, she gives me an *abrazo*, opens her purse and hands me an envelope. "We didn't discuss your honorarium. I trust this will be adequate." She starts away, then turns back. Taking my hand, those bright green eyes challenging me, she says, "I'll be praying every day that God will bring you back to us. Very soon."

In my room the red light on my telephone is flashing. Suddenly I feel guilty; I haven't thought about Moisés since seeing Gabriela Mancini in the terminal!

We don't talk long, just long enough for me to describe the afternoon meeting and assure Moisés I'll be present for tomorrow's service. I fall asleep watching CNN, and dream of feathered snakes, handsome mansions and sophisticated ladies and gentlemen listening intently as beautifully phonetic Spanish flows from my mouth....

When I awake next morning it takes a moment to realize where I am. I shower, dress and go downstairs for a leisurely breakfast in one of the hotel's three dining rooms. No need to hurry; Moisés warned me the service will begin sometime around noon and last at least two hours.

The taxi driver almost gives up on finding Moisés' church. Moisés told me I'd find it in Colonia Azcapotzalco, twenty minutes from the hotel and half a block from a Social Security clinic. There it is! I'd never have guessed Moisés' congregation meets in an abandoned factory if we hadn't seen people streaming into the rundown building. Then we hear the singing. "*¡Muy alegre*" the taxi driver says as he brakes at the curb.

Happy indeed! As I walk toward the entrance I can already feel my spirits lifting.

Inside I find myself in a huge auditorium of unpainted walls and bare concrete floor, vibrating with the excitement of the congregation. The orchestra, made up of half a dozen electric guitars, a set of drums and Moisés' accordion, is deafening. I guess at least a thousand people must be on their feet, shouting out the lively choruses, some clapping, some waving their arms, some dancing in the aisles. Most of the men are dressed in jeans, and the women in flowered cotton dresses. On the platform a dozen attractive young women mark the rhythm. As I'm finding a seat Moisés, pumping his big red accordion, sees me and nods and smiles without missing a beat.

At first I feel alien, almost frightened. I've attended church all my life, but I've never seen anything like this! Nor felt what I'm feeling now. What am I feeling? Something quite different from what I experience each Sunday morning back home when I sing to the accompaniment of a majestic organ and robed choir. The stately, traditional hymns always touch me deeply, and sometimes tears flow. But this…

I'm judging! I will myself to suspend thought and be immersed in the contagious joy of the folk surrounding me. Soon my body begins moving in time with the boisterous cadence of "The Wedding of the Lamb."

Finally, Moisés stands to speak. Fifty minutes into the sermon I become restless, but no one else seems to share my impatience. They're listening intently, punctuating Moisés' words with a constant chatter of "Amen!" Praise the Lord!" "Halleluja!"

At the close dozens of people move toward the platform. A group of helpers join their pastor, praying for the sick and rebuking evil spirits. A thin, white-haired man hobbles to the front on crutches, complaining of rheumatism. They seat him in a chair on the platform and half a dozen people gather around him, placing their hands on his head, his arms, his arthritic knees, all praying at once. Standing to his feet, he takes a cautious step, and a smile lights up his face. Throwing aside his crutches, he shouts "*Gloria a Dios!!* and begins jumping up and down.

Watching, I'm was glad I didn't insist back in April that the medical team remain until Sunday. How would Tim and Chris have reacted? What would they have told the church back home?

It's after two o'clock when Pastor Moisés invites me to come forward and give the benediction. Afterward I'm surrounded by smiling faces and warmed by dozens of hearty *abrazos*.

An hour later I'm seated across from Moisés in a bright VIPS restaurant, pleased we'll have an opportunity for a quiet talk before my flight back to Houston.

"*Señora* Mancini called me this morning," Moisés says.

I look up from my *pollo rostizado*. "I hope I didn't do too badly."

"Are you kidding? She went on and on about how *simpatico* Doctór Kelly was. Finally I had to tell her I'd be late for church if we didn't hang up."

I smile back, not sure what to say. I kept looking for Gabriela Mancini in the service this morning, but soon I understood why she wasn't there. She'd have been uncomfortable in Moisés' church. And reluctant to invite her friends.

Moisés is studying my face. "Now, Doctór Andrés, having met *Señora* Mancini and her friends, it should be easier to respond to God's call, no?"

"God's call, Moses?"

"Just remember, God doesn't have to speak in an audible voice. Sometimes he uses circumstances. Like yesterday, when you stood before a people rich in this world's goods but hungering for spiritual food, and your heart told you God was speaking through you."

I'm choking. Reaching for my cool glass of *sidral* I stammer, "Look, Moisés, just for the sake of argument, let's say I want to come to Mexico City. I'm sure the immigration laws would forbid my moving here tomorrow and opening an office."

Laying down his fork, Moisés leans across the table and lays a heavy hand on my arm. "Doctór Kelly, that's not your problem. Your part is to say yes to God. He takes care of the circumstances."

That night on the plane, a few minutes after takeoff, I look down. How different my feelings from just two months ago! Back then the sea of lights had flamed like the mouth of hell. Tonight they seem to be the footlights of an enormous stage, and Gabriela Mancini is standing there, smiling, beckoning....

CHAPTER 5

▼

DECISION TIME

Margaret and my little grandson Jeff are waiting for me at Intercontinental in Houston. Seeing them is like waking from a dream.

Margaret is petite and blonde like her mother. And like her mother,
deciding on priorities never seems to be a problem for her. When she
enrolled in the University of Houston three years ago she made it clear
she wasn't interested in a career. Somewhere God had a good Christian
man waiting for her, and he'd want her to stay home and be a mother
to their children.

Halfway through the first semester she met Tom, a senior. Two
months after his graduation they married and took a lease on an apartment in Kingwood, where Tom managed a Taco Bell. She became
pregnant immediately. Margaret is the perfect wife, perfect mother...
and yes, perfect daughter.

"Hi, Daddy, Jeff's been driving me crazy!" She gives me a hug and
hands over my grandson, who grins at me and snuggles into my arms.

"I'm anxious to hear about your trip," Margaret says as soon as we
get in the car.

"It was fabulous. Had a great time."

"And that fascinating lady the pastor called you about. Did you meet her?"

"Can you believe it? She met me at the airport, took me to lunch, then to her house."

"Well, I'm going to take you to *your* house and grill you! I can't wait to hear the details."

In my carport she retrieves a big brown German sweet chocolate cake from the back seat of her van and carries it to the kitchen table.

"Tom left this afternoon for a two-day company meeting in Dallas, Daddy. So I just want to sit here a while and have a long talk with you. You've been so busy lately!"

She plugs in the coffee pot and gets Jeff settled in my den in front of a Bambi video. Then we sit down at the table and smile at each other fondly. "Now start at the beginning and tell me everything," Margaret pleads, sliding a huge piece of cake in my direction.

I describe my encounter with Gabriela in the airport, my lecture at her house and the service the next morning at Moisés' church. I don't tell her about the meal in *El Tablillo*. There's a touch of magic in my memory of those two hours, and I'm afraid the enchantment might evaporate if I share it with anyone. And of course I say nothing about the chat in VIPS with Moisés and his insistence that God wants me in Mexico.

When I finish she reaches over and pats my hand. "Daddy," she murmurs, pouring a second cup of coffee, "it's good to see you happy again."

I frown. "Happy? Well, I..."

"Oh Daddy, don't feel bad about being able to smile again. Mama's been gone for eight months now, you know that's what she'd want."

Licking icing from a finger, she says, "Katherine asked if she could come with me to the airport, but I found an excuse for refusing. I wanted you for myself tonight.... She's sweet don't you think?" Margaret takes a long sip of coffee, watching my face.

"Katherine's a nice lady."

"Tell me more about your hostess. What did you say her name was?"

"Mancini. Gabriela Mancini."

"And…her husband?"

"She…she's a divorcee." I can feel the color rising to my cheeks.

My daughter sets down her cup and leaned forward. "And how old is she, Daddy? Fiftiesh? Sixty?"

"Oh no, not that old."

"About your age?"

"A little younger, maybe." I shift nervously in my chair.

Margaret is trying to read my mind! Jeff comes into the kitchen and climbs into his mother's lap.

"Hi, Jeff," I say, "how was Bambi?" I want to hug him for giving me an excuse to change the subject!

"My goodness," Margaret murmurs, checking her watch. "It's way past Jeff's bed time." She gets up, seats him gently on the floor and begins gathering the dishes.

"You go ahead, Dear," I tell her, "I'll get that."

"Sure you don't mind?" She retrieves her purse and takes out the keys.

"Of course not. I'm used to it by now."

I follow her to the door. She stands there for a moment, jingling the keys, her back to me.

"Margaret is something bothering you?"

Turning suddenly, she throws her arms around me. "Daddy, last night I dreamed you called from Mexico City and said you weren't coming home. You…you wouldn't leave us, would you?"

I gently push her away and kissing her forehead, murmur, "Leaving you and my grandson is the furthest thing from my mind!"

"I know I'm being silly. It's just that I haven't gotten used to Mama being gone yet. If you should go away too…"

After I've cleaned up the kitchen I punch in the ten o'clock news. But I hear little, I'm too busy trying to explain to myself why I lied to my daughter.

Finally I lay aside the Sunday paper and go to bed, knowing I'm not going to sleep. When the clock strikes twelve I get up and slide my feet into my slippers. It isn't the French roast coffee that's keeping me awake, I know, but emotional indigestion. So much has happened in the last two days! I boarded the plane Saturday remembering that ghastly encounter with Quetzalcóatl two months before, wondering why I had allowed Moisés Contreras to talk me into breaking my vow never to return.

But two hours later I'd walked out of customs in Mexico City and…

Gabriela Mancini! I stopped pacing, reliving the moment when she stood before me and asked, "Doctór Andrew Kellee?"

I chuckled. Was she the only Mexican who had pronounced my name that way? Probably not. But the way she said it was special, almost like a caress.

And the way her friends treated me! Standing before them I'd remembered Moisés' words on the telephone. The man was right; well-to-do Mexicans did seem to have a special respect for Americans.

But why their insistence that I move to Mexico City? They had no need of an American Ph.D. A city as sophisticated as Mexico City would have more than enough competent therapists steeped in the Mexican idiosyncrasy; an American could hardly expect to be as effective as they. Strange!

I resume my nervous pacing…maybe it wasn't so strange after all…maybe Moisés has already given me the answer to my puzzle: "Don't expect God to speak in an audible voice; listen for God's voice in the things that happen to you."

Did God speak through Gabriela and her friends? Is God daring me to take a leap of faith? My heart is thumping like a bass drum.

I stop suddenly. Just a minute, Andrew! Remember that offer seven years ago of a professorship in Denver? Remember how excited you were; just like you are now? And how about the invitation, a couple of years later, from the counseling center in Los Angeles? Both times you were ready to start packing your bags…until reality punched you in the stomach.

I groan. Every time I reach for the moon I come plummeting back to earth like Apollo Thirteen!"

I walk over and drop down into an armchair. The clock downstairs strikes one. "Oh boy, I'm really far out this time. At least in Denver and Los Angeles they were offering me a salary. They wouldn't even allow me to dig ditches in Mexico City."

"…Dr. Andrew, how you'll get by is not your problem. Your part is to say yes to God. The rest is God's problem."

Moisés again—daring me to put God on the spot.

Have I ever in my life put God on the spot?

No, never.

And if I don't this time, will I ever have the opportunity again?

I push myself up from the chair, feeling like I'm wrestling a 300 pound gorilla. I stand for a moment, swaying. Reaching out for the chair, I steady my self.

Well, why not? When I did the marathon and the sky dive I put myself on the spot, and I didn't let myself down. If I put God on the spot, will God do less?

Grinning, I strike a heroic pose, and shout "All right, Lord. My answer is Yes!" There, I've said Moisés' magic word! I walk over to a window, swing it open and yell out into the darkness: "God, I said 'Yes'. Now it's your problem!"

The neighbor's dog begins barking angrily, and a moment later the next-door patio is flooded with light.

Quietly closing the window, I ease myself down on the floor and laugh and laugh until my sides hurt.

When I finally crash into bed I fall asleep immediately, at peace with the world, myself and my destiny.

The next couple of weeks are extraordinarily pleasant. My clients seem to be more responsive than usual; two troubled marriages I've almost given up on take a turn for the better.

Katherine and I have dinner several times, and enjoy just being together.

One morning after I've finished with a client my secretary tells me, "Your attorney phoned. Said to call him back as soon as possible."

The next afternoon I'm seated across from my lawyer in his office in The Woodlands. Chip has been exceptionally successful in his profession, and his office brags about it. Every time I wade through the deep white carpet and sit on the chrome and black furniture I find myself checking my tie and inspecting the shine on my shoes. But I like Chip. We belong to the same church and for years golfed together every month or so—until Mary's death. Thankfully, sometime before the accident Chip talked me into drawing up a will. Now the will is being probated. I suppose Chip has summoned me to put my signature on something.

His first words surprise me: "Andrew I asked you over because I need your go-ahead on the settlement of Mary's accident."

I raise my eyebrows. "Settlement?"

"Yes, remember? You gave me your ok to pursue the matter."

I've almost forgotten. One day back in February, when I was at home in the depths of depression, Chip called me about the urgency of pursuing the legal aspect of the accident.

"Here's what they're proposing." He pushes across the desk a sheaf of documents with the letterhead of a Dallas law firm. Flipping through the pages, I blink. I must not be understanding the legal verbiage. I lay down the document and ask, my voice uneven, "Am I reading right? Are they offering me a million and a half dollars?"

"Look, Pal, if you don't think that's enough we'll take 'em to trial. They're scared to death, and—"

"I...I had no idea it would be that much."

Chip throws down his pen and leans back in his chair. "Are you kidding? Under the circumstances most people would be suing for ten. But knowing you, I didn't think you'd want to get involved in a long court fight."

"But to profit from Mary's horrible accident...it's obscene!"

Chip comes around and sits on the edge of his polished mahogany desk. "Look, Buddy, let me tick it off for you: the guy that slammed into Mary's BMW was taking a client out to his club in a company car. He's an executive in a corporation worth billions. Businesses like his are loaded with insurance. Believe me, they're getting off light and they know it."

I drop my head into my hands. "I don't know, Chip...remembering what happened still makes me sick at the stomach."…. Clenching my teeth, I mutter, "Besides, I hate the way people these days sue at the drop of a hat!"

My friend leans over and lays a hand on my shoulder. "Listen, if you'd prefer not to keep the money, then donate it to the church...or an orphan's home. But don't feel bad about taking it; they owe it to you."

Forcing myself to relax, I give him a friendly poke in the stomach. "Tell you what, let me have a couple of days to think about it."

I shake Chip's hand and walk slowly out to my car. I'm about to turn the key in the ignition when I remember...and freeze:

A couple of weeks ago, in the dead of night, I stood in my living room and shouted "Yes!" And laughed about putting God on the spot.

I don't feel like laughing now.

Is God laughing?

Houston's July heat makes the car a steamy sauna, but I'm in a cold sweat. Reaching out I turn the key and the air conditioner kicks in.

Taking my handkerchief, I wipe the fog off my sun glasses and sit for a long time waiting for my mind to catch up with my heart.

After a while I check my watch. Three-thirty; in half an hour my late-afternoon schedule begins.

Not today!

Turning off the switch, I hurry back into Chip's office and dial my secretary. She's grumpy about canceling my appointments on such short notice, but I don't care. I hang up, start for the door, then on impulse turn and ask for the phone again. The church secretary answers.

"Connie, by any chance is the preacher available?"

"He's about to leave for a hospital visit. I'll put him on the line, you can check with him."

Dr. Carlson's strong, reedy voice: "Hi, Andrew. What can I do for you?"

"Is there any possibility I might bend your ear for a few minutes this afternoon?"

"I'll be back from the hospital in an hour. How's that?"

Later, seated across from the pastor, I struggle for a way to begin. Dr. Carlson and I have never been close. Tall, graying, almost skeletal, metal-rimmed glasses pinching a thin nose, he lacks the easy friendliness that seems to come naturally for most Baptist preachers. But the man has integrity. And that long night at the hospital after Mary's accident, while the girls and I agonized in the ICU waiting room, he was seated beside us. Didn't say much, just sat there reading his Bible. And after midnight, when the weary, sad-faced surgeon came in with the fateful prognosis, he wept with us.

Now he sits quietly behind his scarred desk, quiet, intelligent eyes on my face.

"Where shall I begin, Pastor?"

Carlson smiled. "What do you say when your clients ask you that question?"

So I begin at the beginning, and end with my challenge to God a few nights ago. I conclude: "So how do you see me? A bereft widower trying to run away from reality?"

My pastor studies his hands for a moment. "Well, with your training you know better than I the temptation of escapism when people are in a crisis. On the other hand, sometimes God does use tough moments in our lives to open new doors."

I swallow the lump in my throat. "But what if the open door looks like an invitation to betrayal?" I tell him of my visit with Chip. And conclude: "So you see why I'm troubled. With the settlement they're offering I could move to Mexico City tomorrow and never worry about finances. But..." I drop my chin into my hands..."how could I let myself profit from that loathsome accident!"

Dr. Carlson blows out a heavy sigh and pushes back from the desk. "Andrew, all this is a big surprise for me; I had no idea you were going through such anguish of soul about God's will. As for that money..." he takes off his glasses and lays them on the desk..."let me jog your memory a bit. You remember, of course, when the doctor came into Mary's hospital room and told us there was no hope."

"How could I ever forget?"

"And that he asked permission to withdraw life-support?"

"Yes." Unwanted tears are stinging my eyes.

"Do you recall what happened after that?"

"Pastor, what are you driving at?" I feel anger rising in my chest. I've struggled for months to find some measure of peace about Mary's death; why does he want to probe a raw wound?

"I'm sorry, Andrew, but this is important. Remember, Margaret handed you her mother's driver's license and pointed out two words right beside her picture."

I gasp. "Now I remember: 'Organ Donor: yes.'" I'm having trouble breathing.

"You were surprised. Said that Mary hadn't told you about having them put that on her license the last time it was renewed."

I pull out a handkerchief and dab at my eyes. "Well, I don't guess I was really surprised. That's how Mary was, always looking for ways to help people in need."

The pastor says softly, "Do you think those words on Mary's license might help you resolve the problem you're wrestling with?"

"What do you mean?"

"This is painful, I know, but hear me out. Remember? Victoria grabbed the license out of your hand and shouted she'd never give them permission to mutilate her mother's body. She was about to tear it up when you snatched it from her and said..."

"I told her it would be"—a sob constricts my throat..."a worse mutilation to deny her mother's last wish."

Dr. Carlson comes over, and his blue eyes inches from mine, says just above a whisper, "Andrew, what about you? When Mary renewed her license she was affirming that if she should have a fatal accident she wanted her death to be a blessing to others. You refused to let your daughter frustrate that wish. Dare you do otherwise?"

Dropping my face into my hands, I groan, "My God, Preacher, what are telling me?"

The pastor pulls up a chair very close and says softly, "Andrew, my friend, I don't know if God wants you in Mexico. But if he does, I can't think of a better way of taking your dear Mary with you."

At my request the pastor places his hands on my head and prays a prayer I'll never forget:

Eternal God, ruler of heaven and earth, our dear loving
Father. Before your son Andrew was born you had already
mapped out every second of his life. These last months
he's wondered sometimes if you'd forgotten him. But now,
it seems, the bright light of your providence is shining
upon him. Give him the faith to walk in that light. And
wherever the light may lead him give him the abundant grace
of your protecting care. Through Jesus Christ our Lord.   Amen.

The next day, before I tell Margaret, I prepare myself for an angry response. She surprises me. "Daddy, remember that dream I told you about the day you came back from Mexico? Ever since, there's been a little knot in my heart. I guess, deep down, I knew this was going to happen."

She goes over to her desk, picks up a legal pad, and says, "We'd better plan a garage sale."

A week later Victoria descends on me. Storming through the front door, overnight bag in hand, she pushes aside the bric-a-brac Margaret and I have piled on the sofa and plops down beside me. "Daddy, why haven't you called me? What if I hadn't pried the truth out of Margaret on the phone last night? Were you waiting to send me a post card from Mexico City?"

Freckles stand out on her nose like tiny brown beacons, and when I reach over to give her a hug, her auburn hair is crackling with electricity. She stiffens and pushes me away.

"Darling I was going to call you this week. I knew you were busy at summer school and your job and I didn't want to upset you."

I reach for her hand, but she jerks it away. "Don't be patronizing with me, Daddy. I know why you didn't call me. You know what you're doing is absolutely insane and you were afraid I'd come and change your mind for you!"

I'm about to give an answer in kind when I see her eyes blurring with tears. And anyway, she's almost right about why I didn't call her. Not because I was afraid she might change my mind, but because I didn't feel up to facing the verbal barrage I knew she'd let loose. Victoria was a champion debater in Kingwood High and is chin-deep in pre-law at Baylor. She's convinced her God-given mission is to straighten everybody out.

It takes me two hours to convince her I'm not going to budge. At last she gets up, brushes back her hair and surrenders. "All right, then, Daddy, you go ahead. Margaret and I will be here to help you pick up the pieces when you come to your senses."

She stays overnight in what has been her room since her twelfth birthday. The next day she takes a different tact, as if determined to rescue something from a frustrating visit. Why didn't I work out a deal with Margaret and Tom to sell them the house? They're still in their small apartment; wouldn't it be nice to have a guest room to stay in when I come back for visits?

I promise her I'll give it serious thought.

She leaves before noon, a large suitcase in hand packed with faded doilies, a favorite table lamp, old National Geographics…and a dozen other things she can't bear surrendering to the garage sale. For a moment I think she's going to get into her car without giving me a hug. But suddenly she buries her face in my chest and bawls.

She pulls back and blows her nose. Brushing at her hair, she turns down the corners of her pale mouth in a sad little smile. "So Daddy, I guess you're planning to be a celibate the rest of your life!"

I playfully slap her cheek. "That's none of your business!"

"Don't tell me you'd marry a Mexican?"

"Look little girl, let me handle my love life, okay?"

She wrinkles her nose at me. "You're kind of old, but you're still handsome. There are a lot of widows and divorcees in Kingwood who'd jump at the chance to lasso a man like you. Think of the opportunity you're throwing away!"

She jumps into the car, turns the switch, guns the engine, throws it into reverse and is halfway out the driveway when she brakes, sticks her head out the window and yells, "I love you anyway!"

I leave for Mexico a month later.

CHAPTER 6

▼

GOD'S KAIROS

The phone is ringing. I shake myself awake and reach out a wet hand to lift the receiver off the pink telephone resting on a stool beside the bathtub.

"Hello?"

"Mr. Kelly? I'm calling from the dining room. One of our waiters knocked on your door and there was no answer. Are you all right?"

"*Perdón, Señor*, I must have fallen asleep. Please send him back and I'll be waiting.

I replace the receiver, grab a towel and am tying on my robe when the man returns.

"Your food may be a little cold by now, *Señor*."

"No matter, it still smells good." I hand the boy a tip and plop down at the table, suddenly very hungry. No wonder! It's nine o'clock and I haven't eaten since noon. M…m…m…enchiladas suizas, my first since that night in the restaurant with Moisés Contreras.

Taking the last bite, I stifle a yawn. I push back the tray and pick up my watch. Nine thirty. "It's still early," I tell myself, "but I'm bushed. Think I'll hit the sack and get an early start in the morning."

I get up, place the tray outside the door, brush my teeth and fall into bed. Almost before my head hits the pillow I'm asleep....

Margaret's house is on fire and my little grandson is trapped inside! Wheezing, coughing, lungs bursting, I push through the dense black smoke, searching desperately, hope almost gone...

I awake gasping for breath, the blood pounding in my ears. Thank God it was only a dream! But then, jolted by a spasm of pain, I clutch my chest. A heart attack!

No, it must be the enchiladas. I roll out of bed, zip open my suitcase and pour half a bottle of Pepto-Bismol down my throat, remembering stories I've heard of people mistaking a heart attack for indigestion.

Another sharp cramp squeezes my chest and telescopes down my left arm. Does Mexico have a 9ll? I imagine myself on a stretcher, strange dark faces staring down at me.

"Oh God, help me!"

...I'm back in Teotihuacan, standing with Moisés before Quetzalcóatl's temple. "Always remember, Dr. Andrew," Moisés is saying, "Satan is a deceiver. When he's at work things are never what they seem."

Kyrus! He is here in the room, invisible, but so real I can smell his fetid breath....

"Kyrus," I shout, "not this time. I'm covered by the blood of Christ."

Beginning at my heart a delicious warmth moves upward, bathing me in peace, turning my arms and legs to lead. I crumple upon the bed and almost instantly fall into a profound sleep.

The alarm awakes me. Throwing back the covers, I swing my feet to the floor and flick on the lamp switch. Hey, I feel great!

I stand up and reach for the clock. "Five o'clock, time to get on the road!"

"Time!"

I fall back on the bed, remembering...when the alarm sounded I was in the midst of a vivid dream: a noisy grandfather's clock kept swinging its pendulum back and forth, whispering "time... time...time." My heartbeat was keeping time with the pendulum as the strokes became shorter, the rhythm of the words ever more ominous, "time, time, time...."

"Time!"

Time...Kyrus...Kairos!

I jump out of bed. My Greek New Testament—did I bring it with me?

I grab up the car keys and run to the door, unmindful of the icy tile floor. Shivering in the frigid pre-dawn desert air, I throw open the car trunk and grunt as I pick up the box of books I packed the day before the movers arrived. Not many, just enough to tide me over until, hopefully, the rest of my library could be shipped.

Lugging the box into the room, I begin digging, my teeth chattering, not so much from the cold as from excitement. Where is my Greek Testament, did I leave it behind? I turn the box upside down, dumping the books on the floor. There!

Flipping the pages, I try to remember: "Where's that verse? Dr. Wentworth spent an entire class on it, not long before I graduated from seminary."

I was thankful for my pastor's insistence that I do my Ph.D. in a theological school. The Master's in Psychology from the University of Texas was fine, he told me, but a good dose of Christian theology was needed as a healthy complement for all the secular stuff they'd piled on me in the university.

"There!" My finger stabs a red-underlined passage, the last words of Jesus before his Ascension: "It is not for you to know the *chronos* or the *kairos*, which the Father hath put in his own power."

"Young men," after twenty years I can still remember my teacher's scholarly twang, "we have a good English word for *chronos*, time', but nobody has found a word that gives the exact sense of *kairos*. It also refs to time, but in a unique sense. The King James Version translates it "seasons" and Phillips, "dates". Neither is satisfactory. Just remember: when you're reading your Greek Testament and come upon *kairos*: stop, look and listen, because the Holy Spirit is flashing a caution light, warning of a coming crisis, an eminent judgment. That's why Jesus used the word more than once to predict his own crucifixion."

I reach up, pull a blanket off the bed and wrap it around my shoulders, remembering a dark-eyed stranger at the filling station putting out a hand and saying, "My name is Kairos."

"And I called him Cyrus!"

So! Quetzalcóatl knew I was coming! But why had he sent a messenger named "Kairos"?

Reaching for my English Bible, I turn to the concordance. "'Take ye heed, watch and pray: for ye know not when the *kairos* is.' (Mark 13:33). Hm-m-m. Here again the Lord is talking about His Second Coming.

"The *kairos* is near' (Luke 21:8, Revelation 1:3). Again, the Second Coming!" I can feel my pulse quickening.

Flipping the pages, I come to Revelation 12:12, a description of the last days before Christ's descent to earth. "Woe to the inhabiters of the earth and of the sea! for the devil has come down to you, having great wrath, because he knoweth he hath but a short *kairos*."

Could it be? Satan sends a messenger named Kairos to intercept me because there's going to be a collision between Christ's *kairos* and Satan's *kairos*. Here in Mexico! Wow, I need to talk to Moisés!

Throwing the pile of books back into the box, I hurry to the bathroom, splash cold water on my face, fold my pajamas into the suitcase, and ten minutes later am in the hotel lobby checking out....

"Imbecile!"

The Feathered Serpent, his hooded eyes colder than the snow glistening in the pre-dawn darkness, is writhing, hissing, his tongue flicking angrily. Before him kneels Kairos, teeth chattering, arms raised in supplication.

The message from his Lord had flashed on the dark screen of Kairos' evil mind after the bogus heart attack in Saltillo: "Pico de Orizaba. Immediately!"

Pico de Orizaba, the highest peak in Mesoamerica, pierces the clear blue sky like a celestial snow cone, separating the cool, rare ambiance of the Valley of Mexico from the heavy moist Gulf air. Kairos knows of more than a dozen demon colleagues who had their last view of the bright, lustrous earth from this point. Now they're languishing in Quetzalcóatl's boot camp beneath the Zócalo in Mexico City. Will that also be his fate? For five desolate hours in the frigid blackness, awaiting his Lord's appearance, he has tortured himself with that question "Have mercy, Oh Master," he croaks, pulling his black academic robe tighter around his thin shoulders. "Everything was going as you ordered until Dunatos, the Lamb's bully, appeared out of nowhere."

"Incompetent!" A flame rolls from the jaws of the Serpent, melting a circle of snow at the feet of the terrified vassal. "You opened the door for the Lamb's angel. I'd warned you Kelly was covered by the Job Clause."

"The Job Clause." As if his master has touched the key of a computer, Kairos intones in a stilted, metallic voice: "El's Manual, Job l:l2b, 'Behold all that he hath is in thy power; only upon himself put not forth thine hand.' Forgive me, Master, it slipped my mind that I'm forbidden to touch Andrew Kelly's body."

"I thought you'd have no trouble deceiving an American Ph.D.," Quetzalcóatl growls. "But what good is an I.Q. of l000 if you're incapable of remembering my simplest instructions? I should have left you blabbering Marxist nonsense in the halls of the National University."

Sobbing, Kairos plants a slobbery kiss on the writhing tail of his serpentine master: "Please, my Lord, have mercy, I've learned my lesson. I became overconfident. The Lamb's emissary looked so meek standing there beside the gasoline pump."

"Meek!" the earl of the Prince of Darkness screeches, and in the East the timid dawn painting the Gulf sky retreats for a moment. "Have you forgot-

ten the Lamb's boast that the meek would inherit the earth?" Quetzalcóatl flicks his tail angrily.

In his post-Saltillo disembodied state of pure intellect Kairos is nothing more than a dark gray effulgence—lighter than a quetzal's feather. The swish of his master's tail wafts him, like a small cirrus cloud, onto the bare branches of a nearby oak, where he hangs disconsolate, awaiting his fate. Tears falling like raindrops freeze into ice pellets and bounce as they hit the ground.

After a long moment of silence the Feathered Serpent curls up on a snow bank and says, quietly now, "The dawn is breaking. I have no more time to waste with you. Now repeat what I told you in your orientation for this job."

Again, a stilted, academic recital: "El is finalizing plans for the Wedding of the Lamb. Soon there will be a decisive battle between the Serpent and the Lamb here in Mexico where—" he clears his throat nervously, "the Serpent has reigned since the Insurrection. Andrew is a key figure in those plans. He must be eliminated."

"And what did I tell you to do?"

"To give Andrew Kelly such a scare he'd go scuttling back across the Border and never return."

"And you failed me!"

"But my Lord, if I'm forbidden to lay a hand on him…

"The Serpent uncoils like a spring suddenly released, and his ugly nose strikes Kairos square in the face. "You and I know that, but he doesn't." The tongue flicks angrily. "And anyway, the time may come when the Job Clause no longer applies."

Encouraged, Kairos floats down from the tree and stands, head bowed, before his master. "So there is time?"

"The Prince has told me that at least one more President must occupy Los Pinos before the final battle. But we can't wait to dispose of Andrew Kelly; once he learns to trust absolutely in the Lamb you'll never scare him away."

Suddenly the Feathered Serpent is a jaguar! Muscles rippling beneath his yellow hide, he rises to his feet, and terrible, snarling jaws inches from the terrified face of his slave, roars: "See that you don't fail!"

Turning he bounds into space and seconds later is lost in the blackness enveloping the valley below.

CHAPTER 7

▼

A HISTORY LESSON

A glorious morning! The road that in yesterday's darkness seemed fore-boding, threatening, has been washed clean by a cool late night shower and the desert sky is pinking into the first flush of dawn. I glance at my watch. A few minutes past six: with luck I'll make it to Mexico City by sundown. The day should go fast, I've got a lot of thinking to do....

By midmorning I'm so hungry I'm gnawing on an overripe apple I found on the back seat. What an unpleasant surprise: I've covered a hundred fifty miles of battered desert highway and haven't found a place I'd risk for even a cup of coffee. A rusty sign warns me the town just ahead is named "Matehuala". Sounds awful, it's bound to be just like the handful of sad villages I've passed through since leaving Saltillo.

Surprise! Beside the highway, shaded by a grove of palms, is the Restaurant Las Palmas.

Freshly painted a bright green, it has crisp white table cloths, uniformed waiters and strong black coffee served from silver pitchers. I enjoy a generous serving of rich golden papaya and *huevos rancheros* with just enough sauce to make my tongue tingle.

Back on the highway I tell myself I have no right to feel this cheerful after last night's traumas. Kairos…where is he right now, buzzing around overhead? Or setting a trap for me somewhere down the road? Or maybe the failure of the trap he set for me back at the hotel discouraged him and he'll leave me alone for a while. I shrug. I haven't the foggiest how evil spirits work, I only know that at this moment my soul is wrapped in a strange peace.

My eyes sweep the blistering desert crammed with twisted, stunted cactus. I see a group of ragged kids ahead, hair matted with chalky dust, trying to flag down the passing cars. What are they hawking? Looks like dried rattlesnake skins! I want to pinch myself. Is Andrew Kelly, Ph.D., really on this desert road, barreling into a way of life completely foreign to anything he's known before?

Hours later, squinting through the dusk, I see a tall gray pylon identifying a huge Ford assembly plant. I ease off on the accelerator. The traffic is picking up, so we must be approaching Mexico City. A quiet, steady rain is falling vertically from the dark sky. I breathe a sigh of relief when Highway 57 becomes the Periferico, a broad boulevard heading south into town. After half an hour I turn left on Reforma ad minutes later I'm checking into the Maria Isabel Sheraton.

I can't remember when I've ever been so excited.

The next morning I'm seated across from Moisés Contreras in the big man's cluttered office. Last night, after checking into my room, I dialed Moisés' number half a dozen times without an answer. Just before midnight I decided to try once more.

"*Bueno?*" Unmistakable, that gruff voice!.

"Pastor Moisés?"

"Gracias a Dios! What a relief to hear from you, since yesterday the Spirit has been warning me you were in danger!"

Half an hour ago I rang the bell at the sagging wooden door of the old factory building that *Iglesia El Calvario* called home. A passerby would never guess what went on behind this unpainted facade of crumbling stucco, I told myself. The caretaker opened the door and led me past endless rows of worn metal chairs to the Pastor's office behind the platform.

Moisés was seated at his desk talking on the phone. Jumping up, he ran to give me a hearty *abrazo*. "I'll be with you in just a minute, *hermano,* he said, "have a seat."

Easing myself into a worn maroon overstuffed chair, I looked around. The big windowless room with faded blue plaster walls and bare concrete floor smelled faintly of an early morning mopping with pine oil. *El Calvario* moved here a year ago because they were overflowing their small thirty-year old temple. Since then dozens of new people have been flowing into the building every Sunday.

"All right," the pastor bellows into the phone, "I'll expect you this afternoon." Gesturing, he knocks over a stack of letters. I wonder how often he cleans off his battered old desk. The ancient Rheinmetal typewriter at his elbow floats like a ponderous battleship in a sea of scattered papers.

On the wall behind Moisés' head hangs a framed elementary teacher's certificate, and beside it a diploma of ordination. But there's no seminary diploma. A couple of years ago Trinidad Seminary advised him the Faculty had voted not to accept him for a second year of study.

Moisés cradles the phone and pulls up a metal straight chair facing me. "Now, tell me about your trip!" he says, reaching out to drag closer a little electric space heater humming bravely in the frigid office.

Sitting with his knees almost touching mine my new friend listens intently as I tell him about my meeting in the gas station with the scholarly stranger and my escape from sudden death. Taking my little black Greek New Testament from my coat pocket I give him a resume of my exciting ten-minute Bible study in the hotel room, yesterday before dawn. When I stop to catch my breath Moisés jumps up, toppling his chair, and striding back and forth between the desk and a lumpy old brown couch pushed against the wall, bangs a fist into his hand, mumbling "*Dios mío...*"God's *kairos* meets Satan's *kairos...Dios mío, Dios mío*!

"I know it sounds wild, Moisés," I tell him, "but everything I told you really happened. Believe me, I didn't have a bottle of tequila under my car seat!"

Ignoring my attempt at humor, Moses goes to his desk and grabs up a worn black Bible. The swivel chair groans as he plops into it and turns pages furiously until he stabs a verse with a finger.

Squinting at me, his thick black mustache quivering, he says, "Doctór Kelly, I didn't study Greek during the short time I was privileged to be in the seminary. Do me a favor. Take your Greek Testament and translate Matthew 16:3."

I find the passage and slowly read Christ's words: "Hypocrites! Indeed you know how to discern the face of the heavens, but the signs of the—" I pause—"the signs of the *kairos* you cannot."

"*Kairos*! I knew it!" Moisés slams a big fist into the desk, upsetting a glass. Getting up, he begins pacing the room again. Finally he stops in front of me, hands on hips, breathing hard: "My brother, can you doubt God has brought you to Mexico for such a..." he smiles, "a *kairos* as this? Listen: last Saturday, while you were conversing with Satan's envoy, I was at a pastor's retreat, listening to a study on demons presented by a professor from Trinidad seminary. Everybody knew why they had assigned him that topic; every time we pastors get together we end up fighting over what to do about so much demon activity all around us.

"Just as I expected, Dr. Barnes had a warning for us: don't try to confront demons like Christ and his followers did. Demons exist, of course. But the authority to cast them out disappeared with the Apostles.

"I asked the professor if he had ever prayed for anyone tormented by a demon.

"'Look, Brother Moisés,'" he said, waving his Bible in my face, 'let me give you a piece of advice. Exalt Christ and you won't have to worry about demons.'

"Several of the pastors said 'Amen.' Most of my brother ministers don't approve of me; you'll learn that soon enough.

"Then I asked another question: 'Is it possible, Dr. Barnes, that growing up in the United States might have influenced how you feel about demons?'

"His face turned very red. 'What difference would that make? Do you think there are more demons in Mexico than in the United States?' Everybody laughed."

"I said, 'Yes, Doctor, I'm sure of it!'" Several of the men groaned. That's when I read them the verse you've just translated for me. That made them mad. Someone stood up and congratulated Dr. Barnes and his colleagues for expelling me from the seminary.

"Do you see what happened. *Don* Andrés? At the very moment you were facing Kairos on the highway outside Saltillo, God, through this unworthy servant, was rebuking my fellow pastors for ignoring the signs of the *kairos*!"

Raw fear gushes up into my throat, strangling me. I mumble, "But Moisés, do you really believe there are more demons in Mexico than in the United States?"

"Look, Doctór, I'm not interested in a head count of the devil's army. But I have a question for *you*: do you believe Christ is coming soon?"

I sit staring at the floor for a long moment. "Well, Moisés, I'm not a theologian. But that's what my pastor back home preaches, and I have a lot of respect for him."

"Your pastor's right. Our Lord *is* coming soon, and the final battle with Satan has begun. Imagine what that means for Mexico, where Qutezalcóatl and his demons have been in control for millenniums. He's not going to give up his territory without a fight!"

My mouth is dry as a desert! I go to the desk, pick up the overturned glass, my hand trembling, and pour myself a drink of water. Turning to face the big man glowering at me like a John the Baptist, I yell,

"Look, Moisés, I want to make something very clear. I didn't come to your country to pick a fight with the devil!"

(Why am I hollering? I must sound like those pastors at the retreat!)

A grin lights up Moisés' face. "Relax, my brother. Have I ever told you I plan to put you to work as an exorcist? God has other plans for you. But do you think Quetzalcóatl, the lord of Mexico, is going to allow you to invade his territory and walk in his spheres of power without challenging you?

"Come, I want to show you why demons are so belligerent in this country." He walks over to a map taped to the wall behind the old couch.

"This is how the Valley of Mexico looked a thousand years ago," he says, pointing to a large lake set in a hilly countryside. "Tenochtitlan, our modern Mexico City, was once an island in the center of this lake, Lake Texcoco. See how Lake Texcoco linked up with Lake Xochimilco in the south, and in the north, with Lake Zumpango? Together they formed a water system a hundred kilometers long and thirty kilometers wide."

"Hm-m, I don't remember seeing any lakes when we flew into the city back in April."

"Of course not, my friend, the lakes have dried up." He turns to face me. Remember, I told you Tenochtitlan was founded by the Aztecs. Did you know, that according to their tradition, their ancestors lived in a city named Aztlan, at the headwaters of your Colorado River?

"More than a thousand years ago one of their prophets had a vision. He saw a beautiful land far to the south, in a valley surrounded by snow-covered mountains. He told the people their god Huitzilopochtli had created this paradise especially for them. They must go find it!

"Soon after a group of pilgrims left Aztlan and headed south. They crossed the Río Bravo and continued walking through desert and mountains, week after week, month after month. One day the wanderers arrived at an immense lake in the shadows of two lofty, snow-covered mountains. When they saw an eagle perched on a cactus with a serpent in its beak they fell to their knees and gave thanks to their god Huitzilopochtli. This was the sign their prophets had given them the day they left Aztlan!

"There was a great valley, surrounded by mountains, and populated by fierce, warlike tribes. So the Aztecs waded out to a broad island in the middle of the lake, and settled there.

"Life was hard at first; they subsisted mostly on fish and snakes. Then they discovered a novel way of creating rich vegetable gardens: they dug mud from the bottom of the shallow lake, spread it on rafts built of reeds and seeded it. The rich soil produced prodigious crops of tomatoes, carrots, corn and beans. The Aztecs became prosperous merchants, selling their produce to the hungry cities bordering the lake.

"By the time Hernan Cortés and his Spanish *conquistadores* arrived the island of Tenochtitlan had been transformed into a thriving metropolis of broad streets, bustling markets, beautiful gardens and soaring pyramids dedicated to the gods. Wide stone causeways connected the city to the mainland, aqueducts brought water from the mountains and the lake was crowded with boats, some coming with provisions, some going off loaded with merchandise.

"Later, when Cortés and his soldiers returned to Spain they told the Queen that Tenochtitlan was richer and more beautiful than any city they'd ever seen in Europe.

"But the the Aztec religion horrified Cortes' Franciscan missionaries. At the center of the city was the Temple of Huitzilopochtli, a double pyramid constructed on a rectangular base the size of a football field. A hedge of serpents' heads circled the base of the pyramid and a massive stone altar at its summit served for human sacrifice. Facing north a sanctuary painted white and blue was consecrated to Tlaloc, the rain god. Facing south, and decorated with skulls painted white on a red background, was the sanctuary of Huitzilopochtli. Priests bearing sacrificial victims climbed one hundred fourteen steps to reach the altar at the top, shaded by a cement roof decorated with butterflies. At the bottom of the pyramid rows upon rows of skulls welcomed worshippers with macabre grins, and beside them stone bowls held the hearts of recent victims.

I'm staring at Moisés, my heart in my mouth. When he pauses, I manage to say, "What about Quetzalcóatl, did the Aztecs worship him too?"

"Yes, my brother, Huitzilopochtli was their ancestral god, but the emperor Moctezuma was devoted to the Plumed Serpent, so he built him a temple a hundred yards east of Huitzilopochtli's great pyramid. It was constructed in the form of a cylinder, and its door was carved and painted to resemble the jaws of a serpent."

I shudder. "Hideous!"

"That's how Hernan Cortés felt. When he saw skulls and coagulated human blood atop Huitzilopochtli's pyramid, he decided the Aztec gods were demons from hell, and put his soldiers to work razing the temples to the ground.

"But let me tell you the incredible thing that happened afterward! The fathers of my nation erected the seat of government and the National Cathedral upon the ruins of those horrible pyramids where stinking blood-soaked priests carved the hearts out of victims writhing in agony. I've wondered how many scowling demons are flitting about the heads of our leaders these days as they ponder the destiny of our nation. And befuddling the souls of the bishops and archbishops as they celebrate mass in the National Cathedral.

"…You're looking at me strangely, brother."

"Am I? Well, I guess it's going to take a while to digest all this stuff you've been telling me."

Moisés grunts. "I understand. It's taken me half a lifetime. During the years I taught sixth grade in the public schools I spent hundreds of hours doing research in the Anthropological Museum in Chapultepec Park. Now I know why: God was preparing me for a special ministry."

"Casting out demons?"

"I call it spiritual warfare."

I sit studying Pastor Moisés for a long moment. At last I say, "Tell me, Moisés, what's going to happen now? Do you think Kairos followed me here?"

He comes over to stand beside my chair. Placing a big hand on my head, he booms out: "Almighty God, by the blood of Jesus Christ I declare your servant liberated from the power of Quezatlcóatl and his servant Kairos."

Dropping his hand to my shoulder, he gives a squeeze. "I don't know where Kairos is right now, but don't be afraid of him. Remember God's promise: 'The eternal God is your refuge, and underneath the everlasting arms. He will drive out your enemy before you, saying, Destroy him!'"

Moisés returns to his chair and brow furrowed, shuffles absent-mindedly through the papers piled on his desk. I wonder what he's thinking. At last, looking up, he smiles. "Andrés Kelly, it is good to have you with me at this time, the time of God's *kairos!*"

I try to smile back. "And now what?"

"That's up to God. But one door is already open: *Señora* Mancini has called several times. She and her friends are anxious to know when you'll be opening your *consultorio.*"

I feel my pulse quickening. "First I must find a place to live."

"I suppose you'll want to settle in one of the newer areas…La Herradura, or maybe Ciudad Satelite.

"No, Moisés, I plan to have my office downtown. And I'll want to live as close to it as possible; I don't like the idea of a long commute every day."

The pastor looks pleased. "Then you ought to try Colonia Roma. It's old, but well preserved. And only half a dozen blocks from Avenida Juarez, our main thoroughfare."

"Sounds like what I'm looking for."

At Moisés' invitation I kneel with him beside the dusty old couch. Placing an arm over my shoulders, he pleads with God for his fellow servant. As he invokes God's protection over me and the power of his

Spirit within me, I feel warm tears coursing down my cheeks. I can't remember when I've felt so close to God.

Later, driving toward my hotel, I ask myself again what I've gotten into. I told Moisés I haven't come here to fight demons, but why kid myself?

Well, what's stopping me from packing my suitcase and heading for the border?

There it is, the El Tablillo Restaurant! My heart skips a beat, here's where I had lunch with Gabriela Mancini the day she picked me up at the airport. I remember the light touch of her hand on mine while I was saying grace…and her rich, throaty voice. Gabriela doesn't speak Spanish, she sings it, pampering the vowels, slighting the consonants.

So she's been inquiring about me! I sigh. During the past two months I've resisted more than once the impulse to pick up my telephone and dial her number.

No, I'm not ready to leave yet.

Arriving at the hotel I check my watch. Twelve o'clock; they won't begin serving lunch until an hour from now. I'm going to have to re-train my appetite!

I smile, remembering the surprise Gabriela gave me when we said goodbye here in the lobby. When I reached for her hand she hugged me and kissed my cheek. For a moment my head was spinning, then I reminded myself she'd done the same with each of the guests as they left her house earlier that day. I was learning that *abrazo* and "embrace" are as different as the two cultures that birthed them. An *abrazo* can be as warm as an American embrace, or as cool as an American handshake. And it's important to discern the difference!

In my room I slip off my shoes and stretch out on the bed. I close my eyes, but it's a while before I drop off to sleep; my mind is churning with the memory of that unforgettable Saturday with Gabriela Mancini that turned my life upside down.

Chapter 8

▼

An Unwelcome Visitor

I awake to the shrill pealing of the telephone.

"Doctór Kellee?"

Gabriela Mancini! I sit up in bed, shaking the sleep out of my brain.

"*Sra.* Mancini. It's a pleasure to hear your voice!"

"So formal, *Doctór*? Please, It's Gabriela."

…. No, I'm not in Houston, I'm in Mexico City…I spent the morning with Moisés Contreras and….

"Andrés, are you still there?" (She called me by my first name!) "We're excited that you've arrived! I've been calling your hotel since Saturday."

"Thank you, Gabriela, I'm pleased too." I know I sound stiff and reserved. But somehow—I'm not sure why—I'm afraid I might say something I'll regret later.

"All of us here are wondering how soon you'll be taking appointments."

"As soon as I have an office. I'm going to start looking tomorrow."

A moment's silence, as if she's waiting for something. For what? Should I invite her to meet me here for dinner tonight?

"It was...nice talking to you." Her voice is cool. The line goes dead.

I swing my feet off the bed and sit up, feeling vaguely uncomfortable. Is she angry with me? I hope not; Gabriela Mancini is a winsome, fascinating woman, and I want to know her better. But any deepening of our friendship will have to wait, because she's expecting my professional help, and therapy and emotional involvement are a bad mix.

In the bathroom, splashing cold water on my face, I remember Kingwood and Katherine. She refused to see me again after I told her I'd be moving to Mexico City. Later, when I called her, she was polite but distant. I know I hurt her. I'm going to be very careful not to hurt Gabriela!

I smile wryly at my reflection in the mirror. Who am I really worried about getting hurt, Gabriela...or myself?

The next morning I buy a city map and locate Colonia Roma. I'm surprised at how close it is to the hotel. Waiting for the elevator, I debate walking; back in Kingwood I was compulsive about getting in at least twenty miles a week on the green belt that winds through the city. No, better take a few more days to get used to Mexico's altitude and smog.

Colonia Roma is a blend of eighteenth-century stone villas and multistoried apartment buildings. I can see why, centuries ago, they named this *colonia* after Italy's capital city. The broad streets shaded by venerable oaks and lofty eucalyptus evoke images of elegant ladies in horse-drawn carriages. The descendents of those ladies have fled the inner city to affluent suburbs like Pedregal and La Herradura. But the neighborhood hasn't deteriorated like once-elegant buroughs I've seen in the States; the streets are in good repair and the sidewalks swept clean.

Last year's earthquake dealt harshly with Colonia Roma. In every block there appears to be at least one severely damaged building awaiting restoration. But interesting little shops with patches of bright flowers out front make it easy to overlook the earthquake's devastation. I turn into a boulevard with antique street lights clustered like grapefruit on wrought-iron lamp posts. Spotting a news stand I brake suddenly and buy a paper, excited by the intuition that somewhere close by is the very place I'm looking for. Ten minutes later, disappointed, I throw aside the paper. There are only a handful of apartments listed for Colonia Roma nd most of them are for sale.

By Friday I'm ready to give up and start looking elsewhere. I've seen a dozen apartments and they were either too large, too small or too expensive.

But the next day a smiling elderly couple welcomes me into their eighth-floor apartment, and I know my fortune has changed. I like the living room immediately. Spacious, with high ceilings, it has floors of shining Italian marble accentuated by bright scatter-rugs. A wide balcony overlooks a tree-lined street. There are two bedrooms and a rather primitive kitchen with green-tiled floor.

The husband, who has introduced himself as Carlos Medellín, insists I join him and his wife in a cup of manzanilla tea. "*Señor* Kelly, I'm sure we can come to terms. Frankly, my wife and I have been looking for someone like you. We had our place listed for weeks, then, after interviewing a number of inquirers, cancelled our ad. Only yesterday we decided to try once more."

He explains that forty years ago they fled Spain to escape General Franco's dictatorship. Now they want to return to their homeland and spend a year with their families. But they can't bear the thought of leaving their beloved apartment in the hands of people who won't care for it.

Within an hour we agree on a price and draw up a contract. "And, of course, you have a co-signer, *Señor* Kelly?"

"No problem."

Yesterday Moisés warned me I'd need a property-owner as a guarantor:

"If you like, I can do that for you."

"Thank you, Moisés. So you own your home?"

"No, but the church property is in my name."

I must have looked surprised.

"In Mexico, Doctór, a church cannot hold title to property."

"How strange! Why?"

"In 1917 Mexico ended a six-year revolution and wrote a new Constitution stripping the Church of its wealth. All its properties were nationalized."

"You mean the federal government owns the churches? Even those huge cathedrals I see everywhere?"

"That's right. And since the Revolution, whenever a congregation acquires property it must be deeded over to the government."

"But your church hasn't done that?"

"Did you notice there's no sign on our building? Officially we're not a church, but an *Asoiciación Civil*, dedicated to social work. I am the owner of the building and the congregation rents it from me."

"But aren't you afraid—?"

"That the government will discover our deception?" Moisés chuckles. "They know what we're doing, and they don't mind, as long as we're not meddling in politics. *Don* Andrés, we Mexicans are great innovators. If a law infringes on our freedom we find a way to get around it."

The next day, Sunday, I arrive at church early, rental contract in hand, hoping to catch Moisés before he gets too busy. At the front door two young people intercept me.

"Good morning, Doctór, the girl says, "I'm Rebeca and this is Juan. We have the pastor's permission to speak with you."

At first I'm surprised they knew who I am, since I've only attended here once before. Then I remind myself I'm probably the only American who's visited this church in months—maybe ever. Even with my mustache and Cajun skin I must stick out like a red bird in a cotton patch!

Rebeca loops an arm in mine and leads me to three chairs placed in a circle at the rear of the auditorium. Nobody's there, except for a few people on the platform setting up the sound system.

"Please have a seat, Doctór."

I suspect I should be irritated by such imperiousness but I'm not. Rebeca, a pretty, large-boned girl almost as tall as I, has enormous brown eyes and a smile that would charm Beelzebub himself. Dressed in jeans and a bright maroon sweater, she radiates energy and good humor.

Seated at my side, she reaches out and lays a hand on my a arm. "*Hermano*, I'm President of the students' Bible class and Juan is the Vice-President. The Lord has placed an important matter on our hearts and we felt we should speak to you about it immediately."

"That's right, Doctór," Juan says eagerly. Rebecca's companion appears to be about twenty. Quite dark, he is shorter than Rebeca and his black eyes study me with a deep intensity. "Our church has over a hundred university students, all of us anxious to learn more about the Word of God." Juan pauses to catch his breath.

"You can imagine," Rebeca continues, "how difficult it is to find a qualified teacher for our class. When we invite non-believers we want them to hear someone capable of exposing the lies Marxist professors have sown in their minds.

"So imagine," Rebeca's smile is compelling, "how proud we would be to invite our classmates to lessons given by Andrés Kelly, Doctór in Philosphy."

I smile to myself. What a clever setup! Rebeca lures the fish to the boat, Juan sets the hook and Rebeca reels him in. But the joke's on them; they don't know how eager the fish is to get hooked!

Fifteen minutes later Rebeca and Juan take me to their class. Meeting behind a curtain strung on haywire at one side of the spacious auditorium, they're a noisy, enthusiastic bunch. There must be nearly a hundred of them when the class begins, pretty evenly divided between male and female. Rebeca and Juan lead an animated round table on

God's call of Abraham. During the thirty minutes the class continues hardly a minute passes without the curtain being pulled aside to admit latecomers.

A heated discussion erupts when someone suggests that Abraham disobeyed God when he took along his nephew Lot. "Didn't God tell him to 'leave behind your people and your father's household'?"

After a few minutes Rebeca stands to her feet, holding up a hand to quiet the crowd. "Sorry, but time is up. I want to make a proposal: let's ask Doctór Andrés to give us the answer to this question next week. That is, if we decide to invite him to be our teacher."

Isn't she going to tell the class who I am? Of course not, they already know! Don't be dumb Andrew, they've already discussed the pros and cons of inviting an American psychologist to be their teacher.

Someone shouts, "*Bravo!*"

The entire class stands and applauds enthusiastically, and soon they're crowded around me giving me handshakes and *abrazos*.

Does this mean I'm elected? Flabbergasted by this Mexican version of a democratic election I smile at them, feeling like a Yankee *cacique*. Does this mean I'm accepting their invitation? I guess it must!

Afterward, Rebeca loops her arm through mine and leads me to a seat near the front of the big auditorium. The noise is deafening as guitars, accordions and a big keyboard tune up for the service, and an eager crowd flows in and fills the seats.

"*Bienvenido, hermano!*" I find myself popping up again and again to receive a welcoming hug.

Rebeca seems oblivious to the competition as she keeps up a steady stream of conversation. I learn she's the eldest of six children, that her father owns a vegetable stand in a nearby market, and that she is in her second year of studies in business administration at the UNAM, the national university.

She remains at my side during the song service, singing at the top of her voice, clapping, raising her arms. Twice she pushes her way to the aisle to whirl in time to the contagious, exuberant hymns of praise.

After nearly an hour on my feet my legs are aching. I'm relieved when the pastor steps to the microphone and begins his sermon on the healing of the woman with the flow of blood. It's obvious the song service has not drained his energy, he paces back and forth trumpeting his message, waving his arms. And leaves no doubt about what he believes: the same Jesus who delivers sinners from hell after death also delivers them from Satan and sickness while they're on earth.

Halfway through the sermon I glance sideways at Rebeca, and when she smiles I notice for the first time the dimple in her cheek. It strikes me she has the same brash, irrepressible energy as my daughter Victoria. But she has something else that Victoria lacks: an amiable, engaging femininity.

After the service I corner Moses long enough to get his signature on the lease, then head toward my car half a block away. One good thing about this church; so few of its members can afford automobiles there's no parking problem! I swing along humming to myself, thinking about the new friend I've acquired this morning. Yes, Rebeca and I are going to be friends; I can tell she likes me. Otherwise, why would she have spent so much time with me?

Or maybe…suddenly I stop. Did Moisés put her up to it? All at once I'm feeling foolish.

"Doctór Andrés!"

I turn to see Rebeca hurrying toward me.

"Please, I would like you to meet my mother."

The plump, attractive woman at Rebeca's side looks surprisingly young for the mother of a college student. She smiles shyly at me. "*Hermano*, please forgive my daughter for being such a bother this morning."

I smile back at her. "She was no bother, *Señora*, my morning was incredibly brightened by the young lady the pastor commissioned to be my hostess."

Seeing Rebeca's dark cheeks redden, I know my intuition is right, and am surprised by the pang of disappointment tightening my stomach. So Dr. Andrew Kelly is not as sophisticated as he appears! He's been blind-sided by a pretty creature young enough to be his daughter!

"*Mamá*," Rebeca says "you go on ahead. I"ll catch up with you."

"All right, *Hijita*, but don't be long. I'm sure the doctór has plans."

Rebeca stands blocking my path, her huge brown eyes just inches from mine, the corners of her mouth turned down. "So. The pastor told you."

Hands on hips, I wrinkle my nose at her. "No, the pastor didn't tell me. Do you think I'm so dumb?"

She reaches over, takes my arm, and falls into step beside me. "Know something, Doctór Kelly? I'm happier than ever we persuaded you to be our teacher. You're a very intelligent man!"

"I guess you know Pastor Moisés is extremely anxious for you to be a part of our church. And he's afraid you may be tempted to go to another congregation a bit more—conventional."

"So he assigned you to work on me."

She squeezes my hand. "The pastor believes the Lord has given me the gift of persuasion."

"No doubt about it. Especially with unsuspecting men, right?" Playfully, I push her away from me.

We have arrived at my car. When I reach for my keys she places herself between me and the car door, arms folded, no longer smiling. "I'm glad you're not angry with me. But let me tell you something, Doctór Kelly: we elected you to be our teacher because we wanted you. We're obedient to our pastor, but we would never entrust our class to a man we couldn't respect. Believe me, everybody is ecstatic that you've accepted our invitation."

"I'm glad to hear that."

"And Doctór—"

"Yes?"

Her eyes dancing, Rebeca's pretty face dimples into a smile. "The pastor did not order me to sit by you in church; that was my idea."

Tuesday night *Señor* Medellin calls: he and his wife will be on the 7:00 A.M. flight to Madrid the next morning. I can pick up the apartment keys from Julio, the building superintendent.

The next day I hurry to get to the apartment before the regular afternoon downpour. I've already learned not to be on the street in the afternoon without my umbrella. Bothersome, but it has an "up" side. From June through October the rains are Mexico City's natural air conditioner: by four P.M. you need a Jacket and at night you sleep under a blanket.

I brake in front of the building. Julio, a dark bear of a man with bushy black hair and one arm, meets me at the door. "*Buenas tardes,* Doctór Andrés," he says, smiling a welcome, "I'm at your orders."

I put him to unloading the linens and dishes Margaret insisted I bring along. I argued it was unnecessary, but now I'm glad she was so stubborn. I've checked the linens in some of Mexico City's best department stores and they're coarse and expensive.

Several hours hours later Julio and his wife stand expectantly at the apartment door. "*Servido, Señor*", Julio says.

Muchas gracias," I reply, placing a thirty peso bill in Julio's hand. Ten dollars is probably overly generous for an afternoon's work, but I was surprised at how much Julio was able to do with only one arm. And his wife Mathilde, a willing helper, mopped the tile floors till they shined. After Julio and Mathilde depart for their tiny rooftop apartment I grab a sweater and ride the elevator to street level. Outside, I find the rain has ended. Buttoning my sweater I breathe in the fresh cool air, remembering how hot and muggy Houston was the day I left. I spend an hour browsing in the shops, and return with milk, freshly ground coffee from the mountains of Cordoba, and a bag of rich sweet breads.

When I open the door of the apartment and switch on the light a quiet peace envelops me. I'm home! Running a hand over a plump, well-used upholstered chair, I smile contentedly. Nothing fancy, but I'm fortunate the Medellins wanted to leave their furniture. Ever since the Mexican consulate in Houston advised me I wouldn't be able to import my things I've been dreading having to buy everything new.

I walk over to the sofa and stand studying two paintings on the wall above it. One pictures the streets of colonial Mexico City. The other is of a red-tiled village with two snow-covered mountains in the background.

The mountains! I hurry to the broad windows overlooking the balcony and pull the brightly flowered curtains aside. Yes, there they are, Mexico's fabled volcanoes, Popocatépetl and Itzlacihuatl! I was awed by them back in April when I saw them through the window of my plane as we were coming in for a landing. Haven't seen them since, they've been hidden from view by the thick veil of smog wrapped around the city. But the afternoon rain has dissolved the veil and...surprise! there they are!

Rising majestically from a high plain fifty miles to the southeast, the snowy summits seem only a whisper apart. The ancients named the mountains Popocatéptl and Iztlacihautl, and worshipped them as gods. Looking at their frosty peaks reflecting the last pink rays of the setting sun, I can understand why. They seem more a part of the limitless blue sky than of the earth.

According to an ancient myth Prince Popocatépetl and Princess Iztlacihuatl were betrothed to marry. One day on the field of battle Popo received a tragic message: his sweetheart had died of a sudden plague. Studying the silhouettes of the mountains one can make out Itzlacihuatl lying in death. Her lover Popocatéptl kneels beside her, head bowed in mourning.

I shiver. All of Mexico's history, even her mythology, seems to be immersed in disappointment and tragedy. I close the curtains and shuffle slowly to the kitchen, my mind troubled. A curious chill, like an omen of doom, has invaded my snug little kingdom. I plug in the coffee pot. Waiting for it to perk, I find myself glancing furtively at the dark corners of the poorly lit room, as if expecting to see—what? Shadows of Quetzalcóatl or his ambassador Kairos?

That road map…what's it doing on the table? Oh yes, I picked it up from the car seat when I arrived this afternoon. But look! I make a face. The map is folded so that the city of Saltillo is staring up at me, circled in red. Before leaving Houston I marked it as my goal for the first night. I had no idea…shuddering, I grab it up and shove it into a cabinet drawer.

"The only thing I don't like about this apartment is the kitchen," I grumble to myself. "How did the Medellins put up with it? That greasy old black two-burner gas stove—they must've brought it from Spain forty years ago! And the grimy water heater that grumbles like an old man with indigestion! Tomorrow I'm going to buy some white paint…and a sassy light fixture to take the place of this depressing 60 Watt bulb dangling over the table."

I flip the switch of my little radio, and the strains of *Claire de Lune* warm the chilly kitchen. Listening to the familiar music, I imagine myself back home tuned in to FM 82. My spirits buoyed by the fragrance of fresh-brewed coffee, I pour up a steaming cup and fill a saucer with sweet rolls. I'm about to head for the balcony when a trembling in my knees remind me how tired I am. The tension of three days on the road and another ten in the hotel has exhausted my reserves of energy. I stagger into the bedroom and switch on the electric blanket.

Gulping down my coffee and sweet bread I take a quick shower and fall into bed. I groan. Lying on this old mattress is like lying on a sack of potatoes! Rummaging for a comfortable spot, I long for my cozy queen-size bed back home. Margaret and Tom must be sleeping on it right now. I'm glad Victoria persuaded me to let them take over my mortgage. Sometimes my younger daughter is a pain in the neck, but she is smart, and has the makings of a good lawyer…

I jerk awake, feeling the anxious thumping of my heart. What?…who?…. There! I hear a faint rustling just outside my bedroom door. Someone is in the apartment! But how? It's eight stories up, and the only entrance is through the front door. I wait, my head raised off the pillow, fists clenched.

Silence…. The bedroom is dark, but a faint glow from the living room windows illumines the open door. Is somebody crouched there, gun in hand, waiting?

The clock's illuminated dial shows 1:19. I lie very still, hardly breathing, hearing only the ticking of the clock, till the black hands move to 1:25. I can't lie here any longer! Easing out of the bed, shivering in the cold air, I grab up my robe and wrap it around me.

Easy…easy…I edge toward the door. Where is that living room light switch? I stop and listen. Not a sound. I ease my hand past the door jamb, feeling for the switch…now!

YEOW! The involuntary yell rising from deep within startles me. My eyes dart to the dark corners of the living room…nothing.

Tip-toeing across the room, my scalp prickling, I reach out and jerk back the curtains. Nobody on the balcony. Where did he go? I stand for a moment, sniffing the air…a musky odor, barely perceptible, but heavy, repugnant. Returning, I make myself keep walking until I stand at the door of the bedroom adjacent to the kitchen…nothing. Funny, the unpleasant scent seem to be stronger here. I want to run from the apartment and lock the door behind me…. No, I'm not going to do it! Now I'm at the kitchen door. It's closed! I know I left it open when I went to bed. He…it…must be inside! I turn the knob and ease open the door, reaching inside, feeling for the switch. There! I'm afraid to push it, something is about to happen, something dreadful!

Through a window overlooking the enclosed patio below a faint light filters into the kitchen, illuminating the table. There's something there! Skin prickling, I lean against the door jamb, steadying myself. Come on Andrew, you can't postpone it any longer. With trembling fingers I flick the switch.

Seeing it is almost a relief. For an instant I want to laugh, but I swallow hard, knowing somehow that my laughter would only be the echo of the demonic laughter that right now must be rocking some corner of Quetzalcóatl's hellish headquarters.

Atop the table, looking ludicrously out of place, sit my blue Addidas, their tongues hanging out like they belong to a pair of weary hounds, the tangled white shoestrings piled beside them. And what's that beneath them? I move closer. No! The shoes sit atop the road map of Mexico I put in the drawer last night. And beside the shoes is an old alarm clock the Medellins left behind. I remember winding it last night and placing it on the refrigerator. But it's stopped, the hands huddled at 7:00 o'clock.

Seven o'clock...time...Kairos!

Suddenly I remember. That awful night weeks ago, seconds before I looked up and saw the eighteen-wheeler bearing down on us, Kairos asked me the time. I lifted my wrist and twisted my head to see the hands in the semi-darkness. I opened my mouth to say "Exactly seven P.M." I never got the words out of my mouth.

Kairos has been here! And has left his signature.

Somewhere I've read that a parable is made of "earthly symbols with a heavenly meaning." Is this arrangement on the table a demonic parable, "earthly symbols with a hellish meaning"?

I need Moisés! But I can't call him at this hour of the night, I'll have to wait.

And meanwhile? No use going back to bed, I'll never fall asleep. I know so little about demons! Where is Kairos right now? Watching me? Plotting his next move?

My eyes remained focused on the table. The knot in my stomach grows tighter. Taking a deep breath I declare: "By the blood of Christ I rebuke you, Satan."

There. I don't know what they mean, but I've said them, the words I heard Moisés use to rebuke demons. And I feel better.

Returning to the bedroom I gather my pillow and blanket and head for the living room to curl up on the sofa. Every light in the apartment is burning…let them burn! I remember the pastor back home saying in a sermon that the devil and his demons hate light.

After a while I doze off.

I awake with a start, surprised to see it's nearly five.

Will Moisés be up yet? Probably. Moisés is a warrior, and I'm sure he must arise very early every morning to prepare for the day's battles. I pick up the phone and dial his number.

The half-ring is silenced with, "*Buenos días*"

"*Buenos días*, Pastor."

"*Hermano* Andrés, I was praying for you this very moment!"

"Really? Thanks, Moisés, I need your prayers."

"Are you in trouble?"

"Big trouble. Can you come over? Right now?"

Only a moment's hesitation. "Of course. I'll be there in fifteen minutes."

CHAPTER 9

▼

A PORTRAIT OF THE ENEMY

I'm seated on the balcony in my bright blue jogging gear, the hood pulled over my head, waiting for Moisés. Soon thousands of automobiles and buses will be flowing downtown, serenading the city with a raucous symphony, but now the streets are peaceful, except for the occasional whisper of a passing car. Shivering in the predawn darkness, I pull the blanket tighter around my shoulders.

The sound of a powerful engine—blocks away, but coming fast. Throwing aside the blanket, I hurry to the elevator, push the down button, and am opening the door just as Moisés' hairy hand reaches for interphone.

"*Buenos días.* Thanks for coming!"

Moisés envelops me in a brawny *abrqzo.* Dressed in jeans, black boots, a black leather jacket and a heavy black helmet, he looks more like a member of a swat team than a preacher. "It's a pleasure, *hermano.*" Even white teeth light up his dark face. "I enjoy being out on the streets early in the morning, before they get mean."

Pulling off his helmet, Moisés guides his big black Harley-Davidson into the foyer. It's spotless, I wonder how much time he spent polishing it last night. A flaming red banner on the back fender proclaims, "*Jesús salva*," and just above it a big black Bible is strapped to the tiny passenger's seat.

Retrieving his Bible, Moisés lays a hand on the flat iron seat. "When are you going to let me take you for a ride?"

"Just give me time. I still don't feel safe on these crazy streets. Even inside my Chevy." I hope my nervous chuckle doesn't tell him how scared I'd be roaring down these wild streets on Moisés big black war horse!

We ascend in silence. The moment we step off the elevator Moisés stops, chin raised, big flat nose flared, sniffing the air. "So, you've had a visitor!"

"How did you know?"

Moisés drops his helmet and it bounces on the green tile of the foyer. He steps into the apartment, shoulders squared like a boxer, head swiveling. Turning to face me, he growls, "No wonder you called me, tell me about it!"

"Not much to tell. I was awakened by a noise a little after one and…come on, I want you to see the message they left me."

Entering the kitchen, Moisés sniffs again, the mole on his nose twitching, and walks over to the scarred old wooden table. He circles the table, head cocked, hands clasped behind him, as if reluctant to touch the strange demon clutter he's eyeing. He asks, "When you went to bed last night did you leave anything here on the table?"

"Nothing. I was so tired I just cleared off the table and put my dirty dishes in the sink." Like a kid wanting to impress his scoutmaster on their first field trip, I add: "Kairos was here, right? Clock=time=Kairos."

Moisés shrugs. "Maybe. Or maybe Quetzalcóatl sent one of Kairos's buddies. Remember, Kairos failed his assignment on the highway. He may be grounded."

He reaches out and lays a and on the clock. "Hm-m-m, interesting. You see where they placed it?"

"On the map."

"Yes, but look closer."

What am I supposed to see? "O-o-oh! They set the clock on the highway just south of Saltillo, where I met the eighteen-wheeler! But what about the shoes?"

"Looks like a warning."

"A warning?"

Moisés reaches out and punches the toes with an index finger. "Look at them: toes pointing toward the Border, tongues hanging out."

I say, strangling on the words: "Message: 'Andrés Kelly, run with all your might for the U.S. Border, and don't look back!'"

My knees have turned to Jello. I pull out a chair, being careful not to bump the table, and ease myself down.

"*Basura*, garbage!" Moisés bellows. With a sweep of his hand he rakes the table clean. "Don't let this bother you, *hermano*. If they were capable of harming you they would have done it last night while you were asleep. Instead, they played this silly game to see if they could frighten you."

"Well, they succeeded," I groan, slumping in my chair. In spite of my warm clothing I'm shivering.

Moisés turns toward me, hands on hips. Fixing his eyes on me, he says, "Brother Andrés, Quetzalcóatl knows he can't lay a finger on you; he's seen how powerful your angel is."

I stare back at him, puzzled. "My angel?"

"A-y-y-y, my brother, for an intelligent man, sometimes you're slow to discern spiritual truths. Tell me again: what happened to you out there on the highway?"

I drop my face into my hands, and eyes closed, mumble, "Well, that monstrous truck was only a few yards away, coming straight at me...I remember squeezing my eyes shut, knowing I was going to die...and then…then…when I came to myself…I don't know how much time had passed…the car was parked beside the highway. I was stunned. I couldn't understand how I had I managed to…"

Staring at Moisés, I say, "So it was an angel?"

He moves toward me and places a firm hand on each shoulder. Bringing his face close to mine, he growls, "*Hermano* Andrés, why are you surprised? Haven't you read God's promise in Psalms:

He shall give his angels charge over thee,
to keep thee in all thy ways.
They shall bear thee up in their hands, lest thou dash thy
foot against a stone."

He steps back "…or thy car against an eighteen-wheeler!"

I shake my head slowly, thoughtfully. "You know, Pastor, I have a doctorate from a seminary, but I'm still in kindergarten as far as the spirit world is concerned. This business about Satan's demons…and now God's angels…has my head spinning. I want to believe all these things you're telling me. But—"

Moisés looks at me for a long moment, then gazes out the window. At last he says slowly, "Doctór, would it help if I told to you that, for many years, I was a disciple of Quetzalcóatl?"

I flinch. "No! So that's why you know so much about the Bearded Serpent!"

"When I was young, I was sure Quetzalcóatl was Mexico's only hope. Only later did I discover he's our curse." His eyes narrow. "We *are* under a curse, you know!"

Shaking my head, I say quietly: "Moisés, there's so much I don't know about you."

The pastor pulls a chair out from the table and sinks into it. "Maybe if I tell you something about my life it will help you understand Quetzalcóatl and his kingdom of darkness."

I nod in agreement. Getting up, I say, "But before you start, let me put on the coffee pot."

Fifteen minutes later we're in the living room, warm sweetbread and coffee on the low table between us. I have no stomach for eating in the kitchen where Kairos…or one of his cohorts…has so recently played out a somber practical joke.

Moisés has pulled off his riding boots and sprawled on the sofa. I'm seated on a straight chair brought in from the kitchen, my eyes so heavy from lack of sleep I'm afraid to trust myself to an easy chair.

"Most of what I know about Quetzalcóatl," Moisés says, reaching for a crusty *caracol,* "I've learned from experience."

He takes a swallow of coffee. "How old are you, *hermano?*"

"Forty-three."

"I've just turned forty. People tell me I look fifty. Maybe it's because of the way I've lived. I was the youngest of five children and never knew my father, he abandoned the family before I was born. It took me until fourteen to finish elementary; like my brothers and sisters I had to spend most of my days on the streets selling *chicles.* We always seemed to live at the edge of starvation.

"At fifteen I became a mechanic's helper. The first two years I didn't even make the minimum wage. Here in Mexico they don't pay apprentices, the twelve hours a day you put in is payment for learning a trade."

Moisés sets down his empty coffee mug, leans back in his chair, and eyes closed, clasps his hands behind his head, pugnacious face melancholy.

"By the time I was eighteen I'd shed enough tears to supply a month of the rainy season. My mother had died of cancer two years before, my brothers and sisters now had their own lives. I was sleeping nights on a straw *petate* in the auto repair shop.

Every Sunday morning I'd get up early and run to the church, kneel before a statue of the Virgin and plead with her to show me a way out of my despair."

Moisés rubs a fist across his eyes, gets up, goes to the kitchen and pours himself a second cup of coffee. When he returns he plops back onto the sofa and continues: "One Sunday morning as I was leaving church I paused in the foyer to read the bulletin board. An announcement printed on rough, yellowed newsprint caught my eye: a block from where I worked a night school was opening. I'd been dreaming for years of returning to school! I crossed myself, sure the Virgin had answered my prayers.

"Soon after enrolling I made friends with two of my classmates, Samuel and Ricardo. One night after classes they invited me to a small restaurant for a glass of *café con leche*. This was a new experience for me, I'd always been a loner. They talked excitedly about a new religion they'd discovered. I was fascinated. This was not an imported creed of sad-faced saints and Latin words mumbled by a bored priest, but a faith as ancient and rich as Mexico itself. A celebration of nature—the nature that makes our country beautiful and fruitful…at least that's what they told me.

"I'll never forget the Saturday I played hooky from work and went with Samuel and Ricardo to Teotihuacan. My heart beat a mile a minute as they introduced me to the pyramids of the sun and the moon. I jumped up and down with excitement when the quetzal whistled his invitation at Quetzalcóatl's temple. When I thrust my hand into the jaws of the Feathered Serpent an electric shock and set my fingertips on fire and exploded in my brain. I was hooked!"

A chill goes up my spine. "So it wasn't my imagination!"

"Of course not!"

I lean forward, shivering, reliving that dreadful moment.

"Moisés, you told me it doesn't it happen that way to everybody."

"No, a lot of people make a joke of it They dare one another to try it, kidding about the terrible things that can happen, then go away laughing."

He pauses, takes a sip of steaming coffee, and adds: "It's almost as if the…the special experience…is reserved for the chosen few. I only wish it had made me sick like happened to you. I would have saved myself a dozen wasted years."

"So you became a follower of Quetzalcóatl?"

"Heart and soul!"

"But a snake! How could you worship a snake?"

"Remember our visit to Quetzalcóatl's temple? The Flying Serpent is a symbol of the rain that falls from Mexico's sky and awakens her soil. I told myself I was not worshipping a serpent, but the miracle that transforms Mexico every year. You'll appreciate what I mean after you've lived through our first dry season; it begins in November and goes on and on, for six or seven months. Everything green slowly wilts into a lifeless brown from April till June the heat is stifling. You begin asking yourself if it will ever rain again.

"Then one afternoon clouds roll in, thunder booms across the mountains, lightening flashes, and the cool, sweet rain splatters down. After that, for the next five months, the downpours come every afternoon without fail and life returns to the earth.

"Do you see why I told myself I wasn't worshipping a snake, but the miracle of life?"

Moisés stands to his feet, stretches, and nods toward the balcony. "Look, dawn is breaking. Come, I want to show you another miracle."

I follow him, wondering what I'm about to see. Outside, we stand in silence for a moment, breathing deeply, filling our lungs with the thin, chill air, still moist from last night's rain. Eight floors below the street lights are blinking out and I hear the low hum of the early morning traffic.

"Look." Moisés points toward the east, to two imperious peaks standing stark against a horizon bathed in the slow-moving blush of dawn.

"*Los volcanes*," I cry, proud of already knowing the label the Mexicans apply to their two fabled mountains, Popocatéptl and Itzlacihuatl.

"Do you see that bright point of light just to the left of Iztla?"

"Venus!"

Moisés grunts approvingly and claps me on the shoulder. "So you've seen Venus before?"

"Sure, it's the brightest star in the sky."

"Exactly! Not long after my first visit to Teotihuacan, my new friends took me to the ruins of an ancient city called Xochicalco. It's not far from here, about a hundred kilometers to the east. There they showed me the temple to Quetzalcóatl, where there's a monument to Venus."

"A monument to Venus in Quetzalcóatl's temple? Why?"

"That's what I asked, and I gasped when they told me Venus is not a star, but Quetzalcóatl, reigning over the heavens."

Moisés is standing beside me, hands on the railing, facing the brightening horizon.

I punch him on the shoulder. "You didn't believe that, did you?"

Moisés turns, smiling. "You asked me the same question about the Flying Serpent, remember? And I told you I was not worshipping a snake, but a miracle."

"And like the rains, Venus is a miracle. For eight months it shines in the eastern sky as the star of the morning, then, it disappears. One day, three months later, it suddenly reappears in the west as the star of the evening!"

"Really? Does that actually happen?"

"Every year without fail!"

"They never taught me that in school."

"And what about the seminary? Did they tell you that God calls Satan the morning star?"

Shaking my head, I stare at him dumbly.

"Come on, I'll show you." Taking my arm, Moisés moves toward the door. "Think we might warm up that sweetbread and coffee?"

In the kitchen I put what's left of the sweetbread in the oven and turn on the burner beneath the coffee pot. Picking up the map, the shoes and the clock from the floor where Moisés had thrown them, I deposit them in my bedroom. When I return Moisés is seated at the kitchen table thumbing through his Bible.

"Sit down, *hermano*, and read this passage." He hands me his big black Bible, index finger on the first verse of the third chapter of Genesis. I read: "Now the serpent was more subtle than any beast of the field which the Lord God had made."

His finger moves down the page. "I'm sure you remember the curse God put on the serpent after he tempted Adam and Eve."

I read: "Because thou has done this, thou art cursed...upon thy belly thou shalt go, and dust thou shalt eat all the days of thy life."

Moisés goes to the stove and brings the bread and coffee over to the table. Pouring himself a cupful, he sits quietly for a long moment, his eyes alert, studying my face.

"Now Doctór, remember that Quetzalcóatl is Satan's representative in Mexico. Do you understand why he gave himself wings?"

Reaching for the coffee pot, I feel the hair on my arm rise to attention. "He was defying God's curse! God told him he was going to crawl on his belly the rest of his life."

"And that's also why he claims to be Venus." Leafing through his Bible, he pushes it toward me. Read what Isaiah says about Satan:

> How thou art fallen from heaven, O Day Star, son of the morning!.... For thou hast said in thine heart, I will ascend into heaven, I will exalt my throne above the stars of God...I will ascend above the heights of the clouds, I will be like the most High."

Moisés closes his Bible, and hands folded, leans toward me. "Do you see now, Doctór Kelly, why I said Mexico is under a God's curse? My *patria* has enthroned a demon god who's in open rebellion against the Creator!"

I stare at my friend, the sweetbread in my throat turning to stone.

Moisés pushes back his chair and goes to the window overlooking the patio. His back to me, he takes a sip of coffee from the mug he holds in his hand. "I love my homeland. But how, except for a curse, could anyone explain why a country so rich in gold and silver and copper and coal and oil and farmlands and rivers and forests, is one of the poorest nations on earth? And why, during all its history, our leaders have blundered from one disaster to another?"

Sighing, he gets up from the table, stumbles to the kitchen window and stares out at the bare yellow wall across the narrow patio. "I served the Bearded Serpent for ten years, never dreaming of the curse he'd brought on our country. Then came the day"...he pauses, his fists clenched—"that terrible day...when Quetzalcóatl betrayed me and the leaders of my country slaughtered the flower of Mexico's youth!"

Whirling, he returns to the table, and slams down his coffee mug.

I have no idea what Moisés is talking about! "That...that day. Tell me about it."

Moisés checks his watch. "It's already eight o'clock. I must be going, I've got a busy day.

And I know you need to start looking for an office. I'll tell you about it another time."

I follow him to the door, unhappy about being left in suspense. "And when will that be, Moisés?"

"I'll need to take you to the place it happened. Maybe we can find time next week."

He gives me an *abrazo*, reaches for the door, then turns. "*Hermano*, I'm praying God will give you your intercessor very soon."

"You mean someone to pray for me?"

"Yes."

"I know my church back home is praying for me. And my daughters."

Moses shrugs. "Of course. But there's someone else. Someone God has appointed to be a wall of protection about you, someone with the gift of intercession."

"But...but...how?"

"You don't need to look for him. Just wait. God will send him to you at the right—" he smiles..."*kairos*".

He reaches again for the door.

"Hasta la vista."

Lake Catemaco nestles in fertile green hills five miles inland from the Gulf of Mexico, its tranquil surface mirroring the bright blue tropical sun. Travelers lingering over a lunch of perch and corn tortillas at the lake's edge cannot hear the demonic murmur pervading this paradise like macabre background music. They'd never guess they're seated at the edge of Quetzalcóatl's field headquarters.

One afternoon eons ago, according to sacred myth, Satan accomplished a monumental work: in a dark cave on Catemaco's Hill of the Mono Blanco he begat one thousand witches. Their descendents, now scattered throughout mesoamerica, have a homecoming once a year.

This is the day.

Seated beneath the gnarled old Sacred Oak atop the Hill of the Mono Blanco *Kairos waits, one of tens of thousands of demons present for the occasion. A few steps away a group of his colleagues, their little black wings whirring noisily, jabber away. They know Kairos is here, but they choose to ignore him.*

"Jealousy," he sniffs.

A century ago the Master assigned Kairos to the National University. His success in making El an object of scorn among professors and students earned him a commendation. Now the word is out he has been chosen for a top secret mission. And given a new name. Everyone else in Kairos' demon brigade is absolutely certain he could do a better job than this bogus professor with his absurd black academic gown. But who would dare protest the decision of Lord Quetzalcóatl? The only way they can show their disapproval is to shun him.

A brooding hush saturates the Hill of the Mono Blanco: absent is the voice of the song bird or the buzz of an insect in flight.

Suddenly a company of witches appears, hundreds of them, some leather-faced, snaggled-tooth, ill-humored, others with the face of an angel and the smirk of a Jezabel, slashing with long-bladed machetes through the twisted green undergrowth of weeds, vines and palmettos, wailing and cursing as they go. They're all caught up in a wild excitement. The gossip is that the Prince Himself will grace the assembly this year.

They seat themselves on the thick green grass, breathless, expectant. Clinging now to an upper branch of the Sacred Oak, Kairos wonders if the witches can see the dark cloud of grumbling, foul-mouthed demons boiling above them. Witches work with demons, but can witches see demons? Kairos has the impression they can't. Every time he speaks with one he feels the witch is looking right through him.

Without warning, Quetzalcóatl materializes. A split second ago the crown of the Hill of the Mono Blanco was empty. Now it is overshadowed by the august figure of the Feathered Serpent, a boa constrictor twenty meters long, his slim, muscular body writhing, scales rattling, tongue flicking, his square serpentine head frowning down on the crowd.

The assembly roars, falls to its knees, and for five minutes the hill vibrates to the frenzied shrieks of the witches and humming black wings of the demons.

At last the congregation quietens, waiting. Will it happen this time? Will the Prince appear?

A thunderous announcement from the throat of Quetzalcóatl reverberates in the surrounding hills: "He who has seen me has seen the Father."

A flicker of silence, then five minutes more of deafening acclamation. But the instant of silence has betrayed the crowd's disappointment, they know that Quetzalcóatl's blasphemous boast means there will be no appearance of the Prince this year!

The gathering falls silent and a gray-haired, portly giant appears on the hill across from the Serpent. Kairos recognizes him as a shaman from one of the lakeside temples. In a shrill, piercing voice he reads from a manuscript:

"Now the serpent was more cunning than any beast of the field that God had made."

Each year the assembly begins with this quote from El's Manual, and as always Quetzalcóatl's vassals erupt in a prolonged ovation, the witches shrieking in ecstasy and the demons waving their wings, stirring up a choking cloud of dust. Above all his other virtues they most admire the Feathered Serpent's guile. Through his craftiness Satan outwitted El in the

Garden and became Prince of the Planet Earth. And Quetzalcóatl is the incarnation of his Satanic Majesty.

At last the congregation hushes and waits anxiously for the reading to continue: an account from El's own Manual of how their crafty Lord bested Him in the Garden:

And the woman said unto the serpent, We may eat of the fruit of the trees of the garden; but of the fruit of the tree which is in the midst of the garden, God hath said, Ye shall not eat of it, neither shall ye touch it, lest you die.

(a scattering of snickers and boos)

And the serpent said to the woman, Ye shall not surely die: For God doth know that in the day ye eat thereof, then your eyes shall be opened, and ye shall be as gods, knowing good and evil.

(loud applause)

And when the woman saw that the tree was good for food and that it was pleasant to the eyes, and a tree to be desired to make one wise, she took of the fruit thereof, and did eat, and she gave also to her husband with her; and he did eat.

(shouts of "Hurrah!", cackles of laughter)

The shaman's voice deepens and his lip curls: And the Lord God said, Because thou hast done this, thou art cursed above all cattle, and above every beast of the field; upon thy belly shalt thou go, and dust shalt thou eat all the days of thy life."

(a roar of indignation, cries of "shame! shame!")

For the second time Quetzalcóatl thunders, "He who has seen me has seen the Father."

Demons and witches unite in a climactic ovation: the witches shout, shriek, scream, dance, and cackle, biting and clawing one another. The demons dart about like drunken bumble bees, buzzing, whirling, doing somersaults, colliding, cursing, groaning, moaning. The Hill of the Mono Blanco shudders as if shaken by an earthquake, the leaves of the Sacred Oak are shredded and scattered as if by a cyclone.

Half an hour passes, and the wild frenzy continues.

At last the Bearded Serpent raises his ghastly head and belches, "*Silence!*"

Instantly, as if at the touch of a switch, the delirium ends.

Again the voice of the Master: "*His Highness, called the Devil and Satan, was cast out into the earth, and his angels with him. And he made himself the Prince of Darkness, which deceiveth the whole world.*"

(again a mumur, the beginning of another ovation)

"*Silence!*" *Towering to his full height, Quetzalcóatl writhes, hisses, and the long red, green and blue feathers at his neck rustle like waves of the sea. His subjects draw back terrified, and a dozen of the younger witches fall to the earth in a dead faint and lie there twitching.*

The Master continues: "*The Great Prince is not gifted with omniscience. Therefore he has appointed viceroys over every sector of the earth. To me, your Master, he has given jurisdiction over Mesoamerica. And to me he has also given the distinction of being the incarnation of himself, the Serpent, the Old Dragon. Who has seen me, has seen the Father!*"

A roar from his slaves, but an impatient flick of the tail silences them, converting an entire company of demons into a whirling a mini-tornado. (Kairos would have been among them if he had not tightened his grip on the tree.)

"*Here I have reigned as the Serpent, bringing honor and glory to the Prince's name. He expects your absolute, unquestioning obedience to me. The time is drawing near. The Lion and his angels are sharpening their swords for Armageddon. Meanwhile, you must wreak havoc, tormenting the world with fears, lies, sickness of soul and body. For him who fails I have reserved chains made red-hot by the fires of Gehenna!*"

"*That is all.... Begone!*"

They all go scrambling, the witches stumbling over one another, the demons bumping together, shoving and cursing in their haste to put distance between themselves and their ill-tempered Master.

Kairos watches with a smile of contempt until the last of the witches has disappeared.

He's anxious to get away; the return to Mexico City will only take seconds, but he always arrives exhausted, because the journey requires an extraordinary burst of energy.

And he arrived here already tired from his excursion into Andrew Kelly's apartment. And disappointed. He'd had such hopes! Kelly was so scared he couldn't sleep the rest of the night. He would have packed and headed for the Border if it hadn't been for Moisés. Moisés! Quetzalcóatl needs to do something about that traitor.

He crouches, preparing to launch himself into flight.

"Kairos!"

Startled, he turns and finds himself staring into the cold, dead eyes of the Feathered Serpent. Damn! He had hoped to get away without a summons from his Master. But no doubt Quetzalcóatl's spies were watching his little drama last night and reported with relish that he had failed again.

An impatient hiss: "Forget trying to scare Andrew Kelly away."

"But my Lord, if it hadn't been for Moisés—"

An angry growl: "Moisés! Turncoat! Ingrate!"

"My Lord, give me your permission and I'll..."

"Don't deceive yourself, not a chance, that traitor has surrendered himself completely to the Paraclete. Listen to me: concentrate on the woman!"

"The woman, my Lord?"

"Yes, the woman Gabriela. She will be Kelly's downfall. One of my most powerful demons, a spirit of anger, has a fortress in her soul. Kelly is trying to destroy his fortress. Make sure he fails!

"So use the woman. She doesn't know it, but she's our ally. Now be gone!"

CHAPTER 10

▼

ANDREW FINDS AN
OFFICE
(OOPS! CONSULTORIO)

"Just coffee, please. I'm expecting a friend. We'll order later."

The waitress, a diminutive Mayan princess in a pink pinafore, smiles and leaves me a menu and a steaming cup of coffee. Yesterday Claudio Rodriguez called and suggested we have breakfast here at Shirley's at eight. It's already 8:10. He'll probably arrive around 8:30, blaming it on the traffic. I'm learning the subtleties of M.S.T. (Mexican standard time). Last Sunday morning the pastor reminded us that the evening service was scheduled for seven o'clock, "to begin at 7:30."

I'll be into my second cup of coffee by the time Claudio arrives. No matter. My soul is being nourished by the noisy, animated conversation around me. Shirley's is on the first floor of the twenty-story headquarters of Banco Comercial, where Mexico City's financial district laps against Colonia Lomas de Chapultepec. In Mexico City you can guess the decor and the menu of a restaurant by its name. If it has an American name like Wings, VIPS or Shirley's you can count on scrambled eggs for breakfast, rather than *chilaquiles* or tripe, which they call pancita, "little stomach". And on weekday mornings the clientele tends to be handsome and well-dressed, like the men and women surrounding me. Looking at them, I remind myself they are the reason God brought me to Mexico City. Those two handsome young men at the next table, for instance, in dark blue business suits and fresh haircuts. They're lawyers or CPA's. In a few minutes they'll push back their chairs and stride across the street to that graceful glass-walled building and ride the elevator to their offices on the tenth or twentieth floor.

People like these will soon be calling my office, requesting an appointment. But my very first client will be Gabriela Mancini! Since arriving at the restaurant I've been acutely aware that I'm just ten minutes away from her elegant home. Admit it. One of the reasons I'm so eager to find an office is to justify seeing her again.

I sigh. She could be here at this moment, smiling across the table at me. Oh, how I wish she were! Me and my professional ethics! Since those two minutes on the telephone a couple of weeks ago her exquisite face has haunted me day and night.

Will she want to see me, after the way I put her off? I wince, remembering how her warm words of welcome turned into a frosty "Goodbye". Since then I've wanted to call her a hundred times. Why haven't I? Maybe I…

"Good morning, Doctór, forgive my tardiness."

Startled, I awake from my daydream. "Good morning."

"*Licenciado* Claudio Gaspar Rodriguez, *a sus órdenes*"

I rise to greet the slim, smiling young man standing before my table. No chance this guy with the faded blue serge suit and frayed collar has an office in that glass building across the street!

"It's a pleasure to meet you, *Licenciado*."

In Mexico *Licenciado* means "attorney." Not only doctors prefix a title to their names; so do lawyers, engineers, architects and teachers.

"Please, call me Claudio. We haven't met, but I was in your class last Sunday. *Magnífico*! I'm going to invite my friends."

After the Mayan princess fills his cup Claudio informs me he has recently completed his social service and now he's ready to go to work. "Following graduation it was my obligation to give a year of free service to the poor. That's how we students repay the *patria* for our education. Only then was I allowed to begin looking for work. An almost impossible task! Our universities are churning out doctors, dentists, and lawyers like *tortillas calientes.* ".

"But I'm one of the fortunate graduates, the church has done me the honor of naming me *asesor* of *Koinonía*, our *Asociación Civil.*

"*Asociación Civil*? The pastor mentioned that name to me the other day. What does it mean?

"It's stated purpose is to help the needy in our society. We call our Asociación "Koinonía". Since it's chartered by the government, it gives us the legal standing the Constitution denies to churches."

"So you administer Koinonía?"

"Yes. And that's why I'm here; the pastor suggested I talk to you before you start looking for an office."

"Sí, Señorita, we're ready to order." I'm pleased at the return of the waitress. I need time to think. I want to be civil to this earnest young man, but I hope we can get this over with as soon as possible. I'm intelligent enough to find an office without his help!

I order scrambled eggs and bacon and Claudio a chicken sandwich. After the waitress leaves I shift nervously in my seat, take a swallow of my lukewarm coffee, clear my throat and say, "I appreciate your offer, Claudio, but I believe I can manage on my own."

Claudio is silent for a full minute, fingering his white napkin, frowning, his Adam's Apple working behind the frayed shirt collar. At last he says, "With all due respect, Doctór, permit me to give you a warning. Within a week after you open your office...if you find someone willing to rent an office to a tourist...Immigration will come knocking at your door. What will you tell them?"

I smile confidently. "That I'm not here to make money; I'll be giving my services free of charge."

Mario picks up his napkin, wipes his lips, takes a deep breath and says, with feeling, "You'll be telling the truth, Doctór, but they're not going to believe you. They'll tell you to close the office or you'll be expelled from the country."

I stifle a surge of anger. "But the pastor assured me—"

"Forgive me, *hermano*, but our federal bureaucracy is suspicious of foreigners. It's important you understand that."

Licenciado Claudio Gaspar Rodriguez reaches over and lays a hand on mine, a broad smile brightening his dark face. "Doctór Kelly, God has sent you to help us in the Kingdom's work. And this morning God has sent me and the *Asociación Civil Koinonía*—to help *you*! Will you let us?"

He spends the next hour explaining his plan....

By the end of the week I've located an attractive suite on the seventh floor of a handsome, modern office building. It's only a ten-minute drive from Colonia Roma and five blocks from El Tablillo, the restaurant where Gabriela entertained me the day we met. Its occupant, a young Yucatecan businessman named Jaime Patt, has just declared bankruptcy and is looking for someone to take over his lease and purchase his office furniture.

As soon as we agree on terms I call Claudio and accompany him and *Sr.* Patt to the office of the owner, Benjamin Strauss. My attorney explains that the *Asociación Civil Koinonía* will sign the lease. Mr. Strauss is pleased. He seems to be relieved that he isn't going to have to ask this American psychologist to prove he has permission to do business in Mexico.

By now I realize how fortunate I am to have Claudio's help. Koinonía's constitution states that its purpose is "to provide encouragement and orientation to the Mexican family." As Claudio remarked when he read me those words at our breakfast, who better to fill that purpose than a psychologist specialized in family counseling? As a voluntary staff member of the *Asociación Civil* I'll have a ready-made explanation for any inquirer knocking at my door.

Two hours later I'm showing Claudio around my new office suite. "This desk at the entrance, of course, is for the receptionist—when I have one." I push open a solid oak door. "And here my is office. I like it because it overlooks a nice little park in front of that huge Liverpool Department Store across the street. And see, I bought Mr. Patt's desk, love seat and easy chairs."

"It's beautiful, Doctór. And by the way, here in Mexico we call the place where a therapist works a *consultorio.* Offices belong to businesses.

Giving the seat behind my desk a twirl, I smile. "That makes sense: I'll be receiving people who come to *consult* with me in my *consultorio.*"

We move into the next room, a spacious salon with folding chairs stacked in the corner. "*Sr.* Patt used this for seminars. I don't know what I'm going to do with so much space; maybe the Lord has something in mind." I examine the rug with the toe of my shoe. "I'm going to replace this worn maroon carpet with something more appropriate, maybe a quiet beige. What do you think?"

"Very good," Claudio says. He rubs the faded blue wall with a long brown finger. "And if you'd like to do some painting I'll get some of the guys in our class to give you a hand."

Back in the reception room I put out my hand. "Claudio, thanks for your help."

He takes my hand, but I can see by his wrinkled brow he has something else on his mind. He clears his throat. "Doctór Kelly, there's another matter. Could we talk for a moment?"

"Sure, come into my *consultorio.*" I smile. "You'll be my first client."

"Uh—another thing: in Mexico people who consult therapists are called patients. Lawyers have clients."

I seat Claudio and take a chair facing him, wondering what's on his mind. He fidgets, picks his fingernails, clears his throat a couple of times and at last says, "The pastor's home is listed as the official domicile of our Association. We were wondering, would you permit us to relocate to this address?"

Seeing my hesitation, he adds, "That doesn't mean I'd be here, I have my own office at home."

Feeling guilty about my reluctance, I say immediately, "Of course. You can even have a drawer of my filing cabinet for documents."

The doorbell chimes. I'm going to have to get used to that doorbell! At my office in Houston people just opened the door and walked into the waiting room. *Sr.* Patt explained to me that here such a preemptory entrance would be considered an invasion of privacy.

I jump up and hurry to the door, expecting to see a stranger I'll have to inform that Jaime Patt no longer occupies this office.

"Rebeca!"

She gives me a hug, her hair damp from the afternoon rain. "Good afternoon, Doctór, hope I'm not interrupting."

I'm surprised at the pleasure I feel seeing this intrepid young lady. We've spoken very little since our first encounter at the church, but her smile tells me we're special friends.

Claudio joins us. "*Hermano,* Rebeca is the secretary of our Association. I told her yesterday about your *consultorio* and the possibility of this being the new home for Koinonía."

Rebeca drops her book satchel on the receptionist's desk and runs a scarlet fingernail over the surface, frowning at the dust. "I was on my way to classes and thought I'd drop by. Hope you don't mind."

Are all Mexico's young people like Rebeca and Claudio and…what was the name of that kid at church that helped Rebeca twist my arm? Here I am, being manipulated again, and enjoying it!

Suddenly I know what I'm going to do. Why hadn't I thought of it before? "Rebeca, If you've got a moment come into my…my *consultorio.* Let's have a little chat."

Claudio's hand is on the doorknob. "Well, Doctór, I'll be on my way. Just let Rebeca know when it's convenient for her to bring over the documents of the *A.C.*.

Seated in my office, Rebeca's huge eyes are bright with anticipation. It occurs to me she must be a classic sample of metiza femininity. Aztec ancestors are present in her tawny skin and high cheekbones. And the small, straight nose and hazel eyes hint at European genes. German, maybe, because she's big-boned and tall for a Mexican female.

"Tell me, Rebeca, what is your class schedule?"

"Four P.M. till ten, Monday through Friday."

"And how do you spend the first part of the day?"

"Mostly I study. And sometimes I help Papá in the vegetable market. But the people there are so crude. I don't like the way the men look at me." She wrinkles her nose and rolls her eyes. "Besides, I took a short business course not long ago and I'm hoping to find work in an office."

Leaning toward her, I catch myself just in time; I was about to lay a hand on her knee. What makes me feel like I've known her for years, that she's the kid sister I never had?

"And what would you say if I told you I'm looking for a secretary?"

She claps her hands. "Are you inviting me to go to work for you?"

I pretend to frown. "Well, since you're the secretary of Koinonía you'll have to spend time here anyway. Maybe we can strike a bargain."

Her face serious now, she reaches out and lays a hand on mine. "Doctór Kelly, it will be an honor to work for you. And if you can't afford to pay me a salary I'll work for free." Her face melts into a smile. "The girls at church will be jealous of me. We all agree you are *muy simpatico.*"

She consults her Mickey Mouse watch. "I still have a few minutes before I need to leave for the university. Anything I can do?"

I snap my fingers. "As a matter of fact, there is."

I go to my desk and retrieve a paper. "Here's a list of people interested in therapy with me. You can start calling them."

She scans the list. After a moment she looks up. "Gabriela Mancini. Isn't she the one who's come to our church a couple of times?"

"Yes. Call her first. Offer her tomorrow at eleven." I feel my pulse quickening.

CHAPTER II

▼

GABRIELA

For the third time I rearrange the two easy chairs in my office. I wonder: do therapists in Mexico sit behind a desk? No matter, I like to sit facing my clients (patients!) with nothing between us; close enough for a quiet intimacy, yet not so close they might feel uncomfortable.

Getting up, I start pacing the office. Two months have passed since that day spent with Gabriela Mancini. Will she be the same person I remember? I was anxious yesterday when Rebeca called her, half expecting her to say she was no longer interested. When she accepted I breathed a sigh of relief.

I check my watch: eleven o'clock, time for the appointment. Maybe she won't show. Maybe she'll pay me back for my tactless treatment of her on the phone.

I straighten my tie. I dressed carefully this morning in a dark suit and conservative tie. In Houston I made it a practice to receive my clients in a sport shirt; Americans seem more at ease if the therapist leaves his tie and white shirt at home in the closet. But I've noticed Mexicans expect more formality from their professionals, as if a suit and tie impart dignity and competence.

A tap on the door and Rebeca sticks her head in, a pleased smile on her bright face. "Doctór Kelly, your patient has arrived."

I move to receive *Sra.* Mancini.

"Dr. Kellee!" She hurries toward me, and taking my hand stands on tiptoe to kiss my cheek.

"Your *consultorio* is splendid! And so well located. Congratulations!"

In an instant I know the memory I've cherished of this woman is not an illusion. Dressed in a chic black wool frock, a white scarf at the throat, just a touch of makeup, she is as elegant and captivating as I've remembered.

"*Sra.* Mancini—"

"Please. Gabriela." Smiling, she takes the seat I offer.

"Gabriela, it's great to see you!"

Her green eyes are regarding me curiously, making me uncomfortable. "I've been worried about the phone call a couple of weeks ago." I say. "That I might have offended you."

Crossing her legs, she pulls at the hem of the dress where it touches her knee.

"To the contrary, your words reassured me. They confirmed my impression that Doctór Andrés Kellee is a man of integrity, a man I can trust."

I want to hug her. Instead, I take a seat opposite her and reach for my yellow pad. The awkwardness has evaporated.

"Your secretary tells me you occupied your *consultorio* only yesterday. Thanks for calling me so promptly. I really need your help, you know."

Tears are welling in her eyes. Once again I'm impressed once again by the subtle blend of sophistication and vulnerability I sensed in her that Saturday we spent together.

"Gabriela, you are one of the reasons I'm sure God brought me to Mexico."

I stop, afraid I've said too much. What is it about this woman that makes me want to gush like an eighteen-year-old?

"And now…" I lean forward, my pen poised, "where shall we begin?"

She reaches for a Kleenex. "Doctór Kellee, is there a cure for schizophrenia? Because sometimes I feel like two completely different persons. I suppose when people look at me they see *Señora* Mancini, daughter of a distinguished family, mistress of an elegant home, owner of Modas Mancini a stylish dress shop patronized by discriminating ladies."

Sighing, she dabs at her eyes. "But when I look in the mirror I see someone else; I see Gabriela, Papá's spoiled little girl; so naive she lived in a dream world for twenty years! And I'm ashamed. And angry. I ask myself what kind of a woman would marry a man, live with him year after year, sleep with him, make love to him…and never realize he's in love with another woman." She looks at me pleadingly. "Do you think you can help me find the answer?"

I scribble on my pad, searching for the right words. "You told me the church granted you an annulment. How long ago was that?"

"Just a couple of months ago. Signed by the same prelate that did the wedding mass."

"So they decided your husband acted in bad faith when he said the wedding vows?"

She makes a face. "Bad faith? That's too polite a term. The man was a cheat, a swindler, a degenerate from the day we married!"

"Want to tell me about it?"

Gabriela has been seated at the edge of her chair, gripping the arm rests. Now she settles back and takes a deep breath.

"If you're going to understand how this absurd thing happened, I need to tell you a little about my family. Grandfather Antonio Mancini immigrated from Italy before the turn of the century, during the Porfirio Diaz dictatorship. He was a humble tailor, but he worked hard, and by the time my father came of age Mancini Suits was a thriving firm.

"My father was past middle-age when I was born. I was the last of three children and the daughter he'd longed for. From the beginning I was Papá's *consentida*, his favorite. He sent me, of course, to a school run by nuns. By the time I graduated from Preparatory, at eighteen, I was engaged to Raul.

"Papá strongly opposed the match. Raul was thirty, the son of a politician and a typical "junior". Do you know what that word means?"

"The spoiled brat of a rich man, right?"

She smiles wryly. "A perfect description of the man I married! Of course my father was right to be suspicious of him, but he had me fooled completely. Raul was on the staff of his father's law firm, and always came to see me wearing a million peso suit with a Mancini label.

"And you know"—frowning, she bites her lip—"while we were courting he hardly touched me. I was so innocent! Doctór Kellee, you can't imagine how jealously a school run by nuns shields its students from the perils of the real world. You may not believe this, but Raul gave me my first kiss after we said our vows." She grimaces, as if in pain. "Ay, that horrible wedding! I still have nightmares when I think about it."

Gabriela reaches for another Kleenex, and I reach for the interphone. "How about a cup of coffee?"

"Good. Just half a cup, please."

While I give Rebeca our orders, Gabriela gets up and walks over to the window. "You're lucky to be right across the street from Liverpool. Have you visited them yet?"

"Just a walk-through. A very impressive department store, as modern and fashionable as anything we have in Houston."

She turns. "One of my chief competitors. Don't tell anybody, but I bought this dress there. Anyway, it's like they're part of the family, since they stock Mancini suits."

Rebeca enters with our coffee. "Sugar, *Señora* Mancini?"

"Just half a spoon, please."

Watching my new secretary I remind myself how fortunate I am to have her. When I arrived this morning the office was spotless, the coffee was perking and she had completed the phone calls I'd assigned her yesterday.

She turns to leave. "Anything else, Doctór?"

"No, thank you."

The door closes quietly.

Gabriela resumes her seat. "How did you get a secretary so fast? And she's so capable. A couple of my friends called last night. Said they had appointments with Dr. Andrés Kellee." he smiles. "They thought they'd make me jealous, but I disappointed them. I told them I was going to be your very first patient. Was I right?"

I smile back "You are indeed!" Feeling the warm glow between us I wonder how long I'm going to be able to maintain this discrete emotional distance.

I clear my throat. "Now let's see, where were we?"

Gabriela deposits her cup on the lamp table. "The wedding. I don't suppose you've attended a Mexican wedding yet, have you?"

"No."

"In Mexico there's an armed truce between the church and the state. Church weddings are permitted, but first you must have a civil ceremony. And the most important moment is not at the end, when the judge pronounces you husband and wife, but about halfway through when he mentions two crucial words.

"If he says '*bienes communes*' the couple will have joint ownership of all their possessions. If he says '*bienes separados*' neither has the right to anything the other brings into the marriage, or acquires afterward."

Gabriela picks up her cup and takes a long sip. Then she sits staring into the cup, as if gathering strength for what she is about to tell me. At last she shrugs and continues: "Raul insisted on *bienes communes*. After all, he pointed out, neither of us had anything to lose, since both families were quite well off. I was surprised by my father's vehement refusal.

I realize now he was planning to will me a large portion of his estate and didn't want my inheritance susceptible to the uncertain fortunes of a politician's son.

"Papá declared there would be no wedding unless Raul renounced his right to my possessions. It became a source of angry confrontations between Raul, his father and my father. I was mortified. The church had been contracted and the wedding date announced. The archbishop had agreed to do the ceremony.

"Why was Papá being so stubborn? I pleaded with him, told him he should be proud his daughter was marrying a man like Raul. But he wouldn't budge a millimeter.

"At last, less than a week before the date set for the wedding, I got down on my knees before my father. "Papá, I love Raúl. And he's right, we're insulting him, insisting on *bienes Separados.*

"Mamá appeared and began yelling at him. Poor Papá! Overwhelmed by his daughter's tears and his wife's threats he caved in.

"The next day the two families and a few select friends gathered in our living room for the ceremony. With Raul and I standing before him, the judge read a homily from his little brown book, in a monotonous voice, as if giving a lecture to a law class. It should have been boring, but it wasn't, because Papá, seated with my mother on the first row, punctuated the homily with mumbled commentaries: 'thief'... 'stupid'...'shameless'...and other words I'm ashamed to repeat.

"I was so tense I was twisting the white carnations off my bouquet, one by one. My father was a nice man most of the time, but when he drank his conduct was unpredictable. And in the last couple of hours, with the help of my two brothers, he'd emptied a fifth of *Don Pedro* rum.

"The judge went on as if nothing were happening. I guess all he wanted to do was finish the ceremony, collect his fee and get out of there. Then he came to those two fateful words. Someone must have warned him about the controversy, because he lowered his head and whispered when he intoned the unexpected words "*bienes communes.*

But my father heard him. He groaned, raised his fist and yelled out something in Italian. To this day I have no idea what he said, but the way he said it left no doubt what he meant.

"Raul's father jumped up and shouted, 'Stop the ceremony! The wedding is off!'

"The judge dropped his little book and Raul squeezed my hand so hard I was sure he'd broken a finger. I began sobbing. My father ran over to confront Raul's father, and toe to toe they yelled insults at one another.

"It took five minutes for my brothers to pull the two men apart."

Gabriela lets out a long, shuddering sigh. "I...I don't remember anything else about the ceremony. The judge must have pronounced us husband and wife because I do remember signing the documents. My father and mother had disappeared, I could hear their angry voices in an adjoining room. At last one of my brothers went for them. When they handed my father the pen, he announced he was signing under protest.

"The church wedding should have been called off, but things had gone too far, now it was a matter of saving face. Besides, I was very much in love, and angry with my father for making such an issue over something so unimportant. Oh, I was so naive!"

I have the feeling Gabriela has forgotten I'm here. She's staring into space, her face very pale. I reach for the pitcher of water on my desk, pour a glass and bring it to her.

Shuddering, she looks up at me as if awaking from a bad dream.

Gulping down the water she moans, "Oh-h-h. I'm so tired! Is our time up?"

I check my watch. "Just about. Anyway, you're too tired to talk any more today."

"You're right. Suddenly I've got an awful headache." She holds out her hand. I help her to her feet, and for a moment she stands very close to me, head down, arms crossed over her chest. I resist the impulse to pull her into my arms.

Feeling light-headed from the nearness of her, I take a step backward. "Would you like me to say a prayer?"

"Oh yes, please!" I take her outstretched hands.

When I return from seeing Gabriela to the elevator Rebeca is waiting for me, eyes wide. (Please, Rebeca, don't ask any questions.) She doesn't. Good girl!

I pause beside her desk. "Well. My first patient. When's the next one?"

"Not till tomorrow. You need to be careful about overworking. Give yourself time to get accustomed to the altitude!"

She dimples. "Anyway, it's my first day, and I have a lot of questions about my work!"

"Let's have at them!" I pull a chair up to her desk, and for the next hour and a half she leads me in an animated dialogue about our Bible class at church, her studies, her family, her boyfriend.

At last she pauses for breath.

"Young lady," I complain, "it's one o'clock and you haven't asked a single question about your work."

She giggles. "There's a place around the corner that sells takeout pizza. Why don't I go get a medium supreme and you can complete my orientation at the table in the seminar room?"

Is this the right way to start off with my secretary? It was never like this in Houston! But this isn't Houston, and Rebeca is more than a secretary. Here we are in our second day of work and she hasn't even questioned me about what I'm going to pay her. It looks like she's adopted me as her special project.

And I've adopted her as my kid sister!

Her hazel eyes are challenging me. "If you don't want to spend money on me you can take the pizza out of my salary. That is, if I'm going to have a salary."

I grin and hand her a fifty peso bill. It's going to be interesting having Rebeca around, it would be all too easy to spend the rest of the day with her, chatting about nothing in particular.

CHAPTER 12

▼

A VISIT TO THE SERPENT'S HEADQUARTERS

"Dr. Andrés…has anyone told you what the angel Gabriel said when the Lord created Mexico?"

Elbows on my desk, hands folded, I study Moisés' face. Should I smile? Sounds like he's about to tell a joke, but his face is solemn.

"No, Moisés, I don't think so."

Rebeca appears at the door. "Pastor, don't you dare! That's a cruel, demeaning story!"

"And that's why the Doctór needs to hear it! It will prepare him for our visit to the Zócalo this morning."

Dismissing her with a wave of the hand, Moisés begins his story: The Lord and Gabriel were reviewing his plans for the creation of the world. The Lord described all the marvelous things he planned to bequeath to Mexico: broad rivers, snow-covered mountains, a country-side filled with coconut palms, banana trees and pineapple, mines of silver and gold, hundreds of kilometers of sparkling beaches. When he had finished, Gabriel protested, "But Lord, why are you giving so much to just one little country. It isn't fair!"

"Don't worry," the Lord said, "I'll make it fair. So fair no other country on the planet will dare complain."

"And how will you do that?"

"I'll populate it with Mexicans!"

"Shame on you!" Rebeca says, shaking a finger at him, "I hate that story!"

I stare at a pen on my desk, trying to hide my discomfort. This isn't the first time I've noticed the penchant of Mexicans for black humor…with themselves as victims. Why, I wonder?

"Doctór!" Moisés interrupts my thoughts. "I've told you Mexico is under a curse. We Mexicans feel it in our bones. That's why we tell so many masochistic jokes. We've been betrayed by our history, it's filled with disappointments and spoiled dreams. Every time it looks like things are going to change for the better, they end up getting worse!"

He goes to the coffee pot and pours himself a steaming cupful. "This morning you'll see an example; we're going to visit the place where fate played a cruel joke on the most powerful monarch in our history."

Last Sunday I reminded the pastor of his promise to take me deeper into the dark history of Quetzalcóatl. He thought for a moment, then answered, "Very well, Doctór Andrés, how about next Tuesday? I'll take you to Quetzalcóatl's headquarters."

Entering the elevator, we wave goodbye to Rebeca and punch the button for the basement parking garage. Downstairs Luis, a smiling young man with a crew cut puts down a thick book, finds my key on a nail behind his cluttered desk and disappears into rows of red and green Volkswagen bugs sprinkled here and there with Dodge Spirits and vintage Mustangs. The Volkswagon bug must be Mexico's national car! They're everywhere. No wonder, they cost a fifth of what you'd pay for the typical American car and use half as much gasoline. I shudder when I hear Luis start my car, floorboard the accelerator, shift gears and take off spinning the wheels. Oh well, I guess he deserves a thrill. He's bored. Two years ago he received a degree in psychology from the National University and he's still looking for a job.

He brakes beside us, tires squealing, opens the door for me and says "*Gracias*" when I drop a peso into his hand.

I steer my Chevy out of the garage onto a narrow side street and bluff my way into the clogged stream of cars on Avenida Escobedo. Half a dozen blocks later I turn right on San Cosme into a churning river of traffic headed downtown. It's nearly noon and the sun is warm, but we ride with the windows rolled up. The rains that have given the atmosphere a daily scrubbing since June have ended. Already the contamination makes your eyes water.

We stop for a red light and a young mother crosses the street in front of us, trying to keep up with a small boy pulling her along by the hand Suddenly I remember Margaret! She called last night asking bout my plans for Thanksgiving. Guilt washed over me. It hadn't even crossed my mind that Thanksgiving was just a few weeks away.

"Would you rather I come for Thanksgiving or Christmas?"

Silence…. "Am I going to have to choose, Daddy?" Her voice rose half an octave: "You've always been with us for both holidays."

I raised my eyebrows, speechless. "Dear, times have changed. You've got your family, Victoria is away at school, and now that your mother…"

Margaret's voice broke. "But can't you see, Daddy? This is the first Thanksgiving without Mom. Must we be without you too?" A quiet sob.

"I'll tell you what," I said, struggling to keep my voice calm, "I'll come for Thanksgiving and we'll talk about Christmas. Okay?"

"Okay, Daddy You know, Victoria called last night, and we talked a long time about you. We're afraid…" the line went dead.

Had she hung up? Should I call her back? No, I'm not going to let her play the role of victim! I've begun a new life and she'll have to learn to accept it.

Moisés interrupts my thoughts. "The Popotla Station is a couple of blocks ahead. We'll take the metro there."

Five million people crowd into the metro, the city's subway, every day. Not surprising, since it whisks you across the city in a fraction of the time it would take by automobile or bus.

Just ahead, a car pulls out from the curb and I swing into the space, breathing a silent prayer of thanks. They don't have parking lots at the metro stations, maybe because most people with automobiles don't ride the metro.

As we walk toward the station Moisés points to the remains of a tree on the other side of a low stone fence. It looks dead, only a bare trunk maybe twelve feet tall, reinforced with concrete and supported by a wooden brace. "That's a popotla tree. Historians call it 'The tree of the sad night.' The metro station is named for it. I don't know why they haven't put up a plaque."

"H-m-m. Sounds like there's an interesting story there."

"I'll tell you about it later."

We've come to the metro entrance. Leaning against the white stucco wall, Moisés points down the street to a complex of massive two-story colonial buildings enclosed in a neatly trimmed green hedge. A column of young men in gray uniforms, rifles on their shoulders, march smartly across a broad expanse of clipped green grass. "That's the *Colegio Militar,* our West Point. The parade ground was once the shore of Lake Texcoco. In the days of Moctezuma you could stand here and see the gleaming white temples of Huizilopchtli and Quetzalcóatl. And from here you could cross over to Moctezuma's island kingdom on a causeway five kilometers long."

When we come to the glass-enclosed booth at the entrance Moisés insists on buying my ticket. I start to argue with him, then remember the ticket costs less than a dime. Taking my arm he steers me through the crowd to a stairway and we cross beneath the tracks to the other side.

"How do they keep this place so clean?" I ask, "no graffiti on the walls, no trash on the floor."

"Look!" Moisés points to a soldier making a long-haired teenager pick up a gum wrapper. "This is federal property and the army sees to it the stations are kept spotless. It works because everybody's are afraid of our soldiers. See that rifle? He wouldn't hesitate to use it!"

A handsome diesel locomotive arrives at the platform, pulling half a dozen bright orange coaches. S-s-s-s…the automatic doors slide open. I hurry forward.

"Careful, Doctór," Moisés calls out to me.

Too late! I find myself flat on my back, bowled over by the crowd disgorged from the train. Nobody in the pushing, shoving multitude seems to have noticed.

"Sorry, Doctór!" Moisés takes my hand and pulls me to my feet. "Are you all right? I should have warned you sooner."

Brushing at my clothes, my cheeks burning, I follow Moisés inside. We find a seat in the near-empty coach. A mother pulls a big-eyed little boy into her lap just as the doors clatter shut and the train jerks forward.

My thoughts return to Margaret's call. After talking to her I had a hard time going to sleep. Are she and Victoria right to be worried about me? Am I becoming obsessed with Mexico and her dark destiny? Maybe so. Yesterday I could think of nothing but this day I'd be spending with Moisés…. But today I've felt a strange oppression, as if something bad is about to happen.

The train is slowing. Looking out the window I see a brightly-lit station that's an exact copy of the one we just left. "Above this station," Moisés tells me, "is the Monument to the Revolution. Pancho Villa and half a dozen of our presidents are buried there."

In less than a minute we're on our way again. "Four centuries ago we'd be at the bottom of Lake Texcoco, and the causeway would be just above us," he continues.

"But now just above us is downtown, right?"

"Right."

"What happened to the lake?"

"It filled up little by little. Remember, I told you about the Aztecs' unusual vegetable gardens: how they piled rafts with mud, sowed the seed and left them floating on the lake. After a while most of the lake was covered with floating gardens.

"As time passed the plants sent down roots and the lake silted up. You've heard about the floating gardens of Xochimilco, haven't you? That's all that's left of Tenochtitlan's magic kingdom!"

At the Palace of Fine Arts station a crowd surges in. When the subway starts up again we're packed tight, unable to move, the mass of people swaying to the rhythm of the train. A little boy sitting on his mother's lap has a tight grip on the back of my seat. I turn and smile at him and he grins back. Suddenly, I'm wishing my little grandson were here. I miss him! How often in the years ahead will he have the chance to smile at his grandfather?

The train slows and Moisés elbows me. "Here's where we get off."

Pushed along by the crowd we climb two flights of stairs and find ourselves blinking in the bright sunlight, at the edge of an immense square. A couple of blocks wide and three long, paved with heavy gray stone, the Zócalo reminds me of pictures I've seen of Moscow's Red Square. Moisés takes my elbow and steers me through the crowd. We pass a dozen ragged men squatting in the plaza beside their work implements, holding crudely-lettered signs: "plumber...carpenter..." brick-layer.

I say, "Moisés, back in my office you referred this place as Quetzalcóatl's headquarters.

Why?"

Stopping, he turns to face me: "Doctór, we're standing at the spot where Hernán Cortés met Moctezuma four and a half centuries ago. I'll bet he and his soldiers were stunned when they saw how Moctezuma had adorned the *Templo Mayor* with thousands of Feathered Serpents."

"The *Templo Mayor?*"

"That's what Moctezuma called the plaza he'd filled with pyramids to his gods. His *Templo Mayor* was only a couple of meters below where we're standing. It made Cortés so angry he razed all those magnificent palaces to the ground."

He points to the northern edge of the Zócalo and an imposing stone cathedral with soaring twin towers. "That's the National Cathedral. Cortés built it with stones from Moctezuma's temples he had destroyed. But you know, he made a tragic mistake: he did nothing about the demons that swarmed in those buildings. They're still here!" He cups a hand over an ear, frowning: "Sometimes I'm sure I hear the flutter of their ugly black wings!

"Come on, let's go." He touches my arm and we move toward the Cathedral. "I wonder how Cortés' soldiers felt the day they marched into Moctezuma's plaza. It was 1519, just twenty-seven years after Columbus' first landing. They had beached their ships on the Gulf coast and hacked their way through five hundred kilometers of steaming jungles, scaled soaring mountain peaks and swum deep rivers. Along the way they were attacked again and again by howling bands of native warriors."

"How many soldiers did Cortés have with him?"

"By the time they made it to Tenochtitlán there were less than four hundred survivors. they had landed on the coast weeks before with twice that number. The audacity of that man!"

"What made him do it?"

"The lust for riches. All along the way people had been telling him Tenochtitlan's streets were paved with gold."

Looking toward the plaza, I can almost smell the rancid smoke ascending from a hundred altars, as Cortés' soldiers pace back and forth in anticipation of the momentous meeting that is about to take place. Their general, representative of the most powerful nation in Europe, will confront Moctezuma II, the supreme potentate of the western hemisphere. I wonder if they realized they were living a hinge of history, a *kairos*?

Just like now!

"Doctór, are you all right?" Moisés is watching me curiously.

Blinking, I drift back to the Twentieth Century. "Yes, I…I'm just overwhelmed by the history of this terrible place."

Taking my arm he leads me toward an imposing two-story building of red stone. Like a gaudy fortress it guards the east side of the Zócalo, polished bronze doors shining in the weak afternoon sun, colorful purple awnings shading its tall shuttered windows.

"That's the *Palacio Nacional,* here the President has his offices. Once Moctezuma's residence stood there."

We halt some twenty paces from the Palace. "This is where the meeting took place. Bernal Díaz, a sergeant in Cortés' army, describes that meeting in a book he wrote when he returned to Europe: the Emperor, his royal head shaded from the sun by a brilliant green canopy, comes striding toward General Cortés on the arms of four great *caciques*. He's dressed in dazzling multicolored robes and his shoes boast sparkling precious stones and soles of pure gold. Dozens of servants go before the him, sweeping the ground and laying sheets of white cloth for his imperial feet. When he arrives at where Cortés stands waiting, he intones:

Our Lord, you are tired, you have wearied yourself. You have arrived at your city, Mexico. You have come among clouds, to sit on your throne. I and the kings who preceded me have been safeguarding it for you.

And now…"Oh come on, Moisés!" The words explode from my mouth, startling me. Moisés, who has been illustrating Moctezuma's oration with exaggerated gestures, stops, startled by my outburst.

Aware of the curious crowd that has gathered, I lean toward Moisés and protest, under my breath, "Am I supposed to believe the great Emperor Moctezuma would give up without a fight? Offer Cortés his throne? It doesn't make sense!"

Pulling me aside, Moisés shakes his finger at me like a teacher admonishing a dull sixth-grade pupil. "What else would you expect, Doctór? Moctezuma thought Hernán Cortés was Quetzalcóatl!"

I glare at him. "Quetzal…Quetzalcóatl? But Quetzalcóatl was a feathered serpent…a…a snake!"

Rolling his eyes, Moisés throws up his hands. "A-y-y, Doctór, how am I going to get you to stop thinking like an unimaginative gringo?"

Rubbing his stomach, he changes the subject: "Doctór, I don't know about you, but I'm hungry! Let's see if we can locate some *taquitos.*"

We turn toward the street.

"*Chicle, Señor?*" A grimy little fist clutching a tiny package of cellophane-wrapped gum is thrust in my face. I step back, painfully aware of the thin, dark-skinned child, his face coated in a film of by a fine of black dust.

Moisés pulls me away. "Don't buy anything. If you do the rest of the kids will drive us crazy!"

Shoving my hands deep into my pockets I shuffle along beside Moisés, my shoulders humped, my spirits sagging. What a depressing, complicated place this is!

A block from the Zócalo we find a tiny restaurant specializing in *tacos al pastor*, shreds of meat sliced from a layered hunk of beef, pork and bacon roasted on a slowly revolving rotisserie and rolled into warm corn tortillas. Slapping on a generous serving of hot sauce, Moisés says, "So you don't believe Moctezuma could have mistaken Cortés for Quetzalcóatl?"

I wave away the hot sauce and bite into my taco. "Look, Pastor, the last time I heard of the Feathered Serpent he had changed into Venus. And now, suddenly, he's a Spanish general?"

Moisés chuckles. "Not suddenly. Centuries had passed since Quetzalcóatl became the Morning Star. The Toltecs had carried their god Quetzalcóatl from Teotihuacan to Yucatan, land of the Mayans. There the Mayans changed his name to Kukulkan, and built him a magnificent temple in the city of Chichen Itzá. And there, according to the Mayans, Quetzalcóatl became a man; a tall, handsome prince with fair skin, blond hair and a beard. Their historians describe how he traveled the countryside preaching temperance and love, exhorting people to forsake war and live in peace with one another."

I shake my head, repulsed by this absurd mythology, last night's oppression closing in upon me like a dark storm cloud. Taking a deep breath, I exhale slowly. "But Yucatan was a long, long way from Tenochtitlan. And Moctezuma had his ancestral god, Huitzilopochtli. Why would he be interested in a faraway god named Quetzalcóatl?"

"You're forgetting, Doctór, that Quetzalcóatl had reigned for a thousand years in Teotihuacan, just a day's journey from Tenochtitlan. We know from Aztec historians that Moctezuma became enamored of the city of pyramids, and visited it frequently. So he was familiar with Quetzalcóatl's miraculous temple. Moctezuma must have become a convert, because he favored Quetzalcóatl above his ancestral god. The high stone wall enclosing the *templo mayor* was decorated with thousands of feathered serpents. And even the stairway leading to the altar atop Huitzilopotchtli's temple was adorned with them."

"But this business of the Feathered Serpent becoming a man!"

"Remember what I've told you more than once? That when you're dealing with Satan, expect the unexpected. Remember: the electrifying news of Jesus Christ, God in the flesh, was about to invade Mexico, challenging Quetzalcóatl's supremacy. There must have been panic among Satan and his demons. What better way inoculate the people against the coming God-Man?"

Moisés signals for the waiter. "Six more tacos, *por favor.*" He turns back to me. "Sometime before the arrival of Hernan Cortés Moctezuma built a beautiful temple for Quetzalcóatl, right next to the temple of Huitzilopochtli. It was different from all the other pyramids in the *Templo.*Mayor Built of white limestone, it was shaped like a cylinder and its entrance was a grotesque serpent's mouth.

"…Here, Doctór, have another taco."

He leans over the table and fixes his black eyes on me. "Then some terrible things began to happen. Moctezuma's kingdom was racked by a series a natural disasters: floods, droughts, earthquakes, volcanic eruptions. The Emperor, a melancholy, superstitious man, believed these catastrophes were the portent of some momentous event just over the horizon. And for some reason—maybe through the influence of his priests—he decided that event was Quetzalcóatl's second coming."

The taco drops from my hand, and I gape at Moisés.

"His second coming?"

"For a long time before Moctezuma's reign a strange, wistful story was making the rounds throughout Mexico: Quetzalcóatl had failed in his attempt to bring nobility and peace to his kingdom. Heartbroken at the rejection of the people, he had disappeared into the mists of the Gulf of Mexico. But before leaving he had left his disciples a promise: one day he would return.

"Now imagine the scene: a runner arrives with electrifying news: a bearded, fair-skinned god, accompanied by a host of angels, has landed on the Gulf coast, borne by clouds."

"Cortés and his soldiers?"

"Of course."

"But...borne by clouds?"

"Can't you guess what the clouds were, *Don* Andrés?"

"The sails on Cortes' ship!"

Moisés reaches for another taco. "Now can you understand why Moctezuma thought Cortés was Quetzalcóatl?"

I let out a long, slow sigh. "I...I guess so. But no, not really. This thing blows my mind!"

Moisés consults his watch. "It's getting late. If we're to see the rest of the *Templo Mayor* we'd better get going." He takes one last swallow of Coke and rises to his feet. Come on," he commands, taking off in the direction of the Cathedral.

My recollection of the rest of that afternoon is muddled. I remember walking past the Cathedral to where the Government had demolished half a block of buildings to reveal the foundations of Huitzilopchtli's temple. And visiting the museum next door with its display of hundreds of artifacts from the *Templo Mayor.*

But I was in a stupor, turning over in my mind all I'd heard this afternoon: Quetzalcóatl, Feathered Serpent and Morning Star, had for thousands of years challenged God's supremacy here in Mexico. And had made himself god incarnate, a burlesque of God's own Son. Moisés was right: who but Satan himself could have invented such a scheme?

And in the middle of it, Andrew Kelly! Shivering in the lengthening shadows, I buttoned my sweater. What am I doing here in this dreadful city? I'd hurry back to my apartment and start packing if it weren't for Gabriela.

Gabriela!

Remembering yesterday, I smile....

"I knew I was going to be late," she said, as Rebeca ushered her into my office, "I should have broken off my tennis game, but I was behind and I can't stand to lose!"

My heart skipped a beat. Gabriela looked fresh and innocent in her rumpled blue jogging suit. Her flushed cheeks and ingenuous smile hardly seemed those of a forty-year old matron recovering from a disastrous marriage.

"Come in, I forgive you." I walked over and gave her an *abrazo.* She smelled of sweet soap and talcum.

Flopping down into an easy chair she kicked off her sandals, and I sat opposite her. Her bright green eyes were studying my face. "What do you do for exercise, Andee—" she giggled, "I mean Doctór Kellee?" I liked the way the corners of her mouth crinkled when she smiled.

"I'm an obsessive runner," I confessed. "I feel guilty the week I don't get in twenty miles. But it's going to take me a while to get used to the altitude. And to think in kilometers, not miles."

"Twenty miles, that's almost thirty kilometers. I'm impressed!" She reached out and touched my hand. "It's good to have you with us, *querido* Doctór. I pray every night you'll learn to like us and our smoggy old city."

My hand tingled where she touched it. I hoped I wasn't blushing like a pimpled teenager. "What about you," I stammered, "Are you...obsessed with your tennis?"

"Maybe so, I spend hours at the club every day. But I guess what I'm really obsessed about are these dreadful hips I inherited from my Italian grandmother."

She jumped to her feet, and hands on hips, did a mock pirouette. "Look at them, aren't they ghastly? I hate them! That's why I knock myself out banging tennis balls and lifting weights."

"*Señorita* Mancini," I answered, "I hadn't noticed. When I look at you I see a graceful, totally charming lady."

"Hmph!" Making a face she dropped back into her chair. "For years I would've given my soul to hear my husband Raul say words like that. He liked to ridicule my hips...and a lot of other things about me. Every time he made me angry I'd grab up my racquet and head for the club. He's no longer around, but I can still hear that mocking voice."

I settled back into my chair. (Time to get to work, Dr. Kelly!) "So Raul was abusive?"

"Not until after we married. While we were going together I could do nothing wrong. But on our honeymoon everything changed. The first night, after we'd..." she studied the hands clutched tightly in her lap, "I won't dignify what he did to me by calling it making love—he turned his back on me and told me I wasn't fit to be a wife, that I was still a *niñita de monjas*...'a nuns' little girl.'"

"You *were* awfully young. Only eighteen. And he was thirty?"

"Thirty-two. But you know something?" Her chin came up, "He was more of a child than I. We spent ten days in Paris, and not a day passed without him calling his mother." She sighed. "I always felt like I was in competition with her."

"Your mother-in-law opposed the marriage?"

Oh no, I was the ideal prospect to keep her dear little son from disgracing his family."

"I don't understand."

Her face darkened. "I found out later—much later—that he'd been carrying on an affair with his secretary for years, and his parents knew about it. Then she became pregnant and he started talking about marrying her."

"And that would have been a disgrace? Why?"

"Because we Mexicans are such hypocrites! Have you watched any of our soap operas on T.V.? How all the rich, glamorous people have fair skin?

"Nobody talks about Mexicans being racists, it's one of our best-kept secrets. But most upper-class families hold their breath when a baby is born, fearful that the genes of an Indian ancestor will show up."

"So Raul's secretary was…"

"*Muy India.* And 'Mamá' couldn't bear the thought of bouncing a swarthy little grandchild on her knee. Raul could have as many dark-skinned lovers as he wished—that was no problem. But they and the children they might bear must remain in the shadows. His duty was to marry someone who could give his mother proper grandchildren."

"So she forbade him to marry his secretary?"

"If he wanted to keep on being her son. I don't know how it is in your country, Doctór, but here the *santa madre* holds incredible power over her sons. Maybe because they see day after day, year after year, how their father mistreats their mother and feel they have a holy mission to make it up to her."

"And that's why Raul began pursuing you?"

"Naive little Gabriela, *niña de* monjjas! It took me twenty years to find out the truth!"

"Doctór, it's time to catch the metro!" I turned. Ten steps behind me, Moisés was standing at the entrance to the station, waving his hand. In the distance I saw the sun slipping behind the twin towers of the great Cathedral.

I hurried back to him. "I'm sorry," I told him, shaking my head sheepishly, "I guess I had my mind on something else."

"I guess you did, *hermano*," Moisés grumbled, starting down the stairs, "I kept trying to get your attention, and finally just gave up."

Following him, I reminded myself that all around me were the still-buried ruins of the *Templo Mayor*. I'd been thinking Hernán Cortés was foolish to invade Moctezuma's territory. But wasn't I just as foolish to be invading Quetzalcóatl's territory! What had I gotten myself into?

CHAPTER 13

▼

A SURPRISING
DISCOVERY

"Doctór! I've been calling you for two hours."

"*Buenas noches,* Moisés, I just got in." I'm breathing hard, I heard the phone ringing from the elevator and ran like mad. "What's up?"

"I'm not sure, but it sounds like it may be something big. Have you met Isaac Sánchez?"

"No, is he a member of the church?"

"He's a deacon. And an engineer at *Construcciones Torres.* His company has the contract for the restoration of the National Cathedral.

"So all that scaffolding we saw in the nave of the Cathedral the other day belongs to them?"

"That's right. This afternoon Isaac called me, real excited. Said he's found something I must see. He's going to show me tomorrow. Want to come along?"

I feel my stomach tightening. Tomorrow's my day off, and I'd been planning to sleep in. "Well, I'd like to, but...does it have to be tomorrow?"

"Tomorrow nobody's working at the site, so we can slip in unobserved."

"Do...do you have any idea what this is about, Moisés?"

"Isaac said something about the Temple of Huitzilopochtli. Remember, we saw the ruins last Tuesday. The Cathedral is right next door, so...look, Doctór, if you're too busy..." I can tell he's getting impatient.

All of a sudden, adrenaline is stinging the back of my hand like hot grease from the frying pan. "Sounds exciting, tell me where to meet you, Moisés!"

A few minutes later I hang up and head for the shower. Looking at my watch, I grimace. It's nearly midnight and I'll be meeting Moisés at nine!

I haven't stopped all day. After my last appointment I drove across town to a *taquería* for supper with half a dozen of the guys from my Sunday Bible class. Had fun, but it's a noisy place, and by the time they brought out the coffee I was tired of all the yelling, so I got up and threw a twenty-peso bill on the table. They kidded me about being a *viejo*. Maybe they're right, I had no desire to stay up with them till dawn.

I shower and go to bed. An hour later I'm still tossing and turning, Gabriela's sweet face floating before me.

This morning was our third session. I found her sitting with Rebeca when I stepped out of my office with a client. Dressed in a white blouse and black slacks, she rose to greet me, eyes shining. "You see, Doctór, I arrived early this time."

Without thinking I pulled her into an *abrazo*, and even though her hair was tickling my nose, didn't want to let her go.

Moments later, seated in my office, she took a sip of her coffee and said, "Andrés, you can't imagine what a relief it is to have someone to talk to. I know God is going to use you to help me understand everything, and..." she set down her cup and looked at me with those penetrating green eyes, "show me how I can get on with my life."

My heart pounding, I checked my notes. "Last time you told me about your honeymoon. And Raul's lover."

Her eyes widened, green melting into amber, and she said, "I still don't know how he managed to fool me for more than twenty years."

I tried to smile. "Believe me, Gabriela, you aren't the first.

There's truth to that old adage, 'love is blind'".

Sighing, she settled back into her seat. "Well, let's go on…. Within a few weeks after our return from that miserable honeymoon in Paris the pattern was established for the next twenty years. Raul was away most days from early morning until late at night. Sometimes, before going to bed, I'd call his office. I wonder now how many times Raul was sitting there smirking when his secretary told me he was unavailable.

"One night toward the end of the first year he came home with lipstick on his collar. I confronted him and he laughed at me. Said I was watching too many *telenovelas*, was he supposed to refuse the *abrazos* of his female clients?

"As much as I hated being lonely, I hated Friday evenings even more. They were reserved for supper with my in-laws. The four sons and their wives were expected to arrive no later than nine. *Don* Emilio, the *papá*, made it his business to arrive an hour later. Regina, the *santa madre*, ruled at the head of the long table like the queen she was. The sons sat to her right, seats assigned according to the family heirarchy. First was Emilio Junior, a paunchy, pompous blowhard, then Ricardo, a muscular showoff who got up every morning at five to work out at the club. He hated his elder brother and was always poking fun at him. I never felt like I knew Samuel, the third in line. He was tall and thin, chain-smoked, never initiated a conversation and communicated in grunts.

"Then came Raul, the youngest. With all his faults, he was the most intelligent, the handsomest and the only brother with personality. And of course, being the youngest he was his mother's favorite.

"We daughters-in-law sat across the table from them, at Papá's side. That is, during the brief moments we were able to be seated. Most of the time we occupied ourselves in serving the meal. It was the same each week: chicken *consomé*, pork roast, and at the end a dessert that Mamá had prepared and hardly anyone touched. Even after the meal was on the table we wives kept jumping up to obey our husbands' orders:

"'*Mujer*, we're out of tortillas.'

"'*Vieja*, another bottle of wine.'

"'*Gorda*, ask the cook if there's any roast left in the kitchen'.

"I always breathed a sigh of relief when the men reached for their cigars. I'd jump up, hurry to the living room and settle myself on the sofa with a novel I'd brought along. The other wives sat around a table in the kitchen gossiping and sipping wine. They were all at least ten years older than me, so we had little in common.

"From the living room I could hear the conversation of the Corona family, still seated around the table. It was always about money. Each son received an allowance, the amount determined by Mamá, and varying from week to week according to her assessment of their behavior. Papá said very little. Occasionally he broke in to curse at one of the sons or to berate Mamá for spending money faster than he could earn it. She'd yell back at him, accusing him of spending less on his family than on his "'street women'".

"Finally Mamá would go up to bed and Papá would slap a pack of poker cards on the table and uncork the first bottle. Within a couple of hours all five men were roaring drunk. From the living room I tried to ignore the curses, the obscene jokes, the belches and the fights erupting every ten minutes are so. After a couple of years I mastered the art of stretching out on the couch with a cushion over my head and getting a few hours of troubled sleep.

"At last, the son who was losing most would complain dawn was breaking and it was time to go home. One by one the couples would stagger out the door, grumbling at one another, heads throbbing."

Gabriela stopped and glared at me. "Go ahead. Laugh. You think it's funny!"

I tried to swallow my smile. "I'm not laughing at you, Gabriela. It's just that…four grown men, still fighting over their allowances from Mamá. Incredible!"

Gabriela got up, stretched, and walked over to the window. Her back to me, she said, "You know, it all seems like a bad dream now. Absurd. A comic opera." Turning, she came to where I was seated.

"Andee, I know I was stupid putting up with all that for so many years."

Tears welled up. "I'm afraid you're going to lose your respect for me."

I took her hand. "Impossible!"

Bending, she kissed my cheek, sending chills down my spine, then sat down again. "Well," she said, letting out a long sigh, "I've finished the prelude. Now for the ugly part:

"One dark, rainy afternoon my labor pains began. I stumbled to the phone and called Raul's office. He was in a meeting, his secretary informed me curtly, and he'd left instructions not to be disturbed. Desperate, moaning with pain, I dialed my mother. She and her chauffeur were there in ten minutes. Mamá sat beside me for nine agonizing hours before I managed to deliver a beautiful little girl with tangled blonde curls.

"Raul made a perfunctory visit the next morning. Not a smile, as if he were angry at me for something bad I'd done. I didn't see him again until three days later when Papá took me and little Angelica home.

"My father was livid. Now in his mid-sixties, he decided the time had come to assure my future. He wrote a will leaving his business to my two brothers and the bulk of his estate to me.

He found a way to void the hated *bienes cumunes* clause in the marriage contract: he established a trust to guard my inheritance until my forty-second birthday, quite sure that by then I would have divorced Raul. Ten years later, two years before his death, he placed the family home in the same trust and purchased a condominium for himself and Mamá. I moved my family into the ancestral home, making it clear to Raul that he was there only by invitation."

"By that time you must have suspected he was seeing another woman."

"Of course! But every time I accused him he belittled me, so what could I do?"

"Did you consider leaving him?"

"When do you decide a marriage is unbearable? My parents, as much as they disliked Raul, never suggested divorce. You'll find out, Andee, that In Mexico people with money tend to recognize the death of a marriage by less drastic means. The husband maintains his *casa chica*...maybe two or three. The wife devotes herself to her children. As the children grow up they become accustomed to a benign matriarchy and a love-hate relationship with their father.

"Husband and wife attend weddings, baptisms and social affairs, playing the role of devoted couple. As the years pass the wife accustoms herself to the fiction, and though her heart is overflowing with bitterness, a public breakup becomes less and less possible."

"You know, Gabriela," I said, "under the circumstances I'm surprised there were more children."

She frowns. "Well, I guess I kept on hoping things would change.

I'd been asking myself if Raul's attitude toward his first child would have been different if it had been a boy. By the time Angelica was five I convinced myself it was worth a try. Within a year Hector was born. But it made no difference.

"So I gave up on him. Late one night when he returned home he was surprised to find our king-size replaced by twin beds."

"You're a very feeling person, Gabriela. How did you manage to continue with just the pretense of a marriage?"

She reached for a Kleenex. "It was hard. I began overeating, and soon I was thirty pounds overweight. Finally, ashamed of how I looked, I joined a club. Began playing tennis several times a week with a handsome, gracious gentleman old enough to be my father."

Gabriela bowed her head. "I guess I'm not supposed to keep anything from my therapist, right?"

"Remember I promised you nothing you could say would make me think less of you."

"Well, Andrés, Cesar…that was the gentleman's name…convinced me to…to begin a relationship. After a few months I packed my clothes, took my children and went to live in his apartment."

"You must have loved him very much."

She shook her head slowly. "I thought I did, but looking back…let's see, that was more than twelve years ago…I realize I was starved for love, a setup for anybody who'd show me a little affection.

"My parents were crushed. And guess what…so was Raul! He began pleading with me to return, promising things would be different."

"And he convinced you?"

"Not Raul, but Papá. For six months he and Mamá refused to speak to me. Then one day he called and invited me to lunch. He made me a proposition: if I'd break off the affair and return home he'd establish a feminine counterpart of *Mancini Suits* and give me full ownership.

"It took a few weeks for him to convince me, but from the day I accepted his offer I threw myself into the enterprise as if my life depended on it. And of course, it did.

"Soon I was making buying trips to New York and Paris. To my own surprise and the delight of Papá I discovered I had a gift for business. Within a year *Modas Mancini* was grossing half as much as *Mancini Suits*.

"And what about Raul?"

Her lip curls. "Raul? The bastard!" A hand flies to her mouth. "Oh, I'm sorry, Andrés!"

I try not to smile. "The name fits…So nothing changed?"

"At first it did. Raul received me back with open arms. Literally. So I retired the twin beds and took the king-size out of storage.

"And guess what? In less than a year a little boy came along!" A spasm of pain contorts her face. "He was an angel! So different from Hector, who at six was dark both in appearance and spirit: self-centered, suspicious, stingy with his affection.

"But Gabriel...that's the name I insisted we give him...seemed to be the incarnation of the angel I named him after. His bright face wore a perpetual smile, his blue eyes were always merry, and he had a thick mop of wavy brown hair.

"With Gabriel at my side and an exciting, prosperous *Modas Mancini* to challenge me, I was almost happy. When Raul returned to his old ways I hardly acknowledged it, except to reinstall the twin beds."

(Shall I ask her? I must...that look!) "But this...this little son Gabriel. Why haven't you mentioned him before?"

The spasm of pain again: "Didn't I tell you the worst part was yet to come?"

Looking at her watch, she winces. "Oh my goodness, time's up. I guess that will have to wait."

I sigh. "I guess it will. Here, let me check my calendar.

"H...m...m...next Wednesday I'll be leaving to spend Thanksgiving with my children."

"Then you must give me enough time Monday or Tuesday to finish my story."

I nod. "Tell you what, I'll set aside all of Tuesday morning for you."

She gives me a hug, and again, a kiss on the cheek. And again, hills tickle my spine.

By ten the morning after Moisés' call we've parked the car and are walking toward the Popotla terminal. Moisés points down the street. "Remember the *"tree of the sad night"*? We saw it last time we were here. Would you like to hear the history behind that name?"

"Of course."

We stop at the pitiful, bedraggled shape that bears only a faint likeness to a tree.

"It goes back to the days of Moctezuma. Some terrible things happened after that incredible meeting between him and Hernán Cortés. The general and his men tried every trick of diplomacy to convince the Emperor to surrender his gold. When he refused they made him a captive in his own palace. Finally, exasperated by his stubbornness, they executed him."

Several passersby have stopped and are listening to Moisés' story.

"The citizens of Tenochtitlán were infuriated. They attacked Cortés and his men, forcing them to retreat over the causeway, fighting for their lives. It's amazing they weren't all killed. When night fell the survivors huddled under this tree, binding their wounds, mourning their losses. It was the worst night of the campaign. Years later, when he wrote the history of Cortés' conquest of Tenochtitlan, Bernal Diaz dubbed the tree '*el arbol de la noche triste.*' The name has stuck."

More passersby have stopped to listen. A policeman is crossing the street to investigate.

Moisés takes my arm. "Come on, Andrés, let's go before we get in trouble!"

As we walk toward the station I ask, "What did they do after that terrible defeat, retreat back to the coast?"

"No, Cortés was a stubborn man. He and his soldiers scoured the countryside and recruited thousands of Moctezuma's enemies. Then they returned and renewed their attack. Within a week Moctezuma's fabulous city was a wilderness of heaps of stones.

After a couple of years, atop the ruins of the *Templo Mayor*, Cortés began the construction of the Cathedral we'll visit this morning."

Fifteen minutes later, as we approach the Cathedral, a dark young man with muscles bulging from the sleeves of his bright red knit shirt hurries forward to receive us.

"Doctór," says Moisés, "This is Isaac Sanchez. He's in charge of the crew working on the Cathedral."

Giving us both hearty *abrazos*, Isaac leads us around back to a fenced-in enclosure. He slips a bill to a uniformed guard and the man unlocks the iron gate and motions us to enter.

"The Cathedral is a national monument," Isaac tells us, "so the government spends a lot of money trying to keep it in repair. An impossible task! The original construction continued for three centuries, and much of it was poorly done. See how the walls are cracked? Inside, the ceiling is sagging in several places, in danger of falling.

"Sometime ago the architects decided it was useless to continue repairing the building without shoring up the foundation. That's what we're trying to do."

We descend a dozen rough concrete steps and Isaac pulls out a large bronze key, turning it in the oversized lock. He slowly pushes open the metal door. Dim 40-Watt bulbs hanging on wires strung beneath the Cathedral floor illuminate a gloomy scene. Centuries ago this must have been a basement, but now it's a wilderness of dusty cobwebs, scattered stones and piles of rubble.

Isaac picks something up, brushes the dust off and hands it to me. I shudder. The dead eyes of a grinning feathered serpent stare up at me.

"We seem to strike one every time we put a shovel in the ground," saac tells me.

Moisés grunts. "Remember what I told you, Doctór? Cortés commanded the people to raze the pagan temples, thinking they were getting rid of the gods and their army of demons.

How wrong he was! The evil spirits simply sank beneath the Zócalo and inhabited these idols like bees in a hive. They consider this their territory. And they're very jealous of it. Isaac, tell him what happened when they were building the *metro,* the subway."

Taking the big dusty icon from my hands, Isaac drops it back onto the pile. "I directed an excavation crew. The work proceeded without problem until we reached the Zocalo. Then unexpected things began happening."

"What kind of things?" I ask.

Isaac winces. "Strange noises, cave-ins, arms and legs crushed by falling debris. Absences for illness shot up. I don't know if the men were really sick or just afraid to come to work. When one of our supervisors died in a freak accident the men went on strike. Finally the route of the *metro* was diverted southward, away from the Cathedral and the ruins of Huitzilopochtli's temple."

Remembering my encounter with Kairos on the highway, my teeth begin to chatter. I'm embarrassed. I want to run for the door, but Moisés sees what's happening and throws an arm around my shoulder.

"Don't be afraid, Doctór, nothing's going to happen. Remember, before we left your office we covered ourselves in the blood of Christ."

Reaching up, he taps the floor over our head. "Listen!" We hear faint footsteps.

"Strange, isn't it? Just above us the faithful are lighting candles and kneeling before statues of the saints. What would they say if they knew how close they are to this den of demons?"

He turns to Isaac. "This is a hideous place, *hermano*. Why have you brought us here?"

"Come with me and I'll show you." Isaac's voice is muffled as he turns and heads toward the eastern wall of the basement. We follow.

"Keep in mind," he tells us, "that this was street level in the days of Moctezuma."

He pauses at the wall, where workers have been digging away the ancient crumbling stones and replacing them with reinforced concrete. Tapping the wall with his fist, he asks, "Pastor, if we could continue our walk, where would we end up?"

Moisés tugs at his chin with thumb and index finger. "Well, I guess we'd eventually reach the spot where archeologists uncovered the foundations of Huitzilopochtli's temple. It's about a block from here." Turning to me, he says, "Remember, Doctór, we saw it last Tuesday."

"You're right," Isaac answers. "It has a long history. A large statue of the Bearded Serpent was discovered there back in 1941. But it wasn't until about eight years ago that archeologists dug deeper and found the foundation of the temple."

For a moment I forget how scared I am. "I wonder what's between here and the temple."

"I began asking myself the same question!" Isaac exclaims, "and I found out. Come on." He carefully maneuvers along the pocked gray wall until we come to a sheet of rusty tin.

Pushing it aside he snaps on his flashlight. "Look!"

I see a small opening into a tunnel leading deeper into the earth. "I talked some of the men into helping me dig this after hours."

Moisés smiles at me. "Let's go!"

Unable to contain my curiosity, I crouch down and follow them into the tunnel.

After a hundred feet or so my fears take over. The dirt walls are going collapse in upon us! Panting, I mutter, "I'm going no farther!"

Isaac yells at me: "Don't give up now, we've made it! He's standing in a dark circular room.

"Look what we found!" Isaac announces when I reach them, directing a beam of light across the room. I gasp. A massive black granite stone fills the center of the room. It's taller than Isaac, and half again as wide. In the beam of the flashlight flecks of light starburst from its smooth, polished surface. Drawing closer I see a giant serpent's head. Fringed by feathers, mouth gaping, it stares back at us with empty, lifeless eyes.

"*Dios mío*," the Pastor murmurs. "What is it?"

"What does it look like?" Isaac answers. Pulling a dirty handkerchief from his pocket, he spits on it and carefully rubs the grinning mouth of the serpent. Sniffing the dark stain, he turns it toward us.

Blood!

"A sacrificial altar!" Moisés exclaims.

Isaac stands before the stone, shoulders squared, chin lifted, and I'm aware for the first time of the classic Aztec lines of his face: large aquiline nose, receding forehead, thrusting jaw. "My brothers," he announces dramatically, "I have waited a lifetime for this moment!"

We watch him mutely, wondering what he means.

"Pastor," Isaac says softly, "do you know how I got my name?"

"No, *hermano*, but why should I? It's not an unusual name, we have at least a dozen Isaacs in the church."

A somber smile creases the man's face. "But how many of your Isaacs have a father named Abraham?"

"That was your father's name?"

"Yes. Before I was born he was called Alberto. But the day of my birth he named me Isaac and changed his own name to Abraham. Know why?" His eyes narrow.

Without waiting for a reply, he continues: "My father was a descendent of an unbroken line of Aztec priests, going back centuries before the Conquest. The priests had a gruesome tradition: the eldest son, the day he was born, was sacrificed upon the altar of Huitzilopocthtli.

"With the fall of Tenotchtitlán, the priesthood no longer functioned. Even so, my ancestors remained faithful to the priestly tradition. The firstborn son would be taken in the dead of the night to the pyramid city of Teotihuacan. There, in a secret ceremony, his heart was carved out and buried in the courtyard of the temple of Quetzalcóatl."

"Lucky you were not a firstborn son!" I murmured.

Looking me squarely in the eye, he answered, "I was! But my father wasn't. My grandfather sacrificed my eldest uncle.

"Thank God, in the next generation a miracle happened. A short time before I was born a Christian friend gave my father a Bible. He was skeptical, but promised he would read it. Soon he came upon the story of Abraham and Isaac. When he read how God stopped Abraham from sacrificing his firstborn, the Holy Spirit spoke to him. He sought out the man who'd given him the Bible, and with tears in his eyes surrendered his heart to the God who had sacrificed his own firstborn that we might have life.

"When I was born he named me Isaac. He was determined that, like the Isaac of the Bible, I would be a testimony to God's grace." He raises his hands in praise to God.

Isaac disappears behind the huge rock and a moment later returns with a small black knapsack. "Pastor, I invited you here hoping you'd help me fulfill a promise I made to my father. As he lay dying he told me a story that his family had passed from generation to generation since the days of Moctezuma:

"In 1487, thirty-two years before Cortés' invasion of Mexico, Moctezuma completed the temple of Huitzilopochtli. In preparation for its inauguration an altar of sacrifice was carved from volcanic rock. Hundreds of soldiers hauled thirty miles and placed it atop the temple. On the day of its inauguration twenty thousand enemy soldiers were sacrificed and their blood poured out on the altar."

He turns and strikes the huge black stone with a muscular fist. "My brothers, this is that altar!"

Moisés and I watch as he unzips the knapsack. Taking out half a dozen candles, he arranges them in a small circle on the dirt floor. Carefully, he lights them. Then he spreads a white table cloth in front of the stone. Upon it he places a wineglass and unleavened Arabian bread.

"Many Saturdays my father would bring me to the Zócalo, and as we strolled by the Cathedral, point to the ground and tell me, 'Isaac, my son, Huitzilopochtli's obscene stone of sacrifice lies buried somewhere beneath our feet. One day you will find it, and when you do I want you celebrate upon it the blood and body of the Lamb of God. By the power of Christ's blood you will break the curse of thousands of years of human sacrifice."

Isaac lowers himself to the ground, his back against the stone, and Moisés and I sit facing him.

My mind is reeling. "Twenty thousand men!" I exclaim. Why?"

Moisés answers, "The gods of the Aztecs were always threatening terrible disasters. To awake in the morning and see the sun was a miracle, because sooner or later the gods Were going snatch the sun away and leave the world in darkness.

"The Aztecs believed that 'life is in the blood', just like the Hebrews. They hoped to postpone the inevitable judgment prepared by their gods with bloody sacrifices. So they were always at war; not to gain territory, but to capture enemy soldiers for sacrifice."

Getting up, he pulls me to my feet. "Isaac, show the Doctór how they did their sacrifices."

Coming over, Isaac pushes me gently until my back is against the altar. The convex shape of the stone causes my chest to arch outward, making me feel fearfully vulnerable.

Isaac stands before me. "Five priests participated in the sacrifice, one holding each of the victim's limbs, and the fifth—" he raises his hand and swings it toward my chest. I flinch, imagining an obsidian knife ripping open my body and a hand reaching in and pulling out my heart.

"The priest held the heart in his hand as it pumped out its lifeblood upon the rock. Then the body was lifted from the altar and flung down the side of the pyramid, where—according to some—it was hauled away and eaten by the populace."

I stagger away from the hideous altar and resume my seat on the ground, sweating, exhausted.

Leaning against the stone, Isaac continues his story: "My father was fascinated by the importance the people of Israel placed on the blood. When he heard the story of the crucifixion it was a revelation:

> the blood of Christ accomplished what the sacrifices of his Aztec ancestors were never able to do. For the first time in his life he felt liberated from the awful dread that had always hounded him."

He rises to his feet. "Pastor, will you help us commemorate our Lord's sacrifice?" Reaching into the knapsack he takes out a worn black Bible and extends it toward Moisés.

The pastor gives us each a piece of the bread, and and reads, "Take, eat, this is my body."

He pours juice into the glass, hands it to Isaac, and reads, "Drink ye all of it, for this is my blood of the new testament, which is shed for many for the remission of sins."

Isaac murmurs "Amen!" and passes me the glass. I take a sip. A surge of joy! "Halleluya!" I pass the glass to Moisés, he sips, turns suddenly, dashes the remainder of the juice against the stone, and shouts, "I baptize you in the blood of Jesus Christ my Lord!"

I can hear his words echoing around the foundations of the cathedral, and imagine Quetzalcóatl's demons scrambling for cover.

▼

CHAPTER 14

THE SERPENT TARGETS GABRIELA

By the time we get back to my office Moisés and I are starving. I hand Rebeca a fifty peso bill. "Run over to *Pizza Pronto*! on Mariano Escobeda and bring us a large Pizza Supreme."

Later the three of us are seated around the big table in the *Sala de Conferencias*. Reaching for a second slice I say, "Moisés, "I'll never forget that communion service. When Isaac asked you to do it, I was afraid you might refuse."

"Refuse?" Moisés grumbles, licking the pizza sauce from his thumb to his pinkie, "And miss the opportunity to hurl down Satan?"

Seeing my puzzled expression, he reaches for his Bible and carefully thumbs through the worn pages till he comes to Revelation. "This is what I'm talking about:

> The great dragon was hurled down…that ancient serpent
> called the devil or Satan, who leads the whole world astray.
> He was hurled to the earth, and his angels with him.
> Then I heard a loud voice in heaven say: Now have come the

Salvation and the power and the kingdom of our god and the authority of his Christ. For the accuser of our brothers, who Accuses them day and night before our God day and night, has been Hurled down.

Moisés pauses. "And there's more:

They overcame him by the blood of the lamb
And by the word of their testimony."

He turns to Rebeca. "*Hermana*, did you understand? How do we hurl down Satan?"

Pounding the table with her Coke bottle, Rebeca answers: "By the blood of the lamb and the word our testimony!"

Moisés turns to me: "Do you see it, Doctór? "That's what happened when we celebrated the Lord's Supper at the bloody altar of Huitzilo-pochtli. We hurled down Satan by giving testimony of our faith in the blood of Christ!"

I squirm in my seat. There it is again, that uncomfortable feeling I always have when people talk about the blood of Christ! As if they're being…what? uncouth? fanatical?

Noticing my discomfort, Moisés raises his eyebrows. "What's the matter, Doctór? Don't you American Christians believe in the blood of the Christ?"

I take a long swallow of my Sprite, trying to collect my thoughts. I don't want to offend Moisés, but I ned to be to be honest with him. Choosing my words carefully, I reply, "Of course we believe in the blood! But we don't talk about it much."

Moisés wrinkles his nose. "Well, you ought to! Did you know the Bible speaks of the blood more than 600 times? The book of Hebrews explains why: 'without the shedding of blood there is no remission of sins.'"

I reply lamely: "Maybe we're squeamish about the blood because it reminds us of ugly things. You know, like war, suffering, death,…."

Moisés beats Rebeca to the last slice of pizza. Grinning, he finishes my sentence "...and healing and life! Or don't you Americans use blood transfusions?"

"Why of course, but...hm...m...m I'd never thought of it that way. When we talk about being saved by the blood of Christ we're saying...we've received a transfusion of Christ's blood?"

Moisés pushes away his paper plate. "Doctór Andrés, even the devil knows a transfusion can be the difference between life and death." Wiping his hands carefully with the big white paper napkin he says, "There's a story I need to tell you. Especially after what we saw this morning."

The phone is ringing. Gathering up the bottles. Rebeca says, "Señores teólogos, I leave the table to you. I must get back to work."

As she hurries from the room I call after her, "How about bringing us a couple of coffees?"

After she's gone Moisés stretches, and yawns. "It's *siesta* time. As soon as I have that cup of coffee I'll be on my way."

Yawning back at him I answer, "But first you're going to tell me a story!"

"Oh yes, of course. Let me see, how does it begin?...."

"One day, so goes an ancient Aztec myth, the sun stopped shining, the stars blinked out—and worst of all—the last man on earth died.

"The gods called an emergency meeting. As they were arguing about what they might do, Quetzalcóatl suddenly appeared. He proposed a solution: they must deliver to him that small reed basket sitting on the table before them, the basket with a small heap of dried bones, all that was left of mankind. Let him have those bones, he told them, and he'd work a miracle; he'd create a new man, and at the same time a new heaven and a new earth.

"The gods were dubious. Dare they believe him? They put heads together and argued for hours. At last they agreed: Quetzalcóatl's proposal, as unlikely as it sounded, was their only hope.

"So with trembling hands they delivered him the basket.

"Hurrying to his castle, Quetzalcóatl took the bones and ground them into dust. With an obsidian knife he slashed his own sexual organ and let his blood drip upon the inert mound of powdered bones.

"There was a stirring in the dust, and a new man emerged! As the man stood to his feet the earth moved on its axis, the sun burst forth in splendor and the birds began singing."

Moisés is watching my face.

"The life is in the blood!"

I turn in my chair and see Rebeca standing at the door, holding a tray with two cups of coffee and the fixings.

"Isn't that in the Bible?" I ask.

"Yes, it is, Doctór," Rebeca comes to the table and sets a cup before each of us. "And it's true, you know. Like the Pastor said, even the devil knows that. That's why he invented the lie about Quetzalcóatl giving his blood to save the human race."

I shake my head slowly. "I guess I shouldn't be surprised. Quetzalcóatl tried to take Christ's place in everything else: the water of life, the light of the world, God incarnate, even the Second Coming."

Moisés stirs two heaping teaspoonfuls of sugar into his coffee. "Now, Doctór, do you see why the blood is important?"

I nod thoughtfully. "I think I do. Blood sacrifices begin early in the Bible, don't they? With Moses and the tabernacle."

"Even before that!" Rebeca sweetens my coffee and hands me the cup. "The Bible says Abel was a keeper of sheep."

I shrug. "I've always figured it was because he liked meat on his table."

"Impossible!" Moisés chimes in, "Don't you know men were vegetarians until after the Flood."

"So. He raised the sheep for sacrifice?"

"Obviously. Abel was the first man to sacrifice blood to his God. Then Abraham and Isaac and Jacob. Finally, God gave Moisés exact instructions about the blood sacrifices. And these continued until Christ came."

Rebeca concludes, "And when John the Baptist saw Christ for the first time he shouted to his disciples, 'Behold the Lamb of God that takes away the sin of the world.' Halleluya!" Executing a pirouette, she heads for the door, singing, "What can wash away my sin? Nothing but the blood of Jesus!"

Moisés and I sit in silence for a while, sipping our coffee. Finally I say, "Now, at last, I think I understand what you meant that day."

"What day, Doctór?"

"Back in April, the first day of our medical mission, when you told the demon possessing that young man. 'I bind you by the blood of Christ."

"So you see now? I was hurling down Satan by my testimony of faith in the blood of Christ."

"And this morning, there at the cathedral, when you told me not to be afraid, that I was covered by the blood of Christ—"

"I was telling you the same thing Moisés told the people when the death angel was on its way: not to worry because they had painted their door posts with the blood of the Lamb.

"And that very night Moisés instituted the Passover Feast. You know why?"

I'm beginning to feel like a nine-year-old in Sunday School! "I guess it was to remind the people they were covered by the blood."

"Of course. And Jesus initiated a new covenant. Remember what he said?" Moisés opens his Bible: "This is my blood of the new covenant, which is shed for many for the remission of sins."

Never again, since that day, have I felt uncomfortable when someone talks about the blood. And that day I learned another useful lesson: Satan and demons and blood are as much a part of Mexico's culture as tortillas and beans.

Demons don't have lungs. So Kairos is quite comfortable waiting for Quetzalcóatl at the bottom of the Enchanted Lagoon.

The patron saint of the witches, La Virgen del Carmen is a dark-skinned demoness with a Mona Lisa smile and the charm of an Old South plantation mistress. She is the caretaker of the Enchanted Lagoon, a peaceful cove on Lake Catemaco. When Kairos arrived a few moments ago she received him graciously and led him to her parlor, a dark underwater cave where turtles, eels and moccasins swim placidly about, unimpressed by their distinguished visitor.

As always, Quetzalcóatl is late for their appointment. Kairos doesn't mind. He feels content among the familiar icons that identify this place as demon territory: goat heads scattered about and small ivory dolls sprawled in imitation of coitus.

This is his first visit to the Enchanted Lagoon. Demons gossip that it has an exact replica in Columbia, and another in the Atlantic Ocean that humans call the Bermuda Triangle.

Abruptly, a gigantic dragon blocks the cave entrance for an instant, then propels himself to where Kairos is waiting. Kairos is not surprised that Quetzalcóatl has materialized as a dragon; since he is a viceroy of the Great Deceiver, the Bearded Serpent possesses the faculty of instantaneous transformation. At a given moment he can present himself as a rattler or a python or a jaguar…or a dragon…or as any of the hundreds of gods that adorn the high places throughout Mesoamerica.

"Rise, slave!" As always, Kairos' Lord looks angry, disapproving. Waiting, Kairos had allowed himself to fantasize a smile or a word of commendation. Now he wonders why he tortures himself that way. His Demonic Lordship never smiles; he is incapable of smiling. There is no kindness in this grim world of the Old Dragon! How could there be? The Serpent's purpose is to make his servants miserable, to provoke sniveling, groveling fear.

"Andrew Kelly's kairos has arrived!" Quetzalcóatl announces, and celebrates his wry humor with a belch of steam that sends a jet of bubbles bouncing against the ceiling of the cave.

"See to it that Kelly is back in his homeland by the end of the year." A long tongue of flame hisses from his nostrils, setting the water to boiling. "And let me warn you: I will not tolerate failure!"

Trembling, Kairos attempts a bow, but the buoyant water frustrates him. He ends up wiggling his arms like the flappers of a turtle, his face wrapped in the soggy academic gown.

"Just tell me what you want to do, my Lord, and I'll obey."

"The subject has fallen in love with the woman Gabriela."

Lifting his chin, Kairos intones, in the unctuous voice of a learned academic, "Am I correct in thinking our Lord has been taking advantage of this human weakness ever since the Garden of Eden?"

Quetzalcóatl grunts, "Stop thinking and listen to me."

"Yes, my Lord." Kairos suppresses a surge of anger. Why must his Master repay the slightest display of dignity with these dreadful put-downs?

"I have already told you that one of my spirits of anger has established a fortress in Gabriela Mancini's soul. Kelly thinks his therapy has vanquished that spirit, but he's mistaken.

"And something else: like most females in Mesoamerica the woman is a disciple of my mother, the great Tonantzin. Of course, she would deny it." He belches again, pleased with his own cunning."

He erupts in a boisterous, humorless laughter, and ten thousand online demons join in. For a full minute the waters of the lake churn with their laughter. On the lake's placid surface, a boatload of fishermen scream in terror as waterspouts suddenly erupt around them.

Drawing close, Quetzalcóatl whispers in Kairos' ear: "And now I will let you in on another secret: we have allies entrenched in Sra. Mancini's house."

Kairos' brow wrinkles in surprise. "In her house, my Lord? But how is that possible? When she became a disciple of the Lamb, he placed a guardian over her household."

"Even so, Gabriela Mancini is about to face a crisis that will destroy her and her pious boyfriend! Remember El's warning to Moses: he visits the sins of the fathers upon their children to the third and fourth generation!"

"Now this is what you are to do...."

By the time Quetzalcóatl completes his instructions his vassal is exuberant, eager to return to Mexico City and initiate the project. This time he will not fail!

CHAPTER 15

▼

GABRIELA'S HEART

"Today I'm going to tell you about the worst thing…and the best thing…that ever happened to me."

I awoke this morning looking forward to my meeting with Gabriela. Even though I'm working with a dozen clients now, my week revolves around Tuesdays and Thursdays, the days she comes for her appointments. And today is going to be special, because last week we agreed to spend the entire morning together.

"This is the picture I took of Gabriel the day before…" she catches her breath and reaches for the box of Kleenex sitting on the coffee table. "It was his third birthday," she says, dabbing her nose. She hands me a photograph of a smiling little boy clutching a bright yellow banana-shaped balloon to his chest. Abundant brown hair curls over his ears, his mouth is stained with bits of chocolate cake and pink punch, and he's surrounded by a dozen grinning kids.

"The next day began like any other. I got up early, gave Gabriel his breakfast, turned him over to Marta, his *nana* and left for work. It was hard leaving him that morning. The night before, when I put him to bed, I had promised I was going to find a way to spend more time with him. I loved him so much! Sometimes I'd awake at night and in my inner ear I could hear the beating of his heart, in perfect time to the beating of my own. It frightened me; was it right to love another person so much, even if he was your own flesh and blood?

"Around noon I looked up from my desk, surprised. Why was my heart beating so fast? I had to see my son! I advised my administrator I was leaving, and started for the door. Then, impulsively, I returned to the office and dialed home. One ring...three...five.... Finally Marta answered, out of breath. Lupita the cook had gone to the store, she explained, and she was in the yard with Gabriel when the phone rang. Gabriel was going to be ecstatic when she told him his *mami* was coming home!

"My heart pounded 'run! run! run!' I hurried out to the car, started the motor and took off, tires squealing. Why was I so scared? I looked down at my wrist watch: one o'clock. I'd be home by 1:25. I drove like a person possessed, and by 1:20 was rounding my street corner.

"Then I heard the wail of a siren. No!

"Since the day of his birth, there had been an invisible link between Gabriel's soul and my own. I always felt him near, even when I was in London or Paris.

"But suddenly the line connecting us had gone dead!

"I slowed, waiting for the speeding ambulance to pass, then swung in behind it. My sense of urgency was gone, and in its place a hot coal was searing the pit of my stomach."

Gabriela's usually lively face is like the face of an aged gravestone. Closing her eyes she hugs herself, as if to embrace her precious son. I pour her a glass of water. She takes it with trembling hands and gulps it down. She burps. She covers her mouth, the gray in her face blushing into red. "I'm sorry, it's been months since I've talked about Gabriel's death. I...I thought I'd gotten over it. Guess I was wrong."

I want to take her into my arms, hug her, tell her everything's going to be all right. Instead I say, "Look, if this is too much for you we can..."

"No. I want to talk about it. Now. I've waited so long for somebody who...who could really understand." Her eyes fill with tears. "Oh, Andrés, I thank God for sending you!"

I'm bathed in tenderness for this enchanting, vulnerable woman.... What's happening to the professional objectivity I've struggled so hard to maintain?

We sit quietly, waiting. Finally she takes a deep breath. "I'm ready to continue now...I won't try to describe what I felt when at last they let me see my little Gabi's crushed, broken body. They were sorry, the doctor told me, his heart had stopped beating by the time they'd gotten him to the emergency room. They'd tried everything to bring him around, but it was too late.

"I was shivering violently. They wrapped me in a blanket and made me swallow a pill. I couldn't think, couldn't cry.

A nurse bent over me. 'Is there someone you'd like us to call? Your husband, maybe?'

"'No, I...'

"Marta! I must call her! When I spoke to her just a few minutes before I heard that dreadful siren, Gabriel was still all right.

"The nurse led me to a telephone and I dialed the number of my home, feeling strangely calm now, as if a logical explanation from Gabriel's *nana* would make all the pain go away.

"'Marta?'

"'*Señora*! We've been waiting for you, something terrible has happened! It's Gabriel, he's...'

"'I know, Marta, I'm at the hospital. Gabi...Gabi...'a sob rose in my throat, 'he's gone, Marta.'

"There was a thud as she dropped the phone and I heard her screaming to Lupita, then the sound of wailing.

"By the time she got back to the phone I was so angry I was shaking again. It was her fault! If she'd done her job my little son wouldn't be lying here, his body already cold and stiff!

"Marta! I screamed at her, "they tell me a car hit Gabriel. Where were you?"

"'Oh, *Señora*, I'm sorry, I'm sorry!' Sobbing, Marta told me what had happened:

"After hanging up from my call she ran back outside where she'd left Gabriel. The front gate was open and he was nowhere to be seen. She raced to the gate, but before she could get to him there was a squeal of brakes and the thump of metal against flesh.

"Suddenly it hit me like the blow of a sledgehammer. It wasn't Marta's fault, it was mine! If I hadn't called her away from Gabriel I'd be home right now, holding him in my arms!"

"'*Señora?*' I could barely hear Marta's voice, it sounded faint, far away.

"I dropped the phone and crumpled to the floor."

I get up from my chair, go over and kneel before her, taking her hands, kissing them gently. "Gabriela, I'm so sorry. Are you sure you want to go on?"

She leans over and kisses my cheek, her sweet face, moist with tears, tender against mine. "Oh yes, yes," she whispers in my ear, "I want to go on. We must not stop now. This is something I've needed to do for so long!"

I take my seat again and she continues:

"I remember little of what happened the next few days: long, exhausting talks with family and friends, the unbearable funeral, consultations with the police who were trying to locate the hit-and-run driver. I spent the rest of January and most of February in the hospital. Finally I went home and began the agonizing process of deciding if life was going to be worth living without my Gabi. Worst of all was the awful guilt gnawing at me day and night. I had killed my little son. If only I hadn't made that call!

"Every day I spent hours at Gabriel's grave. I was too distraught to drive, so my daughter Angelica would take me to the cemetery and leave me for a while, then return and plead with me to go home. Then I'd..." She pauses. "Is something wrong?"

Gabriela leans forward and looks intently into my eyes.

So she's noticed! Struggling to keep my voice calm, I ask her, "The accident, Gabriela, it happened in January?"

"Yes. Why?" She leans closer.

"Do you mind if I ask the date? Can you remember?"

She wrings her hands. "How could I ever forget? It happened on a Friday—Friday the sixteen of January."

I feel my heart thumping. I stand up and trip over the coffee table as I make my way to the window. I lean out, watching a tear falling downward, drifting toward the street far below. On Friday Gabriela lost the love of her life. The next day I lost the love of *my* life!

Gabriela places her hand on my shoulder. "Please, Andrés, tell me. Did I say something wrong?"

"No Gabriela, of course not. I'm just feeling a little ill." I take her hand and pat it gently, reaching for a handkerchief in my back pocket.

"Andres, you're crying. Here, let me. She takes the handkerchief from my hand and gently dabs my eyes. I want to weep on her shoulder, let her weep on mine, I long to comfort her, let her comfort me. But I must not, not today. I return to my seat, unable to speak.

Gabriela sits across from me. "Please, Doctór, if you're not feeling well—"

I will myself to smile at her. "I'll be all right. Just give me a moment."

In a month, maybe, I'll be able to talk about this remarkable coincidence. But for now I'll stow my feelings. Maybe tonight I'll take them out...and meditate on the Providence that has brought this extraordinary woman into my life.

Gabriela is studying my face. "Please, I'm worried about you. Why don't we..."

I shake my head. "No, I'm feeling better now. And besides, I haven't heard the good part you promised!"

Leaning back in the chair and brushing a stray wisp of hair from her cheek, she sighs. "First, I must tell you about Raul."

"How did he take the death of his son?"

"To this day I'm not sure. By that time we were hardly speaking. I was afraid he'd blame me. He didn't. Neither did he attempt to console me. At the funeral I was appalled by his lack of emotion. Surely he must be grieving! I couldn't understand. Until...." She pauses, the color rising in her cheeks.

"Until what?"

Lowering her eyes, she nervously fingers a button on her blouse. Finally she speaks. "Raul and I were no longer sleeping together. He'd moved all his things into another room while I was in the hospital. I was relieved, I'd been trying to work up the courage to tell him to do that very thing.

"One day after he'd left for his office I walked by his room and saw he'd forgotten his brief case on his bed. Impulsively, I opened it. I don't know what I was looking for, his soul, maybe."

Blinking away a tear, she continues, "I'd lived nineteen years with this man and knew less about him than the day we married.

"I zipped open a pocket deep inside the brief case and pulled out a photograph...a 5 X 7 of Raul seated beside a dark, attractive woman and behind them, four smiling faces. The tallest was a young man maybe twenty years old. His hair, combed straight back, was fine and black like Raul's. The smallest, her hand on Raul's shoulder, was a little girl of about six. Looking at her, I gave a start. She had a dimple at the corner of her mouth, the same dimple that had attracted me to Raul as a sixteen-year-old.

"No doubt about it, this was Raul's family. His *real* family. I felt soiled, betrayed, stupid—and very, very angry. I wanted to call him and tell him to come home so I could scream at him, pull out his hair.

Instead I calmed myself, found a phone book and flipped through the yellow pages.

"Within a couple of weeks the detective agency confirmed what I suspected. Raul had carried on a relationship with the woman since before we were married. He had fathered her children. He had even purchased her a handsome two-story home in Ciudad Satelite.

"I said nothing to Raul. But I stayed awake nights plotting ways to pay him back for shaming me. I was outraged that he had made me his victim. And furious at myself for allowing him to do so.

"I knew at once what I must do: initiate divorce proceedings. I engaged an attorney. A few days later his secretary called and told me the *Licenciado* wanted to see me at once. I took my time driving to his office, sure he had bad news for me.

"I was right. The lawyer seated me in his plushest chair, cleared his throat and dropped the bombshell: I couldn't divorce Raul, because five years before, he had divorced me!

"I was so upset I jumped up and knocked over an elegant crystal lamp."

I gape at her. "But how? How could Raul have divorced you without your knowledge?"

"After we'd picked up the pieces, I asked my attorney that same question. He assured me that what had happened to me was not uncommon. In Mexico you can buy almost any kind of justice you want, if you have enough money to pay for it."

"But after so many years! What finally made Raul decide to divorce you?"

"Maybe the other woman threatened to go public with their relationship. Maybe she figured if she couldn't be happy neither should I."

"But why did Raul to keep the divorce secret? It doesn't make sense."

"Oh yes it does! Remember his mother? She was very old and feeble by then, but he was still afraid of her. He must have convinced his lover to keep things under cover until his mother was gone."

"What a grotesque compromise!"

Gabriela nods. "When I returned from the lawyer's office I went into Raul's room and carried everything outside and piled it in the yard: his clothing, shoes, books, even the sheets on his bed. Then I called him and told him to come home immediately, that something terrible had happened. When his car screeched into the driveway I had a canister of gasoline ready. I soaked the pile, stuck a match to it and handed him the reports from the detective agency and the attorney.

"The fire was still burning when, without a word, he got into his car, backed it out and left. I haven't heard from him since."

The intercom buzzes. "Doctór," Rebeca says, "it's been more than an hour. I thought you and the *señora* might like some coffee."

I'm glad for the respite. I need a moment to calm my anger, to remind myself I'm Gabriela's therapist, not her defender.

After Rebeca leaves we sit silently looking at one another, sipping our coffee. I can feel the caffeine kicking in, lifting my spirits.

"Now," Gabriela sets down her cup and smiles at me. "Let me tell you about the day I met Rosario."

"Rosario? Who is she? Is she the good news?"

"She's an angel."…the corners of her mouth turn down in a wry grin…"although you'd never guess it. Talk about an angel in disguise….

"I'd been pushed to the edge of a cliff and was hanging on by my fingernails. The day came when I decided to let go. Life had no meaning for me now. My business no longer challenged me. My two surviving children didn't need me. Angelica was in her final semester at the university and engaged to a nice young man. Hector had become so much like his father I felt sure he'd soon want to go live with him. I had buried both my parents the year before. I wasn't needed any more!

"For weeks I had saved back my sleeping pills. One Saturday morning I picked up a refill at the pharmacy. I eavesdropped on a mother making plans with her children, all the time rehearsing in my mind my own plans for that night after the children had gone to bed.

"Remembering the refrigerator was empty and there's be nothing for the kids when they got home, I stopped at the supermarket. Heading toward the checkout counter my basket collided with that of a thin, red-haired woman with a cigarette tightly clamped between her lips.

"Watch where you're going!" she growled, scowling at me.

"I was in no mood for an argument, I just wanted to get home and shut out the world. Besides, I could see the lady was Spanish. My mother had warned me when I was growing up: 'never pick a fight with an *española*!'. So I turned away, paid for my purchase and headed for my car.

"As I was climbing in I saw the woman coming my way. Oh no, she wanted to continue the quarrel! I started the motor and put the car in reverse. But the woman ran over and tapped on my window. Reluctantly I lowered the window.

"'Please,' she said, 'forgive me.' I was surprised to see that her sharp, thin face had softened and those bright blue Spanish eyes were filled with compassion.

"'Don't do what you're thinking!' she whispered. And she handed me a little book she held in her hands. 'This is a New Testament. Read the Gospel of John; it will change your mind!'

"She turned and walked away."

"I drove home, my hands shaking. I had never been a religious person. At the parochial school they had taught me all the things you'd expect, but after graduation I only went to church only for weddings, funerals and Christmas Eve.

"But at that moment I was sure God had sent an angel to save my life."

"As soon as I got home I shut myself up in my bedroom and flipped through the little book until I found the Gospel of John. I don't know if I'd ever held a Bible in my hand before, all my life I'd heard people say it was boring and nobody could understand it except priests and monks.

"I began reading, and soon was fascinated by the way it spoke to me. Jesus' conversation with Nicodemus stunned me. The Samaritan woman at the well was my sister! When I read about Mary and Martha weeping over their brother's death I was sure they would have been able to understand my own grief. The thirteenth chapter captured me; I spent more than an hour reading and rereading it, bathing my sick soul in Jesus' love.

"Then, when I read Jesus' promise "I will not leave you orphans, I will come to you," an incredible thing happened: beginning at the hurt in my heart a warm feeling moved outward, slowly saturating my body. I knew it was that blessed Comforter pushing out all the pain, frustration, anger and loneliness that had accumulated the last twenty years.

"I read the words of the Savior: 'Peace I leave with you. My peace I give unto you...let not your heart be troubled, neither let it be afraid.' I read the verse once, twice, three times, then three more times aloud. I fell on my knees beside my bed and whispered, 'Dear Jesus, I accept your peace.' And in that moment I was flooded with his love and his forgiveness." She pauses, and placing a hand over her heart, whispers, "He's been here ever since!"

Until this moment Gabriela and I have spoken little about her faith. Now, for the first time, she has allowed me a glimpse into her soul. She sits quietly for a moment, head bowed, hands folded in her lap, then she looks up, her face glowing with a sweet tenderness.

"After my encounter with the Savior I fell into a peaceful sleep. When I awoke, hours later, I was still seated on the floor, my head cradled on the bed. And I knew I was no longer the Gabriela Mancini that had decided there was no reason for living." I reach over and squeeze her hand. "Gabriela, I'm so glad for you."

"I looked at my watch," she continues, "and saw it was two minutes past midnight. But no matter! I must dial that telephone number on the cover of the little Testament.

"At the first peal of the phone Rosario answered. 'Hello, little lady from the store,' she said, 'I don't know your name, but I was sure you'd call!'

"Brushing aside my apologies for the lateness of the hour, she told me to wait for her, she'd be at my house in fifteen minutes.

"We stayed up the rest of the night talking. We're now best friends. Doctór Andrés, you must meet her."

I nod. "Did she explain how she knew what you were planning to do when you bumped into her at the store?"

"Have you heard that many, many Catholics are discovering the Bible? Rosario was one of them. Recently her Bible study group had been examining the spiritual gifts. Her classmates agreed she had the gift of discernment."

"She took you to Moisés' church?"

"Yes, she attends when she or someone she knows needs a special ministration."

I smile at her. "And the rest is history."

"Yes, dear Doctór, the rest is history. And here I sit with Andrés Kellee, the man God sent to complete the work the Holy Spirit began when I met Rosario." She gets up, steps over to my chair and hugs my neck....

Thursday Gabriela takes me to the airport. We have lunch at Wings, a noisy restaurant with bright red table cloths and models of ancient biplanes decorating the walls.

When they announce my flight Gabriela accompanies me to the gate. That's where it happens.

We come together for a parting *aabrazo*, and I feel a sharp twist of anguish in my heart. I don't want to leave her! My arms ache when I release her and reach for my carry-on. I stumble over to the line of passengers. Just before I reach the gate I turn for one last glimpse.

Her eyes are fixed on me, chin lifted, lips parted. I want to run back, grab her arm and tell she must come with me....

As the plane thunders down the runway I remind myself I'm Andrew Kelly, American citizen, on my way to celebrate the most American of all holidays with two daughters, a son-in-law and a grandson. It's Thanksgiving, and I'm going home.

Moments later I crane my neck and squint downward through a veil of brown smog at the disappearing skyline of the largest city in the world, populated by millions of bronze-skinned people speaking a language I'm still struggling to master...a city infested by a host of malignant spirits.

And I'm surprised by what I'm feeling: this is home!

On Thanksgiving Day Victoria, chattering about her problems at school, plops a turkey leg on my plate. I learn that Margaret and Tom are ecstatic about living in the home where she grew up. Over our pumpkin pie I tell them about the good things that are happening to me: my apartment, my church, my fast-growing clientele. But nothing about Quetzalcóatl and his spirit world.

And of course, nothing about Gabriela Mancini.

CHAPTER 16

▼

IN LOVE...BUT AFRAID
TO COMMIT

"Ouch!" My big toe collides with the wheel of the swivel chair. I'm pacing nervously from window to desk, like an expectant father. It's 10:54. In six minutes Gabriela will step through the door, and I have no idea what to expect.

After returning from Houston last night I struggled with the yearning to call her. I went to bed, but when I closed my eyes all I could see was Gabriela's sweet face. Finally I reached for the phone. The luminous clock caught my eye: two-thirty! Groaning, I slammed down the receiver and spent hours turning in my bed like a the grill at a *tacos al pastor* restaurant. Sometime before dawn I drifted off into a troubled sleep.

"You're in love!" I say to my reflection in the window, "Why don't you admit it? Are you worried about being disloyal to Mary? It's been nearly a year since her death, she wouldn't want you to go on grieving forever!"

Rebeca's voice on the intercom: "Doctór, Señora Gabriela has arrived."

Wiping my sweaty palms on my pants, I answer, "Send her in."

"*Buenos días*, Andee."

Manicured fingers carefully shutting the door, she gazes at me, her full lips curling in the hint of a smile. Does she hear the pounding of my heart?

She stops an arm's length away. "How was your trip?" Face raised to mine, her voice is deep, throaty, and her dark hair is fragrant from her morning shower.

"Gabriela, I've missed you!" I reach for her, and she comes into my arms.

"Oh Andee, I've missed you too," she murmurs.

She takes my face between her hands and pulls me close. On tiptoes, she gently kisses my lips. "*Andrés, mi amor!*"she whispers in my ear. Her breath on my face is warm and sweet.

We stand for a long time locked in each other's arms….

I pull away. "If we were in the United States," I tell her, only half joking, "I'd be in danger of losing my license. A therapist is not supposed to fall in love with his patient." We sit facing each other, knees touching.

Sparks light up her green eyes. "Don't worry. Until this moment nobody would have guessed. You hid it well. I've been worried for weeks that the man I cared so much for had no interest in me!"

She brings my fingers to her lips. "But since last Thursday at the airport I've been praying that what I thought I saw in your face was not my imagination." She winks. "And when I came through the door a moment ago I knew it was true, I was no longer just your patient, I was the woman you loved!"

Releasing her hand, I push back my chair.

Her eyes widen. "What's the matter, Andrés? Did I say something…"

"Oh no, my love." I reach out to caress her cheek. "Nothing you could say would ever offend me. You're witty, charming, adorable—"

She laughs. "Is that why you're frowning?"

"No, it's just that I've been thinking about Raul…" I shake my head. "What kind of a man is he? How could he live with you for twenty years and not be madly in love with you?"

She wrinkles her nose. "Please, Andrés, must we talk about Raul?"

"I'm sorry, but your ex-husband sounds like the most stupid man on earth!"

Sighing, she gets up, and going to my desk pours herself a glass of water. "There's something I haven't told you: after the birth of our second child I felt Raul's attitude changing; I could tell he was beginning to care for me. Then suddenly everything went back to the way it was before. I never was able to explain it to myself…until long afterward, when the private detective gave me his report. What he told me…" The words stick in her throat, strangling her. Raising the glass to her lips she gulps down the water.

I stand behind her, gently massaging her shoulders, wanting to cradle her in my arms and tell her I'll never let anyone hurt her again. "I'm sorry, I shouldn't have brought it up."

Leaning into me, she takes my hands and presses them to her cheeks dampened by tears.

"No, Andee, you need to hear this."

"So what did the detective tell you?"

"That Raul's…lover…is from Catemaco."

"Catemaco? Where's that?"

"A village in the state of Veracruz. It's famous for two things: a beautiful lake and evil witches."

I return to my chair, I need to sit down! "You believe Raul's lover is a witch?"

"I'm sure of it." Taking her seat, Gabriela sets the glass on the coffee table, hands trembling. "Several of her neighbors told the detective she'd done love potions for them. And limpias."

"*Limpias?*"

"A ceremony for breaking another witch's curse."

I lean forward. "Are you saying this woman has kept Raul in love with her for over twenty years through some kind of witchcraft?"

She shrugs. "I wouldn't call it love. It's more like...what's the word you psychologists use?...co-dependency. Witches are experts at mind control. So with Raul it must have been easy. Remember, I told you how his mother had him under her thumb as long as she lived."

A cold finger rakes my spine. "I'm surprised this...this witch didn't try to harm you."

The color rising in her cheeks, Gabriela stutters, "I...I believe she did. One day the maid came to me with something she'd found in my yard: a clay doll with a needle piercing the heart. She was frantic, and insisted I go to a witch immediately for a *limpia*."

"Did you?"

"No, I laughed and told her to throw the doll in the garbage. She and the other maids did everything they could to try to change my mind. For months afterward they kept waiting for something bad to happen to me or my family."

"Nothing did, of course."

Biting her lip, Gabriela mumbles, "Before the year was out I lost my little Gabi!"

I reach for her hand. "Surely, Gabriela, you don't think..."

Her fingernails bite into my hand. "Oh Andee, I refuse to let my mind believe it. But my heart...more than once I've asked myself what would have happened if I'd listened to my maids. Maybe today—"

Seeing her eyes brimming with tears, I break in, indignant, "Look Gabriela..."

"I know what you're going to tell me: superstitions like that belong to the life I've left behind. You're right, of course. But the feelings are there just the same."

I could kick myself. Why did I have to mention Raul? Jumping up, I pull her to her feet. "Enough of the bad stuff! We ought to be celebrating, this is the day we declared our love...a day we'll remember as long as we live!" Taking her in my arms I dance her about the room until we're both giggling out of control.

She stops to catch her breath. "You're right, Andee, let's celebrate!"

"Got any suggestions?"

"How about dinner at Rugantino's tonight?"

"Only if it's the fanciest restaurant in town!"

"Well maybe it's not the fanciest, but its pasta is out of this world, and it has candlelight and violins."

"Sounds perfect! What time shall I come by for you?"

"How about eight o'clock?"

"I'll be ready!"

I check my watch. "We have a quarter of an hour before my next appointment. "Care for a cup of coffee?"

Eyes dancing, she nods. I pick up the interphone.

A moment later, pouring the coffee, Rebeca is looking at us curiously.

I smile to myself. Let her wonder!...

Parking my Chevy in front of Gabriela's gabled villa, I wish I could have my big blue Lincoln back just for tonight.

Gabriela greets me at the door dressed in a black pants suit and a snowy white silk blouse. When she kisses my cheek her soft, fine hair tickles my nose. I'm about to take her into my arms and smudge her lipstick when a cute, willowy blonde enters the room. Angelica has her mother's eyes and a friendly smile. She's wearing jeans and a bright red sweater with sleeves pushed up to the elbows. Offering me her hand, her green eyes examine me from head to foot. I wonder what her mother has told her about me.

"And where is your brother?" Gabriela asks. Angelica shakes her head impatiently. "Oh he's upstairs looking at the tele, Mother. He's sulking tonight." She turns. "Please excuse me, Jorge is on the phone."

"Her boyfriend." Gabriela rolls her eyes. "They're at school all day together, I don't know why they have to spend two hours on the phone every night."

At the door Angelica pauses. "Now you two behave yourselves. And Mother," she adds, her face suddenly serious, "don't forget to talk to the Doctór about—you know."

"Hector!" Gabriela calls. No response. A maid appears from the kitchen. "Would you like me to knock on his door, *Señora*?"

"No, never mind. Let's go, Andrés."

In the car she tells me, "I don't know what I'm going to do with Hector. He's become so rebellious."

"You say he's fourteen? A tough age. The breakup of his parents must have been rough on him."

"Terrible. Ever since we found out about Raul's other family he insists he hates his father. But Raul still comes for him every other Saturday and they spend the day together. Whenever he gets angry with me he tells me he's going to go live with his father. This afternoon when I told him about our date he threw a fit and started calling me names. Help me, Andee, what should I do?"

"Sounds like he still has hopes you and his father will get back together."

"Maybe so. Oh, I wish life weren't so complicated!"

Rugantino's occupies the cozy basement of an old red brick office building. Besides the violin Gabriela promised, the restaurant boasts a guitar and an accordion. As we enter they're playing a spirited rendition of The Blue Danube, interrupted by a little green parrot with a yellow beak that pops out of a wall clock to advise the diners it's nine o'clock.

The hostess leads us to a shadowy corner and a round table so tiny our knees touch. A waiter comes over and lights the tall, thin white candle.

While Gabriela rolls her Fetuccini in a big spoon, I try not to slurp my onion soup. "Andee, now that we…we've confessed our love, is that going to complicate my therapy?"

I gaze at her for a long moment. Gabriela's face is exquisite in the soft candlelight; I can't imagine any other widower in the entire world who wouldn't be envious of me. I sigh. "Probably. I should insist you find another therapist."

"Don't you dare! Don't even think about it!"

"Well, let's give it a try. Let's see if we'll be capable of tending strictly to business when you come for your appointments. Frankly, I'm skeptical."

Laying down her fork, Gabriela reaches for my hand. "My dear Andee do you remember what you told me at the beginning? That we'd begin by diagnosing my problems and understanding what caused them. Then we'd apply God's medicine. Don't you think we've about finished the first part?"

Like a sixteen-year-old on his first date, I'm having a hard time concentrating, afraid that at any moment I'll say something ridiculous. "I guess we have."

"Then can't God can use our love to make his medicine even more effective?"

I smile. "You may be right, Gabriela."

She hunches forward. "Andrés, please remember I still have hurts that need healing. Sometimes such strong feelings surge up inside I think I'm going to have to recall every day of those twenty years Raul deceived me so that, one by one, so I can forgive him for them."

"*Sus platillos, Señores.*"

The waiter places a platter of smoked salmon between us, and to one side a sauce of chopped tomatoes, chile and onions, a dish of guacamole, the inevitable sliced lemon, and of course warm wheat tortillas wrapped in a white napkin.

I serve our plates. "Now where were we? Oh yes, you were talking about your anger."

"Why can't I get rid of it? When I took Jesus into my heart I was sure he'd washed away all those bad feelings. Then a few days later I remembered something awful Raul did to me and there was such a rush of bitterness I felt sick with surprise. The next Sunday I visited Moisés' church and requested a prayer of liberation. I was fine for a week or so, then those same bad feelings returned. What's going on?"

Leaning across the table I brush her cheek with my lips. "Let's talk about that at your next appointment, okay?"

She smiles wryly. "Here I go again, bringing up my troubles! I'm sorry." Signaling the waiter, she tells him, "*Más vino tinto, por favor.*"

Watching her sip her wine, I'm reminded of the cultural gulf that still separates us. For Gabriela wine with her meals is as natural as a glass of water. I've told her I don't like the taste of alcohol. But I suspect much of my distaste springs from the prohibitions of my mother, who rejected her Cajun Catholicism when I was a child, and with it a long list of Cajun customs she thereafter designated "sins of the flesh."

Later, after he has cleared the table, the waiter arrives with the pastry cart.

Pushing aside her wine glass, Gabriela exclaims, "Know where I want to eat my dessert? In the *Plaza de Garibaldi!*"

"Something special about the place?"

"You haven't been there? Then we must go. Right now! You must see the place where all the mariachis congregate."

Gabriela insists on driving. It takes us less than fifteen minutes. The *Plaza de Garibaldi* is thronged with noisy groups of musicians dressed in dark blue suits, bright red kerchiefs and gaudy, broad-brimmed sombreros.

"People come here to contract the *mariachis*," Gabriela explains. "For a fee they'll slip up to the window of your true love or your mamá on her birthday an hour before sunrise and serenade her with *Las Mañanitas.*"

Seated at a sidewalk table, Gabriela orders *pastel de mil hojas* and I ask for *pastel de tres leches*. A group of smiling serenaders arrives offer-

ing their services. For twenty pesos they entertain us with *cielito lindo,*
La Golondrina, Rancho Grande and *El Zopilote Mojado.*

It's too noisy to talk. I'm content to listen to the boisterous music
that sounds a lot like Texas country played in a minor key, drink cup
after cup of thick *café de la olla and* watch my beloved as she sings
along with the mariachis.

At last I say, "It's nearly one. Maybe we should be going."

"Oh, must we? I wish this night could go on forever."

Reluctantly I give one of the young men my ticket so he can bring
the car. Still singing *Cielito Lindo,* Gabriela gets behind the wheel.

I'm a little concerned…is it safe? I've never seen her so giddy, must
be the wine. She puts the car into drive and spins the wheels into the
still-busy street.

I lay a hand on her arm. "By the way, Gabriela, what was it Angelica
wanted you to talk to me about?"

Wheeling back to the curb she applies the brakes. "*Santa Madre,* I
had forgotten! I won't be able to face her in the morning if I don't tell
you about it. Where can we talk?"

"How about my place?"

"You don't mind?"

"Of course not, I've been wanting to invite you over."

"This is where I live, Gabriela," I say, opening the door to my apartment. I'm self-conscious, comparing it with the spacious manor she
calls home.

She walks to the middle of the living room, does a slow spin and
declares, "It charming. And so homey. I love it! When are you going to
invite me to move in?"

I smile, trying to picture Gabriela Mancini, heiress and CEO, frying
my bacon and eggs in the ugly little yellow kitchen.

We make ourselves comfortable on the sofa. Gabriela snuggles up
and lays her head on my shoulder. We're content to enjoy a peaceful

silence broken only by the occasional soft whisper of a car passing on the street below.

After a while Gabriela murmurs, "We're both so content, maybe I should tell you about Angelica's problem some other time. Anyway, it's so bizarre you may think I'm imagining things."

Sitting up, I turn to face her, taking her hands in mine. "Now you've really got my attention! Tell me. Right now!"

She takes a deep breath. "It began the night you arrived in Mexico City. Remember, I called you at your hotel, and you acted...kind of strange. Afterward, I had a hard time going to sleep. I'm sure I wouldn't have slept at all if I'd known what was going on below me.

"Angie lives in an apartment we fixed up for her in the basement. It's very homey, with a nice living room, a tiny kitchen, a bedroom and bath.

"The next morning she told me what had happened: her little dog sleeps on the floor next to her bed. About midnight he awoke her growling. She sat up, afraid someone had broken into the house. Then, in the dim glow of her night light, she saw the torso of a huge man floating down the stairs, about two feet from the foot of her bed. Imagine: no legs, just an ugly scowling face attached to a thick, hairy chest.

"She opened her mouth to scream, but no sound came out. Her little dog was running in circles, barking his head off. Then the... ghost...just evaporated.

"Gabriela got up and made herself a pot of coffee and spent the rest of the night trying to explain to herself what had happened. She didn't believe in these things! Her Marxist professors at the university had convinced her that any notion of a spirit world was nothing more than superstition."

Gabriela's lips are trembling. I feel goose bumps rising on my arms.

I say, my voice unsteady, "Are you sure Angelica didn't just have a nightmare?"

"Yes, I'm sure! Let me tell you the rest, and you'll understand why.

"We all had a hard time going to sleep the next night. But nothing happened. After a week I was telling myself Angie must have imagined it. Then, late one night I was awakened by the sound of a crash. I grabbed my wrap and ran to the stairs. Halfway down I stumbled over the remains of a lamp. Angelica was on the floor beside her bed, crying hysterically. Her visitor had returned and she'd thrown her bedside lamp at him.

"I insisted she move into our guest bedroom. Two nights later her little dog awoke her growling. When we went downstairs the next morning Angelica's apartment was clammy and cold, and you could feel an evil presence.

"A couple of weeks went by without another incident. Then just three nights ago there was a loud explosion. I jumped out of bed and ran into the hall. I bumped into Angie. We were hugging each other when my fourteen-year-old came trudging up the stairs, a shotgun in his hands. Said he'd seen the apparition and shot at him.

"He confessed he'd been sleeping on Angelica's couch the past two weeks, the gun at his side. I called a repairman the next day to fix the hole in the stairwell."

Suddenly angry, I get up from the couch and stand looking down at Gabriela. "Why haven't you told me about this before?"

She shakes her head. "Oh Andrés, I've wanted to. But I'd already shared so many horrible things about me and my family. I was afraid my…my ghost story…would be the straw that broke the camel's back, that you'd think I was crazy."

Sitting down beside her, I pull her into my arms. Her head on my chest, I remember the strange happenings here in my own apartment not long ago. Was it just a coincidence?

Turning to me, her face very close to mine, Gabriela continues: "In the last couple of days I've remembered happenings in my childhood, things I'd shoved back into some dark closet of my mind. Things that may throw light on what's been going on in my house. It has to do with my grandmother. Do you want to hear about them now, or is it too late?"

Her eyes plead for permission to continue.

I pat her hand. "No, please go on."

Settling back, Gabriela speaks slowly, thoughtfully: "The house first belonged to my grandparents. Until I was ten, we lived there with them." Her smile fades into a frown. "I love it now, but when I was a child I imagined seeing scary, scaly creatures crouched in the shadows that seeped at dusk into the huge high-ceilinged rooms.

"I'm sure my fear was rooted in what was going on upstairs: my grandmother had converted the attic into a shrine to the Virgin Mary and filled it with candles and statues. When I was very small I liked to visit her sanctuary; the burning candles breathed out a pleasant fragrance, making the room warm and soothing to my little girl heart. But after I almost died, my grandmother's shrine was never the same."

"You almost died?"

Gabriela shivers and huddles closer. "I think I was about five when I fell sick. I'm not sure what I had, but it must have been pneumonia; you've seen how chilly and damp our *colonia* gets in winter.

"The time came when my parents despaired of my life. My father refused to let them take me to the hospital. I was the apple of his eye, and he wasn't going to let me out of his sight. So they turned the house into an infirmary. The doctor visited me every day and a nurse was always at my side. The priest came often, and I don't know how many times my grandmother said the Rosary over me. I remember the sensation of sinking ever deeper, deeper into a dark, icy well.

"Then one day I heard my grandmother arguing with Mother outside my door. Later she entered my room accompanied by one of our cooks, a very old, wrinkled Aztec lady as dark as polished mahogany, who'd been with the family since her youth. On a table at the foot of my bed, beside a likeness of the Virgin, she set a small ugly statue of an Aztec god."

"Huizilopochtli?" I ask.

Gabriela looks at me, eyebrows raised. "How did you know?

I shrug.

"Grandmother placed a small wooden crucifix on my forehead and the old cook laid a tiny stone replica of the Feathered Serpent on my chest."

She pauses. "Since you know about the Aztec gods, I'm sure you've also heard of Quetzalcóatl."

"Yes, I've heard." I resist the temptation to say more.

"My grandmother recited the Rosary, then the cook went into a long pagan litany, chanting in her native Nauahtl language and dancing about."

"And what happened?"

She hesitates, then takes my hand, her eyes begging me to believe: "Andee, within twenty-four hours I was feeling much better, and in a week I was up and about again."

"Incredible!"

"My father told me years later the cook had been insisting for weeks that her Aztec gods could heal me. My grandmother resisted until she got so desperate she was willing to try anything. But she insisted the Virgin and the crucifix also must be present."

My mind is racing. "So what do you think? That when your grandmother and the old cook brought together the crucifix and the Feathered Serpent, they liberated some kind of exotic healing power?"

Gabriela throws up her hands. "Oh Andee, I don't know what to believe. I do remember the arguments that followed between Mother and Grandmother. Mother told her she'd sold her soul to the devil. Said Grandmother had opened up our house to evil spirits, and we'd never be able to sleep in peace again.

"My grandmother, on the other hand, seemed to have undergone some kind of mystical experience; she began mixing her devotion to the Virgin with prayers to Quetzalcóatl. I visited her shrine in the attic only once after that, and it gave me chill bumps. It was evil smelling, filled with black smoke. I never wanted to return."

I sit mulling over what this woman has told me—the woman I want to live with the rest of my life. How different the worlds we grew up in! At last I say, "So you think your grandmother's shrine had something to do with what's been happening in your house?"

She nods. "When my grandmother became a disciple of the Plumed Serpent our house became Satan's territory. And now that I've become Christ's disciple Satan has sent one of his evil spirits to torment us." She reaches over and turns my face toward hers. "Andee, what do you think? Am I right?"

I'm silent for a long moment. Should I tell her what I really think? That the problem in her house is *my* fault—that Quetzalcóatl is getting back at me by harassing the woman I love?

At last I say: "I think your mother was right. Your grandmother's compromise with Quetzalcóatl opened the door to the devil."

Looping her arm through mine, Gabriela hugs it to her body and smiles at me, her eyes moist. "Andrés, I'm so glad I have you." Then she adds. "Can you help us?"

I whistle softly. "I'm sure there's something we can do, but I don't know what. Let me talk to Moisés and I'll get back with you."

She squeezes my hand. "Thank you for believing me. I was so afraid you'd…." She stifles a yawn.

I chuckle. "Right now I think it's time I get you home."

Moving closer, she touches her cheek to mine and nibbles at my ear. "What if I tell you I don't want to go home?"

Suddenly she's in my arms and I'm kissing her, swept by a passion I haven't felt since years ago when I'd take Mary in my arms and….

Pushing her gently away, I mutter. "Whoa, we're headed for trouble. I'm taking you home right now!"

Thirty minutes later we're nearing her house. She's been very quiet, her head on my shoulder. When I brake for a light she stirs and sits up. "Andee, I have a fantastic idea! Next week I have a buying trip to Paris. Come with me."

I chuckle. "And what will the neighbors say?"

She's silent for a moment. "I guess I'm asking you to marry me."

I'm no longer sleepy. Dear God, I love this woman! I know you've brought us together…and the way I felt a little while ago when she was in my arms! Why should we be apart any longer?…. Careful! How often have I warned engaged couples to take time to get to know each other? That most of the things married people fight about are the very things that attracted them to each other before they married?

Gabriela's voice trembles with excitement: "Let's see, this is Wednesday. We can go down to the courthouse today and get our license and make an appointment with a judge to marry us no later than Friday. Meanwhile I'll have my travel agent make a reservation for you on my flight and…" she giggles—"change my hotel room in Paris to a double."

I want to marry this woman! But be honest, Andrew, are you sure Gabriela has healed sufficiently from her divorce to begin another marriage?

"Andee!"

I jump. "What?"

"We just passed my street."

I make a U-turn in the dark shadows of the elegant elms lining Avenida Reforma and return to her street. In front of the massive stone wall fronting her house she reaches over and touches the horn. Almost immediately the garage doors swing open. Poor maid! Since Gabriela called her from my apartment and got her out of her warm bed she's been waiting to push the button when her *señora* arrived.

As we enter the house three chimes of the clock break the silence. Gabriela takes my hands in hers, and her face flushed, eyes shining, says, "O-o-h, we've talked the night away, and we've got such a busy day ahead!"

How am I going to tell her? How am I going to explain that I love her with all my heart, that I'm aching to possess her, but that I'm not ready to marry her?

A shadow darkens her face. "Andee…we are in agreement, aren't we?"

I take her face in my hands and kiss her lips tenderly.

"Gabriela, I love you, I desire you desperately, I want to marry you. But we need to…"

Clinging to me, she buries her face in my chest. "Please, *mi amor*, please. This has been the happiest day of my life. Don't spoil it!" A shudder agitates her body. "Andee, I want every day of my life to be just like this one."

I hug her to me. How dare I hurt this precious woman? But dare I be unfaithful to myself…to her…to our future together…to what I've learned during decades helping others to have healthy marriages?

Rocking her in my arms, I beg God to give me the right words. "Dear, sweet Gabi, I love you so!" A sob tears at my throat.

She's reading my mind. She knows what I'm about to say. "Then let's not wait. Please, Andee, I'm so…so afraid. Let's get married right away. If we don't, something awful is going to happen!"

I take her hand and lead her to one of the overstuffed chairs in the living room. Falling to my knees I lift her chin and force her to look into my eyes. "Gabriela, listen to me. When we marry I want it to be perfect. I love you too much to rush into something before we're ready. I don't want us to waste years trying to work through problems we should have solved before we said the vows."

The sparkle fading from her eyes, she pushes me away and gets to her feet. "Doctór Kelly, you're a brilliant marriage counselor, I knew it the first time I heard you speak. Maybe that's why you're such a sorry lover: when the time comes to take a chance on love you remember all the wise advice you've given others."

An icy hand grips my throat, strangling me. I'm about to lose the woman I love! Reaching out, I pull her to me. Her body is stiff and cold. I plead: "Look, Gabriela, forget everything I've said. You're right, let's get married. Right away!"

She pushes away from me, hurries over to the front door, and opens it. "It's late, Doctór Kelly. We both need to get some sleep...."

When I open the door to my apartment the phone is ringing. It's Gabriela! "Andrés, I'm not going to be able to sleep unless I ask you to forgive me." I can tell she's been crying.

(Oh God, you've given me this woman! Now give me the right words to say to her!)

"My darling Gabriela," I say, my voice breaking, "I'm the one who should ask forgiveness. I..."

"Andrés, you're the nicest man I've have ever met, and I love you with all my heart. But you're right, we *are* so different. It would be foolish to think about marriage."

"Not foolish, my love, just a little premature."

"Maybe some day...?"

"Some day soon," I say, "very soon."

Her voice breaks. "Yes, *mi amor*, very soon."

But I know she doesn't believe it.

A hundred times after this day I'll reproach myself for being. "too good a marriage counselor to take a chance on love!"

CHAPTER 17

▼

BETRAYAL

Juventino, Gabriela's gardener-chauffeur opens the heavy oak gate for me. Gabriela catches her flight to Paris this morning. A week ago I wouldn't have dreamed of taking her to the airport, but now I can't imagine not doing it.

Hector and I place Gabriela's bags in my car while the maids are frantically jotting down Gabriela's last-minute instructions. It's my first time to see Hector. He's short, chubby, dark-skinned, and a moment ago he glowered at me when I offered him my hand.

Angelica follows Gabriela and me to the car. She kisses her mother, then to my surprise, turns and plants a kiss on my cheek.

When we're on our way Gabriela says, laughing, "My daughter really likes you! I'm glad she has a boyfriend. If she didn't, I'd be jealous."

"Angelica's a doll. But Hector wishes I was dead!"

"It's not you, Andee. Right now he's angry with all father figures. Just give him time."

"Does Angelica know you told me about…the unwelcome visitor?"

"Yes. And I promised her you're going to help us. You will, won't you?" Gabriela checks her lipstick in the sunshade mirror.

"I'll do my best. By the way, when will you be back?"

"I'll be here for our Thursday appointment."

I turn onto the *periferico* and head south toward the airport. "I'm going to miss you. I'm afraid I'll be looking for you to walk through the door Tuesday at eleven."

Gabriela moves closer and loops an arm through mine. "Has Rebeca told you who'll be there in my place?"

"No, is it somebody I know?

"It's Rosario. Remember, the person I met in the supermarket. The angel God sent to save my life. I've been wanting you to meet her."

"And I've been wanting to thank her."

Gabriela squeezes my arm. "She needs your help, Andee."

"Husband trouble too?"

"Yes. And I'm sure it's not all his fault. Rosario's probably not the easiest person in the world to live with. You'll see what I mean when you meet her."

"Flight 397 now boarding."

We kiss goodbye. Clinging to me, Gabriela whispers, "I still wish you were going with me!"

"So do I, my darling." I wait for her to reproach me, but she gives me a final hug and heads toward her gate. Long after she disappears from view I stand there, my eyes burning, wishing I'd found the courage to obey my heart.

Sunday after church I corner Moisés long enough to invite him to breakfast the next day. It's tough getting his ear Sundays. When the service ends a dozen people are standing in line waiting to talk to him. I'm usually tied up half an hour or more myself. There's always at least one student wanting to follow up on something I said in class.

Next morning I decide to walk to my appointment with Moisés. It'll give me the opportunity to stroll through the Zona Rosa, Mexico City's Bohemia. The restaurants there are always thronged with people with nothing better to do than while away their time chatting over a glass of wine or a mug of black coffee.

To my surprise Moisés is waiting for me. We'd made an appointment for eight-thirty, so I wasn't expecting him before nine. By Mexican Standard Time I'm five minutes early!

He rises and gives me a hearty *abrazo*. Over coffee we comment on our encounter last Monday with Huitzilopochtli's gruesome altar. Isaac, he informs me, had his men cover up the secret tunnel the next day, afraid his boss might be unhappy if he discovered his excursion into archeology.

I bring Moisés up to date on Gabriela and her neighbors. I say nothing about our personal relationship. Gabriela and I have agreed that for the present our love will remain a precious secret between us.

"Speaking of *Sra.* Gabriela," I tell him, "she's the reason I asked you to meet with me this morning."

When I've finished my account of the bizarre apparitions in Gabriela's house, Moisés sits contemplating his empty coffee cup. At last he says very quietly, "Doctór, do you remember the vision that I called you about back in August?"

"Of course, the one about me walking through the front door of *Los Pinos.* I've asked myself a dozen times, 'Why me?'"

I know why he's brought this up. Just like me, he suspects there's a connection between his vision and that fearsome torso floating down Angelica's staircase!

"*Señores*, your *chilaquiles.*"

The waitress sets our meal on the table. "Careful, the plates are hot."

Chilaquiles are the Mexican counterpart of American ham and eggs. I've learned to like these hot corn tortillas stuffed with cheese, herbs and chile almost as much as *enchiladas suizas.* But today I have no appetite for them.

Moisés reaches over and touches my arm. "Let's ask the Father for his wisdom."

We bow our heads.

When his prayer is finished Moisés grabs up his fork and digs in with relish.

I pick at my food, lay down my fork and take a sip of lukewarm coffee. For the first time since arriving in Mexico City I find myself wishing I were back in the peaceful, predictable world of Kingwood.

Belching gently, Moisés wipes his thick lips with the white napkin. Looking at me intently, he says, "My brother, don't be afraid. That's what Quetzalcóatl wants. He knows that God reached over into your *patria*, plucked you up and brought you to Mexico to play a part in the final victory of the Lamb. That's why he wants to scare you away."

I push back my plate, irritated by Moisés' complacency. "Well, maybe I ought to be afraid!"

"*No, gracias, Señorita.*" Waving away the waitress, the Pastor bends tensely over the table. "My brother, when we're afraid we insult God. Don't you know the same God who brought you here will provide you the resources to do his work?"

Smiling now, Moisés takes a paper place mat and begins sketching a battle plan....

An hour later I'm paying the cashier when Moisés asks: "Where's your car, did you park it in the garage?"

"No, I walked. And you came on your *moto*?"

He stops and looks at me.

Oh, oh! "No, thank you, Moses, I'll walk."

"Still not ready to take a ride on my black stallion, Doctór?"

I resent his patronizing smile! "I'm not afraid of your motorcycle, Moses. I just feel like walking today."

As I move away he calls after me, "In a hurry?"

I turn back. "No, not especially."

He comes over and lays a hand on my shoulder. "We've left something unfinished since October, remember?"

"How could I forget that story you told me about you and Quetzalcóatl?"

"For me to explain to you how it ended we'll have to go to *La plaza de las Tres Culturas.* can spare a couple of hours,…(that mocking smile again)…if you've got the guts to ride with me!"

I allow him to propel me downstairs to the parking garage and his big black Harley-Davidson. Minutes later we're on *Avenida Juarez* in a turbulent river of automobiles, taxis, buses and trucks. Seated behind Moisés, my arms wrapped around his bulky waist, my nose pressed against his back, I try to convince myself we're not in imminent danger of annihilation. Mexico City's streets are scary enough in a car, but at least you can roll up your windows and shut out most of the sounds and smells. Astride Moisés' bouncing black stallion there's nothing to soften the roar of busses, the blaring of horns, the stench of black smoke vomited by diesel engines. Eyes closed, I dedicate myself to repeating the Twenty-Third Psalm.

After awhile I open my eyes and sit back. This is fun, even better than the roller coaster! I give an exuberant yell and Moisés, grinning, stabs the sky with a "V" sign.

"Here we are!" Moisés shuts off the noisy engine and kicks down the stand. I put a foot to the ground, waiting for my spinning head to reconnect with my body.

"They call it "The Plaza of the Three Cultures." You can see why, can't you?"

Before us lies a broad stone-paved square, framed on the north by a venerable Spanish cathedral, on the south by the gray ruins of an Aztec pyramid, and on the east by a glass-walled high rise apartment building.

As we walk in the direction of the pyramid he takes up the story he left unfinished six weeks ago in my apartment: "The four years following my conversion to the Feathered Serpent were busy and exciting. Days I worked in the shop and nights I attended classes. Weekends I dedicated to learning more about my Lord Quetzalcóatl, making frequent visits to Teotihuacan, spending long hours in the Museum of Anthropology, thumbing through the card catalog in the University library. One summer I made a pilgrimage to Yucatan and the Temple of Kukulkan."

We stop, gazing up at the Aztec temple. Studying the pile of crumbling gray stones I try to imagine what it must have looked like centuries ago. I see red-robed priests with feathered headdresses bending over naked, struggling victims, and watch rivulets of blood trickling down the steps of the pyramid. Arms folded, broad dark face melancholy, Moisés is also studying the ruined shrine. I'm sure he must see the ghosts of his ancestors kneeling before an evil demon-god who demanded everything and gave nothing.

Moisés looks back over the plaza. "Doctór, imagine a cool evening the second day of October, 1968, just ten days before the beginning of the Olympic Games. Five thousand university students have gathered in *La Plaza de las Tres Culturas* to celebrate their love for the *ptria*. By now I'm in my second year at the National University. Like everyone else here I'm angry because our government seems unwilling to do anything about our economic stagnation and the obscene corruption sucking the life out of our country.

"We've come to draw a line in the sand: our leaders must promise us they're going to make radical changes. Immediately. If not, we'll turn the Olympics into a public relations disaster. We'll tell the people of the world the truth about our country."

I break in. "And all those young people gathered here in the plaza—were they followers of Quetzalcóatl like you?"

He shrugs. "Oh no, most of them were dedicated Marxists. We disciples of the Feathered Serpent were a tiny minority."

"Then why were you here?"

"Like them, we wanted to change our country. But there was something more important. We had a secret: Quetzalcóatl was about to fulfill the prophecies about his Second Coming. He would appear this very night, here in the *Plaza de las Trtes Culturas*."

"Oh come on, Moisés, did you really believe that?"

Moisés pounds a fist into his chest. "With all my heart; we had the word of our prophet!

The weekend before, at a retreat on the peak of Ajuzco, our leader had fallen into a trance. This is what he saw:"...Moses raises his arms dramatically..."thousands of young people gathered in the *La Plaza de las Tres Culturas*. Suddenly an earthquake! The cathedral crumbles. The high rise shatters and falls flat. But everyone in the Plaza is staring, at this temple, astonished. Quetzalcóatl stands on the peak of the temple, and it holds firm beneath his feet. The multitude drops to their knees in submission to our Lord.

"Can you imagine how we felt as we awaited Quetzalcóatl's appearance? We could hardly breathe from the excitement!"

He pauses. "We'd been here a couple of hours, many of us spaced out on marijuana, singing folkloric songs, applauding the rousing speeches, cheering ourselves hoarse...then all at once our blood turned to ice water, as we heard the put-put-put of approaching helicopters. Moments later they were circling overhead. It was too dark to see them, but the noise was deafening and the wind from their props raised a blinding cloud of dust.

"Everybody stopped singing, stopped talking...stopped breathing...sensing that something awful was about to happen.

"Except for us, the small, tight circle of Quetzalcóatl's disciples. We were shouting, pounding each other on the back, still sure our lord's appearance was just moments away.

"Abruptly the plaza was illumined by a blinding light from the circling helicopters." He points toward the square. "I was standing about ten meters from here. A kid at my side fell to the pavement. I dropped to my knees beside him, and when I saw blood oozing from his chest I screamed out in shock. Now, above the roar of the engines, I could hear the staccato bursts of machine guns overhead.

"I jumped to my feet. All around me people were yelling, running in circles. Above the noise I heard the pounding of boots and saw swarms of soldiers piling out of trucks, beginning to encircle the square. I could hear the pop...pop...pop of small arms fire.

"One of my friends shouted for us to run for Quetzalcóatl's temple. Half a dozen of us locked arms and sprinted toward it." He points to tiny nicks in the stone. "By the time we got here, bullets were splattering against the wall."

"We weren't afraid of the bullets, they couldn't touch us, we were the Feathered Serpent's chosen people! We began climbing the pyramid, singing, anxious to be on top when Quetzalcóatl appeared. I was dumbstruck when one of my companions screamed with pain and tumbled to the ground. Then another, and a third.

"Somehow I made it to the top. I stood up, ready to shout out my welcome to Quetzalcóatl. Suddenly a powerful blow to the shoulder spun me around. I was like a man in a dream, this couldn't be happening to me! Losing my balance, I fell to the ground. When I came to myself I put my hand to my shoulder, and felt a warm sensation. Seeing red blood trickling from between my fingers, I almost passed out. I could hear the shouts of soldiers and the cries of the wounded on the other side of the pyramid. But I'd fallen into the shadows and no one seemed to know I was there." Moisés voice breaks.

"Struggling to my feet, I ran for my life.... Finally I found myself on a quiet street, alone except for a few strollers unaware of the horror taking place only blocks away. I sat on a bench, my hand clutching my shoulder, hot tears running down my cheeks, trying desperately to stop the flow of blood.

"I kept waiting for the sound of ambulances going to aid the wounded. But nothing. Then I knew: There would be no ambulances!"

As if awaking from a bad dream, Moisés shakes himself and pushes away from the pyramid. Massaging his right shoulder, he says, "Let's go!"

We cross the square, surrounded by laughing children and mothers peacefully wheeling their babies over stones long ago scrubbed clean of the blood of Mexico's young dreamers.

I buy a couple of Cokes from a vender (here they still sell Cokes in big green bottles) and we seat ourselves on a hard stone bench. Moisés resumes his story: "I managed to get treatment at a small private clinic, with no questions asked. They assured me I'd be all right in a few days. Sometime before dawn I took a bus out of town. I shivered with fear every time we stopped, afraid soldiers would board the bus and question me about the bandage."

"The next day, in a small village far from the capital, I bought a copy of the *Excelsior*. On the front page I found an article entitled "Fierce Combat When the Army Disperses a Meeting of Rebels". The government had reported twenty dead, seventy-five wounded and four hundred arrests. I knew that was a lie, there must have been hundreds of deaths.

"I spent the next six months wandering through the countryside, avoiding the cities, terrified of being picked up by the army. I felt like the star of a sad, drab movie shot in black and white by a poorly focused camera.

"Toward the end of my exile I ran into a boy who had been present the night of the demonstration. He told me a story that made my teeth chatter: along with hundreds of other survivors, he had been forced at gunpoint to load the dead and wounded into army trucks, then climb in beside them. Just before dawn the trucks arrived at an army camp deep in the mountains of Michoacan. They laid the wounded on straw mats covering the dirt floors of adobe huts. The dead were buried in a common grave.

"For weeks the prisoners were beaten and interrogated daily. Finally they were released under the threat of death if they should ever speak a word of what had happened.

"Ten days after the massacre the Olympics were inaugurated with great fanfare. Millions of people all over the world watched as a cloud of white pigeons filled the air over the shiny new *Estadio Olímpico* and thousands of smiling school children entertained with folkloric dances. Our President welcomed the athletes of the world to Mexico, a peaceful, happy nation, presided over by a benign government."

Gritting his teeth, Moisés takes a last swallow of his Coke. "During the following years I lived the life of a vagabond. Worked just enough to survive. Hallucinated on *hongos*, smoked pot, sniffed glue. Another President was elected and he too promised a new Mexico. Like most other Mexican young people I felt betrayed, not only by our leaders, but by our own idealism. Mexico was under a curse and there was nothing we could do about it!

Standing to his feet, Moisés stretches his arms to the clear blue sky. "Then, praise God, a miracle changed my life! One Saturday night I was walking down a back street, a beer in my hand, wondering how I could while away the hours before I'd fall into a drugged sleep. I passed a small, ugly church. A kid with a crooked grin handed me a tract and invited me to enter. I stopped and glared at him, wanting to slap his silly face. How could he be so happy? Didn't he know what a mess the world was in?

"I glanced at the building behind him. Like most other evangelical temples I'd seen, it looked more like a warehouse than a house of worship. On impulse I threw down my beer and followed him inside.

"I was surprised to find the place packed with young people, singing boisterously, clapping their hands in time to an ear-splitting combo of electric guitars, accordions, bass viols and tambourines. Between songs one kid after another would run to the front, grab the microphone and shout out his testimony about how Jesus had freed him from drugs and given him purpose for living.

"I was fascinated. These people were telling me they'd found what I'd been searching for all my life! And they'd found it in a person I'd heard of all my life, Jesus of Nazareth. But this Jesus was different from the Jesus I had rejected; not a sad, defeated martyr but a conquering hero who, according to them, was always with them wherever they went, whatever happened.

"That night I decided I wanted what they had.

"I became part of a family. Most of my new brothers and sisters had been hooked on drugs, just like me. They were young, loud and undisciplined. As we criss-crossed the country preaching to anybody who would listen, I was excited to see young people by the hundreds leaving drugs and demons to embrace the same Jesus Christ who had changed my own life."

Moisés picks up our Coke bottles and returns them to the vendor. "That was twenty years ago," he concludes.

I glance nervously at the motorcycle standing at the curb, preparing myself for another wild ride.

"A lot of things have happened since then. I finished my studies, taught school for ten years, became pastor of a church...and a couple of years ago found myself face to face with Quetzalcóatl again...now my enemy."

He comes over and crushes me in a hug. "And now the Lord has sent his chosen disciple to work with me!"

A moment later, seated behind him, I open my mouth to ask a question, but Moisés kicks his black stallion into life and the roar of the engine swallows up my words.

CHAPTER 18

▼

DISASTER

Rebeca flips through the desk calendar to Tuesday morning as we chat about last Sunday's worship…the surprising things that happened during the free-wheeling praise…the electric moments at the close of Moisés' hour-long sermon. Rebeca, the kid sister I never had has now become Rebeca my best friend. It's always fun talking with her.

Finally I say, "Well, we'd better have our prayer, it's time to go to work."

We join hands and ask I God's blessing upon the week we're beginning. Rebeca whispers "Amen." In the same breath she adds, "Doctór, your first patient this morning is *Sra.* Rosario Montemayor." She starts for the door, then turns: "She's a friend of *Sra.* Gabriela."

"Yes, I know, Gabriela told me she was coming. Did you reconfirm the appointment?"

"I called her yesterday. Very interesting. She sounded like the typical *Espanola rica.*"

"What do you mean?"

She laughs as she heads for her desk, "Strong-willed!"

Ten minutes later Rebeca escorts Rosario into my office. Thin and taut, straight blond hair falling to her shoulders, she surveys me with cool brown eyes. Taking the seat I indicate, she extracts a package of Virginia Slims from her purse.

I fidget. Shall I tell her? I don't want to make her mad, but...I will!

"*Sra.* Rosario, I'd prefer you not smoke in my *consultorio*."

"Oh?" Frowning, she shrugs and throws the pack on the coffee table. "You Americans and your phobia about cancer!" She rubs a thumb over her tobacco-stained fingertips, "Know what? If I stopped smoking, in a month I wouldn't be able to get into my clothes.

"But never mind." Her face softens, and she makes a stab at civility: "I've been wanting to meet you, Doctór. Gabriela has talked so much about you."

I smile back. "Gabriela told me about how you met. Fascinating!"

"Isn't it though? And did she tell you the awful thing she was planning to do that very night?" Crossing her bony legs, Rosario launches into a description of their meeting in the supermarket and Gabriela's conversion long after midnight. Five minutes into her account she reaches over, shakes a cigarette out of the pack, lights it and continues without missing a word.

Rebeca was right, here's a woman accustomed to having her own way!

When she has finished her story she leans back, purses her thin lips and blows a lazy smoke ring toward the ceiling. "I don't deserve Gabriela. She's been a Christian only a few months, and already she's left me behind!"

Checking her watch, she sighs. "*Caray!* Half my time is gone and I haven't told you why I'm here."

Rosario lights her third cigarette. "It's my husband, Wilbert. I'm crazy about him; he's handsome, charming, and generous. But—" her voice becomes shrill: "he's also a shameless womanizer!"

Wilbert, she informs me, is a helicopter pilot. For the past four years he's been flying the President and his cabinet around Mexico City. "When he first got the job I was excited. Then his boss, an army general, began dragging him along on all-night drinking parties. Worst of all, he introduced Wilbert to a bad woman."

"So you think he's been unfaithful?"

"I know he has!"

"And what does he say?"

"Oh, he denies it. Please, would you talk to him?"

"Of course, if you can you persuade him to come in."

Her brown eyes flash. "He knows better than to refuse me! Two years ago there was another woman, and I threw him out of the house. After three weeks they called me from the hospital where he was recovering from an alcoholic binge. When I went to him he begged me to forgive him and promised never to betray me again."

"And now he's broken his promise."

She nods sadly. "What am I going to do with him? He's like a spoiled child. Since his mother passed away I've felt more like his mother than his wife."

Getting up, I say, "Then I'll be expecting him. And afterward I'll want to talk with you again."

I put out my hand. "It's been nice meeting you, Rosario."

She stands to her feet, ignoring my hand. "Before I go, Doctór, I have a question."

"Yes, of course."

Her chin comes up and her eyes narrow: "Do you love Gabriela?"

Annoyed, I stare at her.

"Don't tell me it's none of my business," she mutters, "I'm the only real friend Gabriela has in this world. Her parents are dead and her brothers think only of themselves."

"Look, Rosario, I know you mean well, but..."

"Doctór Kelly, Gabriela is a brilliant businesswoman, it's incredible what she has done with *Modas Mancini*." Her lips tighten. "But you know as well as I that where men are concerned she's still in kindergarten. Look what she let that husband do to her!"

"Believe me, Rosario, I'd never do anything to hurt Gabriela."

She moves toward the door, her frosty eyes never leaving mine. "I hope not. But frankly, I have my doubts about a romance between a Mexican woman and an American man. They're just too different!"

On Thursday Gabriela calls half an hour before her appointment. "Andee, I'm home!"

"Welcome, *mi amor*, I've been expecting your call. Looking forward to seeing you!"

"I've got a problem. I'm still so woozy from jet lag I'm afraid to try to drive in the traffic. Would you forgive me if I don't make it for my appointment this morning?"

I try to hide my disappointment. "Of course. But I hope I can see you soon."

She kisses the telephone. "The sooner the better, I've missed you so! I'm wondering if…before she left for her classes this morning Angie begged me to insist you come over today and do something about this ghost business. She still refuses to sleep in her apartment. Of course I told her you probably had other plans."

My heart picks up. "Let's see. My last appointment is at four. Would you feel up to company by…say, five-thirty?"

"Wonderful! Angie will be ecstatic." She giggles. "And so will I! Angie doesn't get home until about six-thirty. That will give us an hour to…" she giggles again…"to say hello."

I'm surprised when Gabriela herself opens the gate for me, dressed in dark slacks and a crisp white blouse, looking nothing like the travel-worn executive I expected to see. She greets me with a warm hug and a kiss. "I gave my help the afternoon off. I don't know what you're going to do, but I'm sure they wouldn't understand."

A brightly flowered teapot whistles a welcome when we enter the kitchen. "I've been sipping manzanilla tea all day, trying get over my jet lag. If you prefer something with caffeine just tell me."

"No, manzanilla tea's fine, I've had a tough day." I don't tell her the real reason for my nerves: what if I fail this afternoon? What if, in spite of the instructions Moisés gave me, that hideous demon refuses to leave?

She opens the oven and brings out a pan of savory pastries. "You like our Mexican sweet breads so much I thought you might enjoy something from a Paris bakery."

Seated in Gabriela's kitchen, enjoying a warm sweet roll stuffed with raisins and nuts, watching her animated face as she tells me about her trip, all is right with the world.

After a while Gabriela pauses and reaches for my hand. "Did Rosario keep her appointment?"

"Yes, she did. And you were right, she's a...a very interesting person."

"And what did she say about you and me? Rosario's a good friend, but I was praying she wouldn't infect you with her pessimism." She leans over and places her cheek next to mine.

"Things are going to work out between us, you'll see. In the meantime, let's just—"

"*Mami*, I'm home!" Angie hurries in from the living room.

"Doctór Kelly, I saw your car outside. *Gracias a Dios!!*" She hugs my neck. "I haven't slept well in a week. My boyfriend Jorge was fussing at me today about the dark circles under my eyes. I'm so looking forward to moving back into my apartment!"

(I'm wishing I were as confident as she!)

"Now tell me, dear Doctór, what are you going to do?"

I push back my chair. "First, I want to see the room where your mother was sick for so long."

The three of us climb the winding staircase to the second floor and Gabriela leads us to a door at the end of a long brightly-lit hall. "After I became ill my mother moved me from my own room to this one," she says, opening the door to a small, high-ceilinged room furnished with an antique chest of drawers and a narrow iron bed with starched white sheets.

Pulling back the blinds she says, "Mother put me here so I'd be away from the noise of the house. Now it's reserved for guests. I haven't used it in years, but the maids are under orders to clean it weekly."

I can tell she's as nervous as I am. She keeps chattering, smoothing the bed sheets, running a finger over the chest of drawers.

I reach for her hand. "Gabriela, your grandmother made a pact with the Feathered Serpent in this room. Are you ready to revoke it?"

She takes a deep breath. "I am!" Reaching for her daughter's hand she draws her close. Angelica's eyes, very wide, are fixed upon me.

Taking a folded white sheet of paper from my coat pocket, I read carefully and slowly the words Moisés wrote for me at our breakfast: "By the blood of Jesus Christ…we bind the spirits…occupying this room." My voice gets stronger with each word, but I wonder if Gabriela and Angelica can see how the paper in my hand is trembling.

I continue: "We declare…null and void the pact made in this room…with Quetzalcóatl…and we consecrate this house…to the Lord Jesus Christ. In the name of the Father and the Son and the Holy Spirit."

The two women whisper "Amen!" and Angelica crosses herself.

"Now, Gabriela, it's your turn." I hand her my Bible and she reads in a loud, clear voice the words I have marked for her: "As for me and my house, we will serve the Lord." And again she says, "Amen!"

We're silent for a long moment. I can feel the tension melting away and a refreshing peace filling the room.

"Now," I say, "Let's go up to the attic."

Gabriela gasps and her hand flies to her throat. "Oh Andee, do we have to?" She eases herself down on the bed. "I…I don't think I can do it."

"But why? What are you afraid of?"

"How can I break the promise I made to my father? When he turned this house over to me he made me swear never to open up the attic again."

"Mother," Angelica cries, "if you're going to leave that lock on the attic door, then put another one on the basement door. I swear I'm not going back down there!"

"*Hijita mía*, I know how you feel, but what can I do? It's a sin to break a promise." She pauses, and I'm surprised to see her lips quivering. "Besides, the room has been closed for more than fifteen years. Some terrible things went on up there. That's why Papá put a lock on the door and made me promise never to open it again."

Sitting down beside her on the bed I take her hand and say gently, "Gabriela, don't be afraid, God is with us. Remember, we're about to chase out a gang of demons that have headquartered in your attic for fifteen years!"

For a long moment she remains with her head bowed. When she looks up my heart melts; I can see in her pale face the sadness she's lived with for twenty years.

"You're sure nothing bad is going to happen?"

"I guarantee it!"

(Later, I'd regret those words.)

She sighs and kisses my cheek. "All right, my love, I'll open the door. But I still don't feel good about it."

She gets to her feet. "It's been a long time. I wonder where I put the key."

We follow her to her bedroom and she rummages through the drawers of an ancient armoire. At last she comes up with half a dozen rusty keys held together by a faded yellow ribbon. "My father gave me these the day he and Mother moved out. One of them fits the lock on the attic door."

"*Mami,* should I get a candle?" Angelica asks, her eyes wide.

"Yes, Dear, please do. It's going to be very dark up there."

We follow Gabriela downstairs to the kitchen, then begin climbing a long flight of narrow wooden stairs. "This stairway was built for the household help. Back then they quartered the maids in the attic. It's very steep, so be careful."

At the top she hands me the keys. "Please, Andee, you do it. I'm still afraid."

The door is secured by a large, rusted padlock. I try several keys without success. At last I manage to force a long brass key into the lock.

"Looks like this is it. Ready?"

My hands are sweating and there's a hard knot in the pit of my stomach. I'm supposed to be playing the role of brave man of God, but at this moment I feel like a scared six-year old. hat will happen when I open the door?

The key turns slowly and the lock pops open. I remove it, turn the knob and pull open the door.

Whoosh!

Suddenly we're enveloped in a dark, churning cloud of tiny flailing wings, and sharp beaks emitting a shrill, unending screech. I've opened a funnel into hell!

"E-e-e-k—*murciélagos!*" Gabriela screams. She loses her footing and stumbles backwards, and I catch her just in time.

Behind her, Angelica is shrieking and flailing with both hands. Dozens of bats have clustered about her, beating at her face with little black wings, pecking at her lips. Many are clinging to her hair, fiendish little faces grimacing at me.

"*Dios mío, Dios mío,* help me! Help me!"

I try desperately to get to her, but Gabriela is blocking the narrow stairway, wailing, wringing her hands.

"Gabriela, let me by. Please!" Pushing her aside I reach out for Angelica, but just as my hand touches hers she crumples and falls backwards. I watch in horror as she tumbles downward, head and elbows smacking every other step until she lands with a resounding thump on the hard tile floor.

I stand for a moment grasping the railing, my knees turned to water.

"Angelica!" I yell, and propel myself down the stairs, stumbling, falling, flailing the wall and the railing.

Finally I reach her. I can see she's unconscious. Kneeling over her I call her name, pat her face gently. Oh God, how could I have been so stupid? I was so confident I had Quetzalcóatl on the run.

"You lied! You said nothing bad was going to happen!" Gabriela is over me, beating at me with her fists.

I turn and grab her hands. "Gabriela, calm down, take it easy."

"You've killed my little girl!" she sobs. "You lied to me, Andrés! How could you?"

"Gabriela, call an ambulance. Right now!"

Turning back to the limp figure on the floor, I'm relieved to find a pulse, weak, but regular. The trickle of blood from her nose is not reassuring.

Returning from the telephone, Gabriela falls to her knees beside her daughter and covers her face with kisses.

"*Mi hijita, mi hijita*, speak to me!"

I take her shoulders gently. "Be careful, my love, don't move her. Her neck may be—"

Her face contorted, Gabriela screams at me: "Murderer!" Sobbing, she jumps to her feet, shouting as she runs for the door: "The ambulance, the ambulance, I'll wait for it outside!"

I wet a hand towel in the bathroom and bathe Angelica's face, praying she'll open her eyes. But she lies where she fell, eyes closed, moaning softly now. I want to pick her up from the hard kitchen floor and carry her into the living room, but I know I dare not.

I keep waiting for the sound of an ambulance. At last I force myself to leave Angelica for a moment and run to the front door.

Gabriela is pacing back and forth at the gate, hugging herself.

"Gabriela," I call.

She turns.

"Please, don't worry," I plead, "Angelica is going to be all right."

The cold, pale face staring back at me is the face of a stranger.

CHAPTER 19

▼

REJECTED

I'm surprised. The dirty-faced little kid is still standing beside my car, right where I left him at ten this morning. He'd ambled over the moment I parked in front of the English Hospital.

"Watch your car, Señor? So they won't scratch it or steal your radio."

I agreed. And here he is, six hours later, waiting patiently for his *peso*.

When I hand it to him he tells me the bad news: "You're not going to be able to cross Avenida Constituyentes, *Señor*. There's a pilgrimage."

"A pilgrimage?"

"*Sí, Señor* in honor of the Virgin. Tomorrow's her day, you know. They're on their way to the Basilica."

"The Virgin again!" I complain to myself.

"Are you all right, Sir?" The boy is staring at me curiously.

Leaning against the car I massage my chest, trying to rub away the pain. It's been there since last night, when I discovered why eyes that were once warm with affection had suddenly become angry and hostile. Because of the Virgin! And half a block away there's a parade in her honor!

I reach out and pat the kid on the head. "Keep an eye on my car. Think I'll walk over and see the parade."

I button my coat against the chilly afternoon breeze. The rainy season ended a couple of weeks ago, and now the unwashed skies are gray with a thick smog that makes my eyes water. Sniffing, I pull out a handkerchief and wipe my nose. My head has been throbbing since yesterday. Am I catching a cold?

Strolling slowly toward a river of impoverished humanity flowing down the wide avenue just ahead, I remember what I read in the paper this morning: tomorrow is the *Día de Guadalupe,* the most important holiday of the year for millions of Mexicans. Not many people on the sidewalk, but the street is jammed with marchers, the men dressed in stained white cotton duck and the women in dark skirts and multicolored blouses. Their broad, dark country faces are stoic, unblinking brown eyes fixed on some object in the distance. The barefoot women, many with babes in arms, shuffle slowly, relentlessly, ignoring the kids swarming around them.

On tiptoe, I stare up the street from where the marchers come. I groan. No sign of an end; how long am I going to have to wait?

"*Paciencia, Señor!*"

I turn to face a handsome gray-haired gentleman standing at my side. Dressed in a natty gray wool suit, he looks out of place on this garbage-strewn street.

He smiles at me. "You have someone in the hospital? So have I. I asked my wife's permission not to visit her today. I knew what a mess the streets would be in. But she insisted I come, so here I am, stuck in the crowd. *Ay, las mujeres!*"

He checks his watch. "Looks like I won't make it back to the office before closing time."

Throwing up his hands, he chuckles, "*Así es la vida!*"

"All these people, where do they come from?" I ask.

He studies me for a moment, his eyes friendly "American, right?" Without waiting for a reply, he continues: *"Señor,* today you are gazing at Mexico's soul."

He points westward, toward the mountain peaks looming in the distance. "That's where they come from, hundreds of tiny villages between Mexico City and Toluca."

Before us, a group bearing a bright banner of the Virgin of Guadalupe breaks into song. These are uneducated country people, so it's not hard to understand why they cling with fanatical faith to this miracle-working Mother of God. But...I shake my head...what about Gabriela Mancini, wealthy woman of the world, recently liberated by faith in Jesus Christ...how do you explain her obsessive devotion?

Tears spring to my eyes. Have I lost her forever? My mind goes back to yesterday's nightmare:

After they place Angelica in the ambulance, strapped tightly to a stretcher, Gabriela runs toward her car. I beat her to the driver's seat.

"Gabriela, give me the car keys," I tell her, my hand out.

"Out of my way, *Andrés*!" She bites off the words.

"You're in no condition to drive!"

As the ambulance speeds down the driveway and turns into the street, siren wailing, she beats at me with her fists, screaming at me to get out of the car.

At last, as the sound of the siren becomes ever more distant, she tosses me the keys, goes around to the other side and climbs in.

"Faster, faster!" she urges, as soon as we're on our way.

"Gabriela, I have to be careful in this traffic. Anyway, we won't be able to see Angelica for a while."

She glares at me.

The receptionist at the desk directs us to the emergency waiting room. Seated beside Gabriela, I try to make conversation, but my words fall to the ground.

At last a young intern approaches us. "We've done X-rays and a cat-scan," he tells us. "No broken bones, but there is a severe concussion. We're hopeful there's no damage to the spine."

"When will she regain consciousness?" Gabriela asks.

"No way of knowing, *Señora,* hopefully within twenty-four hours.

A nurse leads us to the ICU. Angelica lies very still, her face pale as death. An ugly purple bruise stains her forehead.

She makes no response to her mother's tearful pleas.

I take her hand and say a stumbling prayer. When I open my eyes Gabriela is staring out the dark window, her face cold and expressionless.

The nurse returns. "I'm sorry, but you'll have to leave now. Why don't you go home and get some rest? We'll call you if she comes to."

I follow Gabriela to the waiting room. Wordless still, she sits down and reaches for a magazine.

I take the magazine from her hand and kneel before her, my eyes inches from hers. "Gabriela," I whisper, "it's time we talked."

She's staring into my eyes, biting her lip, her face crimson with anger. I'm deeply shaken, I've never seen her like this!

"Look, I'm sorry for what happened. If only I'd known!"

Her lips curl into a bitter little smile. "No, you didn't know, but you thought you did! And I believed you. Because of you, my daughter may be paralyzed for the rest of her life!"

Desperate, I plead with her: "Gabriela, don't shut me out. At a time like this we need each other." I reach for her hand.

She pulls her hand back. "*Andrés* Kelly, I thought I had found a man I could trust. I was wrong. There's nothing for us to talk about."

Conscious of the curious stares of people in the waiting room, I sit down beside her, watching her thumb listlessly through a ragged old *National Geographic.* At last I say, "It's nearly midnight. Let me take you home. Remember, you didn't lock the house, and by now the maids are gone for the weekend."

Sighing, she gets to her feet. "Very well, maybe I'd better go."

At her house, I'm surprised when she says, "Please come in for a moment."

Inside she heads for the kitchen, flipping the light switches as she goes. I follow her as she climbs the steep stairs to the attic. At the top she slams the attic door shut, slips the padlock back into place, secures it, and keys in hand, turns to face me.

"I'll never open this room again! I knew I was making a mistake when I let you talk me into breaking my vow to my father."

"But Gabriela,..."

Gritting her teeth, she pushes me in the chest, and I grab the railing to keep from falling backward.

"Let's go downstairs," she sobs, "there's something I want to show you, then you must leave."

I follow her to her bedroom. She opens a drawer of the ancient armoire and drops in the keys. When she turns she's clutching a small porcelain image of the Virgin of Guadalupe, her eyes brimming.

"In the hospital, while we waited for news about Angie, I kept trying to explain to myself why this terrible thing had happened. Then it came to me: remember, this afternoon I found the key to the attic in the armoire. There in the same drawer," she grimaces as if in pain, "I saw my dear little Virgin, where I had left her months ago. My heart skipped a beat. Mother gave me this statue at First Communion, and ever since it has been my most precious possession. I slept with it next to my cheek when I was a school girl, and it comforted me those long years of mourning a ruined marriage." She kisses it and hugs it to her chest.

"The Virgin was always in a place of honor, here atop the armoire. Then one Sunday I attended Moses Contreras' church and he preached about idolatry. Still in the enthusiasm of my...my conversion, I hurried home, my heart breaking, took down the Virgin and hid her in the drawer. I had not seen her since.

"That's why, when I glimpsed my dear little *madrecita*...so alone and sad...I wanted to press her to my heart and beg her forgiveness. But I knew what you'd say.

"I snatched up the keys and was about to close the drawer when...she catches her breath..."it happened!"

"What happened, Gabriela?

"I saw a tear rolling down the Virgin's cheek!"

I stare at her, my mouth open.

"I know, you think it was my imagination. That's what I thought too, at the moment. But now I know better: the Virgin was weeping because I had betrayed her."

Unable to speak I reach out to touch her arm, but she jumps back quickly, as if I might contaminate her.

(Last night I called Moisés, and he wasn't at home. Moisés, why aren't you here? Something horrible is happening and I don't know what to do!)

I say weakly: "Gabriela, are you forgetting what God has done for you these past months? How your life has changed? How your heart has been filled with a peace you never had before?"

She pushes the drawer shut, and still holding the statue, walks into the living room. "Sit down, *Andres*, and listen carefully." She seats herself on the sofa and I take a chair facing her, my heart pounding, wishing I could sink through the floor.

Kissing the image again, she says, "You have a saying in English, 'Blood is thicker than water'."

I nod dumbly.

"That's what I've learned today. My parents, grandparents and great-grandparents prayed to the Virgin. They taught me that faith in the *Guadalupana* is what makes us true Mexicans."

She sobs. "My brothers were right! They warned me I was going to be punished for abandoning my birthright.

Her voice softens: "*Andrés*, I know you mean well; you're not an evil man like Raul. But you are a *gringo*, so even with your Ph.D. in psychology, you'll never be able to understand the soul of a *mexicana*. I was foolish to think you might. Now I understand I can't trust you…any more than I could trust Raul."

She gets to her feet. "Now go. Please."

I jump up, and before she can retreat, reach out and pull her to me. "Gabriela I love you. I can't let you do this!"

Gently now, she pushes me away, staring at the floor, lips trembling.

I lift her chin with a finger, but she refuses to look at me. "Gabriela, you've said some awful things, things that have hurt me deeply. But I haven't heard you say you no longer love me."

Her voice is just above a whisper: "Please, *Andrés*, go. I'm very tired."

I turn away. "All right, Gabi, whatever you want. But you're wrong about us. God brought us together, and I'm not going to let you go! Sure, I have a lot to learn about Mexico and Mexicans. But I'm trying. Give me a chance!"

Without replying she walks toward the door. "Come on, *Andrés*, I'll open the gate for you…."

How long have I been standing here on the street? The parade has ended and the traffic is inching along to the sound of impatient horn blowing. I head back toward the hospital.

At my car the kid grins and holds out his hand. I give him a second *peso* and climb in behind the wheel, but I'm in no hurry to leave. Where will I go? It's five now, and I've been at the hospital since ten.

It hasn't been a pleasant day! When I arrived this morning Gabriela was seated in the waiting room talking earnestly with her two brothers and their wives. The men came over to stand, one at each side of me, glowering at me.

I had the impression they were about to invite me outside, but Gabriela hurried over, took me by the arm and led me to the other side of the room. "*Andrés*, my brothers are very angry with you. You'd better leave."

I stiffen, clenching my fists. I'm prepared to take on the entire family, right here in the waiting room, if that's what they want.

Gruffly I ask, "Have you seen Angelica?"

"Not yet." She checks her watch. "Visitation is in half an hour. The nurse tells me she had a quiet night, but still hasn't regained consciousness."

"Gabriela," I say, my voice firm, "I care very much about Angie, and whether your family likes it or not, I'm going to stay here until there's some news!"

I find an empty chair, and my back to Gabriela and her family, open my newspaper. I've slept very little, and have to fight the feeling that all this is just a bad dream.

To my surprise Gabriela saves the last ten minutes of visitation for me to accompany her into ICU. Her daughter is still unconscious, but when Gabriela calls her name I'm sure I see a flicker of the eyelashes.

When we return to the waiting room her brothers have left, I suppose to go to their jobs. Her sisters-in-law are in and out, but they never leave Gabriela alone with "the enemy." For them I'm an outsider who has taken advantage of Gabriela's vulnerability. Now that she has come to her senses they're determined I'll not have another opportunity to deceive her.

I turn the key in the ignition. After a day of waiting in vain, not only for a change in Angelica's condition, but for some sign that Gabriela will become again the woman I've known and loved, I'm exhausted. Might as well go home.

CHAPTER 20

▼

A VISIT TO THE BASILICA

"Circle the *Monumento de la Raza*, Doctór, and take Insurgentes. We're not far from the Basilica now."

After the nightmare of the past two days it's good to be with Moisés Contreras. As usual he's in good humor, and I can feel my depression melting away. It was very late last night when I finally got hold of him and confessed my failure at Gabriela's house. And my heartbreak over her rejection.

I had expected him to be critical. Instead, he said, "Doctór, if I had been present I would have done exactly what you did."

"But it was a disaster!"

"Agreed. But why blame yourself? What more could you have done?"

"There's an innocent young woman in the hospital because of me!"

"Shame on you, *hermano*, for pushing her down the stairs!"

In spite of myself, I chuckled.

"No doubt about it", Moisés grumbled, "Satan won this time. But remember, he only won an inning; the game's far from over!"

"But I'm worried sick about Gabriela; I'm afraid we've lost her."

He was silent for a moment. "Maybe you expected too much of her too soon. You know, most Mexicans feel closer to the Mother of God than to the Son of God."

"Really? Why is that?"

"Christ seems so far above them they're sure they'll never quite be able to please him. But the Virgin is Jesus' beloved mother, and just like our own mother, she's patient with us when we make a mistake. And ready to speak a word for us when we've failed her son. So they try to stay on her good side."

"Then it must have taken a lot of faith for Gabriela to pack away that little statue in the bureau drawer."

"Of course it did! And all the time her family was warning her the Virgin was going to punish her for her betrayal."

"So when Angelica fell down the stairs…"

"Gabriela decided her family was right after all!"

"But what am I going to do? I imagine you've already guessed the truth: I love Gabriela. And I know she loves me. Everything was going so well!"

Moisés grunted. "Doctór, you've got to learn how it is here in Mexico: when things are going well, look out, something terrible is about to happen!"

"Is that what you meant when you told me Mexico is under a curse?"

A long pause. "Moises," I said at last, "are you still there?"

"Yes, *hermano*, I was going over my agenda in my mind. Look, I can change plans for tomorrow morning. Can you? It's time for me to take you to where the curse began."

I wonder how many people are unhappy with Moisés this morning for last minute cancellations. As for me, I canceled all my appointments for the week. I've fallen into a dull depression. I'm in no condition to help others until I get my own head straightened out.

"Park here," Moisés says abruptly, "We'll walk the rest of the way to the Basilica."

Dodging traffic, we walk down the narrow, crowded street. The sidewalk is teeming with people, some shopping, some standing around talking animatedly, others waiting at the corner for the next bus. The cool morning air is heavy with the scent of food. We pass a taco stand and next to it a vender is selling fried pig skin garnished with a fiery red sauce. My mouth waters, remembering the "cracklin's" I used to eat at my aunt's farm in Louisiana when I was a kid.

Moisés points ahead to a couple of imposing buildings dominating a broad enclosed plaza. "The old cathedral to the right was constructed in the sixteenth century. A few years ago they put a chain on the door…too many cracks in the ceiling. To the left is the new Basilica, completed about ten years ago."

I'm struck by the contrast between the two churches. The older building is a twin-spired Gothic cathedral, typical of colonial church architecture. The newer one is a strikingly modern structure of handsome gray stone, its bronze roof stained a dirty green by Mexico City's infamous smog.

"This is a good day for a visit," Moisés says, as we enter the gate. "Yesterday would have been impossible, with thousands of pilgrims camped out, filling the square and blocking the streets. But I wish you could have seen the dancers."

"I saw some yesterday in a pilgrimage on Constituyentes."

"You did? And did you understand what was going on?"

I shake my head.

"All that leaping about to the sound of flutes and drums was in honor of a blood-thirsty goddess named Tonantizin."

I stop and stare at him in surprise. "Not the Virgin of Guadalupe?"

"Well, that's what most people think. They don't know that most of the dances were invented by the worshippers of Tonantzin, Quetzal-cóat's mother. He points to a knoll rising behind the ancient cathedral. "That was her home, the hill of Teepeyac. For more than a thousand years pilgrims came here to dance before her shrine. Then the Virgin of Guadalupe appeared and everything changed."

"The Virgin of Guadalupe took the place of Tonantizin?" How did that happen?"

We stop at the entrance of the new basilica. "That's what you're about to see!" He takes my arm and pushes me gently through the open door.

There are only a few people inside, some standing reverently before the altar at the front, others kneeling in the aisles. On the wall above the altar hangs the object of their devotion, a small painting of a dark, pleasant-faced young woman, her head covered by a shawl.

"The miracle that turned Mexico upside down!" Moisés whispers.

"That little painting? What's miraculous about it?"

Several people turn and stare at me. Moisés takes my arm and steers me toward to door. "Sh-h-! While we're climbing to the top of Tepeyac hill I'll explain."

As we walk toward a long stairway spiraling up to a chapel at the crest of the hill, Moisés begins his story...

At daybreak on Saturday, December 9, 1531, Juan Diego, an Aztec peasant, was walking up Tepeyac hill. Suddenly he was startled by the sound of celestial music. Halting, he listened in wonder, imagining that somehow he had been transported to heaven. When the music ended he heard a voice calling to him in Nauhatl, his native tongue: "Juan, dearest of my little children, where are you going?"

Looking up he saw a beautiful young woman standing in a bright white cloud bordered by a rainbow, its colors formed by rays of blazing light.

She said to him: "Dear little son, I love you. I want you to know who I am: I am the ever-virgin Mary, Mother of the true God who gives life and maintains it in existence. He created all things. He is in all places. He is Lord of heaven and earth. I desire a temple at this place where I will show my compassion to your people and to all who sincerely ask my help in their work and in their sorrows. Here I will see their tears; I will console them and they will be at ease.

"So run now to Tenochtitlan and tell the Lord Bishop what you have seen and heard."

Juan Diego ran all the way to Tenochtitlan and described his vision to Bishop Fray Juan de Zumarraga. Skeptical, the Bishop demanded a sign.

On Tuesday, December 12 Juan Diego returned to Tepeyac. The Virgin was waiting for him. She told him to climb to the top of the hill and gather as many roses as he could find. He knew there were no rose bushes on the rocky hill, but he obeyed, and to his amazement found dozens of bright crimson Castillian roses, which he gathered in his burlap apron.

He returned to the bishop. When he unfolded his apron the roses tumbled to the floor. But the Bishop was staring at an even greater miracle: imprinted on the apron, called *ayatl* in Nauhatl, was an image of a beautiful lady exactly as Juan had described her.

We come to the top of the hill and enter the chapel built on the very spot where Juan Diego had his vision of "Our Lady of Guadalupe." On its walls artists have painted brilliant murals depicting the six apparitions of the Virgin.

Outside again, we lean on the balustrade, watching the people below. A poor family walks through the gates, and a wrinkled, white-haired old woman falls to her knees and begins a slow, painful crawl toward the church.

Groaning, Moisés slams a fist against the railing. "God forgive us!"

The grandmother has paused, and one of the family is rearranging the rags tied around her knees.

"What does it mean?" I ask. "What is she doing?"

"They call it a *manda*. Sometime in the past the old lady asked the Virgin for a miracle. Now she's walking on her knees from the gate to the altar to show her appreciation for the granting of her petition."

"And what does the Church say about all this?"

"It depends on whom you ask."

"Let's go." Moisés pushes me gently toward the steps.

"They say the abbot of the Basilica denies that Juan ever existed. On the other hand, Pope John Paul has begun the process of canonizing him. And not even the skeptical abbot would suggest doing away with the adulation of the Virgin. She's a gold mine."

We stop beside a stone pathway leading to a rose garden. Just in front of us the grandmother is dragging herself slowly toward the door of the ornate Cathedral, her wrinkled face twisted with pain. Two of the family, obviously concerned, try to lift her to her feet. She shakes them off, and crossing herself, moves one knee a few inches before stopping again. Behind her splotches of fresh blood stain stones recently swept clean of last night's celebration.

"Come on," I plead, my heart thumping, "let's go around them. I can't stand this." Tears are burning my eyes; I'm overwhelmed by the contrast between the beautiful murals I saw in the chapel and the ugliness of the scene I'm witnessing now.

As we head across the plaza toward the gate, Moisés spits out: "At least, when I was a disciple of Quetzalcóatl, I knew what I was doing. These people are worshipping the Feathered Serpent and don't know it."

He stops suddenly in front of me, blocking my path, and hands on my shoulders, warns me: "Doctór, when you see anything attractive in Mexico's popular religion, scratch the surface and demons will pop out!"

When we're back on the street, I take a deep breath. It's as if we've entered another world. "Why doesn't the church stop all this?" I ask.

"Maybe they will sometime in the future. More and more priests are opening the Bible to the people. But it's hard to break a commitment to the past. The Virgin of Guadalupe burst upon Mexico at a critical time and offered the hierarchy a way to become a successful church. The hierarchy must have believed it was providential."

We claim a couple of stools at a taco stand, and while we sip Cokes, waiting for our orders to arrive, Moisés continues his history lesson:

When Juan Diego appeared before Bishop Fray Juan de Zumarraga, the new kingdom that Hernán Cortés and his soldiers had carved out with bloody swords was only a dozen years old. The *conquistadores* had leveled the *Templo Mayor* in Tenochtitlan. They also destroyed all the shrines they could find in the countryside, including Tonantzin's temple here in Tepeyac. In the footsteps of the soldiers came Dominican missionaries zealously proclaiming their faith.

But the people resisted; there were few converts. When reports of Juan Diego's vision began circulating, the clergy scorned it at first. Then the Virgin appeared to Juan Diego's sick uncle and told him her name.

That changed everything.

Moisés takes a *taco al pastor* and crams it with a rich sauce of chile peppers, onions and tomatoes. Taking a huge bite, he challenges me: "Guess what her name was."

"The Virgin of Guadalupe, of course."

"No, that's her Spanish name, they gave that to her later. But it wasn't what the people called her at first. Remember, Juan and his people spoke Nauhatl. So the Virgin had given him her name in his native tongue. When the priests heard it, it must have rocked them back on their heels!"

"Why?"

"Because the Virgin told Juan her name was *Maria Tecoatlaxopeuh*. That name means: 'The one who crushed the serpent'!"

"Quetzalcóatl!"

"You guessed it! Can you imagine what happened? The news spread like wildfire: María, Virgin Mother of God, had appeared to one of their own at the sacred hill of Tepeyac and announced that she was taking the place of Tonantzin and her son the Feathered Serpent."

"It must have looked like a Godsend to the Church!"

"And to the peasants too. Their king Moctezuma had been defeated and their gods dethroned. A powerful new goddess was exactly what they needed. Within six years nine million people were baptized into the Church.

"The Virgin of Guadalupe became the guardian of Mexico's soul. During the war of independence against Spain three centuries later the patriots marched under the banner of the Virgin. Emilio Zapata's agrarian reform movement in your country had the *Guadalupana* as its rallying point. And now you see shrines to the Virgin everywhere: in homes, on the sidewalks, in stores."

I'm silent for a long moment, trying to digest all I've seen and heard today. Thinking aloud, I say, "But the Virgin of Guadalupe didn't really crush the serpent, did she?"

"No. Her takeover provided the peasants an attractive alternative to giving up their old gods. Instead of abandoning them, all they had to do was baptize them with Christian names."

The man behind the taco stand has been listening, and now he frowns and stares at us. I elbow Moises and dart my eyes toward our unfriendly host. "Let's get out of here!" I mumble.

As we walk the two blocks to the car I'm silent, lost in thought. My heart is a heavy stone. Gabriela, why? Why can't you see what's behind your beloved little statue?

Seated in the car, I pose the question to Moisés. He answers with another question: "Doctór, have you seen many monuments to the Resurrection here in Mexico?"

"No, I haven't. But I've seen a lot of statues of Jesus on the cross, covered with blood, a terribly sad expression on his face."

"They call him *El Cristo Limosnero,* the beggar Christ! Not an inspiring male role model, is it? Maybe that's why so few men here take their religion seriously. On the other hand, the model for women is the beautiful, compassionate Virgin, grieving over the Son who has broken her heart."

A light flickers on in my mind. Starting up the car, I ease out into the traffic.

Moises is quiet, aware, I suspect, of the struggle for understanding churning within me.

We're almost back to *Monumento de la Raza* when I say thoughtfully, "So I failed Gabriela, and she turned to the Virgin for comfort."

"A lesson you can be sure she learned from her mother...and her grandmother...when their men failed them. You see, Doctór, the macho syndrome has bequeathed to Mexican men the role of breaking their women's hearts. You can bet on it that Gabriela's father had lovers. And that she heard her mother complain about it a thousand times.

"And that her mother's sons learned from their father. And that their wives fuss at them and cry about their infidelities—just like their mother did.

Slowly it's making sense to me. "And Gabriela married, and..."

"And found herself repeating the role of her mother. But all the time, the Virgin was there to comfort her. She didn't like what was happening to her, but at least it was familiar.

"The role of the wife and mother is to suffer, to be a noble martyr just like the Virgin. That's why many Mexican women are vaguely uncomfortable with happiness. When things seem to be going right she intuits that something must be wrong, because that's not real life!"

I grunt in pain, as if Moises has punched me in the stomach. "Are telling me that Gabriela was...uncomfortable with the happiness she found in her new faith...and with me?"

Moisés shakes his head vigorously. "No, I'm not saying that. But she must have been wondering how long it would last. Here in Mexico, when a person comes to know Christ, it's important they begin immediately a maturing process, or they'll fall back into the old patterns they inherited from their families. That's why a new Christian needs to become part of a family of faith. Gabriela didn't do that, did she?"

"No, she didn't. And I worried about it."

"Maybe you understand now why our worship services are so jubilant. People need to get together at least once a week and celebrate the victory we have in Christ."

A week later I take Continental Flight 205 for Houston. Angelica is home now, but every time I've called the maids have told me the *Señora* is out.

It will be good to spend the Christmas holidays with my daughters. Victoria has agreed to take the week off from her job in Austin to be with us. I suspect she and Margaret are planning a blitzkrieg to persuade me not to return to Mexico. After what's happened, that may not be as hard as they think.

CHAPTER 21

▼

A DISTURBING VISIT HOME

"You're thinking about leaving us, aren't you?" Rebeca reaches across the table and touches my hand, her soft brown eyes clouded with concern.

Laying aside my slice of pizza I give her hand a squeeze. "If I don't leave, Rebeca, you'll be one of the main reasons."

Shivering, I button my sweater against the cold and pull the little electric heater closer. Since returning from Houston a couple of days ago I haven't been able to get warm. I'd complained about Houston's chilly, damp weather, but compared to what I'm feeling now Houston was Oahu!

Half an hour ago I sent Rebeca out for pizza rather than shiver through lunch in a cold, drafty restaurant. Besides, I treasure any opportunity to spend a few moments alone with my best friend. She's already squeezed the truth out of me about Gabriela, and listened, quite fearfully, I thought, as I described the peaceful days I enjoyed back home with my family.

I had only one client this morning and I'll have just one this afternoon. Everybody who can, Rebeca tells me, has left Mexico City for Acapulco or Zihuatanejo. This city's smog is always at its worst in January; I'm tired of watching the TV weather men describe the "atmospheric inversion" that dooms us to putting up with a contamination more than double the United Nations' emergency index. This year it's so bad the schools have extended their end-of-the-year vacation until February. Everyone remaining in the city seems to have a runny nose or inflamed eyes. Rebeca musters a smile. "I missed you while you were in Houston. Did you miss me?"

"Of course I did. You've got me spoiled; I couldn't make it without you to keep my life in order." My chuckle becomes all at once a hard knot in my throat, strangling me: Gabriela! Why can't you be as uncomplicated as my sweet friend Rebeca? Ever since meeting you six months ago I've been on an emotional roller coaster. And your face keeps surfacing in my mind at the most inopportune moments—like now, when I want to give all my attention to my friend.

I haven't worked up the courage to call Gabriela since my return. How much longer am I going to put up with this? The two weeks I spent in Kingwood reminded me that the option of returning to the orderly, peaceful existence I once knew is still very much alive.

When I got home Margaret had the guest room ready...our bedroom, mine and Mary's.

Nothing had been touched since my short Thanksgiving visit. Except for one addition: they had gone to the company where my furniture is stored and rescued my worn blue recliner.

When I sank down into it and closed my eyes I was flooded with memories of Mary cuddled in my lap, her head on my shoulder, while we watched the Rockets playing in the Summit or the Oilers getting mauled in the Astrodome. It wasn't fair; with the tragedy of Gabriela so fresh on my conscience I felt terribly vulnerable. Margaret and my grandson Jeff were standing nearby, and I was sure they couldn't miss the pain in my face.

Margaret twisted the knife: "You know, Daddy, you're going to have to decide about your furniture. It smelled so musty I'm sure some things are beginning to mildew."

She was right; Mexican immigration had made it clear they weren't going to allow me to import my furniture. In their obtuse bureaucratic way they let me know they were aware I wasn't a simple tourist. I got the idea that for the present they were allowing me to get by with it, but that I'd better watch my step because at any moment an official could appear at my door with a deportation order.

But my ex-partners…what a contrast! When I visited their offices the day before Christmas they charmed me with fruit cake and coffee and friendly smiles. I found myself confessing to them that sometimes, sitting with a client in Mexico City, trying to comprehend the Mexican soul, I felt like a visitor from Mars.

"So," Harold, the Senior Partner said, and I suspected he had rehearsed the words with his colleagues, "is it possible your sabbatical will not be extended indefinitely?"

"My sabbatical?" A big gulp of coffee went down the wrong way and I was seized with a fit of coughing. I managed to protest: "Who said anything about a sabbatical? I told you…"

"Let me be frank, Andrew. We're asking you…" smiling, he reached out and touched my arm, "no, we're begging you…come on back home where you belong. You can't imagine the vacuum you've left. The new man who took over your suite was competent enough, but he just didn't fit in. We were relieved when he moved out a couple of weeks ago."

"You mean…?"

Carl, the youngest of the partners interrupted. "We decided not to look for a replacement until after we'd had a chance to talk with you. Look,"…pulled his chair closer…"we know it was tough losing your wife. But it's been a year now, and…"

I was feeling uncomfortable. In a moment somebody was going to mention post-traumatic shock and suggest we thumb through the DSM Manual for a possible diagnosis!

I pushed back my chair. "Look, guys, it's been great, but they're expecting me at home."

Getting up, Harold laid a hand on my shoulder. "Think about it, Andrew. And give us a call before you leave."

Victoria blew in that night. She hadn't been able to come for Thanksgiving, so she was loaded with questions. Lawyer-style she sat across from me at the kitchen table puffing on a cigarette, conducting her inquisition…about my practice, my office, my apartment, my lifestyle.

At last she got up, poured herself a third cup of coffee, and turning suddenly, as if to catch me off guard, asked, "What about your romantic life, Daddy? Are you dating?"

I gaped at her, trying to formulate an answer that wouldn't require the baring of my soul.

Margaret, who had been sitting at the end of the table, more an observer than a participant, broke in: "Daddy, have you seen any more of that lady you met on your trip last August?

I could feel my face reddening. "Well, as a matter of fact…"

Snuffing out a cigarette in her coffee cup, Victoria grinned and winked at me: "You old Romeo! Show us a picture!"

As they passed around the photograph I watched their faces. Victoria looked disappointed; I was sure she had hoped for a wrinkled hag with a couple of teeth missing. Margaret looked worried. Tom, Margaret's husband, who had just walked in the door from a game of golf, whistled in admiration. "Wow, where'd you find her?"

I made my description of our relationship as spare as possible: Gabriela had come to see me because she was working through a divorce. They were not to get any ideas; we'd had some meals together, but it probably wouldn't go any further. The more we got to know each other the more we realized how different our backgrounds were.

Two-year-old Jeff was pulling at my pants leg. I put him on my lap and wrapped my arms around him. At the airport he'd refused to come to me, and on the way home had stood on the seat studying me, as if trying to convince himself we'd met before. Now, looking at his fresh little face, I told myself we'd probably end up being friendly strangers if I remained in Mexico. Was that the kind of grandfather I wanted to be? Was it worth it?

Christmas morning, after we'd opened our presents, I excused myself, put on my running gear and walked half a block to Kingwood's lush green belt. The air was crisp and clean, the early morning sun was filtering through the pines and squirrels were already out seeing what they could scare up for Christmas dinner. I shifted into an easy jog. People I met smiled and said good morning. Life was so much simpler here, running in Mexico City's Chapultepec Park I'd never dream of speaking to people I passed.

I picked up my pace. What did I have in Mexico to keep me from coming back home?

There was Moisés. I'd never met anyone quite like him. If God had prophets in the Twentieth Century, Moisés certainly fit the job description. And he was convinced God had chosen me to be a key player in Mexico's destiny. Heady stuff! I wasn't sure just how much I believed him, but suppose he was right? On the other hand, was I ready to bet my entire future on someone else's opinion of what I ought to do?

I was running comfortably now, breathing easily, feeling the euphoria that always kicked in about this time, making it an ideal moment to tackle tough problems...

I remembered the moment of strange joy that August night when I jumped to my feet, ran to the window and shouted "Yes!" to the entire world. That was the closest ever in my life to actually hearing God's voice. Would that experience qualify as a divine call? Mary was always the spokesman for logic in our marriage; what would she have said?

Would she have warned me of the danger of imagining a divine encounter as an antidote for my desperation?

And then there was Rebeca. The thought of her affection for me, absolutely pure and unselfish, refreshed me like a Galveston beach breeze on a sticky July day. Most of the university students I stood before each Sunday morning were a lot like her, motivated by a disingenuous idealism, eager to hear words of hope for themselves and their beloved *patria*, ready to give themselves to anybody providing that hope.

Gabriela! My toe hit a root and I stumbled, almost falling. A passerby hesitated for a moment, perhaps wondering if a boomer was about to have a heart attack.

I picked up my pace. What had made me fall in love with Gabriela? I'd been attracted to clients in the past, but had always been able to talk myself out of it. Of course, Mary was always there, so any temptation had little hope of surviving more than a few seconds.

Mary! Life was so simple with her. I remembered last Christmas when I returned from my run and she was seated at the kitchen table reading her Bible. She welcomed me with a quiet, affectionate smile and we sat sipping our coffee and talking about plans for the day.

But Mary was gone. And now there was Gabriela, intelligent, attractive, in love with me and my God. Obviously my counseling had done little to eradicate the spiritual cancer eating away at her soul. How else could I explain this contradiction: loving me…and welcoming whatever excuse to push me away?

I had arrived at the lake, the halfway point on my favorite four-mile run. I could make out early-morning golfers on the other side, teeing off at the first hole. Slowing to a walk, I checked my pulse; a perfect aerobic 130. And I wasn't even breathing hard! Surprising how easy it was to run at sea level after becoming accustomed to Mexico City's mile-high atmosphere. I turned aside and flopped down on a wooden bench beneath a huge oak.

In that instant, with the clarity of sudden insight, I knew: God had placed Gabriela in my pathway as his signpost. If she was capable of loving me, of being my partner for life, Mexico would become my home. If not…

The next morning I called my ex-partners and asked them to hold the door open until the end of January.

CHAPTER 22

▼

GABRIELA SAYS NO

"Don't give up, Doctór, we're going to find her!" Rebeca is seated across the desk from me, chin set, her big brown eyes bright with determination.

I'm trying to believe her, but a week has passed since my return and I still haven't been able to contact Gabriela. I call every day, a maid answers and tells me the *Señora* is away on vacation and they have no idea when she'll return.

"I hope you're right, Rebeca. I've got to talk to Gabriela and persuade her to change her mind."

"And if she doesn't?"

"I don't know what I'll do!"

"I'm afraid *I* know. And I'm not going to let it happen!" She reaches for the telephone.

"Who are you going to call? Not Gabriela's house!"

She wrinkles her nose at me. "Just wait. You'll see."

"Hello, is this the residence of la Señora Gabriela Mancini?"

"Let me speak to the *Señora*, please. This is *Telégrafos de Mexico*. I have an urgent cable for her."

"No, I cannot give you the message, I must speak to her personally."

Rebeca places a hand over the receiver. "If she's home, she'll come to the phone. Ever hear of anybody not being curious about an unexpected telegram? And if she's out of town...just watch me!"

.... "Oh, I see, she's in Ixtapa. Then please give me the name of the hotel."

.... (Indignantly) "Look, *muchacha,* I don't care what the *Señora* told you. This is official business of *Telégrafos de México* and we have a telegram from Paris that has to do with the *Señora's* company. She'll be very angry if she doesn't receive the message...(Hand covering the mouthpiece) "She's talking to someone, probably the other maid... "All right, let me write that down. Hotel El Presidente, room 304. Thank you very much."

The next day I'm lying on the beach in front of my hotel in Ixtapa, baking in the warm Pacific sun. But the sun does nothing for the chill in my heart; have I made a mistake, rushing here to confront Gabriela?

Yesterday Rebeca had no such misgivings. As soon as she hung up she insisted on calling a travel agency and reserving a room in a hotel next to Gabriela's. So here I am, at the Ixtapa Sheraton, surprised by my daring...and feeling a bit foolish. What do I do now, go knock on her door and demand a reconciliation?

I shouldn't have come! Gabriela came here to avoid me; what am I going to accomplish by forcing the issue?

Pulling myself up in the beach chair I bury my feet in the warm sand and gaze out over the quiet Pacific surf. So peaceful! And a beautiful day. I have to pinch myself to remember it's January here in Ixtapa, just like in cold, smoggy Mexico City. The travel agent congratulated me on my choice of Ixtapa. Much more tranquil here, he told me, than in Acapulco or Cancun. Well, then, I'll just enjoy it. I'll forget that next door is the woman I love, holding my destiny in her hands. If God in his infinite mercy plans to use Rebeca's subterfuge to bring us together—

"Doctór Kelly, I knew it!"

I jump, almost falling out of my chair. Standing beside me in a stunning yellow two-piece bathing suit, her long golden hair reflecting the bright afternoon sun, is Angelica.

Bending, she hugs my neck, then pulls up one of the reclining chairs scattered about under the *palapa*. "After *Mamá* made the fourth call to Paris this morning and no one owned up to sending a cable, I said to myself, 'It's Doctór Kelly. I knew he wouldn't give up so easily!' So I came down to check out the beach. Of course I didn't tell *Mamá*. She's still trying to convince herself she hates you."

Angie's friendly smile leaves me speechless. The last time I saw her she was lying pale and unconscious in a hospital bed, and I was feeling like the worst criminal on earth.

At last I blurt out: "Angie, you look great! Are you all right?"

Jumping up, she stands on tiptoes, hands on hips. "Look at me: no scars! Better than new!"

"And you're not angry with me?"

"Oh, Doctór, don't be silly, why should I be mad at you? How were you to know *abuelita's* spooky old attic would be filled with *murciélagos*? If anyone was to blame, it was *Mamá*, for leaving it sealed up so long!"

"And…your mother?"

She sits down again, her pretty face darkening. "*Mamá*? *Mamá's* something else!"

"Does she ever mention me?"

She lays a hand on my wrist. "Doctór Kelly, I'm worried about her. She's gone back to being that angry, depressive woman she was years ago after she found out about *Papá's* other family. And no, she doesn't talk about you. And I don't dare. But I can tell she thinks of you constantly."

I say quietly, trying to keep my voice from breaking: "I love your mother very much."

"And she loves you, I'm sure of it! After your arrival in September she was a different person. Before, her work seemed to be the only thing that had meaning for her. Then you became the center of her life, and it was wonderful seeing her so happy. But now…" Leaving her chair, she comes and sits beside me, taking both of my hands in hers. "Tell me, Doctór, where are you having supper tonight?"

"I hadn't thought about it. Why?"

"Why don't you eat at our hotel? Say about nine. And I'll see to it that Mamá and I just happen to pass by your table."

I stare out across the still blue water, conflicting emotions churning inside me. "I don't know, Angie. She'll be very unhappy when she sees me."

Angelica tosses her head. "Then why did you come here? I thought you wanted to see *Mamá*?"

"Well, yes, but…" Dropping her hands I shake a fist at the bright blue sky.

"Then don't get cold feet now. Just be thankful you didn't fool me with that silly telegram trick." She jumps to her feet. "I've got to go, Preston is waiting for me."

"Your boyfriend?"

"No, Preston's a Canadian student I met a few days ago. Nice guy." She turns and calls over her shoulder, "Don't forget. Nine o'clock."

Sitting nervously in the dining room of the El Presidente sipping *jugo the piña* in mineral water, I wonder what I've gotten myself into, taking the advice of two strong-willed kids young enough to be my daughters; first Rebeca, now Angie. I smile. I guess I ought to be thankful they're on my side!

My back toward the lobby, I'm hoping that when Gabriela enters she won't see me.

The waiter has just poured a refill when I hear Angelica's voice: "No, *Mamá*, let's go a little farther so we can see the beach from our table."

A moment later they're passing me. Turning suddenly, Angelica exclaims, "Doctór Kelly, I can't believe my eyes!"

Stumbling to my feet, I find myself just two steps from Gabriela. She's dressed in white linen shorts and a pale peach blouse, her dark hair pulled back in a short pony tail. The bright crimson of her lipstick contrasts with the pale, sullen face, wide eyes staring at me. My heart gives a flip flop.

Mustering a smile, I take a step toward them. "*Encantado!*"

Angie moves to meet me and gives me a warm *abrazo*, but by the time she draws away Gabriela has stepped back, the color rising in her cheeks.

She opens her mouth, swallows, and when she speaks her voice is low and cold: "So! you're the one behind that bogus cable!"

"Gabriela," I move around the table, "I had to see you!"

Tears spring to her eyes, and for a moment her face softens. But when I reach out for her, she stiffens and draws back. "*Señor*, I told you before: whatever was between us is over. Please, leave me in peace."

"Gabriela, we must talk! Angelica has forgiven me, why can't you?" (People are staring)

She turns and glares at her daughter. "So you knew he was here! I thought I could trust you."

Turning on her heel she stalks away. Angelica throws up her hands, and shrugging, follows her mother, calling, after her. As they disappear, I feel the walls of the dining room crumbling around me.

Hours later I'm awakened by the ringing of the phone. "Doctór, I'm downstairs in the lobby. *Mamá* finally dropped off. Sorry to disturb you, but I didn't want to leave without another chance to talk."

"Leave? Are you checking out?"

"I'm afraid so. Mother notified the desk we'll be taking the noon flight back to Mexico City. May I come over and have breakfast with you in the morning?"

"Please do! How about 7:30?"

"Perfect. See you then."

I roll over and look at my clock: two A.M. Getting up, I throw on a robe and open the balcony door. A crescent moon is painting dark shadows on the receding tide...A somber commentary on my life!

I'm up until dawn, pacing back and forth, pleading with God to explain to me how a beautiful dream could have turned into such a nightmare. Did I just imagine it was God bringing me to Mexico and giving me Gabriela?

Angelica is nursing a *piña colada* when I enter the dining room next morning. I'm surprised to see a smoking cigarette in the ash tray. I know I shouldn't be, the Marlboro man seems to have won the hearts of most university students here in Mexico.

Rising to meet me, she brushes my cheek with a kiss. "I shouldn't have called you so late, I can see you didn't sleep much."

I pull out a chair. "I was afraid your mother might not let you come."

She frowns and picks up her cigarette. "Please, Doctór, I'm not a child! And anyway, *Mamá's* still asleep. She took a couple of pills last night. Been taking a lot of them lately." A long pull on her cigarette: "Why does she have to be so stupid!"

"She must love you a lot, the way she reacted when you got hurt"

"*Mami* and I have always been very close; even more so since my little brother's death. I guess we're more like sisters than mother and daughter."

I wait while the waitress fills my big mug with thick black coffee. "I guess I shouldn't blame your mother. First she loses her mother and father. Then her husband, then her little son. And suddenly, there you are, unconscious on the floor at the foot of the stairs." I reach for my cup. "It must have been...how do you say it here?"

"*El colmo.*"

"That's it, the last straw."

"But I'm all right now. What does she hope to gain, driving away the man she loves?"

"She seems to believe it's either me or her Virgin. If she'd just let me explain. I believe in the Virgin, too. Not exactly as she does, maybe...or you...but—"

Angelica is quiet for a moment, studying her menu. At last she lets it drop to the table. "Look, Doctór, you need to understand something about our family: we've never been very religious. That's why I wasn't surprised by *Mamá's* change about a year ago. As for me, I'm not sure how I feel about the story of Juan Diego and the Virgin of Guadalupe." Shrugging, she grinds out her cigarette in the ashtray. "I guess the same way I feel about the *ninos heroes.* You've heard the story, haven't you? That when the American army besieged the military academy on Chapultepec hill in 1846 the cadets wrapped themselves in the Mexican flag, shouted '*Viva México*' and jumped off a precipice. A lot of students think it's a fable. As for me, it doesn't matter whether the story's true or not; believing it is a part of what it means to be a Mexican."

She lights another cigarette. "And I suspect *Mamá* feels the same way about the Virgin of Guadalupe."

The waiter interrupts. After he scurries off, I say: "Bet your mother's sleeping with her little Virgin hugged up to her chest right now!"

She nods, smiling wryly. "You're right."

"Why has she made such an issue of it, Angie? It's driving me crazy!"

She doesn't answer. When she reaches for her drink I can see her hand is shaking.

"Doctór Kelly, do you interpret dreams?"

Surprised at the shift in our conversation, I say cautiously, "Well, sometimes, when it's necessary."

"I'm scared. That's really why I wanted to talk to you this morning. I was afraid it might be my last chance to...to ask you what it means...this hideous dream I've been having."

"*Servidos, Señores.*" The smiling waiter places our breakfast before us; for me scrambled eggs and bacon, for Angie a chicken salad sandwich. (I've stopped being surprised at what Mexicans consume for breakfast!)

When he has gone, Angelica continues. "As you can imagine, there in the hospital, when I came out of the coma, I recalled nothing about what happened that day on the stairs. Then one night a week or so after I got out of the hospital I asked *Mamá* to help me remember. She reconstructed the story for me. When I went to bed that night I lay for a long time, thinking about what she had told me, trying to remember. At last I dropped off to sleep. And suddenly, in my dreams, I was reliving what had happened: climbing the stairs behind you and *Mamá*…seeing the attic door open…the small black cloud of hideous, grimacing bats…screaming, raising my arms to beat them off…feeling myself tipping backwards…reaching for the railing…then…" Angelica, about to take a bite, puts down her sandwich, squeezing her eyes shut "…then that same horrible ghost that had appeared on my apartment stairs materialized just above me, glaring at me, reaching out toward me, pushing at my chest, sending me tumbling down the stairs."

I drop my fork and stare at her, my skin prickling. "What a gruesome nightmare!"

"Guess what: the next night I had the same dream." She takes a long, shuddering breath. "Now every time I go to bed I'm scared to death I'll see that ghost…either in my dreams, or coming down the stairs at the foot of my bed!"

Reaching again for her sandwich, she says, eyes averted,"Doctór Kelly, Mamá has told me about your class for university students. Would you mind if I came one Sunday morning?"

My head is spinning. "Mind? I'd be delighted. But…"

For the first time she smiles. "Funny, isn't it? My mother, your faithful disciple, becomes a rebel. And her rebel daughter wants to become your disciple!"

I smile at her. "I must admit, I'm overwhelmed."

"Let me explain. *Mamá* talked to me a lot in the last year about her faith, but I wasn't interested. I'd been turned off on religion a long time ago. I couldn't stand the fanaticism of my grandparents and my aunts. And anyway, I was so involved in my studies and my *noviazgo* I didn't have time for anything else.

"But ever since that horrible demon appeared in my apartment I've been afraid. She bites her lip. "Then, that terrifying fall!

"As I was slowly regaining consciousness I had the strangest premonition God was going to say something to me. So when the dream came I really wasn't surprised."

She lights another cigarette. "Crazy words, huh, coming from Angelica, the classic agnostic sophomore! I made the mistake of telling one of my professors about the dream. He laughed and accused me of falling asleep smoking pot. What do *you* say, Doctór Kelly? If God is behind my dream, what is he trying to tell me?"

I reach for her hand. "whatever else he may be saying, dear Angie, you can be sure of this: he's telling you he loves you...very much!"

Late that afternoon I take a fifteen minute taxi ride to Zihuatanejo, a quaint port city that was centuries old before Ixtapa became a gleam in the developers' eyes. After a meal of red snapper *a la veracruzana I* walk the streets, feeling desperately lonely...a lot like I felt the first weeks after Mary's death. Stopping at a corner news stand I purchase a copy of *The News,* Mexico's English newspaper.

"Your change, *Señor.*"

"I...I..."

I'm staring at the newspaper, unable to answer.

"Are you all right, *Señor?*" The man is staring at me, eyebrows raised.

I put my hand out for the change. Still mesmerized by what I saw in the paper, I drag my feet far enough to lean against the wall of a little adobe restaurant. My heart is pounding. I look again at the date on the newspaper: January 16, 1987. I take a deep breath: exactly one year ago today I lost Mary!

Somehow I get back to my hotel. I spend most of the night half asleep, half awake, sunk in a grieving stupor. Today I've relived the tragedy of twelve months ago. The one woman in the world who might have filled the void left by my beloved Mary has made it clear she wants nothing more to do with me!

I'm desolate; an entire year of my life has been wasted. Sitting on the balcony I stare blankly at the tiny lights of small fishing boats anchored far out in the bay. I feel like one of those lights, a tiny spark swallowed up in the darkness.

Finally I shuffle back inside, fall upon the bed and drop into a fitful sleep.

Awaking at eight I dial Aeromexico. No answer. I try again. On the third try they answer and assign me a seat on the late afternoon flight to Mexico City.

CHAPTER 23

▼

GOD SENDS A WARRIOR

Seated at the breakfast table, I find myself smiling at the monotonous drone coming from the scarred old yellow refrigerator. The first few weeks I lived here it got on my nerves, now it's the absent-minding humming of an old friend.

I check my watch: nine forty-five. In five minutes my colleagues in Houston will be closing out their first counseling sessions of the day. I'll try to hook up with them before they get occupied with their second round of clients. No use waiting any longer; might as well call and accept their offer.

Getting up, second cup of coffee in hand, I walk slowly into the living room and ease myself down into the comfortable old easy chair next to the telephone. I'm going to miss this apartment! That painting above the sofa of Nineteenth-Century Colonia Roma, for example; it's become a part of my life. So much so I can picture Maximilliano and his Empress Carlotta seated across from me on the sofa sipping a cup of manzanilla tea.

Don't get sentimental, Andrew! Remember the bargain you made with God back in Kingwood: that if Gabriela changed her attitude it would be a sign you should remain in Mexico City. If not…

I reach for the telephone.

To my surprise, I'm dialing my office. What's the matter with me? Rebeca won't be there, I gave her the week off.

"Good morning, office of Andrés Kelly."

"Rebeca! What are you doing at the office?"

"Doctór Kelly! Are you calling from Ixtapa?"

"No, I'm home. I decided yesterday there was no point in staying any longer."

I hear the disappointment in her voice: "So...it didn't work out."

"It was a disaster! But hey, what are you doing in the office?"

"Oh, I just came here because I needed a peaceful place to do my home work. But guess what: there's somebody here waiting for you."

"But why? I told you I'd be out the rest of the week."

"I know, that's what I informed this lady when she phoned yesterday. But she showed up ten minutes ago, insisting you'd call before the day was out. And she was right! Strange."

Since waking this morning I've had all the enthusiasm of a corpse, but now I suddenly feel a warm flush of excitement. "And she's there with you now?"

"She stepped out just a moment ago; said she was going across the street to Liverpool for a snack. But she left instructions: when you called I was to tell you she'd be right back. Can you imagine?"

I frown. "Is she some kind of a witch?"

Rebeca chuckles. "She looks more like an agent for Avon: fiftiesh, well-groomed. And she has an accent. German, I think. At least her name sounds German—Gelda Lohman."

"Did she say anything about her problem?"

Rebeca groans. "Oh you're the one who has the problem, according to her. Says God told her you need her help."

I'm tempted to hang up, the woman sounds psychotic!

"Are you still there, Doctór?"

But what if God really has spoken to her?

"Shall tell I her to come back Monday?"

Suddenly I'm smiling; so somebody wants to help *me*! "No, I'll be right over."

I reach for my coat.

My hand is on the front door when I remember my call to Houston.... Well, what's the hurry? I promised them an answer by the end of the month; I've still got a couple of weeks.

The woman seated in the waiting room, handsome, large-boned, rises to meet me, hand extended. Penetrating blue eyes light up a square, intelligent face. Her straight blonde hair is cropped just below the ears.

"I'm Gelda Lohman, Dr. Kelly. I appreciate your receiving me this morning. Rebeca told me you were on vacation, but the Lord insisted I see you immediately." Her voice reminds me of the wakeup calls my mom employed to bounce me out of bed when I was a kid.

I return her gaze, unable to break away from the unblinking Danube-blue eyes locked onto mine. I don't know what I had expected, but certainly not this business-like woman at the orders of an exigent divine CEO!

As I usher her into my office, I realize I've neglected speaking to my secretary. I turn. "Good morning, Rebeca."

Standing at her desk, eyebrows raised, Rebeca gives me a smiling thumbs up.

Seated across from me, Gelda Lohman immediately gets down to the business that has brought her to my office: "Doctór, you remember Rosario?"

"She visited me on one occasion. You're a friend of hers?"

"We both attend a weekly interdenominational Bible study." She pauses, as if choosing carefully her next words. "At our prayer time two days ago Rosario mentioned that her husband Wilbert will be coming to see you."

"Is that right? I'd been wondering about him."

"She told us he'd been putting off calling for an appointment, but he'd promised her he'd do it before the end of the month." She pauses again, staring out the window, inspecting the gray January sky. Then her eyes return to mine. "I wonder, Doctór, if you are aware of the importance of his visit?"

Now it's my turn to look away, unsure of how I should react. Should I encourage Gelda Lohman's comments on the problems of one of my clients? And is she questioning my interest in Rosario and her husband? There's an edge of irony in my answer: "It's good of you to want to help your friend with her marriage problems."

She frowns. "I'm not here to meddle in Rosario's affairs." Leaning forward, she lays a hand on my arm. "But when Rosario mentioned Wilbert's appointment with you something happened: the Lord told me I should come see you and offer my help."

She withdraws her hand, but there's a warm feeling where she touched me.

Now a smile softens the corners of her lips. "I must make a confession: the Lord told me you need my help, but I haven't the least idea why. I only know it has something to do with Rosario's husband, Wilbert."

I'm beginning to feel uncomfortable. What does this woman expect me to say?

Her cool eyes are studying me. After a moment she says, "Forgive me, Doctór, I can understand your reserve, you know nothing about me." She takes a deep breath and settles back in her chair. "Would it help if I told you something about myself?"

"I'd appreciate that." I'm relieved to have a respite; twenty peaceful years with my modest Mary has made me impatient with pushy women. But we do have something in common:

"I have the impression that, like me, you were not born in Mexico How long have you been in this country?"

"Since I was eighteen. I spent my childhood surviving the second World War. Afterward, Europe was in such a mess I decided I'd do my university studies in America. I was doubtful how a German might be received in your country, so I applied to the National University here and was accepted."

A courageous woman! "You have an excellent command of Spanish."

"Thank you. I consider myself Mexican now. In the past thirty years I became a citizen, married a Mexican national and raised three beautiful children."

She pauses. "Any more questions?"

For the first time I smile. This woman, whoever she is, is worthy of my respect! "You say God told you I need your help, but you have no idea why. Neither have I. Where do we go from here?"

The intercom buzzes. "Doctór, are you ready for coffee? I've just made a fresh pot."

"Yes, please." Any excuse for a time out!

Rebeca helps us with sugar and cream while we chat about the contamination, the damp, penetrating cold and the abominable traffic.

When the door closes behind Rebeca, Gelda settles back in her chair, and cup in hand, and asks me: "Doctór, do you believe in the gifts of the Spirit?"

"I'm learning. I'm afraid I heard very little about such things before coming to Mexico."

"I can sympathize with you. I was raised by pious Lutheran parents who apparently had never read the twelfth chapter of First Corinthians. I still call myself a Lutheran, but I'm afraid my church in Germany would feel uncomfortable with me, because the Holy Spirit and his gifts are very important to me now." She takes a sip of coffee, and setting down the cup, imprisons me again with those astute blue eyes. "Especially since I discovered the Spirit has equipped me with the gift of intercession."

A small bell pings in my mind…there's something I should remember…what is it?…. Feeling disoriented, groping for words, I stutter: "Intercession…is…is one of…of the gifts of the Spirit? But aren't we all supposed to pray for one another?"

"We are, Doctór. Just as we're all responsible for serving others and doing the work of evangelism. But in the same way God has given to some a special gift for service and to others a gift for evangelism...so also some receive a special gift of God's grace for intercession."

"Are you saying you have come to...to pray for me?"

"I have come to offer myself as your intercessor."

Why this discomfiting feeling?...like the frustration I have when I can't remember a name, or a date, or something important I'm supposed to do?

Suddenly I see Moisés standing at the door of my apartment. He has just given me an unforgettable lesson on the history of *Quetzalcóatl*. How long ago was it?...a month?...two months?

Abruptly he turns back and tells me: "You need an intercessor! I'm praying God will give you one soon."

"Doctór," my visitor reaches for her coffee cup, "you're looking at me strangely. Did I say something to offend you?"

...I asked Moisés how I would know when I met my intercessor and he said, "Just wait. God will send him to you at the right..." (he smiled)..."*kairos.*"

Gelda Lohman rises from her chair, eyes clouded. "Maybe I should go. I'm sorry if—"

I jump up, upsetting what's left of my coffee. "No, please don't go!"

Mopping up the coffee with my napkin, I say, "I still don't understand how you knew God was telling you come see me."

Poised on the edge of her seat as if expecting momentarily words of dismissal, Gelda replies, "I have what I call my spiritual antenna, and I try to keep it in tune with God."

"And the day Rosario spoke of her husband's appointment with me..."

"I can't explain how it happened..." her chin comes up, "I just knew that God was telling me you needed an intercessor!"

A sob gushes up from deep within my chest, surprising me.

I manage to groan: "Gelda, if ever a man needed an intercessor, Andrew Kelly needs one now!"

My eyes closed, I feel my intercessor's hands on my shoulders. She prays a quiet prayer, redolent with an intimate knowledge of the Father. She asks nothing, only affirms her faith in God's work in me.

When she has finished I feel cleansed, at peace. We sit in silence.

After a while she says softly, "Thank you, Andrew."

I look up, surprised. "Why are you thanking me? I'm the one who is thankful."

"Thank you for accepting me as your intercessor."

"I don't I understand."

She dabs at her eyes with a dainty linen handkerchief. "A moment ago I was about to decide you were like my pastor. He has never accepted my gift."

"He doesn't believe in prayer?"

"Oh yes, he's a scholarly, honorable man with a firm faith in God's Word."

"Then why does he reject your gift?"

She sighs. "Hardly a Sunday passes that my pastor doesn't lead the congregation in singing 'A Mighty Fortress is our God.' He believes in the absolute sovereignty of God. So he's repelled by any suggestion that our prayers could affect the way God does things. When I told him, six years ago, that God had given me the gift of intercession and I placed it at his service he thanked me. Then he spent an hour explaining in impressive theological terms why God didn't need my help to accomplish his work on earth."

She reaches over and pulls the last Kleenex from the box. "So we've been living in a polite truce ever since. I pray for him every day, tell him so, and he thanks me. But he never acknowledges there's any relation between my prayers and anything that happens to him. Or anybody else."

"It must be frustrating."

"Not really. Years ago I became a member of the interfaith Bible study group I mentioned. We pray for one another and see many answers our to prayers. I know God has more for me to do, so I've been asking the Lord to lead me to one of his ministers who really needs me. Someone who'd welcome a partnership with me."

I lift up my hands defensively. "I want to make one thing clear, Gelda. I'm not a minister."

She smiles. "My pastor says that the Greek word we translate 'minister' really means servant. Don't you think you qualify?"

That's how Gelda Lohman became my intercessor. And that's why I decided to put my call to Houston back on hold…at least until after Wilbert's visit.

CHAPTER 24

▼

LUNCH WITH ANGELICA
AND JORGE

I can't believe my eyes; the moment I stand up to give my lesson Angelica and her boyfriend enter the room. I should have taken her seriously a few days ago when she asked about my Sunday morning Bible studies! But I was sure Angelica would have no interest in rubbing elbows with the people I call my Christian family. None of them belong to her social class, and the young people in *colonias ricas* are often even more class conscious than their parents.

Yet here she is, her eyes searching the crowded room for a couple of empty chairs. I nod at Rebecca and she jumps up and beckons to Angelica and Jorge, her *novio*.

I'm struck by the contrast between the handsome couple. Blonde, light-skinned Angelica would blend easily into the Sunday morning congregation at my Kingwood church. Until she spoke, few would guess she was not an American. Not so Jorge; he has the straight, lustrous black hair and brown eyes of the typical Mexican *mestizo*. On the other hand, he's not as dark as most of the young men in my class; his skin is the color of an East Texas pine cone. And the set of his shoulders and tilt of his chin reflect that subtle arrogance so common to the Mexican *joven rico*. Someone brings in more chairs from the auditorium. When the class is settled I step to the blackboard and write:

"Today you're going to decide if the Bible is the Word of God."

Turning, I say, "If you had been a university classmate of young Saul of Tarsus, you'd have spent a lot of time studying Greek philosophy. And your professors would have told you that history has absolutely no meaning."

I draw a circle on the board.

"For the Greeks history was a circle, without beginning and without end, an unending cycle of meaningless events repeated over and over again, year after year, millennium after millennium. History was headed nowhere, it offered no hope for a better tomorrow. That's why Paul reminded the Ephesians that before they knew Christ they were 'without hope and without God in the world'."

My students are listening intently, many writing in the notebooks they brought to class.

"What a difference the Bible made!" I walk from the left side of the board to the right, tracing a long line with my chalk:

<u>C   C   R</u>

"The Bible tell us the good news: history is not a circle, but a straight line drawn by the finger of God. It began with the <u>C</u>reation. Its midpoint was the <u>C</u>ross. It will end with Christ's <u>R</u>eturn.

Jorge no longer looks bored; his intense dark eyes are fixed on me, as if trying to decide if he dare believe what I'm saying.

I stroll toward the back of the room, still talking, until I come to Kiko. Baptized a couple of weeks ago, Kiko's a class favorite. They kid him about the way he waves his big black Bible when he's telling people how his life has changed since he gave Christ control. Playfully, I grab the Bible from his lap.

"Tell me, Kiko why do you call the Bible the Word of God?"

Because it is!" he shouts, and the class laughs.

"But why?" I jab my finger at him.

Kiko's brow furrows. "Maybe you'd better answer that question yourself, *Maestro*."

I toss Kiko his Bible and return to the blackboard. Picking up my chalk I write:

$$R = H \times Ii$$

"This formula gives the answer to my question, Kiko: (R) revelation=(H) the history of the world related by Ii a God-inspired interpreter."

"The Old Testament tells the history of Israel. What makes that history special? Why is it different from the history of dozens of other small nations that, like Israel, existed for a while and then were swallowed up by Assyria, Babylonia, Greece, or Rome?"

Somebody answers: "Because the Israelites were God's chosen people."

"How do we know that?"

"The Bible tells us so."

I clap my hands: "You're right. That's why we call the Bible the Word of God. Moses is the author of Genesis. He lets us in on a secret that only God and Abraham knew: Abraham turned his back on Ur of Chaldees to spend the rest of his life in Canaan because God had given him a promise. What was that promise?"

Kiko shouts: "That he would have a son."

A pretty, dark-eyed girl at his side adds: "And that all the nations of the world would be blessed through him."

"That's right!" I exclaim, smiling. "Now you're catching on!"

"Now let's think about the prophets. They wrote the history of their nation. But they did more than simply tell us what happened, they explained WHY things happened. They told us that Israel's liberation from Egypt was God's work, and that her defeat by Babylonia was God's punishment for her disobedience.

"The same thing happens in the New Testament. The Gospel writers describe the life and teachings of Jesus of Nazareth. But they do more: they tell us that Jesus was God's only Son: History+inspired Interpretation=Revelation.'

"So now can you see why the Bible is unique compared to other religious books? It's history…HIS/STORY…God's story…not just a compilation of some revered man's teachings. What makes the Bible different from all other history books? God chose to share his deepest secrets with the men he inspired to write that history."

Jorge raises his hand. "*Maestro*, Our professors claim the same thing for Das Kapital that you claim for the Bible."

"That Karl Marx gave an inspired interpretation of history?"

"That's right."

I shrug: "So what does that say about communism? It's not just a political system, it's a religion!"

A dozen hands shoot up, and we spend the rest of the hour comparing Christianity and communism.

When the bell rings, I sum up our discussion: "Communism and Christianity are at war because they give conflicting views of the meaning of history. Karl Marx claims that man is in the process of creating a paradise on earth. The Bible says the opposite: God has created a paradise in heaven for those who believe in his Son Jesus Christ. Apart from God man is weak and selfish, incapable of living in peace with his fellow man. Winston Churchill agreed with the Bible. He warned that communism is bound to fail because it has a fatal flaw: its founder's naïve optimism concerning man's nature.

I stand before the class, arms folded. "Ask yourself: 'Who can I trust? Marx or God?'"

After I dismiss the class half a dozen students gather around me, anxious to continue the dialogue. I can see Angelica and Jorge standing to one side, waiting to speak to me.

By the time I'm free we have to shout to be heard, because the congregation is singing and clapping just a few yards away.

"Doctór," Angelica says, kissing my cheek, "I don't believe you've met Jorge before."

He extends his hand. "*Profesor,* If you have no other plans, Angelica and I would like to take you out to dinner."

I'm surprised; I had the impression Jorge was not too impressed by his girl friend's gringo psychologist.

En route to the *Parrillada Suisa* I'm thankful I didn't try to persuade Jorge and Angelica to stay for the worship service, it would probably have worn them out. There was an hour of loud, enthusiastic singing, then the pastor preached for another hour. Afterward at least a hundred people came forward for prayer and laying on of hands.

The *Parrillada Suisa* is a popular steakhouse located on one of the city's busiest *glorietas.* These broad traffic circles were invented by Mexico City's engineers in hopes of simplifying the horrendous traffic. They only made things more appalling. Once you enter a *glorieta* you find yourself immersed in a swirling current of cars, trucks and buses determined not to allow you to exit. There are jokes about people who passed from youth to retirement, going endlessly around a *glorieta,* awaiting the opportunity for a dash to freedom. Seasoned drivers have learned there's no appropriate moment for escape; when you come to your street you take a firm grip on the steering wheel and exit, ignoring the blaring horns and squealing brakes.

I brake at the curb and hand my car keys to one of the young valets waiting on the sidewalk. Inside, a waitress leads me to a table at the back of the noisy restaurant.

It's four o'clock and the restaurant is jammed. No telling how long I'll have to wait for Angelica and her boyfriend! The smell of grilled steaks and hot tortillas make my mouth water. I order an *entremesa* of melted cheese and flour tortillas, plus a *sidral,* a sparkling apple—flavored mineral water...

"Doctór, you beat us!" They both give me an *abrazo*. No apology for arriving late; none is expected if you arrive within half an hour of the time agreed upon.

Three hours later, on my way home, I review our dinner conversation. I'd expected Jorge to bombard me with questions about my lecture, but instead we talked about last Sunday's Super Bowl. The advent of cablevision has converted Mexicans into avid fans of American football, and the overwhelming majority are *fanaticos* of the Dallas Cowboys.

By the time the waiter placed our flan on the table we were deep in conversation about the smog and national politics. Jorge and Angelica assured me that Benito Juarez, contemporary of Abraham Lincoln, was Mexico's last honest President.

And the traffic cops!

"It'll never change," Jorge lamented, "our great-grandchildren will still be handing over *mordidas.*"

Angelica reaches for Jorge's hand, smiling. "Don't worry, *mi amor,* by that time the contamination will have extinguished all human life in the Federal District!"

I kept waiting for Angie to mention her mother. Not a word.

By the third cup of coffee I knew why Jorge hadn't asked questions about my lecture: he had none. In spite of his horn-rimmed glasses Jorge was not a Deep Thinker. He was studying Business Administration, and his major preoccupation was how he'd earn a living once the generous allowance from his father came to an end.

I reminded myself that Jorge had not come to the Bible study because of interest in what Dr. Kelly might say, but to please the girl he loved.

Of one thing I'm sure: Jorge likes me. I think he was surprised I'm able to present a class on religion that doesn't put university students to sleep. And thankful that I had spent three hours with him and his girl without trying to make them Protestants.

My new friends hadn't opened their hearts to my Lord as I hoped they might, but the afternoon had been worthwhile, even though it had been painful sitting across the table from a pretty young woman whose smile reminded me so much of the woman I loved. Angelica had given me no encouragement for believing things might get better between her mother and me. Or had she? Turning into the driveway, I remember:

Leaving the restaurant, as I'm climbing into my car Angie hurries over. Giving me a hug she whispers in my ear, "Doctór, Mamá's a *burra*, but don't give up." Then, as she turns away, she blows a kiss and says, "See you next Sunday, *querido padrastro!*"

Upstairs in my apartment I pull out my worn green English-Spanish dictionary and find the word: "*padrastro...* stepfather."

I grin. Thank you, Angie, for the encouraging word!

CHAPTER 25

▼

A RECOMMITMENT

"Have a seat, Wilbert, it's good to see you." Ever since Gelda Lohman's visit I've been waiting for this moment.

Taking a fat cigar from the pocket of his bright lavender polo shirt, my visitor sticks it, like a big exclamation point, squarely in the middle of his broad white-toothed smile.

"I promised Rosario I'd come to see you before the end of the month. Here I am, Doctór, a man of my word!"

Seeing my frown, he adds, "Don't worry, Rosario warned me not to light up in your *consultorio*." Leaning forward, he passes the cigar under my nose. "Sniff that aroma! It's straight from *El Presidente's* private stock. *Don* Fidel sends him a case every month from Havana."

So this Latin James Cagney is Wilbert! At least a couple of inches shorter than his thin, angular wife, Wilbert is ridiculously handsome, his smile as open and ingenuous as a child's. In spite of the biting January chill he wears no jacket, inviting admiration of the biceps bulging from the short sleeves of his flashy polo shirt. (Bet he spends a lot of time in the presidential gymn.) If this is God's messenger, he certainly is an angel in disguise!

"I've been expecting you, Wilbert, ever since Rosario's visit."

Eyes on the floor, he shakes his head. "Ay, that woman, she's driving me crazy." Looking up quickly, he adds, "Don't get me wrong, Doctór, Rosario's a saint. I'd be in the grave by now, if it weren't for her."

I lean forward, trying to get a fix on his shifty eyes. "She says you drink too much."

"She's right. But I swear, Doctór, I haven't had a drink since New Year's Eve." He crosses himself. "And with God's help I'm never going to drink again."

"I suppose you're a member of the A.A.'s?"

Grunting, he bites off the end of the cigar. P-t-o-o! a hunk of brown tobacco lands squarely in the waste basket. "That bunch of drunks couldn't teach me anything I don't know. All I need is God and my woman!"

I repeat for Wilbert my standard advice for alcoholics in denial: he may be doing better now, but he'll be battling this problem the rest of his life. He needs the support of other people wrestling with the same demon. Sure, Alcoholics Anonymous is not perfect, but they do better than any other group I know.

Wilbert is staring at the ceiling, looking bored. (What do I say now? Please Lord, give me a clue!) He lowers his gaze to a spot half a meter above my head. "There's something else, Doctór. I hope you didn't believe that garbage Rosario told you about me and Rosalinda."

"Rosalinda?"

"The general's secretary. For some reason Rosario's insanely jealous of her."

"And she's wrong to be jealous?"

He crosses his heart. "God is my witness; I've got my faults, but I've never been unfaithful to my Rosario!"

Can he see I don't believe him? Even if he can, it probably doesn't matter. I remind myself The only reason Wilbert is here is to get his wife off his back. (Gelda, you told me this meeting was of great importance. Right now I can't imagine why!)

Sighing, I lay my pen on the table. Looks like it's going to take more than one visit to win this guy's confidence. Why waste time saying things that will only turn him off? Might as well talk about something more pleasant.

"Rosario tells me you're the President's favorite pilot."

Frowning, he pulls the cigar from his mouth and leans toward me. Glancing over his shoulder as if someone might eavesdrop, he whispers: "I'm at the call of *El Presidente* twenty-four hours a day, seven days a week.

"I'm on the staff of General Camacho, head of the President's bodyguards, and that's even better than being employed directly by the President. *El Presidente* is one of the most powerful men on earth. Rules over Congress and the courts with an iron hand. Has the power of life and death over every man, woman and child in Mexico. But anybody working for him has a problem waiting in the wings: the Constitution forbids the President's reelection, so the day his *sexenio* ends he's a nobody, and everyone in his employ ends up selling *chicles* on the street!"

On the other hand, he continues, military men like General Camacho don't have to worry about changes of Presidents, because the army doesn't meddle in politics. That's why Wilbert is now serving his third President.

(Gelda, I don't doubt your sincerity, but you were wrong; This man has no message for me!) I stand to my feet. "It's been a pleasure meeting you, Wilbert. Give my best to Rosario."

Clearly relieved his ordeal is over, Wilbert gives me an *abrazo* and heads for the door. His hand is on the knob when I call him back.

"Don't forget Fidel's present," I say, smiling, pointing to the cigar he laid on my table.

"Of course, Doctór, excuse my lack of *educación*!" Retrieving the *puro*, he clenches it between his teeth, turns toward the door, stops, takes a fresh cigar from his shirt pocket and shoves it into my hand. "Take one, Doctór, it would cost you twenty dollars in the States."

My first impulse is to hand it back to him, I hate the smell of cigar smoke! But I thank him for his gift and stick it in my shirt pocket.

Gripping my forearm, he mutters, "*Amigo* I understand now why Rosario wanted me to come see you. You're *simpático*. If ever I can be of help, remember, I'm at your orders." For the first time since he entered my office Wilbert looks me in the eye.

After he's gone I sit staring out the window. What a letdown!

I remember my dad's advice the day I left for college: "Andrew, if you're ever trying to decide whether to trust a man, ask yourself a simple question: 'Would I buy a used car from this guy?'"

I'd never buy a used car from Wilbert!

Driving home late that afternoon, I rub my aching forehead. According to the car radio the ozone index reached 292 points a couple of hours ago. I brake for a light, and the instant the light changes a horn blares behind me. Shifting gears rapidly, I beat out a yellow Volkswagen bug trying to cut in front of me. We end up yelling at each other.

Mortified, I turn into a side street and pull up at the curb. What's wrong with me, I don't do stupid things like that.

"I know, I know!" I answer that nagging voice within me. This is the last day of January, and I've got to call my Houston friends about their offer. Now, more than ever, I don't know what I'm going to tell them!

I slip back into the flow of traffic. All right, I'll stay up tonight until I have the answer, and first thing tomorrow I'll make that call.

Parking my Chevy in the basement, I walk around the corner to the *panadería*. As soon as I step through the door the aroma of cinnamon and spice makes my mouth water. A dozen of my neighbors, aluminum trays in hand, are inspecting shelves stacked with fragrant sweet breads.

There's a world of difference between an American bakery and a Mexican *panadería*. Back home the bakeries shut down before noon, leaving you to supermarket breads that need twenty seconds in a microwave to make them palatable. Here they're still trundling out trays of sweetbreads long after dark, just as fresh at 9:00 P.M. as they were at 9:00 A.M.

Later, in a cluttered little shop next door to the bakery I wait patiently while the talkative owner grinds savory coffee beans trucked in from the mountains of Córdoba.

With my trophies in hand I march home. Now I have the raw material for some creative thinking! At the door I retrieve my mail from the box and shove it in my briefcase.

While the old coffee pot chugs merrily in the kitchen to the accompaniment of a pianist playing Beethoven's Moonlight Sonata, I take a quick shower. Later, in pajamas and robe I sit at the kitchen table. A big mug of coffee, a saucer filled with savory *caracoles* and cinnamon rolls, and a yellow legal pad are my companions. The noisy little electric heater puffs warm air at my legs.

After two cups of coffee and three fat cinnamon rolls I've filled several pages of my legal pad with more than enough arguments to convince me I should leave Mexico and never return.

I go to the stove and pour myself a third cup of coffee. Returning, I slowly read aloud what I've scribbled about Gabriela's rejection. Smiling grimly I print a title in big block letters at the top of the page: "Paradise Lost."

Page two is a critique of Moisés' main argument for my coming: that I'd penetrate the Mexican upper class with my counseling. Wrong! My agenda is filled with names of clients from the privileged *colonias*, but outside of Gabriela, not a single person has invited me to his home.

My stomach churns. I'm feeling neglected these days: Moisés is so busy we've hardly talked since my return from the Christmas holidays. I've resisted the temptation to complain he's left me alone in my warfare with Quetzalcóatl and his demons.

Where's that warfare headed?

Nowhere! The debacle at Gabriela's house has left Andrew Kelly defeated, discouraged, humiliated. His last hope was Gelda Lohman's excitement about Roasario's husband's visit, and that turned out to be a flop. Why should Quetzalcóatl worry about me any more?

The telephone startles me out of my pity party. Who could it be? Perhaps Gabriela has decided to call me.... Stupid! When am I going to stop this foolishness?

"Grandpa, when are you coming home?" It's little Jeff; he's called half a dozen times since Christmas.

"Hi, Buddy, soon I hope."

On the other phone, Margaret apologizes: "Daddy, I'm sorry your grandson's bothering you again. He absolutely refused to go to sleep unless I let him talk to you."

Her next question tips me off to whose idea it really was to call: "It's the end of January; we're on pins and needles around here, wondering what you're going to do."

I tell her I haven't called my ex-partners yet, but I plan to give them my answer tomorrow.

The line goes silent. She's waiting.

"Well, Sweetheart, it's been nice talking to you. Bye."

"Bye, Daddy, I love you." I can tell she's about to cry.

Jeff breaks in, his voice excited: "Grandpa, are you coming home tomorrow?"

"Love ya, Buddy. See you soon."

As I hang up the phone I reach into my pocket and pull out a hand-kerchief. Standing at the stove, I refill my coffee cup, shaking my head. Why should I waste my time trying to think up reasons for staying here?

But I promised myself! I turn to a clean page in my yellow pad.

Half an hour later, laying down the pen, I grab the back of my neck and massage it. I'm frustrated. The page is empty except for the black lines and my head is pounding in time to the angry beat of my pulse.

Yawning, I flop down on the comfy old white couch in the dark living room.

.... I awake shivering. 11:52—I've been asleep nearly two hours! ...might as well go to bed.... I stumble into the bedroom, pull back the comforter and sheet, sit down and bend over to untie my shoes.

"No!" I say it out loud, as if speaking it will convince my body to obey, "I won't go to sleep until I have my answer!"

Groaning, I drag the comforter off the bed, and draping it over my shoulders, stagger back into the living room. I'm so tired. Maybe if I get some fresh air....

Br-r-r, it's cold! Leaning over the balcony, I look down on the street far below. A pale glow from the streetlights filters up through the eucalyptus. It's quiet now, except for the murmur of a passing car. In the distance an ambulance siren is wailing. A chilling breeze blowing in from Popocatépetl's snowy peak bites my nose.

A frigid melancholy seeps into my bones, making me shiver worse than before. Pulling the comforter up snug to my neck I turn around. Leaning with my back against the icy railing I gaze through the blinds into the quiet living room, feeling like an interloper. A pool of light cast by the lamp outlines the shadows on the pillow where my head rested, and I can see a sheet from the yellow legal pad crumpled on the floor where I dropped it when I fell asleep. Home!

There's that feeling again...the same feeling I had in the airport, when I saw Gabriela for the first time...the same feeling I had that midnight in August when I fielded God's dare, embraced it, threw open my living room window and shouted "Yes!"to the world.

Slowly, like a dark valley awakened by the rising sun, my mood brightens. My heart whispers, "Don't forget, you didn't come here for logical reasons you could have written on a legal pad!"

I pull open the balcony door, dash to the couch and grab up the yellow pad. I rip out the "reasons for leaving" and tear the sheets into shreds. Tossing them into the air I watch as the bits of brain-numbing logic float down and settle on the carpet around me. Then I flop down on the sofa, my mind racing....

In the last six months I've become a timid explorer, stepping gingerly, fearfully, into new territory. For half a lifetime God's will was decided by simply weighing the pros and cons and choosing the most logical answer, and it seemed to work quite well. I lived a devout, respectable life...loved my wife and children and did my share of good deeds. But always there was a gnawing intuition of something missing, a destiny not realized.

Is that why, turning forty, I dared to throw myself out of an airplane into the bright blue sky ten thousand feet above the Texas prairie?

Remembering, I chuckle out loud:

Landing face-down in a grassy field I pick myself up, laughing, laughing, laughing. While I'm gathering my parachute Skip, the trainer, hurries over. "Man, what happened, why didn't you pull the ripcord?"

My mouth falls open. "What are you talking about?"

"Did you forget my instructions? I told you to keep your eye on the altimeter, and at exactly forty-five hundred feet pull the ripcord."

I think, "He's joking!" Pulling a handkerchief from my pocket I dab at my forehead. Shaking my head at the blood, I say, "Don't be silly, if I had forgotten your instructions I wouldn't be here."

"My friend, you're standing here because *I* pulled your ripcord. I waited until we passed four thousand feet, and when nothing happened I reached over and did it for you."

I ease myself down onto grass, recalling my jump, reliving what happened:...I'm in a free-fall, but I'm not falling, I'm soaring in an ecstasy of infinite velvet blue, being pulled gently, sweetly toward heaven. In less than two minutes, if I do nothing...!

What happened after that? I can't remember doing anything...just feeling...feeling...feeling...

I'm a man who feels...intensely, passionately...seeing the clown-faces of a bed of yellow and purple pansies grinning at me, my chest explodes with sudden joy...more than once, jogging alongside

Lake Kingwood at dawn, I've shouted with happiness when God picked up his paint bucket and hurled it at the sky.

Now I understand: this feeling is God's gift to me, his window to my soul.

And now, once again…feeling!

So…what now?

I stand there for a moment, breathing hard, swaying slightly, exhausted from so much emotion.

"God, what are you saying to me?" I jump, startled, hearing myself say the words out loud.

Head bowed, eyes closed, I wait. I hear the whisper of a car passing in the street far below. Will the next whisper come from heaven?

Silly! You know God doesn't speak like that!

Exhausted, I gather my legs up on the sofa, and they and strike my brief case, knocking it to the floor.…

My eyes focus on the letters scattered like pale leaves in the circle of light thrown by the lamp. Sitting up, I rub my tired eyes. Oh yes! It's the mail I picked up when I came in. Bending, I retrieve the letters and lay them beside me on the sofa. The light bill…a sale at Muebles Morales…a letter from Margaret…I'm about to rip it open when my eye falls on a small yellow envelope postmarked "Madrid".

No return address. Must be from Carlos Medellin, the owner of this apartment. He's never written before, why now? Oh, oh, did last month's rent get lost in the mail? Or is he raising my rent? Oh no, they're giving me notice that they're coming home to reclaim their apartment!

I tear open the envelope, my hand shaking now.

After the inevitable flowery greeting, *Sr.* Medellin gets down to business:

Because of the frail health of my parents, my wife and I find ourselves obligated to remain in our *patria* indefinitely. That leaves us with the painful necessity of selling our beloved apartment. Our fondest wish is that you will want to purchase it. We saw you fall in love with it, and it would break our hearts to have to place it in the hands of strangers. Please advise us immediately.

I lay down the letter, my heart sinking. Buy this apartment?

Impossible! I've been here less than six months. My future is uncertain. It would be foolish to make such a commitment.

…. But *Don* Carlos is right, I do love this place! My eyes caress the comfortable old chairs resting in the shadows, the bright, quaint paintings decorating the walls, the gay, flowered curtains.

No matter. I'll write and ask Medellin to give me a month to find another place.

In the kitchen the old refrigerator moans sadly in protest.

Tears sting my eyes…FEELINGS!

Impulsively, I reach for the phone…careful, Andrew don't do something on the spur of the moment you'll regret later! Anyway, it's after midnight, you'd be getting them out of bed. But wait a minute, what time is it in Spain? Of course! I'll bet the Medellins are having their morning cup of coffee about this time!

"*Buenos días, a sus ordenes* I'm shocked at how quickly Carlos Medellin answers.

"*Don* Carlos, it's Andres Kelly."

I hear his sudden intake of breath. "Doctór Kelly, *que gusto*! So you received my letter."

"Yes, but—"

"Look, Doctór, I'm not going to beat around the bush. My wife and I have no desire to return to Mexico and haggle with strangers. We want you to have the apartment."

Why is my heart racing? I mumble: "But *Don* Carlos—"

"Doctór Kelly, we're prepared to accept $15,000 in cash as full payment."

I'm surprised, I'd expected him to ask at least $20,000…but I have no business buying an apartment! Then why do I want to jump up and down and yell "Yes! Yes!"

Feelings!

Slipping to my knees, I let my face sink into the beloved, stale-smelling old sofa. It's true, I love this place…it's become my home…one day Gabriela will be sitting beside me on this sofa.

I've been asking God for a sign!

"Doctór?"

"Yes, I'm here."

"We're willing to give you a week to consider our offer. I know it's…"

I swallow hard. *Sr.* Medellin, I don't need time to consider. My check will be in the mail tomorrow."

I'm out of my mind!

Feelings!

Kyros scoops up a tiny ikon of the Bearded Serpent and with all his might hurls it into the darkness. Hearing it shatter against the floor he grunts with satisfaction. Why did Quetzalcóatl have to order him here for a meeting? He despises this place! The Zócalo underworld is the most depressing spot in all of Mesoamerica; non-resident spirits refer to it sneeringly as "Lord Quetzalcóatl's garbage dump."

And as usual, his Lord has kept him waiting. Since arriving hours ago he's been pacing back and forth, grumbling, cursing his misfortune, twisting the skirt of his black robe with nervous fingers until it's a crumpled rag.

Grimacing, he clamps his hands over his ears, trying to shut out the din. Don't these Zócalo demons ever shut up?

Every time he visits this abominable place he goes away with a splitting headache. It never stops, the infernal screaming, wailing, groaning, moaning, complaining, of Huitzilopochtli's ill-humored choir.

Huitzilopochtli's choir is the counterpart of the angelic choir that fills heaven with joyful praise. While the angelic choir celebrates the holiness, love and power of El and the Lamb, Huitzilopochtli's demon choir is consecrated to the iniquitous task of venting the anger, bitterness and impotence of their master.

The Zócalo underworld is the domain of the exiled demon god that humans once called Huitzilopochtli. Long ago this ill-humored, murderous spirit led the Aztecs in an invasion of the land of Popocatépetl and Itzlacihuatl. Did he know that eons before, the Prince of This World had ceded all of Mesoamerica to the Feathered Serpent? Perhaps not, since his dominion had always been in the North, at the headwaters of the Colorado River.

Or was the pilgrimage of his demon army a deliberate attempt to expel Quetzalcóatl and his subjects from this Promised Land? No one knew, not even his most trusted generals. As for the Prince of This World, he seemed to be content for more than two centuries to let the two demon gods continue side by side in an armed truce.

Then the unthinkable happened: Moctezuma II, King of the Aztecs, became a disciple of Quetzalcóatl! When the Emperor erected a gleaming circular temple to the Feathered Serpent beside Huitzilipochtli's own sanctuary, the bloodthirsty god of the Aztecs howled with displeasure and made life miserable for the myriads of demon spirits under his command.

Huitzilopochtli was delighted when Hernán Cortés invaded Tenochtitlan and imprisoned Moctezuma. Seeing this as an opportunity for revenge, he threw his demon army into an epic battle with the spirit army of Quetzalcóatl.

For the Prince of This World that was the last straw. In a tense meeting with his generals atop Pico de Orizaba *he reaffirmed the supremacy of Quetzalcóatl and sentenced Huitzilopochtli and his demon subjects to exile. He gave the rebel god a choice: the steaming jungles of the Amazon or the dark underworld of the Zócalo.*

The disgraced demon god elected the world beneath the Zócalo. Ever since, amidst the tumbled monuments and broken stones of Moctezuma's vanquished kingdom Huitzilopochtli squats, listening to the caterwauling of his discordant choir. He has been here in august exile for nearly five hundred years. He will remain here until Armageddon.

Cautiously, Kyros pulls his fingers from his ears. The cacophony of the sniveling, subservient demon choir has slowly, almost imperceptibly become strangely harmonious. They're chanting hosannas to Quetzalcóatl! Kyros can see his master now in the distance. Quetzalcoatl's lofty serpentine head swivels slowly, black tongue flicking, as his dead eyes survey his trembling subjects.

Kyros is crouched in the northeast corner of the Zócalo underworld, his rumpled black academic robe pulled tightly over his head. He hopes Lord Quetzalcóatl has forgotten their appointment.

Fat chance! He knows his hope is an empty illusion. Just like the hope that springs up in his dark little heart, every time the Feathered Serpent commands his presence…the hope that he will hear a word of appreciation for his good work.

But maybe this time he will! Why not? Andrew Kelly has been cowering like a frightened niño ever since his ignominious defeat in the house of Gabriela Mancini.

An ominous rattling shakes Kyros out of his reverie. With trembling fingers he peeks through a slit in his robe. He gasps.

His yellow eyes are locked into the hateful black eyes of his Master, just inches away. A fierce, jaguar-like growl rumbles from Quetzalcoatl's belly. His fangs drip rancid venom.

The demon scholar decides to take the initiative. Throwing off his robe, he squares his shoulders. "My Lord," he intones, "your humble servant takes great pleasure in reporting that Andrew Kelly is packing for home."

"Incompetent ass!" The brilliant blue and gold feathers girdling the Serpent's neck rustle like wheat in a windstorm.

Terrified, Kyros pulls up his robe and hugs it to his chest. "But my Lord…to…today day Andrew Kelly will talk to the people in Houston…I'm…I'm absolutely certain—"

The black tongue lashes his quivering face, stinging like fire. "Why haven't you stayed at your job? If you had, you'd know! S-s-stupid! Ins-s-s-sane!" A hot, liquid hiss splatters Kyros' terrified face. "Uns-s-s-speakable idiot, the worst possible thing has happened: Andrew Kelly has acquired an intercessor!"

A shiver runs through Kyros' miserable, bony little body, "But…but my Lord, how…how could I have foreseen—?"

A flame flickers in the dead eyes of his Master. "I've been watching Gelda Lohman ever since the Paraclete called her to his side. Tempered by the fires of suffering and disciplined by fasting, she's a stubborn disciple of El's Manual. She's the kind of intercessor we most dread. I knew El was preparing her for something special; now I know what!" He growls his displeasure.

"But Master, why is the Enemy wasting such extraordinary resources on this inexperienced fledgling? First he assigns him one of his most powerful angels. And now one of his most dedicated intercessors. Why, my Lord? If Andrew Kelly were a brilliant prophet or a great evangelist I could understand El's strategy. But he's one of the most unpromising men I've ever had the pleasure of tormenting."

"Idiot!" The evil tail rattles like a dry limb in a cyclone and a blast of foul breath picks up Kyros and whirls him around like a black crow's feather. "Haven't you learned yet? Don't you remember the words of that stubborn missionary, Saul of Tarsus: 'God has chosen the weak things of the world to put to shame the things that are mighty'? Remember Moses, Jonah, Simon Peter? Not very promising men either, were they, when El first laid hands on them!"

Kyros grumbles, more to himself than to his master. "After what happened in Ixtapa, I was so sure. Kelly promised himself—and his God—that if Gabriela Mancini turned him down he'd go home."

Now it's Quetzalcóatzal's turn to grumble: "Except for that interfering woman Gelda he'd packing right now. She knew things were going bad for him and spent the day in prayer and fasting. So the Paraclete set up a vigil around the man, and put to flight my demons of fear and despondency.

"Tonight I was sure the tide had turned in my favor when Andrew Kelly let me help him make a list of all the reasons why he should go home. Then..." Quetzalcóatl lets out a screech of anger that so startles the demon choir it falls silent for a moment, "the Paraclete led him out on the balcony!"

"What happened next, my Lord?"

"Everything! It's the second time Kelly's let the Spirit have complete dominion of his mind, and for the second time El whispered in his ear. Now he's got hope again of winning back his precious Gabriela."

Kyros is aware of the hosts of black spirits hovering about, eavesdropping, black wings whirring, beady eyes bright, teeth bared, grinning at one another in fiendish delight. The Serpent gives an irritated flick of his tail and they scurry away, screeching in protest.

"Now listen!" (Oh no, is his Lord about to send him on another mission?)

"It's time for you to take a message to Cuauhtemoc."

"Cuauhtémoc, my Lord? But isn't he already on special assignment?"

"Never mind, there's no reason why he can't do a little overtime." He smacks his lips. "And I'm sure he'll be delighted with his extra assignment, once he lays eyes on Gabriela Mancini's daughter."

"So his assignment is not Gabriela?"

"No, Gabriela has placed her devotion to the Guadalupana above her love for the Son. Deceiving her was easy."

"So Kelly's hope will be fruitless?"

"Absolutely! Only Angelica could persuade Gabriela to change her mind."

Kyros laughs nervously. "But when Cuauhtemoc gets through with Angelica…"

"Kelly won't have a chance!"

He turns to go, then as if it were an afterthought, swings his evil head back to Kyros' and growls, "And meanwhile, I've opened a fortress in the soul of that traitor, Moisés. His days are numbered!"

▼

CHAPTER 26

CUAUHTEMOC TAKES COMMAND

Gabriela called,. She's coming to see me!

She sounded relieved when she heard my voice; said she'd been trying to call me for over a week. I explained I'd spent Christmas in Kingwood with my family. I didn't tell her how difficult it had been for me to return. That I'd all but promised Margaret and Victoria and my little grandson I'd be back with them for good by the end of the month.

A year has passed since my impulsive purchase of this apartment. Lately I've wondered if it was a mistake.

I haven't seen Gabriela since July. Yet not a day (not an hour!) has passed without my feeling the pain of our separation. Which is harder to bear, the death of someone you love or the death of a dream? I came to Mexico hoping to heal the emptiness left by Mary's passing. Then I met Gabriela, and a new dream was born. But the past twelve months have about convinced me it's time to bury the dream, just as I buried my beloved Mary....

I spent most of the past year trying to keep the dream alive. Within a month of Jorge and Angelica's first visit to my class Angelica invited me to begin a weekly Bible study in her apartment. She'd told university classmates about me and they were interested. I was delighted. I wanted to share the Word with Angelica's university friends. But my heart whispered another reason: my love for Gabriela was like a stubborn, unyielding fever. Perhaps she would attend the classes! Or at least meet me at the door with a smile and a hug.

I was wrong. Gabriela soon made it clear she wasn't going to give me the chance to use my classes as a pretext for renewing our relationship. She had other plans most Tuesday nights. Occasionally she appeared to help with the coffee and cookies, but seemed to make a point of not being around when the class was over.

I called her every week, and every week the maid advised me that the *señora* was away. Yes, she'd tell her I'd called. But my calls were never returned.

The last Tuesday night in February Cuauhtemoc appeared. I had just stood to begin my class when the doorbell rang. Angelica jumped up and left the room. When she didn't return I noticed my students glancing toward the stairs, whispering to one another. Surely, I told myself, she'll be back any moment. From the first lesson Angelica had made it clear this Bible study was her special project. She was always there to welcome her friends, and to open the class with a word that put everyone at ease. I was proud that Angelica had become a disciplined student of the Bible; if I asked a question that stumped the rest of the class I could count on her to come up with the answer.

Refreshment time came and still no Angelica. Jorge went upstairs. In a few minutes Angelica returned with him, but she seemed distracted. I wasn't surprised that everyone found an excuse to leave early. When only Jorge and I remained, Angelica took my arm and pulled me toward the stairs. "Come, there's someone I want you to meet."

The stranger perched at the dining room table beside Gabriela stood when we entered. I paused, startled. Inches shorter than Angelica, his shoulders were absurdly wide and muscular, making him appear almost as broad as he was tall. Dressed in black gym pants and a white

T-shirt, the man's face was swarthy and pock-marked, his straight black hair plastered to his huge round head like the ugly feathers of a pompous vulture.

Embarrassed that I was staring, I walked toward him and and extended my hand. He gripped it with such force I winced. "Cuauhté-moc Luna, *a sus órdenes*," the man grunted, his voice as ugly and threatening as his face.

"*Mucho gusto*," I lied. I still remember how his cold black eyes awakened in me a somber anxiety, like the ominous thunder of an approaching storm.

Gabriela came around the table and looped her arm through his. "This is Dr. Cuauhtemoc Luna, a friend of Angelicas's. We invited him to have dinner with us tonight. Would you like to join us?"

"No thank you, I have other plans."

Gabriela smiled, as if relieved, and my heart contracted. Looking at her lips, I remembered the last time they had touched mine. The woman I loved was beautiful tonight, ivory skin and clear green eyes in striking contrast to the unpleasant man standing beside her, his complacent smile mocking the pain in my heart.

Angelica stepped to the side of her guest. "I'm excited to have Professor Luna as our guest tonight. When he spoke to my gymnastic class a few days ago, I knew immediately my little brother needed to meet him."

Hector was seated at the table, his usually surly face lit by a grin.

"Dr. Luna is your gymnastics teacher?" I asked.

"Oh no, he's too busy for that, he's the personal trainer of the *Señor Presidente*. You can imagine how pleased we were when he accepted our profesor's invitation to speak to our class."

Driving home, I wondered at the scene I had just witnessed. Cuauhtémoc Luna had charmed Gabriela and Angelica. Even I, repulsed by his ugliness, had felt a curious magnetism. I shivered. The man was evil!

The next Tuesday night I arrived a few minutes late for the Bible study. My class was buzzing.

"No, Angelica, not a knitting needle!"

"I swear I'm not lying," Angelica declared, her eyes bright. "Standing there before my class Cuauhtémoc passed a knitting needle right through his bicep! And didn't blink an eye."

"They say here it's mind control," Jorge interrupted, waving a copy of *Señorita!*, a Spanish version of *Playboy*.

"And that's not all!" Angelica continued, "he withdrew the needle from his arm and held it before us, looking at us one by one." Everyone gasped. "Those eyes!" She shivered. "Then he said, 'Angelica, do you have faith in me?'"

The other girls giggled. "And what did you say, Angelica?"

"I said, 'Of course, Doctór!' And guess what he did? He walked over to my chair, took my hand and led me to the front of the class. Then he said, 'Students, Angelica affirms her faith in me. So of course she'll have no objection to my passing this needle through the pupil of her eye!'"

One of the girls screamed, covering her eyes with her hands. "What did you do?"

"I got back to my seat as fast as I could! Later I was ashamed of myself. I'm sure I wouldn't have felt a thing if I'd had the courage to let him do it."

"Oh, hello, Teacher," somebody said. I was jealous; until now nobody had acknowledged my arrival.

"Look, Doctór!" Jorge handed me the magazine he'd been studying.

"Don't look at the cover, Profesor," one of the guys warned, and the class laughed.

The gaudy magazine was opened to an article entitled, "Meet Dr. Cuauhtémoc Luna, Mexico's Master of Mind Control."

While my students continued commenting on Angelica's distinguished new friend, I scanned the story. Accompanied by photos, it described the work of Cuauhtémoc Luna, Director of the Presidential gym in *Los Pinos*. He'd been appointed to the post a year ago when he returned from India, where he had studied for three years under one of the country's most distinguished gurus.

From that chilly night in February until the end of July, my Bible study in Angelica's apartment went downhill. Cuauhtémoc appeared every Tuesday night. Most evenings Angelica gave the welcome and stayed a while, but always, before the class ended the doorbell rang and she ran upstairs to receive her new boyfriend.

Yes, she and the monstrous *maestro* were now *novios*. Jorge, Angelca's ex, continued attending my class, but as the weeks wore on he became more and more forlorn. We made a sad pair, Jorge and I, going through the motions of Bible study but fearful of what was happening to the women we loved on the floor just above us.

The first Tuesday morning in July my telephone rang as I stepped out of the shower. Angelica's voice was apologetic. "I hope you won't mind, Profesor, but we've decided to suspend the Bible study tonight. Cuauhtémoc is giving a lecture at the *Auditorio Nacional* and everybody is dying to go."

When I rang the following Tuesday night the maid opened the door. Angelica would not be present for the class, she advised me; she was attending a supper at the *Restaurant del Lago* with Doctór Cuauhtémoc Luna. He was the featured speaker, and *La Señora* had accompanied them. Jorge didn't come either; he and Angelica had fought, and he'd slammed the front door behind him shouting she'd never see him again.

I went downstairs and sat alone on the friendly pink sofa, feeling utterly defeated, staring at the sputtering logs in the fireplace. The basement, usually warmed by the bodies of a dozen exuberant young people, felt chilly and hostile. It was raining, and I could hear water gushing from the gutters onto the sidewalk just above me.

What connection was there, I wondered between Cuauhtémoc Luna and the dark spirits that still occupied the attic? Of one thing I was absolutely certain: the *Maestro* had been sent by my enemy

Quetzalcóatl to break my only remaining link with the woman I adored. And he had succeeded!

The logs on the fireplace collapsed into coals. The flames diminished to a flicker. It was time to go. I climbed the stairs and let myself out. Angelica could advise her fellow students that Dr. Andrew Kelly would no longer be coming to her house on Tuesday nights. Another man had taken his place. Quetzalcóatl's emissary had won the hearts of the two women of this house.

Since that dreary July night I've heard nothing from Gabriela and her daughter. And made no attempt to call them. But in a few minutes Gabriela will enter my office and sit across from me...in that chair! I picture her leaning forward, smiling at me. My pulse quickens.

I can sit still no longer; I get up and begin pacing the floor. Why is she coming? What does she want? She sounded very agitated on the phone.

Her visit comes like a reprieve from a death sentence. The last six months I've continued my counseling agenda and my classes at church, but hardly a day goes by that I don't I ask myself why I'm here. I see Moisés only occasionally. He's away from the pulpit a lot now. They've invited him speak in Argentina and Brazil...and he recently spent three weeks in Switzerland. Even when we have a few moments together I get the impression he has something on his mind he doesn't want to share. I find myself wondering if I've offended him.

Without my intercessor, Gelda Lohman, I wouldn't have survived this long. After the disappointing visit with Wilbert I wasn't particularly interested in seeing her again. But she called me the next day, and when I told her what had happened (or had not happened!) insisted on coming to my office. She spent two hours carving out a classroom inside my mind, insisting I was wrong to think nothing had happened. Wilbert's visit was engineered by God, so something *had* happened, even though I didn't perceive it.

Since then she has called me weekly and visited me at least twice a month. And more and more I've become aware of the quiet power of her stubborn, unrelenting prayers.

But why this continuing obsession with Gabriela? I should have been able to forget her by now, yet every passing day seems to spike her love deeper into my soul.

I think of home often these days: my pleasant office and the camaraderie of my colleagues, the inspiration of the great anthems sung by our church choir...the quiet, comforting sermons of the pastor...the friendly greenbelt in Kingwood with its fragrant pines and frisky squirrels. And my daughters: the sweet affection of Margaret and the sharp, challenging intellect of Victoria.

I'd gladly drop everything and leave tomorrow. And never return to this demon-cursed city. Except....

Except for Gabriela. As long as I have the slightest hope of regaining her love I'll never leave. Did I love Mary this way? I didn't have to! Mary's love was different, with her I never experienced the quiet hell of tenderness withdrawn. From the day we declared our love Mary was always there for me, understanding, tender.

Oh God, why did you take her away from me?

.... Rebeca's soft, caressing voice: "Doctór, *la Señora* Gabriela has arrived."

I rise to meet her, fearful of what I may feel, what I may say when the woman I love steps into my life again. Will she step on my heart again?

CHAPTER 27

▼

GABRIELA ASKS FOR HELP

I gasp. I've never seen Gabriela like this; it's as if someone yelled "Fire!" and she rushed out of the house to save her skin.

Swallowed up in a rumpled blue gym suit, she pauses just inside the door, the laces of her scuffed white tennis shoes loosely looped together, breathing so hard I wonder if she chose to run up the stairs rather than risk waiting for the elevator.

Her voice breaks, "Oh, Andee, it's so good to see you!" Dark shadows rim her eyes, letting only a glimmer of green shine through.

I don't know what to do. I want to take her into my arms, comfort her, tell her how much I love her. But I'm angry. This woman who called me half an hour ago spent a year refusing my calls!

"May I sit down?" She tugs off the white kerchief tied at her throat and shakes out her hair, letting it fall to her shoulders.

"Of course, Gabriela. Have a seat." I'm standing by my desk, feeling terribly awkward.

"I left in such hurry!" Bending, she reties her shoe laces. My heart catches and I resist the temptation to lean over and touch my lips to the whiteness of her neck. Instead, I pull up a chair and sit facing her. I wonder if she can hear my racing heart?

"I know I look awful," she says, running a hand through her tangled black hair. "An hour ago I got out of the shower and dialed your number. When Rebeca said you were here I couldn't wait. I just blew dry my hair and ran out." Lifting her chin, she tries a smile. "I guess I was afraid you might...oh Andee..." she reaches over and touches my hand (her fingers are ice cubes!) "I've treated you so shabbily I don't have the courage to ask you to forgive me. But here I am, pleading with you to rescue me from my own stupidity."

I struggle to remain cool. I've been praying for this moment since the first time, months ago, I looked into Cuauhtémoc's cruel eyes.

"This...this Cuauhtémoc. What's he done to you?"

She ducks her head. "You knew from the beginning, didn't you, Andee? That *El Maestro* is a wicked man."

I repeat: "Tell me, Gabriela, what happened?"

"I'm so ashamed," she wails. "Why did it take me so long to see the truth?"

I take a deep breath. "Gabriela, once we were united, you and I, and you loved God with all your heart, but—"

She looks up, shaking her head. "Believe me, Andee, I'm not the renegade you think. I meet every week with Rosario for Bible study, and Sundays I go to mass."

I'm not going to argue with her!

Collapsing into the chair, Gabriela moans, "How could I have let him deceive me?"

"The first time I saw him," I tell her, "I knew the guy was just as much a demon as that ghost Angelica saw floating down her stairs."

She winces. "I'm, afraid your right. How else could he have deceived us so completely? And convinced Angelica to break the heart of a precious boy like Jorge. And now do you know what she's doing?"

Closing her eyes, she shakes her head, as if trying to clear her mind. "But first let me tell you about Hector. He's the one that opened my eyes."

"Hector? You mean he convinced you that Cuauhtémoc—"

"No, no, it's not the way you might think." She moves to the edge of her chair, and taking my hands, presses them to her cheeks. "Andee I'm scared."

How can I keep my heart closed against this woman? I pull her into my arms and kiss away the tears. "Tell me what happened, Gabi. We'll face it together."

For the first time she smiles. "Thank you, Andee. When I walked in a few moments ago you scared me. You seemed so cold! I know I deserve it, but..."

I place a finger on her lips. "Sh-h-. Tell me why you're frightened."

She takes a deep breath. "Three days ago I looked deep into Hector's eyes, and instead of seeing my son I saw—" she shudders—"the devil himself."

"But Hector's just a kid!"

"Not any more. You'd have to see him to understand. In the last months hardly a day has passed without his visiting Cuauhtémoc."

"Every day with that charlatan? Why on earth?"

"That's what I ask myself now. But at the time it seemed like the thing to do. Cuauhtémoc began a martial arts class for teens, and named Hector the captain."

"And you weren't worried about what might happen?"

"Not until recently. Oh, Andrés, try to understand. Hector was a flabby, embittered adolescent until *El Maestro* took an interest in him. His father had hurt him so! He was failing in school, had no friends, sassed me. Then, for a while, everything seemed to be changing. Cuauhtémoc told Hector he'd have to do well in school and mind his mother if he wanted to be the leader of his group."

"And he did?"

"Oh yes, he became a model child, and we even stopped fighting." She frowns. "Until I began expressing my doubts about his idol.

"For several months Cuauhtémoc came over most nights for dinner. We'd spend hours at the *sobremesa*, charmed by the Stories he told us about his studies in India, his training sessions with the President. Many times we talked till long after midnight.

"Then, about six weeks ago the nightmare began. One night when he was about to leave Angelica invited him down to her apartment. He didn't go home until the wee hours. I was upset, But the next day when I tried to talk with my daughter about it she became very angry. The following night the same thing happened. Then the next, and the next."

She pours herself a glass of water. "Then one night he...he didn't go home. And it's been that way ever since."

"*Dios mío!*" I hold out my glass and she fills it. "Have you talked with Angelica about it?"

"Oh, I've tried to, Andee, more than once. But our talks always end up the same way—with our screaming at each other. You can't imagine how desperate I feel."

"What about Cuauhtémoc? Have you confronted him?"

Biting her lip, Gabriela says, "I've tried to. But every time, he stops me cold with...his look. You've seen those eyes, Andee."

"But Gabriela, your own daughter! How can you allow that loathsome man to..."

Half rising from her seat, she cries: "Do you think I like it?"

"Forgive me, Gabriela." I reach over and rub her hand. "I considered ordering her out of the house, but why just turn her over to him? Then, about a week ago, something happened...something that made me run to my Bible. I had to find that verse where Paul says we're not wrestling with flesh and blood, but with principalities and powers."

She squints at me, like the light is hurting her eyes. "Andee, what I'm going to tell you is literally out of this world. I'm afraid you'll think I've lost my mind."

"Is this where Hector comes in?"

"No," she says impatiently, "I'll tell you about him later. This is about my *abuelito*."

"Your grandfather? But I thought he was…"

"Of course he's dead. I told you my story was going to be out of this world! Andee, are you sure you want to hear this? It's been so long since we talked I'm afraid…" She's studying my face, her brow furrowed.

I try to smile: "Go ahead, Gabriela, and if I have trouble believing you, I'll let you know."

She takes a deep breath. "Well, I can't ask any more than that. Here goes:

"Four Saturday afternoons ago, as usual, Cuauhémoc was at our house. About five we were in Angie's apartment drinking coffee. My sister-in-law Eunice was with us. Out of the blue she asked, 'Who's playing squash?' Remember, Andee, we have a squash court connecting to the house through a door in Angie's apartment.

"I told her nobody, we were the only ones in the house. But she held up a hand and whispered:

'Listen!'

"Then I heard it: poom…poom…poom…. The sound of a rubber ball hitting a racquet, then bouncing off a wall.

"A chill ran up my spine. We sat there looking at each other, frozen. Finally *El Maestro* got up and strode to the door leading out to the squash court. We followed. He threw the door open and we could see the court was dark. Then…we saw it!"

Gabriela jumps over to my chair, pushes my legs aside and sits on the edge of the seat. "Please, Andee, hold me!"

Wrapping my arms around her, I pull her close to my chest. She's shivering. "Take it easy, Gabi," I whisper in her ear, "everything's going to be all right."

She gives a convulsive sob. "I wish I could believe that!…. Andee, it was so scary! We could see no one, only a tiny red light striking a side wall, then the back wall, then back to the court. And the soft sound of a ball hitting a racquet was even clearer now: poom...poom... poom...poom...."

I'm beyond thinking. I hear myself say: "Just because you couldn't see anyone doesn't mean nobody was there."

Half turning, her eyes huge, she says: "Thank you for saying that, Andee. Several times these last few sleepless nights, I've almost convinced myself I dreamed all this."

I kiss her forehead. "My love, remember the running shoes on my kitchen table? Those shoes taught me demons have a twisted sense of humor. And sometimes they use it to scare us."

She touches her lips to mine. "I feel better already, just hearing you say you understand."

Rising, she paces back and forth. Finally she stops, facing me, hands outstretched, appealing for understanding: "But I still haven't told you yet the strangest part of my story.

"As soon as we saw what was happening Cuauhtémoc pushed us back into the apartment and closed the door. 'You ladies go upstairs,' he ordered, 'I'll take care of this.'

"We were too shocked to do anything but obey. We went into the kitchen, made a fresh pot of tea and sat at the table avoiding each other's eyes. I don't remember anything we said, except for Angelica's comment that she was thankful her brother Hector was at the movies.

"After maybe half an hour Cuauhtémoc walked in, very calm. He told us, as if giving the time of day: 'Your father and grandfather were playing a lively game of squash. They didn't want to leave, said it was like old times.'

"Can you imagine how we felt! When he smiled I wanted to slap him in the face."

Gabriela sinks down to her seat, face ashen. "The three of us sat staring at each other, remembering how my father and grandfather loved to play squash. Ten years before his death *Abuelito* built the court, and until the last year of his life, when he became ill, he and *Papá* spent

Saturday mornings playing like two kids, running all over the place, yelling at each other." A hand grabs my ut, squeezing hard. If I feel like this just hearing her story, what must she have felt, looking at *El Maestro's* impudent face? "When you got your breath back, what did you say?"

"I begged Cuauhtemoc to tell *Papá* and *Abuelito* to go back to heaven, and never come down again."

"I'm sure he had an appropriate reply."

She grimaces. "You should have seen his face. He was enjoying himself! He knew how I was suffering because of what he was doing to my daughter. And now this!"

"Do you know what Moisés would say? He'd say it wasn't your father and grandfather on that squash court, just a couple of demons doing a pantomime."

Gabriela raises her eyebrows. "I hope you're right. Because if *El Maestro* has the power to order my dead father and grandfather around...but no matter—"

She jumps to her feet, waving a fist. "He's gone too far. I'm not going to put up with it any more, not even if Cuauhtémoc Luna is the devil himself! First he stole my daughter. Now..." she gasps, "my son is ready to cut my throat."

I take her hand and guide her back to the seat. "What are you saying, Gabi? Has Hector threatened you?"

She drops her head into her hands, sobbing. I feel helpless, wishing there was something I could do. At last she reaches over, pulls a handful of tissues from the box and dries her face. Taking a deep breath, she continues:

"It happened the night after that business on the squash court. I was so scared I forgot how angry I was with you. I knew you were the only one who could help me! First I dialed your office. There was no answer. Then I tried your apartment. Again no answer. I kept trying until after midnight. It finally became obvious you must be out of the city. I panicked, afraid you'd left for good!

"Day before yesterday I caught Rebeca in the office. She told me you had gone home for the holidays and she had no idea when you'd be back. She sounded so forlorn it frightened me…like she knew you might never return."

She reaches out and wraps her arms around my neck. "Andee, if you can't help me, I don't know what I'll do!"

"I'll do what I can, Gabriela, but first you've got to tell me everything."

"All right." She takes a deep breath. "After the way Cuauhtémoc handled that awful scene on the squash court I decided to take things into my own hands. When Hector came home that night I told him he was no longer going to be able to see *El Maestro*.

"I expected an explosion. Instead, without a word he turned on his heel and marched upstairs to his room."

"I waited a while, wondering what to do. Finally I decided: I wasn't going to let him go to sleep until he promised me he would never try to see Cuautémoc Luna again.

"His door was closed. I knocked, waited a moment, and when there was no answer, pushed open the door."

She pauses, her eyes on the floor, her lips twisted, struggling to find the words. "He was seated at his study table. I couldn't believe my eyes! He had a large hunting knife in his hand and was running it back and forth over a whetting stone. He must have been doing it a lot, because the knife glistened as he moved it.

"I screamed at him: 'What do you think you're doing? Where did you get that knife?'

"He didn't look up, he just kept moving the knife back and forth over the stone. The grating sound of it sent a chill up my spine.

"'Give it to me right now!' I demanded. I stuck my hand out ready to grasp it. He pulled back the knife and hugged it to his chest, and for the first time he looked me in the eye.

"If I live to be a hundred, I'll never forget that look. His face was black as midnight and his eyes burned with hatred! This was my son!"

Her voice quivers: "If we hadn't had that table between us...I doubt that I'd be standing here now!"

A tear slips down her cheek. I wait a moment before I ask, "What happened next? Did he give you the knife?"

She lets out a long shuddering sigh. "No, he laid it on the desk, stood to his feet, and said, in the calmest voice, as if he were talking to a child, 'Mother, you're being unreasonable. Have you forgotten how much I've changed since *El Maestro* has been helping me? You don't want me to go back to failing in school, do you?'

"I was looking at him, seeing the body of my son, but the face and the voice belonged to a stranger. And those eyes, they were mocking me! 'Hector,' I told him, my voice shaking, 'it's over between you and Cuauhtémoc. Now give me that knife.' I was so scared! I was afraid he'd pick it up and plunge it into me!

"Instead, he shoved it so hard it slid across the desk and fell, sticking into the floor. He laughed and flopped on his bed. With his back toward me, he emphasized each word: '*Mujer*...you can take...the *maldita* knife, but...you can't...take away *El Maestro*. Never! I'll live on the street first!'"

Brushing away a tear, Gabriela reaches for my hand. "Andee, that was a week ago. We haven't talked since. He comes downstairs in the morning and fixes his own breakfast. He leaves the house and I don't see him until after dark, when he goes upstairs to his room and slams the door.

"Do you see why I've been so desperate to talk with you? These last three nights with my son locked up in his room and my daughter downstairs in her apartment with her...her lover from hell—I've felt like a captain on a stormy sea, waiting for his ship to go down!"

She drops to her knees, and her face in my lap, clings to me.

Gabriela loves me, and needs me! I should be ecstatic, but a part of me wants to board a plane tomorrow and never come back. Will it always be like this, an unending battle against the curse that clings to this country like the tentacles of an octopus?

But I can't abandon Gabriela! It comes to me like a curtain being pulled aside, a quiet, certain revelation: Gabriela is suffering because of me; Quetzalcóatl is attacking her to get at me.

I slip to the floor beside her and hold her in my arms. I hear the words I'm saying as if they're not mine, as if someone else were saying them: "Cuauhtémoc can only do to you and your children what you allow him to do."

She says, her voice weary: "But I'm so afraid."

"As long as he can convince you to be afraid of him, he has you under his control. But the moment you assert your authority in Christ he'll lose his power over you."

She sits up, folding under her legs, and for the first time I see a spark of hope in her eyes. She listens intently as I outline a plan of action.

CHAPTER 28

▼

A BREAKTHROUGH

"Guess what, Gelda, it's happened!" I know I'm yelling like an excited teenager, but I don't care; Gelda and I have been praying for this for nearly a year.

"*Que Pasó?*", Andrew?" Gelda is German, and I'm American, but the only way we can communicate is in Spanish.

"Wilbert just called, very excited. Says he has something important to tell me. I invited him to come this afternoon at six."

"*Gracias a Dios*! I'll be praying till you phone and tell me how your meeting came out." She could have added, "I told you so!" but she didn't. That's Gelda. In the past nine months she has become my strong right arm.

I hang up smiling, remembering her visit the day following my disappointing encounter with Wilbert. I was angry at her for getting my expectations up, and at myself for believing her. I told her Wilbert was the poorest excuse for a human being I had ever met, and only an idiot would expect God to speak through a person like him.

"Andrew," she said evenly, "if God spoke to Baalam through the mouth of an ass, don't you think he's capable of speaking to you through Wilbert?"

As I tried to think of an appropriate answer she continued: "God told me he's going to use that man to open doors for you. God never lies." And she concluded, "But remember, I didn't say God told me when it was going to happen."

Before the visit was over I no longer had any doubts that Gelda Lohman was the intercessor Moisés had promised long ago.

I appreciate the way she listens quietly, patiently as I tell her about my trials, complain about my disappointments, share my doubts. She seldom gives advice, but after her visits decisions come more easily.

By the time the doorbell rings, Rebeca has left for her classes, so I answer the door. The man standing there is dressed in a freshly pressed, tailored navy blue uniform and a gold-braided pilot's cap. Very impressive! Without the fat stogie jutting from his mouth I wouldn't have recognized him.

"It's good to see you, Wilbert, come in. But if you don't mind..."

"I know, douse my *puro*." Wilbert snuffs out the cigar on the sole of one of his brightly polished black loafers.

"Looks like you're coming from work," I say, waving him to a chair.

"Yeah, and man I'm worn out. Got up at four A.M. to go to the Presidential hangar and check out the 'copter. Since eight I've been jockeying *El Presidente* all over the *Distrito Federal*." Pulling a white handkerchief from his coat pocket he carefully dusts the elegant cap placed in his lap.

"I almost called and postponed the visit, but I knew you'd be anxious to find out why I wanted to talk with you." He grimaces. "And besides, I knew if I went home without seeing you Rosario would kick me out of the house By the way, she didn't call you today, did she?"

"As a matter of fact she did, Wilbert."

He scowls. "If she told you all about it, why am I here?"

I reach over and pat his arm. "She didn't tell me a thing. Just warned me to get ready for some exciting news."

By now, Rosario considers me her friend. I guess she's right, though we fought about her cigarettes every time she came to see me last year.

It was a relief when she finally agreed to try to convince her husband to come for counseling too. But so far, no luck.

I force myself to sit down opposite Wilbert. I'm so uptight I'd much rather be pacing the floor. "Come on, Wilbert, let's have it. I haven't been able to concentrate on anything today, wondering what in the world is bringing you to my *consultorio*."

Frowning, the President's favorite pilot plucks the cigar from his shirt pocket and bites into it with his straight, pearly-white teeth. "Remember, Doctór, I mentioned to you my boss, *el Señor General* Raymundo Camacho?"

"Yes, I remember," I stand up, fidgeting, hands on hips. "Is this about him?"

"Well, in a way. Did I tell you the General is a…um-m-m…*mujer-iego?*"

"A what?"

He grins. "A ladies' man."

Sighing, I resume my seat. (Something tells me this is going to take a while.) "No, you haven't told me anything about your boss."

"Well, he's old enough to be my father, but since he's a big shot, it's easy for him to impress pretty young women." He grins again. "That is, until he met La Novicia Rebelde."

I translate in my mind: "the rebellious novice".… "What on earth are you talking about, Wilbert?"

He takes another bite out of his cigar. "That's the name of a play. It ran most of last year in the Rerforma Theater downtown. There was a movie of it in English…'The Sound of Music.'"

"My wife loved that picture! So he tried to date the star?"

"Right. Her name's Anastacia. Beautiful, isn't it?"

He excuses himself and goes out to the bathroom. Fidgeting, I pour myself a cup of coffee. I've almost drained my cup by the time he returns…sniff…sniff…cigar smoke. I pick up the coffee pot and pour him a cup. "Milk?"

"No, make mine black. And strong." He spoons in three teaspoons of sugar and takes a big swallow, smacking his lips.

"Beep…beep…beep."

"Oops, it's the General!" Wilbert grabs his waist and shuts off the beeper.

"Mind?" Reaching for my phone, he dials a number. "*Sí, Señor General*," he repeats half a dozen times, nodding his head over and over. Hanging up, he growls, "*Dios mío*, something has come up and I've got to go back to the hangar."

"Now Wilbert…" The man's not going to leave me in suspense, if necessary I'll wrestle him to the floor!

Wilbert Montemayor holds up his hand. "No, no, *Don* Andrés, I'm not going until I finish my story. But I'm going to have to hurry."

(Then thank goodness for the phone call!)

When he picks up the thread of his narrative I'm pleased to discover he can speak rapidly and quite clearly when necessary:

In August of last year the General took Wilbert and several of his officers to see a presentation of *La Novicia Rebelde*. They were captivated by the performance of the bright-faced young star who sang in a soaring, exhilarating soprano. Each one of them was sure her dazzling smile was especially for him.

After the curtain calls the General told his men to wait outside a few minutes. "Wish me luck, I'm going backstage to see what the *muchacha* is doing between now and daybreak!"

Half an hour later he returned. "How did it go, *mi General*?" a lieutenant asked.

The big, dark man straightened his broad shoulders and grunted, "*Magnífico*! The *muchacha* is even more charming up close than she appears on stage."

One of the men made an obscene gesture. "So the rest of us going to have to catch a taxi?" The others laughed.

The General scowled. "Oh, I'll be taking her out soon, but not tonight. Her mamá was hovering over me like she thought I was a fox invading her chicken coop. What a pain!"

For the next two months the General pursued Anastacia with military precision. Every night at the close of her performance she found a large bouquet of roses in her dressing room. At least once a week he attended the play, and afterward managed to visit the enchanting young actress…but only for a few minutes.

Finally, in mid-October she agreed to have lunch with him. The next day he confided she was the most intriguing female he'd ever met.

"The woman must be pushing thirty, but she could pass for eighteen. She graduated from college five years ago and then hooked up with a no-good husband. Her divorce became final just a couple of months ago. I guess that's why her mother hangs over her like a black thunderhead. When I took her home she insisted I go inside for a cup of tea. As soon as I sat down I realized it was so the old lady could grill me."

Apparently Wilbert's boss didn't pass mamá's exam. After their first date Anastacia was always too busy to accept another invitation. When the play closed, General Camacho continued calling her. He seemed obsessed with the conviction that his manhood would be compromised if he didn't find a way to take her to bed.

When he called her house the first week of December a maid informed him the *señorita* was out of town.

"And where has she gone?" the General asked, suddenly hopeful. If she was on vacation in Cancun or Acapulco maybe she'd be more accessible!

The maid was silent, as if considering whether she should reveal the whereabouts of her mistress.

The General knew how to handle lowly maids! "Do you know who you're talking to, *Niña*? I am General Raymundo Coronado Camacho Garibaldi, the right hand of *El SeñorPresidente de la República*! Answer me!"

"*Perdóneme, honorable Señor General,*" she sniffled, "I only know *la señorita* left yesterday for the United States to be with her mother."

In the following weeks the General was insufferable, his staff could do nothing please him. Behind his back they speculated over the reason for their superior's behavior. One of them was sure he had fallen hopelessly in love. Another insisted it was nothing more than frustration. The General was an addict who had been introduced to an enticing new drug and until he had the chance to try it out, he was going to make life miserable for all of them.

"A few days ago," Wilbert continues, moving to the edge of his seat, "I arrived early at the hangar, and General Camacho was already there, pacing about. I tried to slip into the command center without him spotting me, afraid he'd be in another of his vile moods. But as soon as he saw me, he boomed out: 'Guess what, Wilbert, I did it!'"

"Immediately I knew he was talking about the *Señorita* Anastasia.

"'Is she home?' I asked, already afraid for her.

"'Yes, she's home,' my boss said, 'and tonight I'm taking her to dinner!' The old man smiled and winked at me, 'without her mother!'

"My heart sank. I'd bet my colleagues the General would fail this time.

"But the next day the General arrived in a fury. 'That crazy woman! In all my life, I've never been so humiliated!'"

Wilbert reaches over, picks up his cup of cold coffee and sips it noisily.

I want to strangle him! "Come on, Wilbert, what did she do? Why was the General so mad?"

He closes his eyes, and chuckling, shakes his head slowly.

"Get the picture, Doctór: the General walks into this elegant restaurant with a charming young woman. The waiters know him, of course; this isn't the first beautiful lady he's entertained here. And everyone recognizes the captivating *Novicia Rebelde.*"

The General ordered the house's best red wine, then, as they sipped, initiated his strategy.

Wilbert explodes in laughter. "I wish you could have been there in the hangar with us, Doctór, when the General yelled '*Muchacha tonta!* and slammed his fist through the wall. You should see the size of the hole he left. We haven't repaired it yet!

"Then he explained that Angelica opened her purse, and he thought she was reaching for a cigarrete. But you know what she pulled out?" Wilbert pauses dramatically, raising his cup in a salute. "A Bible! That's right, a Holy Bible! And right there in the restaurant, with people around them straining to hear, she told him he was a black-hearted sinner headed straight for hell!"

Wilbert takes another sip of his coffee, waiting my reaction. At last I manage to sputter: "Anastacia, talking to him about his soul?" I can't stop shaking my head. "But how...what...had something happened on her trip?"

"That's what I asked the General. He began cursing the United States. Like most military men, Doctór, he despises your country. He was furious at Anastacia for letting some gringo brainwash her."

"The dinner must have been a disaster."

"They never got past than the wine. The General picked up his mobile phone, dialed a number, talked for a moment, informed the *Señorita* that an emergency had arisen, and told the waiter to call her a taxi."

I sit staring at him, trying to digest this sensational news. "What do you think happened to Anastacia on that visit to the United States, Wilbert?"

He says, "Doctór, I don't have to think. I know exactly what happened: she became our sister in the Lord."

"What makes you so sure, Wilbert? Not that I'm taking the General's side...he's a scoundrel. But..." I shrug, wanting to believe, but remembering disappointments in the past with the "conversions" of famous people, "a lot of people run around waving the Bible who..."

"Please! He holds up his hand like a policeman stopping traffic, "permit me to finish my story. When I got home that night I told

Rosario what had happened. She shouted 'Halleluya! glory to God!' and demanded I call the *señorita* immediately."

"Did you?"

"You know Rosario. He drains his cup, belches loudly, and continues: "once she makes up her mind there's no changing it. Yes, I called her."

"I'm surprised you had her number."

Wilbert grins sheepishly. "One day when the General was dialing her I watched his finger and jotted it down. I kidded the other guys about calling her myself and asking for a date.

"I was surprised when she answered; I'd expected a maid. I told her a white lie: that the General had asked me to express his regrets for running out on her. And guess what…she started witnessing to me! When I told her I was also a believer she was suspicious.

"Then Rosario grabbed the phone out of my hand and began talking a mile a minute. I waited around until I saw I'd never get the phone back; Rosario was quoting Bible verses and preaching at her like mad."

He holds out his cup. "I'm bushed! "Any coffee left?"

"You sit right there and I'll bring the pot." I jump up and fill his cup. When I spoon in his three helpings of sugar my hand is trembling.

"What happened next?" I ask, afraid he'll check his watch and tell me he has to leave.

"When I got back from my shower Rosario had hung up. Man, was she high! They'd talked without stopping for almost an hour. She told me *Señorita* Anastacia had invited her to come for a visit."

He empties his cup with one swallow, wipes his lips with the back of his hand and says, "Then she told me something that surprised me…and that's why I'm here, Doctór. Said she opened her mouth to accept Anastacia's invitation and all at once she was strangling. While she was trying to get her breath the Lord told her *you* should visit Anastacia, not her!"

I'm staring at Wilbert, speechless, as he reaches for the phone. "Doctór, guess what? *Señorita* Anastacia is expecting a call from you!"

I listen, dumbfounded, as he greets her. Then he hands me the receiver. I stammer that I'm looking forward to meeting her. A sweet, golden voice tells me she and her mother would love to see me tomorrow at five.

Wilbert looks at his watch. "*Ay*, I've got to go. The General's going to kill me for taking so long."

I hardly hear him, overwhelmed by the intuition that, after tomorrow, my life will never be the same.

CHAPTER 29

▼

ANASTACIA!

I press the bright brass button in the white stone wall.

No answer.

I punch the button again, harder.

"*¿Quién?*" I jump at the shrill voice of the maid on the interphone.

"Andrés Kelly."

"*¿Quien?*"

"Doctór Andrés Kelly!"

"*Un momento.*"

The buzzer finally sounds and I push open the gate, expecting to see a uniformed maid waiting at the door. Instead I'm startled by the vision of an angel ascending from below, first, auburn hair, then a smiling face.

Here in *La Herradura* the architecture is different from Gabriela's *colonia*, just fifteen minutes away. There, imposing stone mansions lift their heads in arrogant splendor above high stone walls. But *LaHerradura* is serrated by deep canyons, so the houses wrap themselves around the hills and hang on for dear life. One can only imagine the form of the residence hidden behind a wall. This house is an example. From the street I saw only a red-tiled roof. Now, inside the gate, I understand why: to get to the first floor I'll have to go down a flight of stairs.

"*Bienvenido*, Brother".

Anastacia hurries to meet me and enfolds me in an *abrazo*, her unruly curls tickling my cheeks. She holds me for a moment, patting my back, long enough for me to catch the scent of jasmine bath powder. Stepping back, she takes both my hands in hers, her smile lighting up the somber January afternoon. "Since Rosario's call last night, Andrés, Mother and I have been impatient to meet you. In your country we were loved by brothers and sisters in Christ. We've been hoping to find the same love in our home town. So you see, you're an answer to prayer."

Could anyone not smile back at that bright, open face? Listening to the music of her voice I remember my Spanish teacher in college exhorting us: "Now class, remember, this is a language that flows from the soul. You don't speak it, you sing it!"

I feel clumsy, tongue-tied. "Anastacia, you...you too are an answer to prayer."

Releasing my hands, she turns: "Come on down, Mother's waiting for us." As we descend the broad, brightly-polished mahogany stairs she says, "I hope you'll forgive me for receiving you in a house coat. When the sun peeked out from behind the clouds a little while ago I couldn't resist jumping in the pool. "Mami's a little peeved because I let the time get away from me."

We step into a broad parlor dominated by a black baby grand piano. The curtains are pulled back from the picture windows, giving a view of green hills sprinkled with white houses.

"*Mami*, this is Doctór Andrés Kelly."

From the dining room Anastacia's mother strides toward me, her hand extended. "Mercedes de los Ríos, *a sus órdenes*, Doctór." The smile is friendly, but reserved. Dressed in a dark pants suit and tailored white blouse, Anastacia's mother is half a head taller than her daughter. Her straight brown hair is drawn back in a knot, accenting high cheeks painted a delicate rose. As her cool gray eyes measure me from head to foot I understand why General Camacho perceived her as a menace.

I take her hand, intuitively executing a half bow.

"My brother, I'm sure Anastacia has already told you how excited we were when we received the call from *Señora* Rosario. Please have a seat. We have so much to talk about!"

She indicates a graceful white satin sofa. I'm thankful I decided to wear a dark suit and conservative tie.

Anastacia is still at the door, tightly clutching a brightly-flowered housecoat around her. "Andrés, I'm going to leave you and mother to chat while I get into something decent."

I watch her leave, surprised at the warmth in my heart for this creature I met only a few minutes ago.

Doña Mercedes takes a seat opposite me. I know she'll reserve her approval until after a respectful inquisition.

"Doctór, *La Señora* Montemayor gave an unqualified recommendation of you." She allows herself a benevolent smile. "Tell me about yourself. I'm intrigued that a man established in his profession, as you obviously were, should want to start all over again in our city."

Beginning with Mary's death, I give her a running account of my life. I can see her gradually relaxing. I explain why I believe God has brought me to Mexico, but omit my ongoing battle with Quetzalcóatl; no sense in straining the credulity of this stern lady!

I pause, fixing my eyes on her, waiting for questions. Instead, she picks up a tiny bronze bell from the table beside her and rings it. A door opens at the far side of the dining room and a maid appears.

"Calendaria, you may bring the tea now."

"*Hola*, have you two become acquainted?" Anastacia, dressed in pleated white slacks and a red silk shirt, skips into the room and flops down beside me.

Reaching over, she touches my hand. "Has *Mami* scared you? She does most men!"

Mercedes smiles fondly at her daughter. "Doctór, you're a psychologist. Tell Anastacia that stern mothers are God's gift to reckless girls like her."

Anastacia smiles back: "And tell *Doña* Mercedes that mothers ought not to make frightening changes in their lives without first warning their daughters! Have you told him yet about what happened, *Mami?*"

"No, I wanted to wait until you were here."

The tea arrives. As we stir in the sugar I ask Anastacia if she has plans for another play any time soon.

She and her mother exchange glances. "It's in God's hands. At present I'm reviewing several scripts. I love the theater, but now that Jesus is my Lord, I don't know if I'm willing to pay the price it demands."

I lean forward, "And now, what are these 'frightening changes' you mentioned, Anastacia?"

Putting down her teacup, Mercedes begins: "I retired from the theater twenty years ago, a widow with a small daughter and no means of support. Here in Mexico, Doctór, very few *artistas* end their careers with much more than a scrapbook of reviews and the clothes on their back. I decided to enroll in the university and learn a profession."

Four years later Mercedes graduated from the University of Anahuac with a degree in interior decorating. Thanks to contacts made during her theatrical career she was soon able to attract a distinguished clientele. Among these was a Mexican industrialist who a few months ago engaged her to decorate a vacation home he was building near Denver.

"I rented a furnished apartment and had a lot of opportunities to practice my English as I lined up sub-contractors.

"Among these was a young couple I contracted for the draperies. From the beginning I noticed something special about Charles and Martha Johnson: they went out of their way to please me, were scrupulously honest…and they seemed so happy!

"One day I asked them why. Martha laughed. 'If you'd like to know, come to our house tonight.'

"By the time I arrived every seat in the Johnsons' living room was occupied, and half a dozen people were seated on the floor. A handsome, muscular young man jumped up and offered me his place.

"What was that thick red book in his hand? As I thanked him and sat down I saw the title in black letters: 'Holy Bible.' I looked around. Everyone else in the room seemed to be clutching that same book! What had I gotten myself into? I wanted to get up and run out the door. But now Martha was introducing me and the people were smiling a welcome. I mustn't make a scene!

"They began singing to the accompaniment of a guitar. I felt my body relax, and my foot began tapping in time with the simple, repetitive choruses about the joy of knowing Jesus. Someone read a passage that described Jesus as a vine and his followers as the branches. A discussion exploded all around me. I sat silent, impressed by the way everybody struggled to apply the study to their everyday lives.

"I considered myself a fairly religious person; I attended mass at least once a month and every now and then went to confession. But I'd always shed my religion at the door of the church. This was different; these people seemed to know the Jesus of the Bible personally.

"I had trouble falling asleep that night. Early the next morning I called Martha and Charles and asked some questions. They invited me to lunch."

Mercedes rings for the maid and she brings a fresh pot of tea and a plate of cookies. Anastacia takes up the story: "When Mami called and told me she had 'met Jesus' I was flabbergasted. My mother had always scorned people who went to mass two or three times a week or had statues of the Virgin in their kitchen. I told myself she'd soon come to her senses.

"I was wrong. She started calling me every day, begging me to come and see what she had discovered. I was terribly concerned; Mother and

I had always been so close, and now I felt alienated from her. I was anxious to bring her home and nurse her back to sanity. My performances the last couple of weeks were a torture."

As soon as she could get away Anastacia flew to her mother. What a surprise! She had been bracing herself for an encounter with an agitated, irrational female. Instead, she found her mother happier and more at peace than she had ever seen her.

"Mami was so-o-o patient with me. At first I yelled at her, pleaded with her to consider what people back home would say. She just kept telling me how her life had changed since she came to know Jesus Christ, not as a religious icon, but as a personal friend."

Anastacia pauses, her face glowing. "Then one morning, after a sleepless night, the Holy Spirit did the same work of grace in my heart that he had done in Mother's."

Anastacia picks up a well-thumbed Bible from the coffee table. "And now we'd like to ask you some questions. May we?"

"Of course. Just remember I'm not a theologian."

For the next hour we talk about grace, faith, salvation, the Christian life, holiness, the Person of Christ, the Holy Spirit. I'm impressed at how well these two women know the Bible after such a short time. Before long I realize that most of their questions are not for their own edification, but to help them decide if I'm a true brother.

At last Anastacia closes her Bible. "I don't believe I have any more questions. Do you, Mother?"

Mercedes looks at me, and I see in her eyes the acceptance she has withheld until this moment. "No, for the last ten minutes I've been praising the Lord. Doctór Kelly, you are a good man bearing good tidings. God has sent you to us; from this day forward *mi casa es su casa*."

Anastacia drops to her knees, takes my hand and pulls me down beside her. Mercedes kneels near us, and the three of us pour out our hearts in thanksgiving.

"Amen!" Anastacia jumps up, runs to the corner of the room in her stocking feet, picks up a guitar, and perches herself on a stool. Strumming, she says, "I learned this song in Denver and translated it into Spanish."

She sings about Jesus, barely whispering at first, increasing volume, accelerating the rhythm until the room is overflowing with a melody so pure, so mellow my heart is in danger of exploding from my chest…my spirit carries me to the green hills of Galilee where I walk with Anastacia and my Lord. I see him feeding the hungry, embracing the little children. I shudder as my Savior writhes on the cross…I tremble as I kneel before my resurrected King, feeling his cool hand on my brow….

More sweetly than I have ever known before, Anastacia has brought me into the presence of Jesus. Seated on the floor, smiling back at that young face luminous with love, I can sense a divine needle knitting our hearts together like Jonathan and David.

"Come with me, Andrés, I want to show you something!"

Taking my arm, Anastacia guides me toward the stairway.

"Don't be too long," Mercedes admonishes, "Supper will be ready in a few minutes." (Oh? I didn't know I'd been invited to supper!)

Descending a long flight of stairs we come to a brightly-lit hallway. "This is the bedroom floor," Anastacia tells me. "It's much too much just for mother and me. Before the breakup of my marriage I dreamed of filling these rooms with my children." She pauses, face clouding. "Maybe some day!…but come, this is not what I brought you down to see."

We descend another flight of stairs, and Anastacia flips a switch. I blink: a high cathedral ceiling arches over a polished tile floor to sheer glass walls overlooking a green manicured lawn.

"What a beautiful place!"

"When we built our dream home *Mami* and I wanted a party room where we could entertain our friends. And where, later, her grandchildren could romp on rainy days." She shrugs. "We had no idea God had other plans."

Striding to the other side of the room she slides open a wide glass door and swings an arm in a dramatic gesture: "*Voilá*!"

My mouth drops open.

"I suppose you've noticed there are very few outdoor pools here in Mexico City. That's because it's so chilly most of the time. An inside pool with a thermal roof is the answer!"

Kneeling on the bright green tile floor I let my hand dangle in the warm water.

Anastacia giggles. "Ever since we got back home Mami and I have been talking about how God must have smiled when he saw us building this floor. He was seeing our party room filled with people listening to the Word of God. As for the pool..." she pauses, her eyes wide, inviting me.

I clap my hands: "Baptisms!"

She gives me an enthusiastic hug. "Now do you see why I brought you down here?"

It's almost midnight when I arrive home. As the elevator door opens on my floor I hear the phone ringing. Fumbling with my keys, I finally get the door open, but just as I reach for the receiver the phone stops ringing!

Grunting in frustration I throw my keys on the coffee table. Who'd be calling at this hour?

Gabriela!

Stop it, Andrew! You've been having this fantasy for months.... But it's not a fantasy now, Gabriela promised to call me when she was ready for our encounter with Cuauhtémoc.... And what if she *has* been calling me? Remember, I went straight from the office to my appointment with Anastacia and Mercedes.

I reach for the phone. A little voice nags me: "You're going to wake her up, Andrew. She's not going to like that!"

Shaking my head I set the phone back in the cradle.

"I don't care!" I say it out loud as I begin dialing.

Only one ring, and immediately: "*Bueno?*"

"Gabriela, forgive me for calling so late, but—"

"Andee! I dialed your number only a minute ago. How did you know?"

"I just knew." My throat constricts, making it difficult to speak.

"Andee, (She clears her throat. Is she having trouble with her emotions too?) "I called to tell you I'm ready."

I grip the phone. "Did...did you make an appointment with him?"

"Yes,"...a long pause..."he's coming over tomorrow at eleven. I hope you..."

"Of course I'll be there. Look, shouldn't we talk first? I can come right now, if you want!"

A quick intake of breath. She speaks slowly, as if talking to herself, her voice so soft I cram the receiver to my ear, straining to hear: "I'd love to have you come...and never leave me again." Her voice breaks. "But I'm afraid...look, why don't you come tomorrow about ten?"

I sigh. "Okay, I'll be there." Why do I feel so close to tears?

"Goodnight, my dear, sweet Andee."

Something about her voice, affectionate but muted, leaves me with a dull foreboding that keeps me wide-eyed until I hear the clock strike two.

▼

A VICTORY AND A HEARTBREAK

I arrive at Gabriela's house a little after ten. It's reassuring to know she's expecting me. The memory of the last time still haunts me. I can still remember how it felt to be all alone, and finally to leave, rejected and defeated.

"Are you sure you're ready for this, Gabriela?" I ask her after we're seated in the parlor.

"I'm at peace, Andrés, I've spent a lot of time reading my Bible and praying. Remember what you told me: Cuauhtémoc can only do to me what I give him permission to do."

As we chat like old times I resist the impulse to tell her how much I love her. That can wait.

After a while she looks at her watch. "It's almost eleven-thirty. Maybe he's guessed why I want to see him and won't show up."

"He'll be here. Even if he's suspicious, I bet he'll come anyway, just to twist the knife in your back."

The doorbell! The maid scurries in from the kitchen. We hear Cuauhtémoc's guttural voice: "*La Señora* is expecting me."

Sí, *Señor*, come in." The big man advances into the living room, then pauses when he sees Gabriela seated in a rocking chair, a Bible in her lap. Bowing slightly he says, "Here I am, *Sra.* Gabriela, *a sus órdenes.*" Dressed in a rumpled black gymn suit, he looks even more loathsome than I remember. My nose tells he hasn't taken time to shower after his morning workout. What impertinence!

And what a contrast with Gabriela, dressed in pristine white, her dark, freshly shampooed hair glistening, a blue kerchief at her throat— the incarnation of wholesomeness.

"I suppose you remember Doctór Kelly." Gabriela motions toward me and Cuauhtémoc turns. Seeing me, his lips tighten.

I smile at him. Never have I felt more at one with this woman I love. Just minutes ago we read Christ's promises: "Whatever you ask when you pray, believe that you have received it and you shall have it.... If two of you shall agree on earth as touching anything that they shall ask, it will be given to them by my Father who is in heaven."

"Have a seat *Maestro*," Gabriela says softly, indicating a straight chair brought in from the kitchen. Her visitor obeys, his body rigid, fists clenched. This is the way Gabriela wanted to do it, and I agreed. It's her house that has been violated, so she has the right to call the shots.

"Look, Señora, I don't know why you...and the doctór...wanted me to come here, but—"

Gabriela leans toward him, spearing him with her eyes. "Be quiet and listen, Cuahtémoc, I have something to say to you!"

Sitting behind him I see his shoulders tensing. I fidget, wishing I could see the man's face.

Gabriela opens her Bible. "You've told me, *Señor*, that you read the Bible. Maybe you remember this verse from the forty-first Psalm: "Even my own familiar friend, in whom I trusted, who ate my bread, has lifted up his heel against me."

Cuauhtémoc half rises from his seat.

"Sit down, *Maestro*, I haven't finished!" Her voice is still quiet, but edged with steel. "Some time ago my daughter invited you into our home, and I welcomed you with open arms. You ate at my table, convinced me you were our friend. But soon you took away from us the love of God's Word that we had learned from Doctór Andrés. Then you won the love of my daughter and converted us into strangers. And now," her voices rises, "you've made my only son my enemy!"

She gets up from her chair, brandishing her Bible. "*Hombre maldito*, do you know what a lioness does when an enemy invades her lair?"

From behind, I imagine Cuahtémoc's dark face flushed with wrath, black eyes burning.

"Answer me!"

Cuahtémoc's body stiffens, his hands clenched. What's he going to do? I rub my sweaty palms on my pants legs, ready to spring to her defense.

Gabriela slams her Bible shut, and clutching it to her breast, cries: "You won't answer? Then I'll tell what she does: she rips him apart!"

Cuauhtemoc pushes back his chair, toppling it. I'm about to step to Gabriela's side when I'm surprised to hear his voice, soft, pleading. "*Señora*, yesterday you called and invited me to your house. I was delighted, because we haven't had the opportunity to talk much recently. But now...what a surprise! You accuse me of terrible things! What has this...*caballero*..." he half turns, lip curled, "been saying to you?"

"Nothing that I hadn't already said to myself, Cuauhtémoc, when I saw the hatred in my son's eyes and suddenly realized you're a disciple of the devil!"

A growl rumbles from some deep chamber within him. He reaches for her, but she steps back and trips, falling into her chair.

Instantly, I'm beside the woman I love, emboldened by an authority I've never felt before: "Cuauhtémoc, look at me!"

Fists clenched, eyes bulging, he glares at me.

"Tell me your name, son of Satan!"

Like a cornered lion, he bares his teeth. "Go to hell!"

Hands on my hips, my eyes boring into him, I shout: "Cuauh-temoc, the lady of this house has declared it: you are Satan's disciple. You have no place here!"

Sweat pours from his face, puddling on the white tile floor. He opens his mouth, his lips move, but no sound comes out.

I challenge him: "I dare you: say 'Jesus is Lord!'"

Dreadful obscenities vomit from his mouth. He curses Jesus of Naz-areth, taunts Gabriela, boasts of his power over her children, and chants in a high, sing-song voice a hymn of praise to Satan and Quetzalcóatl.

"Enough! In the name of Jesus Christ shut your foul mouth!"

My face is inches from his, and the heat of his body is like the fires of hell.

His jaws clamp shut, twitching, unable to open, his face purple. He clenches his fists, shoulders heaving, as if struggling against a powerful, invisible foe.

In that moment my heart tells me that Gelda Lohman is on her knees, face lifted to heaven. I'm no longer surprised at this awareness of invincible authority.

Stepping back to Gabriela's side I take her hand. "In Christ's name, we declare this house God's domain."

Gabriela says, in a strong, clear voice, "*Maestro* Cuahtémoc, you are no longer welcome here. Out of my house!"

He stands for a moment, trying vainly to open his mouth, the fire going out of his eyes, jaws going slack. Turning, he rushes out the door.

I pull Gabriela to her feet. Her face pale, she whispers, "Andee, what of my children? Will they be free from that man now?"

I want to invite the woman I love to celebrate. Together we have met the enemy and overcome! Let's shout for joy, dance before the Lord! But looking at her I know she's in no mood for celebration, she's too concerned about her children.

I kiss her damp forehead. "Gabriela, your children will be free when they do what you just did: tell Cuauhtémoc they're no longer going to be his victims."

She sighs. "I guess you're right." She looks up at me, eyes brimming. "Andee, I was so proud of you!"

Taking my hand, she says, "Come into the kitchen. I told the maid to prepare a *merienda* for us. I don't know about you, but I had no appetite for breakfast."

Sitting at the table, munching warm, rich *chilaquiles*, I'm ready to open my heart to her. Gabriela has come back to me, confessed she needs me. We can talk about marriage now! I'm afraid I may do something ridiculous, like sweeping her up in my arms and dancing around the room!

Instead, I reach across the table and take both her hands in mine. "Gabriela, *mi amor*, I'm ready now!"

She frowns. "Ready? Ready for what?"

"Remember? More than a year ago you said, 'Let's get married!' I told you we needed to wait awhile. We've waited long enough. Let's do it!"

I jump up and pull her to her feet. But when I try to kiss her she gently pushes me away. "Please, Andee, so…so much has happened today I'm exhausted. Sit down. I'll make a pot of tea."

Puzzled by her reaction I return to my seat, my heart thudding. Something is wrong! Something bad! I can feel it!

I watch Gabriela at the stove, her back to me. Her movements are jerky, and she keeps shaking her head. Is she rehearsing what she's going to say to me? I try to convince myself she's just worried about her children.

She brings my manzanilla tea and sets down her own cup across the table from me.

I reach for her hand. She withdraws it quickly.

"Gabriela, what—?"

Stopping me with an uplifted hand, she raises her cup to her lips, takes a gulp and sets the cup down so hard it overflows into the saucer.

"Andee..." her lips are trembling. "I...I just can't talk today. Could I see you in your *consultorio* tomorrow?"

I stand to my feet, relieved she's bringing this strange, painful dialogue to an end.

"Tell you what. I'll cancel my eleven o'clock appointment. I'll be expecting you."

Rebeca's voice on the interphone: "Doctór, *Senora* Gabriela is here."

I rise to receive the woman I love. I slept hardly at all last night. Had only a strong black cup of coffee for breakfast.

A moment ago I took my pulse: eighty-eight. Usually it's in the mid-fifties, proud trophy of a veteran jogger. I don't know what it is, but something awful is about to happen! I'd like to be in Chapultepec Park right now running...running...running....

"Good morning, Andee." The dark rings under her eyes tell me she didn't sleep well either.

We sit facing each other, knees touching. I want to reach out and take her hand, but I know I must not.

At last she raises her eyes and says, just above a whisper,"Andee, this...this is so hard. I don't want to hurt you. But it's not right to...to keep secrets, is it?"

My heart skips a beat. "Secrets? Do you have a secret, Gabriela?"

She reaches for a Kleenex. "It's only right to tell you, Andee." She fumbles with a button on her blouse, refusing to meet my eyes. "These last few months I've been...going out...with someone."

I stare at her, struck dumb. At last I manage to murmur, "What are you saying, Gabriela? That you don't love me anymore?"

"His name is Gregorio. I want you to meet him, Andee, he's such a nice man. Older than me, but strong and reliable, and very much in love with me."

I think I'm going to throw up!

Her hand touches mine. It's cold and stiff, the hand of a stranger. I pull back, not wanting her to touch me...until she laughs and tells me this is a cruel joke.

"Andee, dear Andee, I'm so sorry!"

I know I sound like a petulant six-year-old: "You haven't answered my question."

"No, Andee I...I haven't stopped loving you." She dabs at a tear rolling down her cheek.

I jump up, and my arms outstretched, plead with her: "Then why...? Gabriela, this is crazy!".

Tears are splotching her blouse. "Andee, you're a good man, the best man I've ever known. But you still don't understand my heart, do you?"

(I must stop shouting at her!) My knees trembling, I sit down again. "I thought I knew your heart, Gabriela, I thought it belonged to me. In spite of all the bad times we've had, I've kept telling myself you loved me just as much as I love you, so things were going to work out." Now it's my turn to reach for a Kleenex. "Looks like I was wrong."

"You weren't wrong, about my loving you, Andee." Shaking her head, she blows her nose, "that's the problem, I love you too much."

I cock my head, trying to make sense of her words. She continues: "Andrés, you're a therapist, you ought to understand what I'm talking about. Don't you remember the problem I had with Raul? I was crazy in love with him when we married. That's why, in spite of all the terrible things he did to me, I was unable to leave him."

I break in, feeling the heat rush to my face. "But I'm not Raul!"

"Of course you're not. I know you'd never intentionally do anything to hurt me. But Andee, we're from two different worlds. It's just not going to work out. It's time we faced up to the truth!" She buries her face in her hands.

"That's why we keep on having so many problems. I can't bear the thought of living with you, loving you with all my heart and hurting you...and being hurt...because we're so different."

I push back my chair, angry now. "This is ridiculous!"

"Is it, Andee?" She's crying, but I don't care. I want her to hurt as much I'm hurting!

"Imagine," she continues, "we're married, and we're about to go to bed. How would you feel about the little porcelain Virgin lying on my pillow?"

I stare at her dumbly, unable to answer. (Careful, Andrew, don't say anything to widen this gulf that's already opened between us.) Before I can find the right words she continues:

"There's something else. Rosario told me, after we began the Bible study here in my house that sooner or later you'd be talking about becoming a church. I said nothing at the time, but..." Taking a deep breath, she reaches out, then quickly withdraws her hand. "Andrés, I don't think you've caught on that...that my religion is not something just between me and you and God. It's my culture, and all I've inherited from my family: I could never betray my parents, my grandparents, my great-grandparents.!"

I say quietly. "Are you telling me, Gabriela, that your family and your traditions are more important to you than the man you love, more important, even, than...?"

"Go on, Andrés, say it, Rosario has said it to me more than once: 'more important than the Christ I love'?"

I reach out and take her hand. Oh God, why is she crucifying herself...and me...like this?

"Rosario's said some terrible things to me, Andee. She's threatened me with hellfire if I don't change."

I squeeze her hand. "I'm sure of one thing, Gabriela, the same Savior that lives in my heart lives in yours. But..."

"But if we married, you'd expect changes from me, wouldn't you?"

I'm silent, remembering my visit with Anastacia and her mother. I can't imagine Gabriela agreeing to being baptized in their swimming pool!

"Now do you understand why I feel so comfortable with Gregorio? He was born and grew up in Mexico, just like me. He feels the same way about our traditions."

"I haven't heard you say you love him."

"But I do. In my own way." She raises my hand to her lips. Of course, not like I love you. But I don't want to love him that way, Andee, it scares me!"

"Gabriela!" I shout her name, wanting to pound the table, to shake her, to crush her to my chest, to sob out the pain I'm feeling. This is insane!

"Let me say it for you, Andrés: there's something wrong with me; I'm still tied to the past. I guess you're right." The corners of her mouth turn down in a sad little smile. "Don't you see the favor I'm doing you? I could never make you happy!"

Dropping her hand, I raise my arms to the sky. "All I know is I love you and you love me. God gave us to each other, Gabi. To turn away from our love is madness!"

A tear is trickling slowly, crookedly down her cheek. "Please, Andee, I'm so tired of the struggle. Just let me go!"

I get to my feet and say, very slowly, like a benediction: "All right, Gabriela, I let you go."

Rising, she reaches for her purse. I hold out my hand. Taking it, she brings it to her cheek for a moment, and says, "I'll always be glad to have known you, Andee."

Bitter gall boils up in my throat. "I...I wish I could say the same!" I turn and walk to the door.

My hand on the doorknob, I pause. There's one more thing I must tell Gabriela, the last thing I'll ever say to her.

She's standing where I left her, a hand clutching her throat, eyes very large.

"Gabriela, I'm quite sure I'm doomed to love you the rest of my life. If ever...ever...you change your mind, let me know. As for me, I'm going to do everything I can, from this moment, to avoid seeing you or hearing of you ever again!"

I open the door and she rushes past me, sobbing now…

Rebeca is standing behind her desk, frowning. I can see like she's about to cry too. "Oh, Doctór Andres," she moans, "I thought…"

"I…I thought so too. I guess we were both wrong!." She reaches out for me. Suddenly I'm bawling.

Thirty minutes later I'm on Reforma, headed toward *El Desierto de los Leones*, a national park on the western fringe of the city. I'll hide myself in that wooded wilderness until this volcano boiling in my heart simmers down.

I told Rebeca to cancel my appointments for the rest of the day. How could I talk to anyone about their problems? I must concentrate on this new resolve to feel nothing, to shed not another tear, to lose not another minute's sleep.

I can do it, I can! After all, it's the only way I've been able to survive as a counselor. I've had to learn how to listen to my clients, suffer with them, cry with them, then walk out of the office and leave my feelings behind. Right now I must allow the same thing to happen to the searing pain in my own heart.

One more thing: I will not allow myself to fall in love again. Oh, I'll go on loving people, I must. But I will not, ever, fall in love again.

Gabriela is right. It hurts too much!

CHAPTER 31

▼

ENTER CARLOS

Umbrella time again! It's June, and the rainy season is here. Every day around three or four big black clouds trundle in from the Gulf. By midnight the clouds move out, and sometimes from my eighth-floor balcony I can spot a star or two over Mount Popo. Every night I sleep under an electric blanket. Often I dream of Anastacia…silly, happy dreams, and we're laughing, touching, enjoying one another…

What a surprise! Until a month ago I'd never have imagined Anastacia and I would be *novios*. It began with a midnight phone call. I'd spent three hours with Anastacia and Mercedes and a dozen others who now meet at their house every Tuesday night for Bible study.

"Still awake, Andrés?" I was surprised to hear Anastacia's voice. I was *not* surprised at stir of pleasure I felt; lately, I'd been thinking of her a lot.

"Mami and I are still too excited to go to bed. We've been talking about your lesson about the joy of being a Christian. You remember, that's what attracted us to those people in Denver."

Knowing Anastacia makes it easy for me to talk about joy! I've never see her without a smile, except for those moments when she's talked about her short, painful marriage.

"Speaking of happiness," she continues, "do you think the Lord would mind if you and I had some fun tomorrow night? *Mami* just reminded me that somebody gave us tickets to a delicious comedy at the Reforma Theater. She has other plans, and thought you might like to go with me."

"I'd be delighted!" I answer, pleased that "*mami*" feels her precious daughter will be safe with me!

The next night Anastacia's entrance into the theater where she had been *La Novicia Rebelde* created a murmur of excitement. After a dozen autographs the lights dimmed and we were swallowed up in blessed anonymity. When Anastacia reached over and took my hand my heart thumped and I felt like a sixteen-year-old on his first date.

The play, like most Mexican comedies, was downright silly. Nearly all the jokes were plays on words and I missed the punch line a lot of times. But the best part was having Anastacia at my side. Every time she burst out laughing, her fingernails biting into my hand, I laughed too at the sheer joy of being with her.

We slipped out just before the curtain calls and had supper at a small, noisy restaurant featuring lime soup and *sopes*, Yucatecan dishes. And laughed again as she explained with gestures and mimic some of the jokes I'd missed.

It was after midnight when we got to her house. I opened the car door for her and she hugged me and held me for a moment. "Oh Andrés, I had a gre-e-at time. You're so much fun!"

A moment later at the gate she dropped her keys and I picked them up and dropped them again. We laughed nervously like two kids who know they're going to be fussed at for staying out too late. And we jumped when the patio light suddenly flashed on.

"Have a good time?" Anastacia's mother was standing at the top of the stairs.

"Great, Mami, you should have gone with us." Anastacia giggled softly and squeezed my hand.

The following Friday I took her to lunch, and since then we've been going out together two or three times a week. We seldom talk about our feelings. Probably because both our hearts are in slow, painful therapy from the hurt of recent disappointments. We simply enjoy each other, celebrating the music we make when we're together. No deep discussions about love and life…and our embrace when we part could be mistaken for the touch of dear friends.

But I know what I feel for this beautiful woman is more than friendship…Beautiful?…The first time I saw Anastacia I might not have used that word to describe her. Her face is a bit too rounded and her figure too generous for the cover of a fashion magazine. But she *is* beautiful, a comeliness that flows from within, energized by her passion for God, reflected in the glow of her cheeks and the sparkle in her eyes.

Anastacia has little of the sophistication you'd expect in a child of the theater. When she smiles it reminds me of the happy innocence of the little girls decorating Mama's Campbell Soup cans when I was a kid. At twenty-eight she has no memories of shameful affairs to lament, no hidden secrets of alcoholism or mind-bending drugs.

And it's not difficult to understand why she's elected to accept the authority of the autocratic mother dedicated to protecting her daughter from the errors that flawed her own life. Before Anastacia was born, Mercedes' name was featured constantly on the marquees of Mexico City's theaters. While starring in a production of "Fiddler on the Roof" she fell madly in love with a handsome Greek sea-captain vacationing in Mexico. After only two weeks together he sailed away, promising to return and marry her. A cruel twist of fate shattered her dreams: One dark, stormy afternoon she stumbled upon a story buried in the international section of *Novedades*. Her lover's steamer had caught fire at sea and gone down with all hands. The next day she learned she was pregnant.

The only keepsake that remained was a snap-shot of her captain and his gorgeous red-haired mother. Inscribed on the back was a note: "From Anastacia to my beloved son." When the wrinkled red-haired baby was born it seemed natural to name her after her grandmother. Mercedes never married, choosing rather to consecrate her life to the daughter bequeathed by the only true love she had ever known.

Mercedes is a woman to be admired…and feared? Sometimes I ask myself if the iron will that fuels her dedication to her daughter…and now to her newfound faith…will cause problems in the future.

I have discipleship studies with Mercedes and Anastacia twice a week. One wants to glean every detail of Gospel facts, the other every ounce of God's love. Mercedes' passion is walking the walk. Anastacia's passion is saturating her heart with God's love so she can pour it out in song and prayer.

She's still struggling with whether she should continue her theatrical career. More than once I've seen her toss aside a script some has asked her to consider, commenting: "Will I ever again find a role I can feel comfortable with?"

And then there is Carlos. He attends our Bible study for the first time in July. Arriving late, he perches on the shadowy staircase sweeping down into the party room. A handsome young man, he's taller than most Mexicans, with broad shoulders and an abundance of wavy chestnut hair. He sits silent, without movement or involvement. Every time I glance in his direction his dark, unblinking eyes are fixed on me, his face expressionless. What does that look mean? Is it suspicion? Several times Anastacia glances in his direction and smiles. I decide he must be a friend of hers checking out the American who now shares so much of her life.

Eddie and Lupita, faithful members of our group, pose a question to me after the study. As we talk I see Anastacia approaching the newcomer. His gaze meets mine for just an instant, and again I feel the appraisal of those unblinking eyes. Later, glancing in his direction later, I'm surprised to see he's disappeared.

"You see, *Mami*, he did come!" Anastacia exclaims after everyone has left.

"Un huh…what a surprise!" Mercedes answers in a monotone. "But he's so cold and…intellectual!"

"Oh Mother, you just don't know him, he's not like that at all!"

I interrupt: "I guess you're talking about that good-looking guy sitting on the staircase,"

"His name's Carlos," Anastacia declares. "And he is handsome, isn't he?"

"Almost too handsome."

A blush tints her throat. "Don't worry, he's already spoken for. We're just friends. While I was working in *La Novicia Rebelde* he came backstage and invited me out. We've seen each other half a dozen times. He's the nicest man I've met in ages."

"Now that Orpha's gone maybe he'll be coming around more," Mercedes says.

"Who's Orpha?" I ask.

"His girlfriend. She's a ballerina, tiny and pretty, like a miniature painted on a sea shell. Left a week ago for her second year in a school of dance in New York. Carlos says Amalia Hernandez has promised her a job when she finishes her studies."

"Amalia Hernandez?" I scratch my head. "The name sounds familiar."

"Ever been to a performance of the Ballet Folklórico in the Palace of Fine Arts? Amalia Hernandez is the Director."

"Wow! Orpha must be very good."

"She is. Amalia Hernandez has one of the finest ballet troops in the world; every year they tour the United States and Europe. Anyway, I wanted to present Carlos to you, but he was in a hurry." Smiling, she squeezes my arm. "The truth is, he's not too happy about what the gringos in Denver did to Mami and me."

I try not to show my discomfort. Every time someone uses that word gringo I feel like a spy in enemy territory. "Think he'll be back?"

"You can bet on it! And next time he'll probably have some questions for you. Look out, he's quite brilliant!"

The next Tuesday Carlos returns…late again…this time with a new black Bible under his arm. Anastacia sits beside him on the staircase and helps him thumb through the pages.

Afterward, Carlos descends the stairs, walks briskly up to me and hand extended, introduces himself in classic Latin style: "Carlos Suarez Ramirez *para servirle*, Doctór."

I search his steel blue eyes for hostility, but find none. Rather, I think I see an assertive integrity that says "I've got nothing to hide, how about you?".

We small-talk about the weather, until he abruptly shifts the conversation: "Could you have lunch with me tomorrow?"

Surprised, I accept immediately.

"I've been praying for this!" Anastacia exclaims as soon as he's gone. "I hope you can convince him he needs Jesus. I've been trying, but he has too many questions."

I say thoughtfully, "I think he's trying to decide if he can trust me. Tell me a little about him."

"He's a classic Mexican yuppie. Graduated from the *Universidad Anahuac* with a Masters in Business Administration two years ago, and now he's assistant manager of a downtown Paris y *Londres* department store. Teaches calculus nights at the *Universidad de las Américas*. Tells me they're trying to convince him to come on full time as head of the department."

"Doctór," Mercedes says, "we need men like Carlos. So far Eddie is the only male in our group."

I say a hearty amen. I've mostly dealt with women since coming to Mexico; most men seem to have little interest in the spiritual. In Moisés' church women outnumber men three to one.

The next day I'm on my second *naranjada* when Carlos arrives. He orders a *sidral*, and almost immediately the sparring begins. He questions why I would be in Mexico working for a third of what I could earn in the States. His face softens when I explain I'm making a fresh start after the death of my wife.

I learn he's the youngest of seven children. Like many other Mexican families, his is one-parent; his father moved out when he was small. His eyes cloud as he speaks of a dad who comes once a week to leave his mother her allowance and play chess with his last-born son. I make a mental note to encourage him in the future to talk more about his family.

As we dip into our onion soup I ask, "And our Bible studies…what do you think about them?"

He lays down his spoon. "In all my life, I don't suppose I'd held a Bible in my hand more than two or three times until that first night with you. I was baptized when I was a baby, of course, but like most university students I came out convinced Marxism was the answer to my country's problems."

Frowning, he picks up his spoon. "And like most of my friends, after a couple of years in the real world I've already discovered how unworkable socialism is. As one of our cynics has said: 'Anybody spending four years in a Mexican university without becoming a communist has no heart…and anybody who's still a communist five years after graduation has no brains.'" He smiles wryly. "So I guess the only thing I really believe in right now is my ability to get ahead in the world."

"But you did come to our Bible study."

"Because of Anastacia. I wanted to find out why she's changed so much."

"You don't like what has happened to her?"

"I haven't decided yet. Most of all, I don't want her to lose her love for the theater. You haven't seen her onstage, have you?

"No, I haven't had the pleasure."

Carlos smiles. "Imagine Pavorotti as a soprano and you'll have an idea. The way she projects feeling...honesty...sincerity. Fantastic!

As if embarrassed at betraying so much emotion, Carlos drops his eyes and concentrates on his soup.

We eat in silence for a few moments. Then I say, praying for the right words: "It sounds like integrity is very important for you."

"Look, Doctór, I don't know how it is in your country, but here, by the time you're my age, it's hard not to be a skeptic. Your mother has seen to it you touch all the bases on religion: communion, confirmation, mass every Sunday. And all the time you're observing your father: never at home on weekends...running after other women...unable to talk with you about things that matter. You finally decide religion is for women and children.

"And in the university they teach you the only thing worth getting excited about is the proletarian paradise Karl Marx promises."

"Before I came to Mexico I took for granted everybody here was religious."

"Most of us are—in a very superficial way. In 1917, when our last revolution ended, they wrote a new constitution decreeing a radical separation between religion and real life. Have you read about your President Kennedy's visit to our country in the 1960's? Sunday morning he and his wife attended mass, but our President had to wait for them outside. If he had entered the *Villa de Guadalupe* with them, they would have impeached him!"

"Why on earth?"

"A visit by the President to the church would have been considered a compromise with the enemy. After all, that's what our revolution was about."

We attack the fetuccini. After a while Carlos lays down his fork and asks the question I've been expecting: "Tell me the truth, do you really believe these things you teach about God and Jesus Christ?"

"With all my heart." "But how can you? You have a doctorate in psychology, and psychology is the sworn enemy of religion."

"Carlos, have you heard me pushing a religion?"

"Well," he raises his eyebrows, "you talk about God...isn't that religion?"

"When God came to earth in his son, Jesus, his worst enemy was the religion of that day. Remember, the religious leaders condemned him to death."

He leans back, pushing away his empty plate. "Doctór, I'm surprised that a sophisticated man like yourself takes the Bible seriously. How can you? It's so antiquated. And filled with myths and contradictions."

"How do you know that? Have you studied the Bible...for yourself?...or have you accepted uncritically the stuff you've heard in school?"

He shrugs. "A good question."

"And if your teachers were wrong about Marxism, isn't it possible they're also mistaken about the Bible?"

For the first time he smiles. "I guess that's what I'd like to find out."

"Look, Carlos, when I was in college I had my own intellectual doubts. A book by a Christian philosopher named McDowell cleared up a lot of things for me. I have a copy in Spanish. If I lend it to you will you read it?"

Frowning, he picks up his fork and digs into his *pastel de tres leches*. He takes a bite, then spoons sugar into his coffee. He sips it, grimaces, and stirs in another spoonful, takes a huge swallow, sets the cup down and squares his shoulders.

"Tell you what, Doctór, I'll read your book if afterward you'll answer all the questions I'm going to have for you!"

I stick out my hand. "Agreed!"

We finish off our dessert in silence. Finally I push away my empty plate and say, "Tell me about Orpha."

He raises his eyebrows. "Not much to tell. We've been going together for several years. I know she cares for me, but I've about decided she'll never stand up to her parents. Tell me, Doctór, why are Jews so clannish?"

"So she's Jewish?"

"Yes, and her parents absolutely refuse to entertain the possibility of her marrying a Gentile."

I shake my head slowly. "Carlos, I wish I could offer you hope."

He takes a long sip of his coffee. "It's tough. We really care for each other, but there seems to be no future for us." Glancing at his watch, he exclaims, "Oops! Where did two hours go, I've got to get back the office! And I'm sure you have your patients."

Outside we chat while waiting for our cars. When Carlos' Cougar arrives he surprises me by pulling me into an *abrazo*. Apparently he has surprised himself also; he releases me quickly, slips into his car and takes off spinning the wheels.

They meet, Quetzalcóatl and his lackey, Kyros, in the courtyard facing Teotihuacan's unimpressive Temple of Quetzalcóatl. It's high noon and the city of pyramids is crowded with tourists, but of course no one sees these potentates of the dark kingdom. The Feathered Serpent purses his thin lips and emits a high shrill whistle, and what happens next takes Kyros' breath away: the stone wall of the temple slides apart like a curtain, revealing a wide marble staircase spiraling downward. Queztalcóatl, who has spoken not a word to his slave spirit, slithers into the opening and as soon as Kyros follows, the wall closes behind them. Kyros expects darkness, but to his surprise a bright sliver of the noonday sun, penetrating an invisible opening at the peak of the pyramid, strikes the jewelled walls of the marble staircase and explodes into a thousand tiny spotlights. A covey of quetzals, resplendent in their choir robes of red, blue and gold, line the sparkling staircase, singing hosannas to their Lord. They descend a thousand steps, enter an immense domed hall, and Quetzalcóatl ascends a golden throne and coils upon it in august splendor. Kyros falls to his scaly knees, trembling. From the corner of his eye he perceives, just beyond the throne, the mouth of a dark abyss. There hundreds of serpents slither and coil, their rattles muffling the dreadful sound of the moans and shrieks filtering up from the depths of the abyss.

This is Quetzalcóatl's throne room! Why has his master brought him here? With one flick of his tail, Kyros knows, he can send him tumbling into the abyss.

Kyros' colleagues, grinning evilly, have warned him of this place, a parable of Satan's deceitful genius: from without, the temple of Quetzalcóatl appears quite harmless and inviting, but once you enter you find yourself at the gateway to hell.

Every spring and fall equinox tens of thousands of seekers flow into Teotihuacan to bask in the strange power radiating from the Pyramid of the Sun and the Temple of Quetzalcóatl. But like all Satan's promises, the sweet fragrance of peace and joy lasts for only an instant, to be replaced by the stench of hopelessness. Coiled on his throne, cold eyes resting upon Kyros, Quetzalcóatl declares: "Andrew Kelly will die!"

"But…but Master," stutters the emaciated spirit professor, "the day you commissioned me you warned me of the Pact of Job. You said I could do anything to Kelly except take his life."

"Andrew Kelly will die!" The domed throne room vibrates to the rumbling of his voice. The quetzals become silent and the serpents turn and crawl away into the darkness.

"But how, oh mighty Lord?"

"You will go to Oaxaca, the province of Thanatos, and warn him that Kelly is coming."

Thanatos, the only spirit in Mexico exempt from the Pact of Job!

Trembling, Kyros pulls his wrinkled gray robe tight around his thin shoulders. "I understand, Master, I will go immediately."

"And afterward, you will report back to me here. If Thanatos fails…" Quetzalcóatl tips his head toward the menacing black abyss.

"But Master," (His teeth are chattering) "it would not be I who failed, but Thanatos!

The Bearded Serpent rears up on his tail, head brushing the vaulted ceiling. "Enough of your excuses! Why have I been so patient with you? This time you must succeed, the time is getting short."

"It's not fair!" Kyros whimpers.

"Don't talk to me about fair! El's man will soon open an office in Los Pinos, the armies of heaven are in training for Armageddon and the heavenly choir is in rehearsal for the Wedding of the Lamb…" Quetzalcóatl hisses out a volcano of foul-smelling gasses—"and you're whining to me about being fair!"

With a flick of his dreadful tail Quetzalcóatl sweeps the miserable little spirit off the marbled floor, up the shining stairs and out of the temple. Kyros lands hard, scattering half a dozen stones cluttering the courtyard.

"Myron, did you feel that? A startled matron from Mississippi cries to her husband.

"Did I feel what, woman?" "That hot breath of air gushing from the pyramid. It smelled like spoiled turnip greens!"

CHAPTER 32

▼

WHO IS CELSO?

"Doctór, this is Tatiana," Anastacia tells me one Tuesday night after Bible study. "She works for a neighbor and they asked me to see if you could help her."

"Please, Doctór, don't let him do it to me again!" The small, dark young woman grabs my hand and kisses it fervently.

Dressed in the neat uniform typical of maids in La Herradura, Tatiana appears to be in, perhaps, the sixth month of her pregnancy. Reaching out to take her hand, I'm surprised to feel it trembling.

Seated on the sofa, she tells me her story:

Four years ago she came to Mexico City from her small village in the nearby state of Oaxaca, nurturing the dream of becoming a nurse. Thanks to the recommendation of a family friend, she was able to enroll in a nursing school.

Raymundo was gardener and chauffeur for the family where she worked. Before long they entered into a common law *libre unión*, living in a tiny apartment on the roof of their employers' home. Hot summer nights before the beginning of the rainy season they escaped their stifling apartment to sleep on straw *petates* stretched under the stars.

"I'll never forget the night it happened," Tatiana murmurs, reaching over to clutch Anastacia's hand. "Sometime after midnight I awoke with a start. A handsome young man was standing at the head of the stairs, staring at me.

"'Come, Tatiana,' he said, beckoning to me. Looking down, I saw that Raymundo was sound asleep."

"You'd never seen him before?" Mercedes asks.

"No. If only I'd known, *Señora*, that it was *El Chamuco*!"

I flinch, recognizing the nickname Mexicans give to the devil.

"I don't know why I went to him, it was like I'd lost control of my will. He took my hand and led me downstairs. We walked the streets for a long time, his arm around my waist. I felt so safe with him. And excited and happy!

"He told me his name was Celso and that my Aunt Consuelo had sent him. Aunt Consuelo is the *curandera* in the village where I grew up. For a fee she casts spells. And she can cure spells placed on people by other witches, using things like eggs, chicken entrails and secret words she learned from her mother and grandmother.

"As I listened to Celso I found myself believing him and wanting to please him. Suddenly he stopped, took both my hands in his and told me something that made my heart skip a beat: he was going to help me with the exam I'd be taking at the nursing school the next day.

"I stood with my mouth agape, staring at him in the light of the street lamp.

"Seeing my surprise, he added: 'Your Aunt Consuelo knows you're worried about failing your test tomorrow.'

"It was true. Just the day before the Director of the school had called me in and warned me I'd be suspended unless I raised my average. I was frantic, I didn't want to be a maid all my life. Besides, I couldn't bear the thought of returning to my village a failure.

"I asked him how he was going to help me. He touched my face tenderly and said, 'Tomorrow you'll find out. I'll be waiting for you at the school gate.'" She blows her nose on the Kleenex Mercedes hands her.

"Tatiana, you rest for a moment while I bring us something to drink," Mercedes says. Hurrying to the kitchen she returns bearing a tray filled with mugs of strawberry *atole*.

The four of us sit without speaking, sipping the thick, soothing beverage, Tatiana holding the steaming mug in her hands, warming them.

After a moment she continues: "The next day when I arrived at school Celso was waiting for me, just like he'd said. As I approached he reached out and touched me and…when I came to myself I was nearing the house where I live. I was exhausted, and I could tell by the sun that several hours had passed. Then I saw my hands:…they were stained with ink! I knew what had happened, and I trembled.

The next day the teacher returned our test papers. I had made a perfect grade! I saw her looking at me, her lips tight, and knew she believed I had cheated. Of course I'd cheated, but not the way she thought: the person seated at my desk the day before was not myself but Celso, an angel of *El Chamuco* clothed in my body.

"I told myself the next time he appeared I'd tell him I wanted nothing more to do with him.

"That night he came again, smiling as before, whispering my name. Before I could stop myself I was at his side. He held out his hand, I took it and…the next thing I knew I was standing beside my *petate* in the pale glow of dawn.

"A few months later I found myself pregnant with Raymundo's baby. Celso was furious! He insisted I get an abortion. I screamed at him that he'd never make me do such a horrible thing.

"The baby died two days after it was born. The doctors couldn't explain it, but I knew why.

"I graduated from nursing school at the head of my class. Only I knew the reason: every time I'd had an exam Celso had taken my place. They assigned me to the cardiology department of the *Hospital de la Raza*, the finest government hospital in the city.

"Celso continued his visits, several nights a week. Sometimes I could feel Raymundo looking at me strangely. How much did he know?

Those nights I was away with Celso, was my body still there on the *petate* beside Raymundo? I didn't know. Every morning when I awoke I vowed this was the day I'd tell Celso to leave and never return, but I couldn't get up the courage.

"I guess I was selfish: more than once I had a patient they said couldn't survive the night, and Celso took over my body and nursed him back to health. People began whispering that God had given me a miraculous healing power. All the patients wanted me to be their nurse.

"When I learned I was pregnant again I trembled. I soon found out I was right to be afraid; Celso told me flatly he was going to kill my baby. I pled with him, prayed to the Virgin. I insisted on having the baby in my own hospital, under the care of our best doctors.

"But it happened again.

"And now," she touches her stomach, "in two months the baby will be born, and…" her voice breaks, "Celso tells me he's going to kill my baby again. I resigned my position at the hospital and went back to working as a maid so I could tell him that now I owe him nothing. But he pays no attention. Please, help me!" Dropping her face into her hands, she sobs.

That night I dial Moisés' number. I don't dare tackle Tatiana's problem alone, it's far beyond anything I've experienced. Besides, I welcome this excuse to call on Moisés. We seem to be drifting apart. When was the last time we did anything together? Remembering, I shake my head. It was that visit to the Cathedral of Guadalupe, more than a year ago!

Not that we've had problems. He gives me a warm *abrazo* every Sunday, and quite often he calls me to the platform to lead in prayer. He knows most of what's been happening to me. But he always seems to be so busy! The last six months or so I've had the feeling something's on his mind, something he doesn't want to share with me. Every time I suggest a meal or a cup of coffee he has a conflict….

Darn, he's not at home! I tell his wife I'll stay up till he calls. She sounds very tired. Poor woman, living with a man like Moisés must be tough. Sunday mornings she sits at the back of the church nursing the latest baby, looking very lonely....

The phone jars me awake.

"Doctór, are you all right?" Good, he's worried!

I tell him about Tatiana, afraid he'll insist I take care of the problem myself. I'm pleased when he begins asking questions.

Finally he says, "When can I see her?"

"How about next Monday?"

There are five of us: Anastacia and her mother, Tatiana, Moisés and myself. Tatiana gently rubs her belly as she repeats her story for Moisés. I can see he isn't surpised. He explains that this isn't the first time he's ministered to a demon-possessed person whose grandmother or aunt was a witch; usually that's the origin of their problem. But Tatiana has a special problem, he warns her. She renounced exclusive rights to her body when she agreed to lend it to Celso. She shouldn't be surprised he's angry about her having another man's baby.

Tatiana sits silent, her face pale, hands trembling.

Moisés turns to Anastacia and Mercedes: "*Hermanas*, I need your help. Please go into the kitchen and uphold us in prayer."

They grab their Bibles and get up immediately. I wonder if they feel like me; we've spent the day praying and fasting, but I'm still nervous about how this is going to turn out.

Alone with Tatiana and me Moisés bows his head. I see his lips moving. Is he speaking in tongues? I attempt to pray, but my mind wanders. It's so filled with questions I'm unable to concentrate.

I watch Tatiana out of the corner of my eye. Her body is rigid, eyes staring. Slowly, I'm aware that a faint bitter smell is stinging my nostrils. Suddenly afraid, I fall to my knees and pray in a frantic whisper, unaware of the words I'm saying.

Moisés voice booms out, startling me: "Foul son of the devil, tell me your name!"

I slip into a chair, shivering. Moisés is bent over Tatiana, his face inches from hers. She's still staring into space.

He holds up his Bible. "Tatiana, kiss God's Word."

She grimaces and turns away.

Moisés addresses the demon, exhorts Tatiana, prays, calls on me to pray. An hour passes...and another...and all the time I'm aware of an unseen presence, dark, menacing.

The clock on the wall strikes ten. Suddenly Moisés shouts, "Tatiana, say 'Jesus is Lord!'"

Her eyes focus on him for the first time, her lips open and she grunts, "Je...Je...*Jesús*..." and falls to the floor, writhing, groaning.

Kneeling beside her, Moisés says in a quiet, strong voice, "By the blood of Jesus I command you, unclean spirit, release this woman!" Tatiana sits up, her eyes clear.

"I'm so tired!" she whispers.

Moisés pulls her to her feet, muttering, "Well, I guess we've done all we can do tonight." He calls to the two women. They come into the living room, their faces gray with weariness.

"Did...did anything happen?" Mercedes asks.

"At least he made his presence known," Moisés answers, "we'll continue tomorrow night."

The next morning when I arrive at the office, Rebeca informs me my first client has canceled. "But no problem, someone else has just reserved the hour."

"Who?"

"Me!"

I look at her, concerned. "Got a problem?"

"I think we both have, Doctór." I'm surprised to see tears welling up in her eyes. "Do you remember how it was when you first opened your office? There were only a few patients, so we had a lot of time on our hands. Sometimes you'd send me out for pizza and we'd sit and talk for hours."

"Of course I remember. Thanks to you I got a great introduction to Mexico and Mexico's people."

"Back then I was so proud to be working for you. I felt more like a special friend than a secretary. But now it's almost like you've forgotten I'm here." She reaches for a tissue and dabs her eyes.

I take her hand. "Looks like we need to talk. Let's sit down in y my *consultorio.*"

When we're settled, she says, "First, tell me about last night. I was praying for you."

As I describe the two hours with Tatiana and her persecutor, my friend's eyes are fixed on mine, her face mirroring the emotions I'd felt the night before. Rebeca no longer attends the Bible studies in *La Herradura.* At first she skipped her Tuesday night classes so she could be present. Later she begged off, saying she couldn't miss any more classes. I suspected there was another reason; she seemed to feel uncomfortable with Anastacia and Mercedes and their friends. Funny thing, Rebeca is as intelligent and attractive as any of them, but her skin is a bit darker and she sometimes uses words not in their vocabulary. I'm still perplexed by Mexico's subtle social prejudice.

After a while she falls silent, studying her hands.

"Anything else on your mind?" I ask.

Still looking down, she says, "Dr. Andrés...uh...did Pastor Moisés seem...uh...all right to you last night?"

"What do you mean?"

"Have...have you noticed anything...different...about him lately?"

Dare I share my recent concern for the pastor with another member of the church, even my best friend? Finally I say, "Well, he has been a little withdrawn lately. Maybe he's working too hard."

She seems to be searching for words when the doorbell rings. I'm quite sure this conversation will be continued later.

That night when we arrive at Mercedes and Anastacia's they greet us with disturbing news: Tatiana won't be coming. Raymundo arrived a few moments ago to inform them she's ill.

Mercedes' face is a storm cloud: "I don't believe a word of it! He's the problem; he's forbidden her to come!"

Moisés sets his jaw: "Take me to them!"

Anastacia and I stay behind. She's serving me a manzanilla tea in the kitchen when the front door opens. We jump up and hurry into the living room. Mercedes enters, followed by Moisés and Tatiana. A moment later Raymundo comes in, feet dragging. I study his face: is he angry or scared?

"Pastor Moisés explained to Raymundo that he must choose," Mercedes tells us, her face grim. "Either he helps Tatiana rid herself of this demon, or he loses her forever!"

Moisés takes Raymundo's arm and guides him to a chair. "Raymundo, sit here quietly. Whatever happens you must not interrupt. Tonight we're going to see if we can persuade *Don* Celso to manifest himself."

Refusing the chair Raymundo goes to the farthest corner of the room, plops down on the floor and draws his knees under his chin as if pulling up a drawbridge. No doubt now about his feelings now, the man is scared!

"Brothers," Mercedes tells us, "we'll be in the kitchen pleading with the Almighty to make this the night of Tatiana's liberation!"

After they've left I look at Tatiana. Seated on the sofa, she has lapsed into that same semiconscious state I observed last night. I've brought my cassette, Moisés wants to record tonight's session.

Going to the far end of the sofa I drop to my knees as Moisés reads aloud Ephesians 6:12, "For we wrestle not against flesh and blood, but against principalities, against powers, against the rulers of the darkness of this world, against spiritual wickedness in high places."

Closing his Bible, Moisés looks upward: "Holy Spirit, help me. Reveal the truth!"

Then he says quietly, "Celso, only Tatiana has seen you until now. You've been in hiding long enough; stop being a be a coward, reveal yourself!"

Tatiana is still staring into space.

Moisés puts his hand on Tatiana's shoulder and commands: "Vile spirit, God's Word calls your master 'the Deceiver'. You're like him, a deceiver, aren't you? You and I know Celso is not your real name."

What's he trying to do? Bowing my head, I attempt to pray, but I'm shivering, my nostrils tingling with the same acrid smell.I remember from last night.

Moisés taunts the enemy: "Lying, cheating spirit, show yourself. You're ugly and stupid, not handsome and intelligent, as Tatiana thinks you are!"

The clock strikes ten.

Click! The tape runs out and I turn it over.

"*Hoc es corpus!*" The voice is deep, sonorous.

My head jerks up. Who said that? Moisés? No, it wasn't Moisés' voice. I look at Tatiana. Her body is rigid, arms raised as if in invocation.

"*Hoc es corpus.*" Tatiana's lips are moving; the deep, liturgical voice is emanating from her throat! Slowly she rises from her seat, smiling now.

"Celso!" she murmurs, in her own voice now, and starts for the door. Raymundo jumps up to intercept her, but Moisés waves his arms frantically and he slides back down to the floor, his foot thumping impatiently.

Almost to the door Tatiana stops, still smiling, and reaches out to touch...what? Another hand? Her lips move, whispering.

Abruptly she drops to her knees, hands clutched in supplication, "Celso, please, no!"

She nods her head, "Yes, I promise, I promise!" and crumples to the floor, sobbing.

Moisés motions to Raymundo again to remain seated. After a moment Tatiana sits up, moving her head slowly from side to side, as if in a dream. "Celso, he was here!"

Moisés goes to stand beside her. "Did he threaten you?"

"Yes," she moans, "he said he's going to leave me and never return, unless I…"

"What did you promise him, Tatiana?"

Shaking her head, she refuses to meet his eyes.

Reaching out, Moisés lifts her chin. "Look at me! What did you promise him?"

"That…that I'll not come back here again. Please, leave me alone, I can't live without him!"

"Tatiana, listen to me: Your Celso is a liar and a cheat, an ugly, murderous spirit from the fires of hell!"

She shakes her head fiercely. "That's a lie, Celso is my special friend. Nobody has ever helped me like Celso!"

Moisés roars: "And he murders your babies!"

She lets out a shrill cry and covers her face with her hands: "*Dios mío*, what am I going to do?"

"You're going to tell him he's been lying to you. You're going to demand he tell you his real name!"

"*Hoc es corpus.*" That deep, pontifical voice again, followed by a raucous laugh and a stream of unrecognizable words. Latin? Greek? Hebrew, maybe?

Suddenly unseen hands lift Tatiana up, screaming, then drop her. She lies sprawled on the floor, moaning.

This time Moisés makes no attempt to stop Raymundo as he rushes over and cradles her head in his lap, mumbling soothing words.

She sits up, shaking her head. "What happened?"

"Please, Doctór," Moisés says, "tell the ladies they can come in."

When we're all seated Moisés speaks sternly: "Tatiana, there's something you haven't told us!"

She's on the sofa beside Raymundo, head resting on his shoulder. "What do you mean?"

"When was the first time you had trouble with this evil spirit, Tatiana?"

"I told you. Celso appeared to me the first time about two years ago."

"Tatiana, it's time to tell the truth."

"But I…"

"Tatiana!" His voice is angry. "How many times did your Aunt Consuelo give you a *limpia* for demon possession?"

Ducking her head, she mutters, "Many times…but…but it did no good."

Moisés tells us: "Last night as I worked with Tatiana the Spirit kept whispering in my ear, but I couldn't discern what he was saying.

"When I awoke this morning the truth came to me: this spirit calling himself Celso possessed Tatiana long before she came to Mexico City, and…"

I interrupt. "But don't you remember, Moisés? Tatiana told us Celso first appeared to her here on her roof top."

"My brother, that deep voice speaking through Tatiana's mouth. You heard it, didn't you?"

"Yes, I heard it."

"But when Tatiana was talking with Celso, did you hear his voice?"

"No, I heard nothing."

"Neither did I. Don't you see? This handsome, smiling young man who has so charmed Tatiana is a masquerade, created for her benefit alone."

"You mean Celso exists only in Tatiana's mind?"

"Not exactly." He turns to Tatiana. Eyes very big, she's clutching Raymundo's hand. "Young lady, I'm going to ask you again, when did you first begin having problems?"

"She sighs. "Please, Pastor, I'm so tired."

"We'll soon be finished. You must help me; answer my question. When…"

She heaves a deep, shuddering sigh. "I… I first remember feeling…another presence…when I was twelve. I once heard my mother say it began the day the *padre* died."

"The *padre*?"

She sighs. "Pastor, it's very complicated. You'll have to ask my mother."

"Your mother is still alive?"

"Yes, she and my father have never left my *pueblo*, Santa Catarina de la Cruz."

"Where is that?"

"In the mountains about three hours south of Cuernavaca."

Moisés turns to me. "Doctór, we must visit Santa Catarina de la Cruz. Can we make the trip in your car?"

"Of course, When do you want to go?"

"How about day after tomorrow?" He turns to Tatiana. "Can you get permission from your *señora* to accompany us?

"I…I guess so." She looks scared.

"Then do it! And Raymundo, you must go with us also."

"*Sí, Señor.*" He's looking at Moisés with new respect.

There's a question I'm anxious to ask Moisés, but first we must dismiss Tatiana and Raymundo. Standing at the door, Moisés orders Tatiana: "If Celso appears tonight or tomorrow tell him to leave you in peace, that you want nothing to do with him."

"I'll try." I can see she's still unconvinced.

After they've left I run the cassette back. There it is: Moisés is speaking and…"*Hoc es corpus.*"

"*La misa!*" Mercedes and Anastacia, who'd been absent when the demon spoke, say it at the same time.

"Yes, my sisters," Moisés replies, "the mass." He turns to me. "Have you ever attended a Catholic mass?"

"No, but aren't those words Latin? I'd swear I've heard them before."

"Probably in your seminary studies. When the priest is saying the mass, he takes the wafer and intones in Latin, '*Hoc es corpus*', 'This is the body'. And in that moment, all true Catholics believe, the bread becomes the body of Christ."

"But why would a demon…"

"It looks like our enemy has a sense of humor. Remember, I was taunting him, daring him to produce Tatiana's 'friend', Celso. So what does he do? He tells me in Latin, 'The body's here!' as if mocking me for not being able to see Celso.

"So Tatiana's demon speaks Latin!"

"Yes. And after the Latin, he said some other words I didn't understand. Doctór, run the tape back again."

I jab the rewind button. "It's only a jumble of sounds to me," I say. "But it does seem to be a language."

Moisés snaps his fingers. "Doctór, I'll bet Professor Barnes can tell you what it is!"

"Professor Barnes?"

"He teaches Hebrew Old Testament at Trinity Seminary. Specializes in Semitic languages."

"Isn't he the one that gave you such a hard time at the pastor's retreat a couple of years ago?"

Moisés smiles. "The same. But he'll be fascinated by the tape. And don't worry, even though he's a narrow-minded old gringo, he's a Christian gentleman. Go see him tomorrow, Doctór, before we make our trip. You may get a clue to what we're going to find in Santa Catarina de la Cruz!"

CHAPTER 33

▼

A DEVASTATING ACCUSATION

The only thing "Mexican" about Trinity Seminary, Moisés has warned me, is its colonial setting; the faculty is almost exclusively American. Denominational leaders complain about gringos molding their fledgling pastors, but these gringos have doctorates, and for most young theologs that's more important than their national origin.

I turn off the Toluca highway onto a narrow, pot-holed blacktop winding upward through a forest of green firs. After a couple of kilometers I nod my head, relieved. That cluster of whitewashed Spanish colonial buildings ahead must be the Seminary! Ten minutes later I'm standing at the open door of a tiny high-ceilinged office. Seated behind a scarred oak desk piled high with papers is a balding, sandy-haired man, a red pencil clenched in his big hairy fist.

"Dr. Joe Barnes?" I ask, breathing hard from three flights of narrow stone stairs.

He rises to greet me. "Dr. Kelly! Come in, please, come in, I've been expecting you."

I'm relieved to see a friendly smile; he sounded rather tentative a while ago on the phone. Giving me a firm handshake and a squeeze of the shoulder, he pulls out a chair. He's taller than me, and thicker at the waist. According to Moisés Dr. Joe (José!) Barnes arrived sixteen years ago with the gold ink barely dry on his Doctor of Theology degree. Now he's the veteran of the staff and Dean of Studies.

Seated again behind his desk, my host pushes a pile of papers aside. "Have trouble finding us?"

"Not really. You have a beautiful campus."

"It *is* lovely here," he grunts, rubbing his hands together, "but it's a job keeping warm this time of the year."

I shiver in agreement. Ever since stepping out of my car into the thin, frigid air I've been wishing I'd brought my topcoat. The professor is dressed in a heavy brown wool suit, a bright red tie peeking out from inside a thick black knit pullover sweater.

Resting his elbows on the desk he leans toward me, his bright blue Irish eyes studying me. "So. This is Dr. Andrew Kelly, our fiery rebel's associate pastor!" He waits for a response.

"Hardly associate pastor, Dr. Barnes, I'm a layman."

"I know, I know...Psychologist. The good Lord must have sent you. Maybe you'll been able to talk some sense into old Moisés." He chuckles.

I remember my decision, driving over, to avoid any confrontation with Moisés' ex-professor. I open my brief case and lay a cassette on his desk. "As I told you on the phone, Dr. Barnes..."

"Joe."

"Thank you. And I'm Andrew. Anyway, here's the cassette I mentioned. I'd like for you to listen and see if you can make some sense out of it."

I press the button. Immediately, a deep pompous voice: "*Hoc es Corpus!*"

The professor jumps, scattering the papers on his desk.

"Latin! What is this, a *misa*?"

"Sh-h-h...listen."

A moment of silence, then suddenly a gush of harsh guttural words.

"Good Lord! It...it sounds like..." Barnes ejects from his seat, circles the desk and hunches over the cassette, breathing hard.

"Play it again, boy." Joe Barnes is back in his Alabama piney woods and the hounds are about to tree a possum. He listens intently, nodding, a smile playing on his lips. Finally he returns to his seat and grabs a pen and a sheet of paper.

"Just one more time, please." He writes furiously, muttering "Uh-huh...uh-huh."

At last Barnes leans back in his chair, rubbing his broad, freckled forehead. "Dr. Andrew, I'm absolutely flabbergasted. If I didn't know you're an honorable man I'd be tempted to think this was a trick."

"So! You recognized the language?"

Joe Barnes clears his throat, shakes his head, opens his mouth, shuts it. "Andrew, tell me where you recorded this."

I describe the two dramatic nights in the living room of Anastacia and Mercedes. Halfway through, Dr. Joe pushes himself up from his chair and paces back and forth in the cold, cramped office, grunting and shaking his head. When I've finished he sits down again, clears his throat several times, and at last says: "And this young woman, Tatiana. What can you tell me about her?"

"She lived in a small country town all her life, until a few years ago when she decided to come to the city and make herself a nurse."

"And...and that deep masculine voice. You're sure it came from her? There's no way.?"

"No way! Look, you still haven't told me what language she...he was speaking."

"Aramaic," he grunts, his eyebrows raised, as if doubting his own words. "As you know, that's the language the Jews spoke in the time of Jesus."

I feel the skin prickling on the back of my neck. "And what was...the demon...saying?" There, I've used the word!

I watch his face, waiting for him to contradict me. He says, "Just words, nothing that made sense. Almost like a vocabulary drill…" Sighing, he moves nervously in his seat. "So we've got this country girl with little more than a grammar school education speaking like a…" he pauses, frowning…"like a sixteenth century monk!"

"In a deep bass voice!" I add, hoping to elicit a smile from the professor. But he looks like he'd prefer to cry.

Going to the window he stands for a moment gazing out at the lush green hills. Finally, sighing, and without turning, he says, "I suppose Moisés has told you the Seminary's position on demons."

"Well…he told me about the talk you gave at the pastor's retreat."

Returning to his desk, Barnes sinks back into his seat. "The timing of your visit is curious, Dr. Kelly, very curious. A couple of weeks ago we invited an anthropologist from the National University to our annual faculty retreat. He shook us up. Accused us Americans of being brainwashed by the western scientific world view. Said we need to listen to the Mexican people more."

I lean forward, forcing him to look me in the eye. "What do you think? Could he be right?"

He turns his hands palms up. "I don't know what to believe. Maybe the Lord's trying to tell us something. Look, Kelly, I attended a Christian college and a Bible-believing seminary. They taught us demons were a First-Century phenomenon, and that when the last Apostle died demon possession ended."

Sighing, I sit back in my chair, wanting to yell at him. Instead, I say quietly, "Look, Joe, as I said, I'm no theologian. But I have studied psychology and I can guarantee you no psychologist I've ever met would be able to explain what's on that tape. As for you theologians," I pause, not wanting to offend my host, "it looks to me like you need to listen to that anthropologist."

Dr. Joe picks up his red pencil and taps it on the desk. "So what are you and Moisés going to do?"

"What would you do?"

Getting up he unplugs my cassette and carefully winds the cord. Handing it to me, he growls, "I guess I'd go to Santa Catarina and try to find an explanation."

"That's exactly what we're going to do," I say, getting to my feet. "Will you pray for us?."

Joe Barnes comes around the desk and takes my hand. "You can count on it. And when you return, call me and tell me how it came out."

Are those tears in his eyes?

Back on the highway, I impulsively I turn toward Toluca. Two hours until my first appointment...yes! I can make it if I push it a little.

I feel like indulging myself. The man who humiliated my pastor has all but admitted he was wrong! I have every right to eat a steak at *El Paraiso Escondido*.

Ten minutes later I pull into a grassy parking lot and walk down a long stone stairway to a rustic straw-roofed restaurant nestled beside a tiny lagoon. My heart is thumping, remembering. Gabriela! She taught me to love this place.

Sipping a *sidral* at a table overlooking the pond I remind myself it's been more than a year since I was last here with Gabriela. And there's the same young woman who snapped our picture, my arm encircling Gabriela's shoulders, our cheeks touching.

Gabriela insisted on paying for the photo herself. "I'm going to put it on my dresser, and every night I'll give you a goodnight kiss!"

I wonder if the picture's still there? If so, it's being upstaged by her little statue of the Virgin of Guadalupe!

I sigh. I haven't heard from Gabriela in months now. But why should that surprise me? She has a new *galan* who's rich, Mexican, and thinks and feels just like her. She must be deliriously happy!

"Ready to order, *Señor*?"

I order the same filet mignon I had the last time I was here. Anastacia would love this place, I must bring her soon. What a blessing she's been! Unlike Gabriela, Anastacia seems to agree with me on just about everything. No doubt about her commitment to the same faith I hold and to our small, loving flock.

And to me? Is she in love with me? Am I in love with her? I sigh. Not yet, I'm afraid. I'm still working at falling out of love with Gabriela. Some day I'll awake and find I'm free. Meanwhile…picking up my napkin, I dab at a teardrop staining the immaculate white tablecloth…

Oh no, it's one-thirty! Who was I kidding, thinking I could enjoy a leisurely meal and still arrive on time for my first appointment?

…. The tires squeal on a sharp curve. Whoa, slow down! I ease off on the accelerator. Thinking like an American again! If there's one thing people here are accustomed to it's waiting.

At 2:10 I press the button on the elevator, knowing I'll blame the traffic for being late, even though it was my fault.

Why is the waiting room empty? "Did *Señora* Martinez cancel?" I ask Rebeca.

She answers softly, scribbling on a pad. "No Doctór, I was the one who canceled your afternoon appointments; I was sure that's what you'd want."

One look at her face, and I know something's wrong.

"What's happened, Rebeca?" I reach for her hand. Sniffling, she dries her eyes with a Kleenex.

My heart skips a beat. Is it her family? Am I in trouble with the government? Has Margaret or Victoria called from Houston?

She nods toward the closed door of my *consultorio*. "Alicia and Monica are inside. They…they want to talk to you."

Taking my arm, she ushers me into my office. The two girls, both members of our Sunday School class, are huddled together on the love seat. Alicia is a thin, timid first-year sociology major. Monica, a pretty young divorcee, is completing a course on computer technology and has a part time job in a government tax office.

She speaks first. "Doctór Andrés, it took us a long time to get up the courage to come. We're so ashamed; we know you're going to be disappointed in us. But Rebeca keeps telling us we're wrong to keep our guilty secret."

Rebeca, standing near the window, nods.

"What secret, Monica?" My mind is racing...what's going on?... what's happened to these girls?

Alicia says, her voice high, squeaky. "We've put off coming, Professor, because we're afraid you're not going to believe us. He'll probably deny it, so it'll be his words against ours."

Oh oh, sounds like she's going to accuse one of the guys in my class!

"But we know how much confidence you have in Rebeca, and when she promised us she'd vouch for us..."

"Girls, I'll listen to whatever you have to say. But of course I'll have to hear the other party's side too."

The girls look at each other.

Monica says, "We know how much you respect him. We did too, until..."

An icy finger rakes my spine. Oh no, they can't be about to accuse...

"Remember, Monica," Alicia sobs, "it's just as much our fault as it is his."

Rebeca comes over and sits at my feet. Looking up at me with those huge brown eyes, she says softly, her voice breaking, "Doctór Andrés, do you remember, I asked you a few days ago if you had noticed anything different about the pastor?"

God in heaven, where is this headed? I say, hardly recognizing my voice, "Yes, Rebeca, I remember."

Monica mutters, "I know he must be suffering too. Believe me, Doctór, we're doing this as much for his sake as ours."

All right, let's get this over with! "Girls, are you here to accuse the pastor?"

"They're not here to accuse anybody," Rebeca protests, "they're here to ask you to help them head off a scandal that can destroy our church!"

I remind myself I'm here to counsel, not to judge. I take a deep breath. "All right, girls, just tell me what happened."

Rebeca says, "Monica, you first."

The young woman raises her chin, and still avoiding my eyes, begins: "As you know, I divorced a little over a year ago. I don't need to tell you about the problems of a divorcee; that's why, six months ago, I decided I needed the pastor's help to keep my life straight. I began going to his office once a week for prayer. One day, as I was about to leave, he gave me an *abrazo*, and…" she makes a face. "*Profesór*, you know how pure and holy the Christian *abrazo* is. But sometimes a person tries to make it something else. That day, I felt something…different. Afterward I told myself it was my imagination.

"The next time, when it happened again, I tried to pull away, but…" her eyes drop, "Doctór, I must be honest with you…I found myself liking it. In a moment we were kissing passionately.

"After that…" she moans…"every time I came to the Pastor's office he locked the door and we…" she sobs, unable to go on.

"Are you telling me, Margarita, that you had relations?"

"Yes, *Maestro*."

"More than once?"

"Many times, until a few weeks ago when I finally got up the courage to confide in Rebeca and she convinced me to stop going to his office."

Alicia's accusation is even more devastating. Her relation with the pastor began months before Margaret's. Moisés complained to her that he was under a lot of stress. He convinced her God had given her to him as a balm for overwork. When she became pregnant she considered killing herself, but the pastor arranged an abortion.

I want to run out of my office, jump in the car and drive…drive…drive…. Maybe I'll wake up and find all this was just a nightmare. We can't be talking about the man responsible for my being here in Mexico, the man I've honored as the only true prophet of God I've ever known! No, it's impossible!

But I know must go on. "What about your parents, Alicia? Have you told them?"

"I told my mother a few days ago."

"And what did she say?"

"She cried, of course. And insisted we tell my father immediately. I reminded her he has an awful temper and might do something terrible to the pastor. So she agreed to wait until after I'd talked with you."

I sit, my head bowed, unable to speak, my world crumbling about me.

At last Rebeca says, "Please, Pastor, may we pray?"

On our knees we pour out our hearts to God.

When we've finished Alicia asks plaintively, "Do you believe us, Doctór?"

I groan. "Alicia, I'm sorry to say I feel I must believe you."

"Will you help us?"

I heave a big sigh. "Tell you what. I'll talk with the pastor. Then we'll see where we go from there."

Monica moans, "Oh *Maestro*, forgive us. We're your *discípulos* and we failed you!"

An hour later, when the door closes behind the two girls, Rebeca looks at her watch.

I say in a weak voice, "You're going to be late for school. (I'm thinking, "Please don't go, Rebeca, I need you!")

She's watching my face. "I think maybe I should skip class this afternoon."

"I think maybe you're right!" Abruptly, our arms are around each other and we're both bawling. Afterward we sit in silence, unable to put into words what we're feeling.

Finally, we're ready to talk. We agree that Moisés' ministry to Tatiana and her husband must have priority for the moment. But we know we're sitting on a powder keg, I'll have to do something before Sunday.

I find myself thanking God for the miracle of our friendship. We've spent many hours alone together in this office, Rebeca and I, and not once...

She must be reading my mind. "Doctór Kelly," she says, reaching for my hand, "I want to thank you."

"For what, Rebeca?"

"For being my friend. Just my friend. When I'm with you I feel so secure." She smiles. "My boyfriend feels the same way about you and me. He has never..."

I pat her hand clumsily. "Rebeca, I'm no saint, but God has been gracious to me."

She squeezes my hand. "You're wrong, you know. You *are* a saint!"

A deep peace is moving through my body, healing the pain, and I thank God again that my friend decided to skip classes today.

CHAPTER 34

▼

FACE TO FACE WITH
Thanatos

"This is the day the Lord has made, let us rejoice and be glad in it."

Thank you, radio preacher! I don't know your name, but I'm glad you got up so early this morning to remind me. Turning down the volume, I repeat the verse twice, three times, four times...How will this day end?

This day is different from any I've ever lived before. In the past the moments that have changed my life came uninvited, unexpected, surprising me. Not this time. I already know that years from now, perhaps for the rest of my life, I'll be living the consequences of what happens today.

I whisper a prayer, asking for courage and peace.

Guiding my Chevy through the pre-dawn traffic toward Anastacia's house, I keep telling myself not to worry. "Easier said than done!" a little voice mocks me. Within a few hours, in a tiny village in the mountains, we'll come face to face with Tatiana's tormentor. Afterward, I must confront the man God used to bring me to Mexico. The accusations I must make against him will probably destroy his ministry...and end forever our friendship. Groaning, I slam my fist into the steering wheel.

Moisés is wheeling his big black motorcycle through the gate when I arrive. I'm glad to see Anastacia greeting him, I'm not yet prepared to face him alone.

Anastacia welcomes me with a hug. Smiling, she asks, "How about a *cafecito*, Doctór?" Always cheerful! Does she sleep with that same quiet smile on her lips? Following her downstairs to the kitchen, I wonder if some day I'll discover the answer to that question. Only the Lord knows!.

Mercedes greets us: "*Buenos días*, brothers." She leads us to the bright kitchen, where the table is already set. As Moisés and I enjoy *café con leche* and warm sweet breads she makes an announcement. "Anastacia and I have been wondering what our contribution to this day's enterprise would be. Last night the Lord told us: prayer and fasting here at home."

Smacking his lips, Moisés nods. "Very good, *hermanas*; above everything else, what we need for this day is prayer…prayer…prayer. Besides, it will be better if there are not too many of us in the car. On the way to Santa Catarina I'll be dealing with Raymundo and Tatiana about their salvation."

I'm thinking: Good! Maybe Tatiana and Raymundo will decide to spend the weekend in Santa Catarina with her family. If so, Moisés and I will be alone on the return trip and I can get on with this miserable business I've been trying to prepare myself for.

Twenty minutes after a final prayer with Anastacia and her mother we pass the toll gates on the west side of the city and begin the long sweeping ascent into the green mountains separating Mexico City from Cuernavaca. In the back seat Raymundo and Tatiana are very quiet. I can only imagine what Tatiana must be thinking; it's been three years since she left home.

Moisés turns in his seat to face his captive audience. He speaks in a low, firm voice: "Tatiana and Raymundo, we must prepare ourselves for what lies ahead. Are you ready?"

Tatiana answers, her voice pitiful. "No-o-o-o, *Señor*, I am *not* ready. This thing we are doing is very dangerous. I'm afraid!"

Moisés says sternly, "You're right to be afraid, Tatiana. But I'm going to tell you how to take Jesus into your heart. If you do, you'll no longer be afraid."

Opening his Bible to the book of Romans, Moisés reads Paul's warnings about sin and its consequences. Then he invites me to quote John 3:16.

"Tatiana, will you ask Jesus to come into your life? Right now?"

She doesn't answer.

"Tatiana, don't be foolish!" Using the backrest as his pulpit, Moisés pounds a big fist into his Bible. "Don't face your enemy alone."

Still no answer. I'm surprised when Raymundo interrupts: "Señor Moisés, can I invite Jesus into my heart?"

"Of course you can!"

"Then I want to do it."

Moisés must be as surprised as I am. Till this moment Raymundo has seemed a very reluctant participant in everything. "Tell me, Raymundo, what has changed your mind?'

He answers immediately: "The other night when you were talking to Tatiana about Jesus…." In the rearview mirror I see him place a large, work-worn hand on his chest, "…I felt something right here. Was that Jesus calling me?"

Moisés grins and says, "I'm sure it was, Raymundo. Look, I'm going to say a prayer. If you agree with what I'm saying, repeat the words after me.

"Jesus, I know I'm a sinner…and that you died for me on the cross…I open the door of my heart…please come in."

As Raymundo prays, stumbling over every word, I watch Tatiana's face in the rearview mirror. Absolutely no expression. She's still not ready!

We've passed the crest of the mountain and are descending toward Cuernavaca, a toy town three thousand feet below us. Lower than Mexico City, Cuernavaca's benign climate produces abundant splashes of red and purple bouganvilla year-round. It's a favorite refuge for people burdened by the tensions of the world. In the 1860's Emperor Maximiliana and his beloved Carlota maintained a vacation home on one of its green hillsides. In the 40's and 50's it was an elite hideout for Hollywood stars. Now, on weekends, its streets are jammed with the cars of escapees from the big city an hour to the east.

In Cuernavaca we rent a van with four-wheel drive. Tatiana has warned us cars self-destruct on the rocky mountain road leading to her *pueblo*. She guides us through the narrow streets to a blacktop highway carved into the side of the mountains. Moisés is driving now, doing his best to dodge treacherous potholes that look mean enough to break an axle or swallow up a careless jackrabbit. I'm fascinated by the brilliant fields of roses and gladiolas on both sides of the road. Clusters of workers are harvesting the flowers for shipment to Mexico City's markets. Men in white swing their machetes, and following behind, women in white blouses and bright skirts, red, purple and orange, tie the flowers into huge bundles.

Within an hour the blacktop has become an almost perpendicular rutted dirt lane. "How much farther, Tatiana?" Moisés asks, after another forty-five minutes of kidney-jarring ascent.

"We're very near now, maybe a couple of leagues."

We've already passed half a dozen *pueblos*, their tiny thatched houses built of stones grubbed from the countryside. We seem to be the only travelers, save an occasional ox cart or *burro*.

We round a bare, rocky hill and abruptly, just below us, a tile-roofed village materializes in a barren setting of scrubby pines. Tatiana cries, "My pueblo, *ay*, how pretty!"

We enter its main street, scattering squawking chickens and squealing children. An indignant hog rouses himself from a puddle in the
middle of the street and waddles away, complaining in a deep bass
voice.

A man slouched on the doorstep of a grubby *cantina* salutes us with
his bottle of *pulque*. Tatiana waves timidly at a solemn-faced housewife
standing in the doorway of her hut of whitewashed stone, and, unsmiling, the woman raises a flour-covered hand.

"Keep straight ahead," Tatiana says, "my family lives on the edge of
town."

A moment later she exclaims, "Look! Our church! Isn't it beautiful?"

I'd seen the twin moorish towers and massive stone walls from a
couple of miles away. Traveling in rural Mexico, I've been surprised
more than once by the crumbling elegance of churches in unlikely set-
tings, reminders of colonial days when the countryside was teeming
with people and the church had authority to draft laborers at will.

Because there is neither telephone nor telegraph service in Santa
Catarina de la Cruz, Tatiana has warned us, she was unable to advise
her family of our visit.

We stop before a sagging wooden gate in a low, crumbling stone
fence. Beyond it a thatched stone house squats in a rock—strewn yard
populated by half a dozen kids and as many mangy dogs. Tatiana steps
from the van and the children, squealing, run to embrace her. At the
door of the house a skinny teenager stands immobile, her dark face sullen. She must be wondering what Tatiana has done to merit such a
royal escort.

One of the kids runs into the house and a moment later a short,
frowning, wrinkled woman is standing at the door wiping her hands
on a frayed dirty apron. Gaunt and sallow, hair streaked with gray, she
looks sixty, but I suspect she's much younger.

I shut off the engine and watch as Tatiana walks slowly up to her
mother. She reaches out to hug her, but the woman responds with a
listless pat on the shoulder. They talk for several minutes, her mother

shaking her head. Tatiana's voice rises higher and higher. Finally her mother turns and disappears into the house.

Tatiana returns and says, without emotion, "You may come in now." She shrugs. "Mamá's not too happy about our visit. My father is working in the *milpa* and he'll expect his meal when he arrives home in a little while."

She adds in a whisper, "You must be very careful what you say. If my family learns who you are, you will not be welcome. I told my mother you're from the hospital where I work and have come to interview her about my illness."

Two of the older boys have placed cane-bottom chairs beneath a sickly, almost leafless tree in the front yard. I'm relieved we're not going to have to enter the house; it looks dim and cluttered, and I can see swarms of flies buzzing about the front door.

The old woman returns and sits down opposite us, her eyes fixed on the thin, worn hands clutched nervously in her lap.

Moisés begins, a notebook on his knees, pen poised: "*Señora*, a thousand pardons for coming without advising you, but we are concerned about your daughter's health."

"*Bien*," Tatiana's mother mutters, "but there's not much I can tell you, *Señor*."

"Would you please describe how Tatiana's illness has manifested itself in the past?"

The mother begins, becoming more animated as she talks. For years Tatiana, her firstborn, was in perfect health, she tells us, never giving a moment's trouble, helping care for the brothers and sisters who came after her. Then, at twelve, her problems began. One midnight she awoke screaming, complaining of an unbearable pain in her stomach.

At first they thought it was indigestion, but nothing they did brought relief. Finally, at dawn, she fell asleep, and afterward remembered nothing.

Several months later she had her second attack, this time in the afternoon, falling to the floor, foaming at the mouth.

"We were very frightened and sent for my sister, the *curandera*. *Tía* Consuelo informed us, after consulting with the spirits, that someone had cast a spell upon our daughter. Did we have enemies who would want to harm us? We could think of no one."

The aunt applied her formula for undoing hexes, and little Tatiana rested.

Most of the time after that Tatiana lived a normal life, but the family was always on edge, never knowing when more attacks might occur. And they continued, sometimes at home, sometimes at school. At the insistence of her principal they took her to the Social Security hospital in Cuernavaca. The first diagnosis was epilepsy but further tests disproved this. Then cancer was suspected, but X-rays revealed nothing.

On her seventeenth birthday Aunt Consuelo suggested a change of scenery. Why not send Tatiana to Mexico City?

"That was three years ago," her mother concludes. "Until now we thought she was doing all right...except for the loss of her babies."

She stands up. "That's all I can tell you. Now I must fix dinner for my *viejo*." And she disappears into the house. Moisés and I sit staring at each other, frustrated.

Suddenly, Moisés says, "Tatiana, you must take us to your Aunt Consuelo."

Tatiana's body stiffens, her face flushes. "Oh no! I can't do that! She'll be very angry! When I left she warned me I must never..."

"Don't be foolish!" Moisés interrupts. "Do you think your aunt hasn't already heard you're here? We must see her, the Holy Spirit tells me she's holding a secret in her heart, something she's never shared with anybody."

Tatiana's eyes widen, her lips tremble. She goes over to Raymundo. "Please, *mi amor*, tell these *señores* we must go. Right now. I'm afraid."

I'm surprised when he takes her hand and says firmly, "No, Tatiana, I'm tired of this. I'm not leaving here until it's settled!"

Whimpering, Tatiana turns and hurries toward the van. When she finds the door locked she lets out a thin wail and sinks to the ground.

Raymundo quickly comes to her. Placing a hand tenderly on her stomach, he says, "*Mujer*, if you're not willing to break with Celso for my sake, then do it for our baby's. Do you want that demon to kill this child just like he did the others?"

Tatiana buries her face in his shoulder, sobbing. Raymundo pleads, "Do what I've done, invite Jesus into your heart, then you won't be afraid!"

"Leave me alone!" she cries, pushing him away. Raymundo walks over to where Moisés is standing. Arms outstretched, he complains, "As you can see, *Señor* Moisés, Tatiana is a very stubborn woman!"

Lips tight, Moisés shakes his head.

Abruptly, Tatiana pushes herself to her feet. "All right, I'll take you to my *tía*. But you'll be sorry, she's a very powerful woman!"

Giving Raymundo an angry look, she marches away, in the direction of the church. We follow, a crowd of kids in our wake.

"Children, go away!" Moisés says softly, waving them back.

Most of them turn around, but one of the kids runs up to us: "Cheap, cheap!"

He places in my hands a small, exquisite carving of a snake, its feathers still showing traces of red and purple dye.

"Where did you get this?"

"From over there, *Señor*." He points to a heap of rocks behind the temple.

Tatiana has returned and is standing beside me. "Long ago, before the *padres* arrived, there was a temple dedicated to the god Quetzalcóatl. The *padres* tore it down and built a church over the ruins."

I'm about to shove the idol into a pocket when Moisés rushes up, snatches it from my hand and hurls it against the side of the church, shattering it.

Taking my arm he pulls me aside and growls, "Doctór, have you forgotten that these idols are hangouts for demons?"

"I'm sorry, Moisés. I ought to know by now."

"Yes, you should!"

He turns on his heel and walks away. I shake my head, feeling foolish. Before this afternoon's over I'll be exhorting him to repent of a shameful sin. Yet, he's just made me feel like the worst of sinners!

I hurry to overtake him. He is staring up at the massive wooden doors of the church, Tatiana at his side.

"Let's step in for a moment," he says.

As soon as the door opens I stop, my blood turning to ice. Just a step away is a life-sized statue of Christ impaled upon a cross. A wreath of thorns crowns his head. His eyes burn with pain. Blood streams from his hands and feet. I turn away, tears stinging my eyes.

I jump, startled, when behind me 'Moisés' voice booms out, filling the church, echoing from the altar, "Behold the Lamb of God that takes away the sin of the world."

"Moisés," I protest, grabbing his arm. "What do you mean? This... this thing is horrible, it turns my stomach!"

He pulls back. "Doctór, if you'd lived here four hundred years ago maybe you'd have felt different. Remember, these people came in, tore down Quetzalcóatl's temple and put a Christian church in its place. The Bearded Serpent and his angels were furious with them! Wouldn't you have wanted a cross like this to cling to when they came after you?"

"Celso!" I had forgotten Tatiana. Whirling, I see her standing just behind us, arms outstretched, a smile on her lips. Suddenly the smile vanishes and she grasps her throat, her face twisting in pain, "No, Celso, please, please don't hurt me!"

Moisés hurries to her side. "He's angry with you, Tatiana! I warned you!" He throws an arm around her shoulders.

She falls to her knees, gasping, "*Dios mío*, he's...he's going to kill me!"

"Call upon Jesus!" Moisés urges, kneeling beside her.

She doesn't seem to hear him.

Suddenly Raymundo is there. He picks up Tatiana and deposits her at the foot of the cross. "Tatiana," he shouts into her ear, "Jesus can save you, ask him!"

Taking her limp arms, he wraps them around the cross.

Now she's hugging the cross, tears pouring from her eyes. She whispers, "*Jesucristo mi Señor*, forgive me! Save me, save me, please!"

Her body relaxes and she slips to the floor. Raymundo takes her again into his arms, smoothing her hair, "See, my love, I told you! Celso has gone, hasn't he?"

She reaches out, and hugging the cross, presses her cheek to the nail-scarred feet.

"Thank you, Jesus, thank you!"

Moisés says quietly, "Yes, thank you, Lord Jesus."

.... Consuelo's place is a sturdy hut built of white native stone topped by a red tile roof. Crimson bouganvilla flames everywhere, covering the fence, brightening the walls.

Standing at the gate Tatiana sings: "*Tía...*it's me!"

"Go away, I have nothing to say to you!"

"Please, Tía, I need you!"

A figure suddenly materializes at the door. I'm surprised at her bulk; she must be half a foot taller than myself, and as thick as an oak. The pickled prune of a face, is framed by bushy, uncombed red hair streaked with gray. How old is she? Eighty? ninety? Her black brooding eyes widen when she sees Tatiana is not alone. "There's nothing more I can do for you, *Niña*, return to where I sent you."

She turns back into the house, but Tatiana bursts through the gate and throws her arms around the big woman, sobbing, "Oh Tía, I know you still love me. Please, please, don't send me away!"

Her eyes softening, she waves us inside. The only furniture is a small table and two ancient straight chairs. Consuelo seats herself at the table and motions for Tatiana to sit facing her. The rest of us remain standing.

Moisés, stepping up beside Tatiana, growls, "*Señora*, you must tell me his name!"

She glares at him. "What are you talking about?"

"You could not convince him to leave your niece alone, Consuelo, but I'm sure you know his name."

Her eyes widen. "Who are you?"

"A servant of the Lord Jesus Christ. By his power I can do what you were unable to do! Just give me the name of the spirit that has been tormenting Tatiana."

She stands to her feet, her body trembling now. "You must go. At once!"

Moisés tells Raymundo and me: "You're free to leave. As for me, I shall remain here in prayer until the *señora curandera* gives me the name I'm seeking."

Neither of us moves.

"So you think you can do what I could not?" The old woman sits down, breathing heavily. "Don't you know I also invoke the Virgin and the saints?" She points to a large multi-colored painting of the Virgin of Guadalupe on the wall above her head.

Moisés answers, "They have no power. Only Jesus Christ has authority over evil. But you have sold yourself to Satan! I am a servant of Jesus Christ, Lord of lords and King of kings. That's why I have the power and you don't!"

For the first time Consuelo drops her eyes. Her big hands grip the table.

Tatiana goes to her aunt's side, and taking a hand, places it on her stomach. "Tía, feel my little son. Celso murdered my first two babies, and now he's waiting to kill this one."

Consuelo raises her head. "He calls himself Celso?"

Moisés answers: "That's what he says is his name, but he's lying, isn't he? How much longer are you going to protect the demon that's destroying your own flesh and blood?"

Consuelo heaves an enormous sigh, opens her mouth, closes it. Finally, pushing Tatiana gently toward her chair she mutters, "His name is *Thanatos*."

"*Thanatos?*"

"Yes, and he's very proud of it."

"Moisés," I interrupt, my heart racing, "*Thanatos*" is the Greek word for death!"

Moisés slams a fist into the table. "Then he is well named!"

"His vocation is death," Consuelo says. "He was the ruling spirit here in Quetzalcóatl's shrine until the *padres* came."

"And were there blood sacrifices here?" Moisés asks, "Like in Teotihuacan?"

"Yes. They've found hundreds of skeletons buried around Quetzalcóatl's shrine.

"Woman!" Moisés roars, "how did you get mixed up with this blood-thirsty evil spirit?"

She shrugs. "You must know that one is not a *curandera* by choice. I inherited the office from my mother, as she had from hers. Since the *padres* arrived it has been our task to protect them and the villagers from the power of the dark spirit world. This hasn't been easy.

"When my mother passed her office on to me she told me that the day the Spanish *conquistadores* destroyed his temple, Quetzalcóatl pronounced a perpetual sentence of death against the *padres* that would come to minister here. And he sent *Thanatos* to execute the sentence."

In the years that followed the villagers began noticing a disturbing phenomenon: priests assigned to Santa Catarina de la Cruz would begin acting strangely soon after their arrival. Eventually, they would suffer a violent death. As time passed, it became more and more difficult for the church to find a priest willing to minister here.

"Thirty years ago *Padre* Pablo arrived. He was quite young and inexperienced, but a good man. He had been warned that to come Santa Catarina was to fall under a curse of death but, as he told me, Christ had died for him, so how could he refuse to die for his Lord?"

"So you and *Padre* Pablo became friends?"

"*Sí, Señor*. Just before he arrived my dying mother had passed her ministry on to me. So you might say *Padre* Pablo and I began exercising our offices about the same time."

"Were you able to protect him?"

"I tried to. I pled with *Thanatos*, appeased him as best I could. But the Lord *Thanatos* is very proud. Through the centuries he has inhabited the bodies of many learned clerics and acquired their erudition. By the time *Padre* Pablo arrived *Thanatos* had become a master at manipulating people. I soon found he was only mocking me."

And *Padre* Pablo?"

"He loved to mock him too. Some Sundays as the *Padre* was sharing his homily he would find himself speaking blasphemies."

"And you couldn't help him?"

She shrugs. "I tried. But the time came when I decided it was useless to continue bargaining with *Thanatos*. How I hated him! Every time he appeared I cursed him in the name of the Virgin and the saints, but he would only laugh at me.

"Then one terrible day, almost ten years ago, the *padre* decided he could take it no longer. He…climbed the stairs to the top of one of the bell towers and…and jumped to his death."

She sits for a long moment studying her big wrinkled hands, folding and unfolding them. At last she continues. Her voice is low now, and I lean forward, straining to hear. "*Thanatos* must have guessed that after this tragedy the Bishop would stop sending priests to live in our village. The day of *Padre* Pablo's funeral *Thanatos* came to see me and informed me he would no longer be inhabiting priests. From now on he would occupy the bodies of innocent maidens! And the first would be…" she reaches out and takes Tatiana's hand…"the person I most loved in the world, my dear little niece."

Staring at her aunt, Tatiana gasps.

"And you spent years trying to change *Thanatos*' mind?"

She raises her head, and I'm surprised to see the dead black eyes filled with tears.

"I did, but it was useless. At last a thought occurred to me: *Thanatos* had been assigned to this village. If Tatiana went to live in Mexico City, maybe he would leave her alone."

"But you were wrong!"

She grunts. "Of course I was wrong! *Thanatos* is not subject to time and space. At his master's commands he can travel instantly to Mexico City. Or London. Or Tokio."

Groaning with the effort, Consuelo stands to her feet. Her voice is strong now: "*Señores*, I have told you things I never shared with anyone else. *Thanatos* will be very angry." She crosses herself. "I will be his next victim. But it doesn't matter, I am very old, and weary of this evil world."

"*Doña* Consuelo," Moisés' voice is gentle, "your niece has taken Jesus Christ into her heart. Do the same, and we'll face *Thanotos* together. And we'll win!"

The old woman grimaces. "*Señor* Moisés, invite me to betray my mother and all who have gone before me? I cannot do that. You accused me of selling my soul to Satan. Maybe so, but I abhor the evil work of Satan's angel among my people. And I've done my best to help them. Maybe the Virgin will intercede for me with her Son when I die."

Moisés says sadly, "Very well, *Señora*, I have given you the opportunity and you have refused. I will now direct myself to the demon *Thanatos* on behalf of your niece." Moisés looks around the room. "He is here, you know!"

Consuelo's hands are trembling. "Yes, I know." Her voice drops off.

Moisés lays a hand on Tatiana's head and shouts: "*Thanatos* now I know your name, and through Jesus I have authority over you. By the blood of the Son of God shed on the cross I declare that your power over Tatiana is broken. She belongs to the Lord Jesus Christ!"

Raymundo has come to kneel behind Tatiana's chair, his arms looped around her neck. The air is heavy with tension.... We are watching, waiting. Will *Thanatos* challenge Christ's ownership of Tatiana?

Hearing a groan, I look up. Consuelo's eyes are bulging, her body contorting. "*Hoc es corpus!*" The guttural, mocking voice comes from deep within her chest. "You know my name, Moisés? So what? You have no power over me. My Lord Satan has a stronghold in your soul!"

I watch, thunderstruck, as Moisés crumples to his knees, clutching his throat, his face ashen. My God, is *Thanatos* going to destroy him?

"No, Lord *Thanatos*," Consuelo cries, "don't take me now!" She tries to rise, but falls heavily to the floor. Tatiana runs to kneel beside her, kissing her face.

"*Tía*, speak to me, speak to me! *Tía*! *Tía*!"

Her aunt takes Tatiana's face in her hands and groans, "Trust in Jesus, my love, only in Jesus!" She sits up suddenly, then drops again to the floor.

Raymundo hurries over and places an ear on her chest. Finally, he stands up, shaking his head.

Consuelo is dead. What *Thanatos* is now unable to do to Tatiana's baby, he has done to his old adversary.

Beside me, like a boxer after a knockout blow, Moisés, shaking his head, is pushing himself to his feet. Tatiana and Raymundo are too distraught to even guess at the awful truth about him. As for me, the demonic confirmation of the accusations of Rebeca's friends has my head spinning. I'm dumb with fear, like a man alone on a battlefield, his only ally lying mortally wounded at his side. Where is *Thanatos* now? What will he do?

Raymundo says hoarsely, "Tatiana, we must tell your family."

Weeping, Tatiana mutters, "Doctór Kelly, Raymundo and I will remain here for a few days. Will you inform my employers?"

Suddenly, a deafening peal of thunder!

Raymundo steps outside. "*Señores*," he calls to us, "a storm is approaching. You must leave immediately!"

Hurrying out the door, we see an enormous black cloud churning toward us, stabbed by jagged streaks of lightening.

"Raymundo is right," Moisés yells, "in a few minutes the road will be impassable. We must go. Now."

"Run! Tell my family what happened, Raymundo," Tatiana calls, "I'll wait here with my tía."

As we hurry toward the van, the rain comes down in sheets, stinging my face.

My foot slips on the muddy pathway, and I'm stumbling, falling....

"Doctór, are you hurt?"

I take Moisés' outstretched hand and pull myself to my feet.

He gives me a handkerchief. "*Hermano,* you're bleeding."

I take the handkerchief and mop my forehead. Is the blood an omen? I must convince Moisés to confess his sin and ask God's forgiveness.

It's a matter of life or death!

CHAPTER 35

▼

THE UNTHINKABLE HAPPENS

I've never been so afraid in my life! I'm sure Moisés would hear my teeth chattering if the rain wasn't thundering so on the roof of the van.

We're caught in a storm in a murderer's territory! He's on a rampage because we've robbed him of the woman he loves...or do demons fall in love with humans? I don't know, but *Thanatos* is so jealous of Tatiana he'll kill anybody who tries to come between them...at least, that's what troubled mind is telling me at this moment.

"*Dios mío!*" Moisés spins the steering wheel violently as a gust of wind broadsides the big van, almost sweeping it off the narrow road.

Suddenly a deluge of hail the size of golf balls drums on the roof and clatters against the windshield.

"What next?" Moisés growls, hunkering down over the steering wheel.

I clench my teeth, expecting the windshield to shatter at any moment. The wailing wind drives the rain through the crevices in the door of the old van, soaking me.

Just ahead a tall, thin fir is bent double over the narrow road, its branches reaching out like arms in supplication.

"Look out!" I yell.

Moisés jams his foot on the brake, but too late! A huge branch crashes down on the hood, crumpling it. We duck as it bounces against the windshield.

"Stop, Moisés, stop!"

"Not a chance!" Moisés shouts, "The road is too slippery. We'd never get moving again."

I've learned a lot about the kingdom of evil in these past two years, but there's still much I don't know. *Thanatos* taunted Moisés about Satan's "stronghold" in his soul. How much authority does this murderous demon have over Moisés? Always before, I've felt safe with him, but at this moment I feel terribly vulnerable, aware of an evil, brooding presence.

Topping a rise, we bump downhill. The pounding of the rain lets up a bit. Now's the time to talk!

I turn toward Moisés and shout into his ear: "Margarita and Monica came to see me yesterday."

"Oh?" His foot lifts off the accelerator, and the motor gives a nervous cough.

"I'm sure you know what they talked to me about."

An explosion of breath escapes his lips, melting the thick frost on the windshield.

"*Dios mío!*" The old van slams into a deep hole hidden by the flood, the wheels spin, the motor coughs and almost dies. Moisés pumps the accelerator and the motor roars back into life, the van leaps forward, slithers sideways, teeters on the edge of the road, miraculously rights itself and surges forward.

All the time Moisés stares ahead, gripping the wheel, his lips tight, a muscle in his jaw twitching.

The rain is thundering on the roof again, maybe I shouldn't distract Moisés…but no, I can't wait any longer! "What are you going to do, Moisés? Even *Thanatos* knew about your sin!"

"*Thanatos?*" he bellows, "*Thanatos* is a liar!" He turns and looks at me, his eyes challenging me. Then he says, his voice quieter now, "Doctór, I'm no fool. I've already asked God to forgive me."

"And now…?"

"It's over, done with. The blood of Christ has cleansed me from all unrighteousness."

I remember the stricken faces of Mónica and Margarita. No, Moisés it's not all over with!

I grip his shoulder. "What about the damaged souls your sin has left behind? What are you going to do about that? Those two young women will be nursing sick, scarred consciences for the rest of their lives!"

He pushes against the steering wheel so hard I'm afraid he's going to break it. "Those two young women tempted their pastor! Have they asked God's forgiveness?"

I have no trouble hearing Moisés above the pounding of the rain, he's screaming out his anger.

I lean closer. "Okay Pastor, let's forget the girls for now, let's talk about you. I'm puzzled: how could you carry on a relation with two women of your flock for months, and all the time go about your business as if nothing was wrong? Didn't it bother you?"

We've come to the blacktop highway leading to Cuernavaca. Moisés slows for an instant, and without braking, wheels onto the highway.

His foot jams the accelerator and the van leaps forward, bucking and swaying on the rain-slick road, spraying sheets of water. I'm really scared now, maybe I should lay off. But I can't! I've got to make this man face up to what he's done!

"Tell me, Moisés, is this the first time? Or have there have been other women? You must confess your sin before the church!"

Gritting his teeth, he growls, "Thank you for your advice, Doctór. I will consider it."

I shake his arm, trying to make him look at me: "Pastor," I shout at the top of my voice, "you have no choice, you must act this Sunday. If you don't tell the church, the families of the girls will."

It's getting dark. A damp chill permeates the vehicle, making me shiver. I hug myself, praying desperately, overcome by a devastating sense of loss. Always before, Moisés has been my ally; suddenly he's my enemy. I want to stick my fingers in my ears, suspecting that the roar of the engine and the drumming of the rain are a funeral march, and that this man is intent on killing us!

"Please, Moisés slow down!" He stomps the accelerator to floor, making no attempt to avoid the deep potholes. Every time we strike one the van bucks violently, rattling my teeth.

The van weaves across the road and Moisés yanks it back. I give thanks there's no traffic....

No traffic! We've been on this road for a quarter of an hour now, and haven't met a soul. Something's wrong!

"Idiot!" Moisés roars. A figure is standing in the middle of the highway, waving wildly. Instead of braking Moisés veers to the left, two wheels leave the highway, he fights for control and somehow gets us back on the road. I'm pounding on him, shouting "Stop! stop! stop!"

What happened next I remember only as a dim, flickering video of a bad dream...there's no longer the sound of wheels on the highway...we're airborne!.... An instant later I feel myself catapulted forward, my head slamming against the windshield....

I awake gasping, choking, coughing, kicking desperately at the windshield...I'm drowning, and there's no way of escape....

Is this heaven? Must be. No doubt about it, the figure standing over me is an angel. He doesn't have wings, but he's eight feet tall, and his flowing white robe shines like a full moon.

"Where…where am I?" I try to push myself up, and, exhausted, fall back onto the cold, muddy ground. No, I can't be in heaven, I feel rain on my face…and this muddy clothing is no heavenly robe! I raise a hand to my forehead. "Yi-i-i-! It hurts!"

The giant is smiling now, a friendly smile.

"Who…who are you?" I ask, my voice trembling.

His voice rumbles like a peaceful waterfall: "My name is *Dunatos*. The Father sent me in response to the prayers of your intercessors."

"I…I thought I was dead!"

He kneels beside me. "That was the intention of the enemy, but the Father's not ready for you to come home. He's still got work for you to do, so…" like a caress from God, his breath warms my face…"once again I've come to your rescue."

"Again?"…. *Dunatos'* hand, as light as a moonbeam, is on my shoulder. That hand! One dark night on the highway outside Saltillo it grabbed the steering wheel!

Wrapping his arms around me, he pulls me to my knees. His robe smells of frankincense, and peace flows from him in unending waves, warm, soothing, healing.

I reach up and touch my forehead. The huge, throbbing knot is gone! My hand brushes my shirt. It's dry and spotless now, with the same sweet fragrance as *Dunatos'* robe.

He sets me on my feet. I feel reborn! Above the angel's shoulder a bright star winks at me, and a crescent moon outlines a bank of retreating thunderheads.

"Moisés…do you hear what I hear? It sounds like a choir of angels…Moisés?"

I'm trembling. "Moisés! Where are you?"

Dunatos lays a hand on my shoulder, his voice gentle, "Andrew, your pastor didn't want to be rescued."

"You mean he's…"

"He's with the Father."

"But...but..." I should be desperately sad. Why then this incredible peace?

"Moisés was a valiant warrior. The Father loves him very much."

I whisper, "Is he...is he all right?"

"He was a casualty of the war with Quetzalcóatl. But the blood of the Lamb is more powerful than the schemes of the enemy."

"*Señores, señores!* Are you all right?" I can make out two figures running toward us in the flickering glow of a flashlight.

No, *Dunatos*, don't leave me!

He's gone! Nothing to show I've been rescued by an angel, not even giant footprints in the mud.

I yell: "Here I am, *Señores.*"

I find myself smiling, shaking my head in wonder. How will I explain to these people what happened to me? No broken bones...not even a bruise! And this clothing, dry and unwrinkled, still warm from the ironing board!

CHAPTER 36

▼

Adios, Moisés, Adios, Kyrus

People sit shoulder to shoulder, filling every chair in the huge, drafty old auditorium. Still more are pouring in, packing the side aisles back wall.

It's two o'clock on a chilly, dark Friday afternoon. Already the rumble of thunder announces the approach of the inevitable daily rains. Almost no one in Mexico embalms their dead, so funerals can't be postponed for two or three days like in the States. Federal law dictates a body must be interred within twenty-four hours of death.

I've been so busy helping arrange this funeral I haven't even had a chance to take a nap.

Everything keeps revolving in my mind like a video stuck on replay: the wild ride after we left Santa Catarina de la Cruz…the yelling match with Moisés…the plunge into the river…the encounter with *Dunatos*…wreckers pulling the van from the river…the Red Cross placing Moisés' battered body in the ambulance…. our deacons haggling with the police in Cuenavaca over the *mordida* for the release of Moisés body….

Moisés' widow is huddled with her four children down front row. Every few minutes she wails," *Ay Dios mío.*" I study the faces of the congregation,dumb with shock, eyes red from weeping, unable to accept the death of the dynamic saint who has been the heart and soul of their church.

Only a few of us here know that the spirit of the man whose body lies before us died months ago....

Grandmother Eunice is delivering a eulogy on behalf of the Missionary Society, reminding us that Moisés Contreras was an inspiring preacher, a loving pastor, a tireless, Spirit-filled evangelist, a holy man of God, a model for every man in the church.

I'm dully aware, in my zombie-like state, that I'm feeling more relief than anguish. Until the accident I'd been agonizing over the least traumatic way to present our pastor's sin to the congregation this coming Sunday. It was going to be a nightmare! I was sure some would insist on sending him packing at once, and others would argue for mercy.

But now the man who was hours away from being publicly disgraced is being celebrated as a hero.

Porfirio Gonzalez is speaking on behalf of the deacons. No other man he's ever known, he testifies, had such an anointing of the Spirit. He describes the miraculous moment two years ago when the pastor laid hands on him, and his cancerous liver was instantly healed....

From the hospital in Cuernavaca I dialed Anastacia's number. She picked up the phone at the the first ring.

"*Bueno?*"

"It's me, Andrés." I was aware my voice sounded strange. I still was having trouble accepting I was alive.

"Andrés! Thank God! We've been frantic! What happened, did you have car trouble?"

I paused. "First, let me tell you all went well in Santa Catarina. Tatiana and Raymundo decided to stay for the weekend. I'll explain later."

"Andrés, you sound...where are you?"

"In Cuernavaca, Anastacia…look, Moisés is dead." And choking on the words, I described the tragic accident.

After I had answered all the anguished questions Anastacia and Mercedes could think of I insisted they not drive to Cuernavaca at that hour of the night, assuring them the members of the church would take care of matters there. Yes, I'd call as soon as I got back to the city.

Next, I dialed Rebeca's home number. Thank God it was she who answered the phone, at first muddled from being awakened in the middle of the night, then speechless for a long moment after I gave her the news. We began making a list of the people she should call.

When I was about to hang up, she breathed, "Dr. Andrés, *gracias a Dios.*"

At the moment I thought she was giving thanks for my survival, but moments later it came to me: she was thankful for her pastor's death!

No, not for his death, but for what would be his reputation's miraculous resurrection from the dead….

Kiko, the President of my Students' Bible class, is speaking, waving his big black Bible, recalling the Sunday morning when the Word preached by God's mighty evangelist penetrated his heart.

For the first time I spot Alicia and Monica seated several rows back. They are clinging together, tears glistening on their cheeks. Are they tears of relief?

I glance at my watch: three-thirty. About this time yesterday Moisés and I were running for the van. As long as I live I'll remember that enormous black cloud lumbering toward us, spouting jagged streaks of lightening. Immediately I knew it wasn't an ordinary storm cloud. Now I know it was Satan's executioner!

I shiver. September fifteenth, a date I'll never forget. September fifteenth? Suddenly, it hits me: exactly two years ago, on another highway far to the north, I met Kyros.

I'm the one who was meant be in that coffin! The knowledge comes to me so clearly, so unmistakably, I receive it as a revelation: *Thanatos* had a demon companion on the road with us yesterday. Their mission was to kill Andrew Kelly, not Moisés Contreras. Of course! Moisés had already died!

I need someone to talk to! There's Rebeca, and Gelda, of course. And I can see Anastacia and Mercedes at the back of the auditorium. Suddenly I realize that, with the passing of Moisés, the only confidants left to me are these women.

Bernabé, The chairman of the deacons is presiding. He announces, "And now, Dr. Joseph Barnes, one of our pastor's beloved professors, will read from God's Word."

As Dr. Joe reads Psalm 90, I'm remembering our meeting a few days ago. From Moisés' description of him I had expected an unbending, narrow-minded theolog. But he surprised me. I discovered that just like me, he was struggling to maintain his integrity in the face of life's ambiguities. Would he, maybe, also be looking for a friend?

An hour later, after the last "Amen", Joe surprises me with a warm hug. "Andrew, I hope you'll go home and get some sleep. You look beat."

I'm touched by the concern in his warm brown eyes. "Thank you, Joe, I plan to do that."

He says, his voice just above a whisper, "I've been on pins and needles since our talk the other day. Anything new?"

"Got a spare moment in your agenda this weekend?"

Smiling, he replies immediately, "How about tomorrow afternoon? I'll warm up the old percolator in my chilly office."

Mexicans have mixed feelings about death. On November 2, the Day of the Dead, they make fun of dying, feasting on sweet breads baked in the form of skulls. But when it comes to burying their dead, they're more honest than Americans. No painting of a dead face so people will say, "Doesn't he look natural!" And no artificial grass around the grave to mask the ugly, gray dust to which the body must return....

The graveside service is over, but no one will leave until the last shovel of dirt has been thrown. The shovel has passed from hand to hand, and now it's my turn. I spade up a bit of dirt and drop it onto the coffin.

The last dull rays of the sun are filtering through the smog as we turn away from the grave. Rebeca takes my arm, and I'm surprised by a sob rising in my chest. Then I remember: after we'd buried Mary my daughter Margaret took my arm and together we stumbled over to the car. Rebeca has a lot of Margaret's tenderness, maybe that's why she's so dear to me.

"Let's hurry," says someone in the crowd shuffling out of the cemetery, "I don't want to be in the *panteon* after dark."

Panteon, place of "all the gods." Why do Mexicans use such a curious word for their place of burial? I've never heard anyone call it the "cemetery." On the Day of the Dead the *panteones* are thronged by thousands bearing food for the spirits of the dead that hovering about. No wonder everyone is hurrying to get out of here before dark!

A deep melancholy is settling into my bones.

"Doctór, are you all right?" Rebeca squeezes my arm.

"All I need is some sleep, Rebeca," I tell her. But my tired mind is filled with confusion about Kyros, *Thanatos* and Quetzalcóatl. Will this battle never end? And with Moisés dead, where do I go from here?

Driving home I make a resolution: for me, the memory of Moisés' fatal flaw will be buried with his body. From now on, when I think of him, I'll remember only the good things that were said about him at the funeral.

I owe that to him. Except for Moisés I'd still be in Kingwood, trying to decide why I was born. But the man convinced me the Creator could indeed place his hand on a man's shoulder and steer him to his destiny.

Moisés' life has ended, but not God's purpose for Andrew Kelly. I must remember what I learned from Moisés, if God is going to fulfill his purpose for me.

What was the most important thing I learned from Moisés?

That Christ is coming, very soon!

Trembling as if struck by a sudden fever I brake and pull over to the side of the street. Resting my head on the steering wheel, I feel the fierce beating of my heart. After a while I sit up and stretch. No, this is not a fever, but a divine excitement. Something is going to happen soon! When it does, I must be prepared to recognize it, to act upon it....

Saturday afternoon Joe Barnes sits listening, his elbows on the scarred desk, chin resting on a big fist, eyes never leaving mine. I've decided to leave out nothing.

When I've finished, he lets out a low whistle. "So this...this angel even told you his name!"

"That's right. *Dunatos.*"

"'Powerful, mighty'" He chuckles, the swivel chair squeaking as he leans away from the desk. "Andrew Kelly, your story's ridiculous. But you know what? I believe every word of it! Listen, would you mind telling me a little about yourself? I really know nothing, except that you have a Ph.D. in Psychology from a seminary my profs called liberal, and that you somehow got mixed up with the most cantankerous student that ever got bounced out of this seminary."

I do my best to give him a summary of my life in fifteen minutes, fourteen of which deal with Mary's death and what's happened since.

"I hope you understand, Joe," I conclude, "I'm not trying to convince you of anything. All I know is that, for some reason God recruited me, the most unlikely candidates imaginable...to be a foot soldier in his showdown with the Feathered Serpent."

Frowning, Joe answers, "That 'showdown' business scares me, Andrew. You know, my colleagues and me have been insisting that the First Century was the exclusive setting for God's special miracles. But what if the Final Century has been slipping up on us without our realizing it!"

His lips curl in a wry smile. "At least that's what I'm going to suggest to my brothers tomorrow in our monthly faculty meting. Pray for me."

I whistle. "You're going to tell them you've been teaching your students error? Hope you don't get in hot water."

He grunts. "Are you kidding? You've never attended a Monday morning Faculty meeting at Trinity Seminary. They're going to burn me at the stake!"

Hunching over, he shuffles through a pile of papers on his desk. "But now, let me make a confession. I had another purpose when I invited you here today. Thought you might help me get out of a problem."

Tossing me a letter, he adds, "I accepted this invitation a couple of weeks ago, and yesterday at the funeral my pastor reminded me I'm supposed to preach at my own church the same weekend. As you can see, the letter's from the President of the Pastor's Association in the Yucatan. They want someone to deliver lectures on Pastoral Counseling at their annual retreat next month. I can't think of anyone better qualified than Dr. Andrew Kelly."

I scan the letter, written in a shaky hand on lined notebook paper. "I don't know, Joe, remember, I'm not a preacher."

"Even more reason why you should go. Pastors get tired of listening to other preachers."

The date of the retreat catches my eye. "Tell me, Joe, do you know the date of the fall equinox?"

He raises an eyebrow. "The equinox? What's that got to do with a trip to the Yucatan?" Reaching for a dictionary, he growls, "Don't tell me you check your horoscope before you accept invitations!…Um, here it is, September 22nd."

"Invitation accepted! I've been promising myself for more than a year I was going to visit the Temple of Kukulkan in Chichén Itzá. And guess what? Your pastor's retreat is just a week before one of the two target dates!"

Eyes wide, Joe listens as I tell him the story of the Feathered Serpent's bi-annual "second coming" in Chichen Itzá. It's late when I leave Joe Barnes and start from home. For the first time in weeks I'm at peace. Our last hour together Joe and I opened our hearts and shared how we feel about God, our work, and ourselves. I can't remember when I've felt so at ease with another man.

Sunday morning a couple of weeks later, as I'm preparing to leave for church, the interphone buzzes.

"Good morning, Andrés." No mistaking that voice, it's Anastacia! I'm surprised; we were together until quite late last night.

"Hello, beautiful, what are you doing here?"

"May I come up?"

Of course!"

Two minutes later she's standing in the door, a newspaper in her hand. Dressed in jeans and a white blouse, her strawberry hair brushed and fluffy, she looks as fresh as the bright morning sun beaming through my living room windows.

"Andrés, do you take a paper?"

"Yes, but I haven't picked it up from downstairs."

"Thank goodness, I wanted to be with you when you saw *Novedades*. Come, my love." She takes my hand and leads me to the sofa, makes me sit down, then hands me the newspaper, opened to the Society section.

My heart stops: "Prominent Couple Announces Engagement." They're an impressive pair, Gabriela Mancini and Gregorio Benavides Monsanto. He's a big man, with a square face, heavy jowls and grave eyes behind dark-rimmed glasses. Fifty, maybe? Stockbroker and investment banker. Vice-President of the Rotary club.

He isn't smiling, but Gabriela is! Please, Gabriela, let me see somewhere in those shining eyes a shadow of sadness, a hint that you're wishing it were I there beside you!

Seated at my side, Anastacia is lightly rubbing my back. "Andrés, I'm so sorry!"

I study the man's face, searching for something that might help me dislike him. But no, he looks like a gentleman, a solid citizen, honest and reliable.

What attracted her to him? Not wealth, she has no need of money. His looks? No, he's quite ordinary. Then I remember what she told me: they're two peas in a pod!

"Andrés, are you all right?" Her arms around me, Anastacia plants a kiss on my cheek.

A tear splatters down, blurring *Don* Gregorio's thick glasses.

Anastacia is on her knees, her face close to mine.

"*Mi amor*, I want to spend the day with you. Let's do something crazy!"

My head is spinning. "But…but what about church?"

"God will forgive us. Come on, Andrés you deserve it!"

We haven't yet begun Sunday morning meetings at Anastacia and Mercedes'. At the moment they're attending Rosario's church when they go to church. Most Sundays they have their own devotional at home. As for my Sunday School class, they can get by without me; last Sunday I asked one of the more mature students to do the Bible study this morning.

I get to my feet. "Let's go!"

It turns out to be a crazy day indeed. First we go to Chapultepec Park and ride the *MontañaRusa*, Mexico City's version of the roller coaster, screaming, hands raised, teeth rattling.

"Let's do it again!" Anastacia yells as soon as the car screeches to a halt.

Laughing, holding hands, we run for the ticket booth.

After the third ride we agree we're ready for something more restful. We rent a boat and row like mad, chasing the indignant, quacking ducks.

On the bank we find a spot under a friendly eucalyptus, where other couples are too interested in one another to pay any attention to our hugs and whispers.

Later, lunching in Chapultepec's extravagant *Restauarant del Lago* I put down my fork and take her hand.

"Anastacia, let's get married. Tomorrow!"

She smiles, a tender, bittersweet smile. Squeezing my hand, she says, "Andrés, there's nothing I'd rather do than marry you. But I'm not going to do it until I can have all of you."

"What do you mean?"

She kisses my hand tenderly. "You know what I mean: I saw that big teardrop falling on Gabriela's engagement portrait!"

Searching for words, I take my fork and pick at the pescado a la Veracruzana.

My dear companion mutters, "Gabriela's a fool!"

I swallow hard. I'm not going to cry again!

Popocatéptl!

Kyros balances himself on the crater of Popo's sheer, snow-crowned cone, awaiting the arrival of his master. In the distance the lights of Mexico City have coalesced into an enormous, glittering lake of fire.

Kyros had been expecting this summons, and when it came, he bowed his head like a prisoner receiving a death sentence.

Still fresh in his mind is the warning of a fellow demon the day after his last encounter with Lord Quetzalcóatl: "Your next meeting with Our Lord will be at the mouth of Popo!" His smirking colleague jabbed a companion in the ribs and they snickered.

"What are you talking about?"

"Haven't you heard? An audience with the Feathered Serpent in his throne room is always a last-chance warning. After that the Bottomless Pit!"

Kyros the scholar called upon his erudition: "That old myth's been float-ing around for eons. I personally have researched all the royal archives and found nothing to substantiate it"

"And I guess you also found nothing to substantiate what everyone knows about Popocatépetl....that for all of Mesoamerica, it's the main gate to the Pit."

Not wanting to to pursue this troubling conversation, Kyros drew his academic robe close around him and turned away.

His colleague chuckled. "On your last visit you saw what was on the far side of his throne, didn't you?"

Kyros shuddered, remembering the blast of hot air roiling up from that dark tunnel.

"And you heard the moans, too, I'll bet!"

Kyros uncovered one doleful eye: "Sure, but what does that have to do with Popo?"

"Oh, come on, Kyros, you know the tunnel in his throne room is our Lord's private line to Gehenna." Reaching out, he pulled the faded black robe away from the Kyros' face: "You and your research! You scholars think everything's written down on manuscripts, but you're wrong! The most fearful things are preserved in the mind of our Master."

Unfortunately, his inquisitor was probably right: there's a ton of dread-ful oral tradition floating around the Dark Kingdom, and Kyros suspects the Feathered Serpent encourages it as a means of keeping his subjects in line.

Then there are other myths that simply tantalize. For instance, the one about the day the Prince delivered Mesoamerica to Quetzalcóatl. On that day, so goes the story, tens of millions of demons erupted from the Bottom-less Pit in celebration. The earth people saw only a fiery eruption of Popo. The black lava rock decorating hundreds of square miles around Mexico City countryside commemorates that day. It's fitting that the loathsome bloody altar atop Huitzilopochtli's temple was carved from that rock. And it's sobering that souvenirs made from that demon-infested rock decorate living rooms around the world!

The myth ends with a prophecy: on the day the Great Tribulation begins there will be another eruption of Popcatépetl. Every demon that has been exiled to the Pit since the beginning of the Prince's reign will be returned to earth, to serve as Satan's cannon fodder in the great Battle of Armageddon.

Is Kyros about to be designated one of these disgraced warriors, destined to vegetate in Genenna until the final battle between the Serpent and the Lamb?

Kyros shivers....

From 19,000 feet the stars seem close enough to touch. Especially Venus! All the demon kingdom knows that Venus is really their Lord Quetzalcóatl, so Kyros is not surprised when that brilliant star detaches from the firmament and begins drifting in his direction. He watches fascinated as it sails over Mexico City's glowing lake of fire and comes floating toward Mount Itzlazihuatl, undulating now like a serpent.

"Kyros! My idiot envoy!" From the peak of Itzlazihuatl his dreaded Master's jeer thunders at him, and an instant later Quetzalcóatl is coiling himself around the icy crater, black tongue flicking like a cat-o'nine tails."

"But my Lord, it wasn't I that failed, it was Thanatos!"

"Don't prattle to me about Thanatos! A million years ago the Prince removed him from my jurisdiction, so I cannot punish him. But I can you!"

"But, oh, Divine Perfection, Thanatos contracted Chac-Mol, Lord of the weather, to prepare the setting for Kelly's demise...Chac-Mol guaranteed us the tempest he'd conjure up would raise an impenetrable shield about us. This time the angel Dunatos would not be able to intervene. This time, without fail, Andrew Kelly would die!"

"But who died?" Quetzalcóatl bawls, his voice triggering an avalanche that rumbles down the mountainside.

"Moisés died, my Lord, and you should be pleased; he was one of your most stubborn enemies."

"Pleased? How dare you opine about what should please me! Did I not advise you that I myself was arranging the demise of Moisés? Did you and Thanotos think I needed your help?"

"No, my lord, but he is out of the way now."

"I didn't want him out of the way, I wanted him alive, so I could parade him before his precious congregation for what he was, a fraud, a failure. But because of your muddling they made him a hero! You idiot, you spoiled it all again!"

"But, my Lord…"

Was it a flick of his tail or a lash of his tongue? Kyros has no idea, he only knows he's floating down…down…down into the dark, dismal depths of Popocatépel. Above, the light of the full moon, framed by Popo's crater, shrinks to the size of a half dollar, then the size of a dime. From below a howling blast of blistering air snatches away his treasured black robe, burns it to a whisp of glowing ash, and vomits it upward, out of the mouth of the crater. Gone forever is this badge of scholarship, his entree to the Feathered Serpent. From this moment his name is erased from the Prince's roll of honor. From this moment he will be nothing more than a cipher in the Prince's computer, destined for extinction in that final war of desperation against the Lion of Judah.

CHAPTER 37

▼

THE SERPENT AND THE LAMB IN THE LAND OF THE MAYANS

Like a bird fluttering through a suddenly opened cage door I break free of the last red light and turn onto the Puebla turnpike. It's a beautiful day for travel. The sky is as blue as a baby's eyes, and snow-capped Popo and Iztla are peeking at me through feathery clouds. I lower the window and breathe in the thin, clean mountain air.

If I had taken the 8:00 A.M. flight my plane would be touching down about now in Merida, Yucatan's capital city. By automobile it will take me three days. But no matter, I've waited two years for this. This is way the Toltecs came, about the time of Christ, when they abandoned Teotihuacan and set out for the Mayan empire. Their journey lasted a generation, so why should I worry about a mere three days?

And I'm glad to be going alone. I toyed with the idea of inviting Anastacia and her mother to accompany me, but I have the feeling Anastacia and I can use this time apart to reevaluate our relationship.

I need time to think! I'm still numb from Moisés' fall from grace and precipitous death. I have no idea where I'm supposed to go from here. And besides, there's this curious feeling…this knowledge…that God is going to speak to me on this trip. I must keep my heart open, every moment, for that message.

After a light lunch I leave Puebla behind and turn east toward the Gulf coast. Fighting early afternoon drowsiness, I'm suddenly blinded by an awesome brightness just ahead: Cortés and his tiny army are marching up from the coast, armor glinting in the sun!

I shake myself awake, remembering: Cortés was expecting a fierce battle with Moctezuma's army. He didn't know that the most powerful king in the Americas was at that moment pacing back and forth in the royal palace, ready to receive him with open arms. For Moctezuma believed that Hernán Cortés was Quetzalcóatl, fulfilling his promise to return from heaven. He was sure this mystical messiah would give his people the paradise he himself had not been able to provide them.

What a rude awakening awaited Moctezuma!

Now I can see the snow-covered peak of *Pico de Orizaba*, the highest point in North America, dividing the high, arid plain dominated by Popocatépetl from the lush green coast.

An hour and a half later I'm navigating the hairpin descent from the mountains to the city of Orizaba, my lungs slowly adapting to the tropical air.

The coffee plantations are folding into lush green banana fields when I top a rise and see in the distance white cumulous clouds painted gold by the setting sun. Hovering over the blue Gulf of Mexico they look like huge billowing sails.

I pull over at a lookout point, and let my mind drift back to the fourteenth Century: a group of farmers, maybe on this very hill, are watching open-mouthed as the white sails of Hernán Cortés' ships appear, mingled with low white clouds.

"Look!" one shouts, "three great ships, floating in on the clouds!"

"It's Quetzalcóatl!" another cries, "returning from heaven!" They run to the coast and when the blond, bearded soldiers leave their ships and stride upon the beach, fall to their knees in worship.

Just like Moctezuma, they too were longing for the coming of a divine king who would bring heaven to earth.

No wonder I've got this feeling Mexico has a special place in the Father's plans for his Son's Second Coming! Mexico's history is saturated with the expectation of a Savior descending from heaven....and a heart-breaking cycle of repeated betrayals. Is there any other place earth where, without understanding, people have been so long awaiting Christ's return?

I spend the night in Vera Cruz. My room is comfortably air conditioned, and the steady washing of the surf lulls me to sleep. But I awake half a dozen times, my heart thumping, excited by my new vision of the coming of my Lord.

The next morning I head south toward the state of Tabasco. Outside the refinery city of Coatzacoalcos I park on the banks of a wide, deep river where, according to legend, Quetzalcóatl bid farewell to his weeping followers and disappeared into the mists of the Gulf.

Stopping at Lake Catemaco I find a palm-thatched restaurant that features fresh perch and warm brown corn tortillas. Except for the absence of Alpine snow, the green hills and emerald lake are a picture postcard of Switzerland. Mercedes insisted a stop in Catemaco was a must. Witches from all over the world celebrate their yearly convention here. The placid shores of the lake are dotted with temples where shamans offer daily sacrifices. Witchcraft is tailor made for people victimized by broken dreams. No promise of a savior. No hope for a better world. One is left only to bargain with fate in hope of survival. Tatiana and her aunt Consuelo taught me that sad reality.

At mid afternoon, in the quaint little village of La Venta I stand in the shadow of a colossal gray stone head thirty feet tall. The broad, flat face stares back at me without expression. It has thick lips, a wide nose and cold slanted eyes. A curious helmet covers head the head to the eyebrows.

I blink. The headpiece looks like an export from Cape Canaveral! Who was the model for this strange sculpture? A prehistoric astronaut, perhaps? A chill runs through me. Maybe it's not a coincidence that this monument is near the place of Quetzalcóatl's sudden rapture!

As the sun sinks into the tangled jungle I arrive at the lush tropical city of Villahermosa. This capital of Tabasco has the warm, humid climate of Houston and the cuisine of the Garden of Eden! Seated in the dining room of my hotel, I chide myself for waiting two years to visit this land of absurdly sweet watermelons, luscious oranges, melt-in-the-mouth mangos and papayas, and pineapples that would make Hawaii blush in shame.

I have trouble going to sleep. Is it because of gorging on so much fruit? Or because I can't stop thinking about the side trip I've planned for tomorrow? I opted for a detour because of a book I stumbled on in a dusty little store behind the *Zócalo*. Charles Gallenkamp, its author, recounts the discovery fifty years ago of an incredible royal tomb. After reading the book I knew I must visit that grave!

I awake early and travel two hours over a bumpy jungle road to Palenque. Palenque was uncovered earlier in this century, after being lost in the primeval forest for more than a thousand years. As I pull into the graveled parking lot I see dozens of visitors climbing the Temple of the Sun. Others are snapping pictures of the soaring tower of the Great Palace.

Step by stumbling step I make my way up a seventy-foot pyramid, careful not to slip on the loose stones forming the pyramid's serrated sides. Finally, breathing hard, sweat pouring down my face, I reach the top and enter the Temple of the Inscriptions. Inside I find a narrow passageway leading downward into the heart of the pyramid. I'm all alone. No wonder, the descent into the airless pyramid promises to be even more heart-stopping than the difficult ascent to the top.

Taking one of the fat yellow tallow candles piled on a stone table, I light it and begin picking my way downstairs, my breathing labored, my pulse pounding. A inner voice whispers: "Stronghold of Satan!"

Reaching the bottom at last, I cross a dimly lighted vault, duck my head and step through a triangular opening into a dark chamber. The candle flickers and almost dies. I cup my hand and wait anxiously until it recovers. Then I lift it high, and gasp at what I see: the floor is a beautifully sculptured marble slab some twelve feet long and seven feet wide. Kneeling down, I trace with a finger the figure of a man carved into the center of the stone. About my height, he wears a bright feathered headdress and a necklace of red rubies. Who could he have been, this Mayan King David, this pagan high priest?

Rising to my feet I take a step forward. Suddenly I draw back in horror. I've bumped into a stone cross! Reaching almost to my chin, its horizontal arms are in the form of serpents, and between them perches a quetzal bird with brilliant red and green feathers and a long streaming tail. Biting my lip, I force myself to draw closer. There he is, Quetzalcoatl, represented by a carving of the planet Venus in the white marble wall!

Hot wax is burning my fingers, reminding me that the candle is getting shorter by the second. I shiver, imagining what it will be like if my candle goes out.

Hurrying back to the stairs I begin my climb upward, the words of my Savior drumming in my ears: "As Moses lifted up the serpent in the wilderness, even so must the son of man be lifted up; that whosoever believes in him should not perish but have everlasting life." When I step out into the light I give thanks for a God who "so loved the world".

On the way back to my hotel, I pick up Gallenkamp's book from the seat and, driving with one hand, read again the words of a Mexican archaeologist who discovered the strange tomb. The cross, he suggested, celebrated the Mayan's worship of the maize plant. By dying, the maize gave life to those who cultivated it. I let the book fall back to the seat, and gripping the steering wheel with both hands, say aloud the words of the One who died on another cross: "Unless a grain of wheat falls into the ground and dies, it abides alone, but if it dies, it produces much grain."

I let out a shout and pound the steering wheel. I've just witnessed a prophecy: a millennium before Christ arrived on this continent pagan sculptors carved in stone his message of salvation!

Next morning at the first blush of dawn I plop my suitcase into the trunk for the final leg of my journey. Mercedes recommended I take the ancient coastal route, rather than the more recent inland highway. Soon, the cool fresh breeze blowing in from the Gulf is clearing my brain of the melancholy left by yesterday's dark encounter, and I'm glad I took Mercedes' advice.

I cross on the ferry to Isla del Carmen and lunch on giant shrimp and French fries, then cross again to the mainland and spend the early afternoon cruising sandy beaches fringed by coconut palms. More than once I find myself dreaming of a honeymoon here with Gabriela. And each time, I remember the promise I made myself the morning I left on this trip: I will not think about Gabriela! I force myself to play a grim game: every time Gabriela's face floats up before me I conjure up the solemn, self-satisfied face of her fiancé Gregorio.

The sun is slanting toward the horizon when I leave behind the beaches and palm trees of Campeche and enter Yucatan, the stern kingdom of the Mayans. I've read that the entire peninsula is a rocky spur covered by a thin cap of topsoil, unable to support crops of corn and vegetables like those growing so abundantly in Tabasco and Campeche. So life is hard here.

As I approach the capital city of Merida the road becomes a narrow passage through endless rocky fields of hennequin. This Mayan staple is a cousin of the maguey plant, but unlike its cousin, you can't make tequila from hennequin. The leaves yield a tough fiber that generations ago brought premium prices on world markets. Not any more; hennequin is being replaced by plastics, and now Yucatan's farmers face economic disaster.

I've heard that Merida, the capital of Yucatan, is the friendliest city in Mexico. I soon understand the reason for its fame. After checking into Hotel Caribe I take a walk. What a pleasant city! Strolling down red brick streets swept as clean as a living room floor, I find myself in a gracious tree-shaded square facing the great cathedral. For an hour I chat with a young family come here to escape the heat of their home. Later, at a sidewalk restaurant sipping *sopa de lima*, I'm treated like royalty by the short, smiling waiter.

The next morning at sunrise the host pastor is waiting for me when I come down with my bag. Like most everyone else I see out in the square he's dressed in baggy white cotton shirt and pants. People here get up early, he explains. Farmers must be in the fields by daylight so they can get in a day's work before the sun becomes unbearable.

Halfway to Cancun we come to the rustic encampment where we'll spend the weekend. It occupies a rocky field outside the city of Vallodolid. Before the two days have ended, these simple people win my heart with their unfailing smiles and exaggerated courtesy. In spite of their poverty they present themselves every morning immaculately dressed, the men in spotless white broadcloth and the women in the traditional multi-colored *huipl*....

On the day of the equinox, I awake before dawn, refreshed by a leisurely three days on Cancun's white beaches. The hotel clerk has warned me to leave early. Last year, he told me, more than 40,000 people gathered at Chichen Itzá to witness the Feathered Serpent's descent.

Until recently, no one had suspected the mind-blowing miracle that unfolds in the ruins of this ancient Mayan city twice a year. For a century archeologists had diligently studied the Temple of Kukulkan. They were aware it had been constructed with a unique relationship to the sun, but its meaning remained a puzzle. Then a few years ago a group of tourists visiting the pyramid on the afternoon of the fall equinox discovered its awesome secret.

I arrive an hour before noon and pay ten pesos for the right to park half a mile from Chichén Itzá. For another ten pesos I become part of a guided tour. We visit the remains of the observatory used by the Mayan astronomers to study the heavens and devise a calendar every bit as sophisticated as our own.

They take us to the *Cenote of Itzá*, a sacrificial well in whose depths Chac Mol, the Rain God was supposed to hibernate in divine splendor. I stand on the stone altar from which, in time of drought, wailing priests tossed jeweled maidens into the dark waters in hopes of appeasing the Rain God's wrath.

I check my watch. In two hours the Feathered Serpent will make his appearance! I maneuver to a place a few yards from the pyramid and while away the time studying the immense structure. How many steps? I count them: ninety-one on each of the four sides. I take out my pen: 4 X 9l=364. I add one more step for the upper platform and shake my head in wonder. The exact number of the days of the year!

As I munch a ham sandwich I eavesdrop on the lecture of a nearby guide. The Temple of Kukulkan, he explains, is really two pyramids, one within another. First, the Mayans built a temple in honor of the rain god. When the Toltecs arrived centuries later they superimposed their own pyramid atop of the Mayan structure.

A murmur ripples through the crowd: the sun is forming bright triangles of light at the very top of the staircase. Chills tickle my spine as the triangles begin moving downward, slowly, looking for all the world like an undulating snake.

The lights continue descending until they reach the base of the pyramid, the final triangle fusing with a carved serpent's head. Look! The shadow of the snake's head is moving across the ground. The spectators, some laughing, others screaming, run to escape from the snake's path. Just behind me, I hear the guide's voice: "For the ancient Mayans the equinox was the revival of their covenant with the almighty

Quetzalcóatl. They believed he returned to earth twice a year, bringing fertility and prosperity at the time of the spring planting and the fall harvest."

Thousands of people are responding to the advent of the Feathered Serpent, dancing, waving colorful cloths, and chanting, "Quetzal-cóatl…Quetzalcóatl…Quetzalcóatl!"

Suddenly, the serpent disappears! A dark shadow has raced across the courtyard, blotting him out. The multitude falls silent, turning their eyes skyward.

A brisk Gulf wind has trundled in a big white cloud, and is forming and reforming it like a child with molding clay. Boiling, churning, the cloud changes shape continually, until…

"Look Mommy, a big white lamb!" A little boy is pointing upward, his voice carrying through the still air.

Now thousands are pointing skyward, echoing his cry, "A lamb! A lamb!"

I stare at the sky, my heart racing. I can see it: the fluffy head, the round body, the stubby legs of a celestial lamb floating serenely in an immense field of blue.

"Worthy is the Lamb who was slain, to receive praise and honor and glory forever and ever!" I'm surprised to hear my voice repeating the triumphal words from the book of Revelation.

The little boy turns and stares at me, his eyes big, knowing with a child's intuition that I've spoken a mystery.

A deep reverie, like a ghostly mist, settles upon the crowd. They begin to move away, murmuring now, not of the miracle of the Bearded Serpent, but of the of miracle of the Lamb.…

Long after everyone else has gone, I'm still standing before the Temple of Kukulkan, praising the Lamb.

CHAPTER 38

▼

SOME THINGS JUST
DON'T WORK OUT

"Bye, Jeff, old buddy, see you in a couple of weeks. I can hardly wait."

I hang up and go out to the balcony. I need a breath of fresh air! I'm feeling guilty about lying to my grandson.

The chilly December air doesn't help much. Now that the rainy season's over the sky isn't getting washed clean every afternoon. My eyes are burning. Is it the smog, or because of the way I feel about going home for Christmas?

The truth is I'd prefer not to go at all. I'm a coward, I dread facing Jeff's mother and oh! even more his Aunt Victoria. As always, they're going to give me the third degree about coming back to Kingwood and finding someone to marry. How can I tell them I can't come home? I must remain in Mexico till...till the Wedding of the Lamb.

There, I said it! Funny, I've always thought people who talked like that were fanatics. But in my hotel room in Vera Cruz, the last night of my return trip from the Yucatan, something happened. Thumbing through the Gospel of Luke, I came upon the account of the presentation of the baby Jesus in the temple. When I read his words about Simeon I swallowed hard, put down my Bible, hands trembling, picked it up and read the words again: "It had been revealed to him by the Holy Spirit that he would not see death before he had seen the Lord's Christ."

The Holy Spirit whispered to me, "You will not die before you have seen Christ coming in glory!"

I shook my head. I must be imagining this! But no, there's that whisper again! Clutching the Bible to my chest, I ask myself: did Simeon feel this way when the Spirit spoke to him? I've told no one. But the Holy Spirit keeps witnessing to my spirit that the countdown to Armageddon has begun!

Of course, what my girls really want is for me to marry Gabriela and take her to the States to live. They've never met her, but they've fallen in love with the photos and videos I've sent them. And they've never forgiven me for not bringing her home for their inspection! Though they haven't said so, I'm suspect they feel our problems are my fault, and that if I just asked her she'd melt into my arms.

I guess that's why they weren't upset when I called a few weeks ago and told them what had happened to Anastacia and me....

During the long drive back from the Yucatan I pleaded with God to show me his will. Was it time to accept the loss of Gabriela and move on? I hadn't seen her since January, but through news blurbs in the society section of *Novedades* I kept up with her glamorous life. My heart followed her on buying trips to London, New York or Paris every couple of months, frequent appearances with Gregorio at charity functions, visits to the theater, and dinners at exclusive restaurants.

By the time I arrived home I was telling myself it was time to face reality: Gabriela and I'd had three marvelous months together two years ago, but since then it had all been downhill. It was foolish to keep hoping she'd come back to me.

I must convince Anastacia to marry me!

The day after my arrival I took her to a chic French restaurant on Avenida Las Palmas. I'd worked hard perfecting my strategy. One: I'd tell her I loved her and it was time she admitted she loved me. Two: I'd remind her that the way we found each other was nothing short of a miracle. And three: look how we'd both chosen to make Jesus Christ the focus of our lives!

This time I was going to be stubborn. I'd refuse to accept no for an answer.

Anastacia listened, eyes big, as I described my trip. She stumbled with me down the stairway of the Temple of Inscriptions and cried out in amazement when I described that cross on the tomb. When I told her about the dramatic meeting between the Serpent and the Lamb in Chichen Itzá she got so excited she knocked over her glass of water.

I'd never seen her so exuberant! I couldn't wait to pop the question.

The waiter cleared the table and brought our coffee. Now...this was the moment! I reached for her hand.

She surprised me when she drew back, picked up a spoon and began nervously stirring sugar into her coffee. "Andrés:..." she laid down her spoon and took a sip of coffee, "now it's my turn to tell you something exciting. Something that's happened to *me*."

Disappointed, I stuttered, "I'm s-s-sorry, guess I've monopolized the conversation."

She set down the cup, wiped her lips with a napkin and reached for my hand. "Andrés, a few days ago Carlos and I admitted something we've both been feeling for a long time." A bright smile lit up her face, "We're in love!"

Stunned, I could only stare.

"I...I know what you're thinking, what about Orpha? But she and Carlos agreed to call it quits a week ago. She told him she could never become a Christian. Loyalty to her family was more important to her than Carlos and his commitment to his Messiah.

"The very next morning Carlos came to my house and told me what had happened. When I expressed my regrets I was surprised to see him grinning.

"'Anastacia,' he said, 'you can't imagine what a relief it was for me when Orpha said she couldn't marry me.'

"A relief? You're kidding!"

"'No, I'm not.' Suddenly he was very serious. 'For months I've been asking God to show me a way to break up with Orpha without breaking her heart.'

"Then Carlos got up from his chair, came over to where I was sitting, went down on one knee, took my hand and said, 'Anastacia, I've been in love with you since the first night I saw you on-stage.'"

Anastacia was holding my hand tightly, her eyes pleading for understanding.

I said hoarsely, "And you love him?"

"With all my heart!" She hugged me. "Please, Andrés, give us your blessing! Carlos and I both love you dearly. We're so happy, and we want you to be happy with us!.... Andrés?"

I felt very foolish, remembering the first night Carlos attended a Bible study, and how he and Anastacia looked at each other. At that moment I'd asked myself if there was something between them. But when I learned Carlos was engaged to Orpha I decided it must have been my imagination.

I'm a professional counselor, trained to intuit people's feelings. How could I have been so stupid?

She brushed away a tear. "Please, Andrés, understand us. Carlos wanted to speak to you first, to beg your forgiveness. But I wouldn't let him."

Staring over her head, eyes fixed on a watercolor of the *Niños Heroes* I heard myself say, "I guess you've told him I...I asked you to marry me."

"Yes."

"And the answer you gave me?"

"Yes."

I managed a smile. "And what else did you tell him?"

Her cheeks reddened. "That even though I knew you weren't in love with me, I might have accepted your proposal, if I hadn't already been so in love with him!"

Later, remembering the conversation, I wondered who was more surprised by my sudden laughter, Anastacia or myself....

That night I wrapped a blanket around my shoulders and sat on the balcony for a long time, wondering. I should be angry with Carlos and Anastacia. Why such peace in my heart? Probably because I knew that, in spite of everything, I still wasn't ready to give to anyone else the place Gabriela still occupied in my heart. And maybe because I suspected the union of Carlos and Anastacia would be the spark that ignited our little congregation.

I was right! The next week I baptized Carlos in the swimming pool, along with eleven other new believers. In October we initiated Sunday morning Bible studies. New families began knocking at the door.

Now, every Sunday, Mercedes is surrounded by giggling kids in our new children's department. Anastacia glows as she directs the music. I challenge lifestyles by the truths we discover in my Bible studies. And what most excites me is that Carlos has agreed I should prepare him to share the teaching ministry with me.

No...I'm not anxious to spend Christmas in Kingwood,even though last month ago a gossip columnist sank my last hopes of ever marrying Gabriela. He announced that Gabriela Mancini and Gregorio Buenaventura will be married in February.

Chapter 39

▼

Together Again!

Jolted awake, I reach for the phone in the dark, knocking over the bed-side lamp. The glowing hands of the clock show 3:21 A.M.

It's one of the girls, something bad has happened!

"Hello?" My voice is trembling.

"Andee…?"

"Gabriela! Is that you?" Suddenly I'm wide awake, my pulse pounding. "Where…where are you?"

"Andee, before I die, I want you to know…"

I press the phone to my ear, straining to hear. "My darling, where are you?"

"In Budapest, Andee." (No wonder her voice sounds so far away!) "I'm in a hospital, and before I leave this earth I wanted to beg you…(sob)…to forgive me…I love you, Andee, and I'm so sorry…"

I shout: "Gabriela, I'm coming to you! You hear me?" I hope I haven't awakened my neighbors, but I don't care!

"But Andee…I'm so far away, and so sick! I may not be here when…"

"Listen to me, Gabi! (I'm not going to let her say it again!) "I don't know what's happened, or what they're telling you, but you're not going to die! I couldn't live…" My voice breaks.

"Dear, sweet Andee, do you…really…Still…love me? After…all I've…?" Her voice is fading, like a distant radio signal.

"Gabriela, you can't die, I'm not going to let you!…. Gabriela, are you there?"

"Yes…yes my love."

"Listen, I don't know how soon I can get a plane out, but I'm on my way, Do you hear? I'm on my way!"

"Yes, yes, *gracias a Dios*! I'll be waiting for you. I…"

Silence.

"Gabriela! Gabriela!"

A deep male voice breaks in, saying in heavily accented English, "Mr. Mancini, I am the your wife's physician. She seems to have…lapsed into unconsciousness again."

"Tell me, Doctor, is she going to…?" I can't say the word.

"I must be frank with you, Sir. Her condition is critical. She was unconscious when they brought her in twenty-four hours ago. We discovered she has acute viral pneumonia. We have done everything possible, but…She returned to consciousness a few minutes ago, and her first thought was to call you. It's against the rules in Intensive Care, but under the circumstances…"

"Just…just how bad is it, Doctor?"

"Sir, I recommend you get here as soon as possible. I'm not going to tell you there is no hope, but right now…well, it is impossible to predict the outcome."

I'm drowning in fear, gasping for breath. "Listen to me Doctor. Do everything you can!…no matter what it costs…please, don't let her die! I…I…." I'm shaking so hard I grasp the phone with both hands.

"Believe me, Mr. Mancini, we're already doing everything we can." I scribble madly as he spells out the address of the hospital. "I'll be on the first plane out of Mexico City." I know I'm yelling at him. I want to threaten him with physical harm if he lets my precious love die.

Two seconds after the line goes dead I'm dialing. "Continental?" Within five minutes I have a reservation on the ll:l7 flight for Houston, where they tell me I'll make the connection to Budapest.

At first light I call Rebeca and tell her everything, words tumbling out, unable to stop, mixing Spanish and English, my voice failing several times.

When I pause she says: "*Dear Doctór*, I'm going to the office and spend all day on my knees. May I call Gelda and invite her to come pray with me?"

"Yes, yes, by all means! I was going to call her, but this is better." I can feel the panic receding.

While I'm wolfing down a bowl of cereal I dial Anastacia's number and tell her Gabriela is in Europe seriously ill and I'm flying to her. In the light of what's happened between us recently, her promise to pray for Gabriela and me is especially comforting.

When I land in Houston Margaret is waiting for me. After a hug I reach for my bag, but she catches my arm and exclaims: "Daddy, ever since your call I've been so excited I haven't been able to sit down. For more than two years now, since the first time you told me about her, every time I've prayed for you I've prayed for Gabriela...." she brushes away a tear, "I've known you belong together. And now..." She puts her arms around me and kisses my cheek, "my prayers are answered!"

"Whoa, wait a minute, sweetheart. I'm on my way to see Gabriela, but all I know is she's very ill. And remember, she's still engaged to that guy Gregorio. And besides, the doctor said" "I don't care what the doctor said! Gabriela is going to get well!" She picks up my attaché case. "And forget about this...this Gregorio. Gabriela belongs to you!"

I'm glad there's a layover before my KLM flight to Amsterdam. And I'm glad Margaret left my grandson Jeff with a neighbor. I'm looking forward to two hours alone with this daughter who inherited her mother's stubborn faith.

Sitting very close to me in the restaurant, her arm looped through mine, she brings me up to date on the family: little Jeff is having a great time in pre-kinder. Tom has received another promotion. She calls Victoria a least once a month (Victoria never calls!). No she, hasn't seen her in more than a year.

She asks endless questions about Gabriela. No, I tell her, until her call this morning we hadn't spoken a word to each other since January. Gregorio? All I know is what I've read in the paper: the wedding is scheduled for next month. Yes, I still love her as much as ever. More, maybe.

She reaches up and touches my hair. "You should have gotten a haircut, Daddy, I want you to be real handsome when Gabriela sees you."

I smile at her, shaking my head.

She squeezes my hand. "You know, Daddy, you deserve to be happy...you've gone through so much. Wish I could go with you, I'd sit down with Gabriela and tell her..."

I put a finger on her lips. "Know what, punkin'? I don't think I'm going to need you around to tell Gabriela anything, and don't blame her for the way things have gone, I'm as much at fault as she."

She's studying my face, a little smile on her lips. "I hadn't noticed that touch of gray in your sideburns before. Makes you look distinguished." She pokes me in the ribs. "God put it there to remind you it's time you had a good wife!"

I check my watch. "Guess I'd better go to my gate, the plane leaves in half an hour. Would you say a little prayer for me?"

We bow our heads over the scraps of our lunch and Margaret prays earnestly for a safe trip and for Gabriela's recovery. And she thanks God for the miracle he'll perform while I'm in Budapest.

She holds me for a moment, whispering in my ear, "Now you call me as soon as you find out something!"

"I promise."

She starts away, then turns back. "Don't you worry, Daddy, Gabriela's going to be all right!"

KLM Flight 662 for Amsterdam backs away from the terminal at exactly 4:46 P.M. Once in the air I settle back, able to really believe for the first time that I'm on my way to Gabriela! I watch the bright green line on the monitor moving steadily northward, tracing our flight.

Until this moment I've refused to let myself think about what I may find when I arrive in Budapest. On the flight to Houston I distracted myself talking to an elderly Mexican gentleman nervous about a medical checkup in Houston. Now I will myself to go to sleep. I've been awake since Gabriela's call, and need to rest, so I'll be prepared for what lies ahead....

But I can't sleep. Like a restless surf, thoughts keep pummeling my mind. Why was Gabriela in Budapest?...Her honeymoon! Don't be silly, if she was on her honeymoon she wouldn't be calling me!.... Did she call Gregorio?.... Will he already be at her side when I arrive? But the doctor took for granted *I* was her husband. Had Gabriela told him that?

I'm crazy making this trip, Gabriela is engaged to another man, and it's been nearly a year since we've talked! What if she was so disoriented she had no idea what she was doing...?

No, I reassure myself, she sounded quite rational when she told me she loved me and said she wanted to ask my forgiveness before she...I snap awake...Oh God, don't let her die!

What did the doctor say? "Condition critical...unable to predict the outcome"...I remember something else he said: that they were making an exception allowing Gabriela to call from Intensive Care. What did that mean? A chill spears my chest...was it because she was dying and they needed somebody to come and claim the body?...by now her corpse is lying in a morgue somewhere, cold and lifeless!

Andrew, you let yourself be carried away by the emotion of the moment! Somebody else should have made this trip...a member of her family. What's the point in going all the way to Budapest just to arrange for the shipment of Gabriela's body back home for burial by people who won't even want me around?

Groaning, I push my face into the hard little pillow. No, she's alive, she has to be, God wouldn't be so cruel....

I'm awakened by the arrival of the stewardess's cart. "Doughnuts and coffee, Sir?" I look at my watch: 6:05 A.M. As the hot black coffee shocks my mind back to consciousness I watch the luminous green line on the monitor approaching the British Isles.

An hour's layover in Amsterdam's fog-shrouded Shiphol Airport, then the final leg of the flight to Budapest. I refuse breakfast, I'm so hyped I wouldn't be able to digest scrambled eggs and sausage.

When we land I grab my overcoat and hurry through the fresh snow toward the old red brick terminal. After a yawning official on the other side of a thick, smudged glass stamps my passport I find my bag and hurry to the long line of drab old taxis pulled up outside. Handing the driver the address I've scrawled on a scrap of paper I pray he'll be able to decipher it. The Hungarian I heard in the airport bears no resemblance to either English or Spanish. I breathe a sigh of relief when he nods and shifts into gear.

Half an hour later he brakes before a somber gray building remarkably similar in appearance to many of the Social Security hospitals in Mexico. I hand him a bill I bought in the airport, and not waiting for change step carefully onto the icy sidewalk. Halfway to the hospital entrance I stop, my heart racing, my head floating away from my shoulders. This is the moment I've been waiting for! What am I going to find inside those gray walls? After a while my brain clears and I move ahead very slowly, whispering the Twenty Third Psalm.

"Gabriela Mancini," I say to the young receptionist, pronouncing each vowel very carefully, as I learned to do when I was studying Spanish.

She looks at me, shakes her head and answers with syllables bearing no resemblance to words. Now it's my turn to shake my head.

"Gabriela Mancini...very ill..." I point to my chest: "husband from United States. I must see her."

She hands me a pen and a pad and I print Gabriela's name. Turning, she runs her finger through a file. I see her frowning, and my heart stops for a moment. Dear God, Gabriela has died and they have no record of her! Down the hall an elevator door opens and an orderly emerges pushing a stretcher. On the stretcher...I catch my breath...yes, there's a body under that sheet! Gabriela! My knees buckle.

"Mr. Mancini?"

I turn back. The receptionist is smiling, holding out a slip of paper. I grasp the counter to steady myself, feeling like a condemned man who's just received a stay of execution. Pointing to a bank of elevators across the waiting room she hands me the note. I can understand nothing she's written except for the number "4".

Gabriela must be on the fourth floor....

I'm alone in the elevator, my pulse pounding so hard I can feel it in my throat. During the ten seconds it takes to reach Gabriela's floor I pray out loud, "Lord, I've never needed you like I need you now. Give me strength to face whatever's ahead!"

The doors open, I stumble down the hall past a maze of closed doors and hand the receptionist's note to a large woman in a white uniform. Her face breaks into a smile, she pumps my hand, says something that sounds like "One moment, one moment" and hurries away.

A white-haired nurse comes toward me, smiling. I'm relieved when she addresses me in school-room English: "Welcome. Mr. Mancini, your wife has been so anxious! We kept assuring her you'd be on the first flight from Amsterdam."

I lean against the wall, breathing hard.

"Are you feeling ill, Mr. Mancini?"

"No, no, I'm great! You say Gabriela is expecting me. How…how is she?"

"There has been a remarkable improvement since she talked with you yesterday. The doctor had her moved from ICU to a private room less than an hour ago."

I want to dance, shout hallelujah, jump up and slap the ceiling! Gabriela is *alive*! She's expecting me! I'm going to see her, hold her in my arms!

It dawns on me I haven't looked at a mirror in hours. I ought to at least comb my hair!

"Nurse, I'd like to visit the bathroom first."

"Of course, Sir. It's right down the hall. Take all the time you want." She reaches for my bag. "Let me have this, Mr. Mancini, I'll hold it for you."

"I'll be back in a second."

She's watching me, smiling broadly.

When I look in the mirror a few seconds later I know why. I'm grinning, my red-rimmed eyes shining. I splash handfuls of cold water at my face, dry with a rough paper towel and run a comb through my rumpled hair. It's silly, but I want to extend this blessed parenthesis, knowing I'll remember it as long as I live. I I bow my head in thanksgiving.

A moment later the nurse leads me down the hall and stops at a closed door. "I'll leave you here."

I cautiously push open the door and peek in. Gabriela! She's propped up on pillows, eyes closed, her face and arms very pale. Yes, she must be expecting me: her beautiful hair, jet black against the white pillow, is freshly shampooed and her lips are painted a bright crimson.

As I tiptoe toward the bed my toe bumps the I.V. stand. Her eyes open. "Andee! Andee, *mi amor*!" She half raises from the bed, arms outstretched, her face glowing.

I bend over, taking her into my arms. "Oh Andee," she breathes, "they said you'd be here this morning, but I was afraid to believe them. My darling, I've needed you so much!"

I take her beloved face between my hands, and tears brimming, devour her with my eyes. "Gabi, I'm with you, I can't believe it. Have I died and gone to heaven?"

Suddenly we're laughing, clinging together, and I'm kissing her cheeks, her eyes, her mouth.

Drawing back, she smiles and touches my lips. "Careful, Doctór, remember, you're holding a very sick woman in your arms!"

I rearrange her pillows, take her hands in mine and we talk, words spilling over words, rising to a crescendo, falling to a whisper, trying to say all the things we've been aching to say in the long months apart.

Finally we pause, exhausted. She reaches up a pale hand and caresses my cheek. "Andrés Kellee, I warn you, I will never, ever let you out of my sight again. Yesterday morning when I floated back into life only one thing was clear to my confused mind: if you no longer loved me, wanted me, I would drift away into the darkness and never return, because there would be no reason for living. I had to call you and find out!"

I bend down and gently kiss her lips. "Gabriela, my love, how could we have been so foolish?"

A knock at the door and a nurse steps in. "Mr. Mancini, you will have to leave now. We must not tax our patient's strength."

Swallowing angry words, I force a smile. "Nurse, look at your patient. Does she appear too ill to have my company?"

Her face shining, Gabriela presses my hand to her cheek. "Nurse, this man is the only medicine I need. Don't make him go away, please."

Lips tight, the nurse insists, "I'm sorry, Mrs. Mancini, but we must obey the doctor's orders."

"Miss," I say, "my wife almost died and I wasn't with her, I'm not going to leave her now." I move closer to her, and struggling to keep my voice calm say, "Look, I'm a doctor myself. If you will put me in communication with my wife's physician, I'm sure he'll give his permission for me to remain a few minutes longer."

She shrugs. "Very well, Mr....Dr. Mancini, you may remain half an hour longer. But remember, your wife needs her rest." She slips out, pulling the door shut behind her.

"Shame on you, Andee, telling the nurse you're a doctor!"

"But I am...I just didn't tell her what kind. Besides, I'm not the only liar in this room, or she wouldn't be calling me 'Mr. Mancini'!"

She says, softly, "If you're willing we can fix it so I'm not a liar."

I try to smile. "Gabriela Mancini, are you asking me to marry you?"

"The sooner the better!"

"And...and what about..." I'm choking..."your previous commitment?"

"Gregorio?" She sighs. "You haven't asked me what I was doing in Budapest."

"I've got a million questions, but we can start there if you want."

"Back in September, at a fashion show in Paris, I met a delightful person from here. She invited me to help her in a seminar for businesswomen she was planning for a couple of months later. I accepted."

"But wasn't that going to interfere with preparations for your wedding?"

She smiles. "Exactly. That's why I accepted her invitation. By then I knew I had made a terrible mistake and I was happy for an excuse to postpone the wedding."

I grunt, "So Gregorio wasn't such a great catch after all!"

"Gregorio is a darling and a gentleman. That's why I was so uncomfortable. He didn't deserve what I was about to do to him."

"What did he say when you told him about your change of plans?"

"He was very sad. But I think he already suspected I was having second thoughts. He told me to take all the time I needed to make up my mind.

"After the seminar I stayed on, unwilling to return and face Gregorio. Finally I called him one night and told him the wedding was off. By then I was terribly depressed. Had lost my appetite. Couldn't sleep nights."

"Oh Gabriela, why didn't you call me?"

"How could I? Remember, we hadn't spoken in a year. I was sure you'd found someone else by then. More than once I picked up the phone to call you and beg you to take me back, but I was terrified! I was so afraid you'd say you no longer loved me."

Shaking my head, I lean over and kiss her forehead. "It makes me sad to think of you here all alone, needing me. And me there in Mexico City, wanting you so! If only…"

"One day I awoke feeling feverish and faint. I called the hotel desk and asked for a physician. As the doctor checked my vital signs and listened to my lungs I saw him frowning.

"Miss Mancini," he said sternly, "you should have called me days ago!" Picking up the phone he dialed a number. I heard him say, "Send an ambulance immediately. This is an emergency. I repeat, this is an emergency!".

I remember nothing more…until the next morning when…when it happened."

She pauses, her eyes closed.

"What happened, Gabriela?"

"I was awake, but not really awake, I seemed to be floating in space. Below I could see my hospital bed and a group of doctors and nurses working over my body.

"But I was drifting upward…upward…feeling a peace so beautiful I couldn't possibly describe it…and in the distance, I could hear beautiful music. I knew it must be a heavenly choir."

Her eyes open wide and she takes my hand and squeezes it hard. "I hope you'll believe me, Andee, "I…I saw…Him!"

"You saw Jesus!"

She kisses my hand "You do believe me, my darling? Yes, yes! He was waiting for me, his face shining with love. I remember hurrying toward him, my hands outstretched, eager to feel his touch…Then, all at once, his face clouded.

"…And I heard myself calling, 'Andrés, Andrés!'

"I opened my eyes to see the faces of the doctors and nurses. They were staring down at me, their eyes wide with surprise.

"Everybody began speaking at once. I couldn't understand what they were saying, but I could tell they were shocked that I had returned to consciousness.

"I heard myself saying in my poor English, 'Andrés, I must speak to Andrés!' and I could feel tears running down my cheeks.

"One of the doctors asked me in English about the Andrés I was calling when I returned to life. I told him Andrés was my husband and I had to speak to him at once. Guess what, Andrés? Jesus had told me…not in words, but in my heart, in one split second…that my destiny on earth had not been fulfilled. Immediately I knew what I should do. I should call you and tell you I loved you and needed you….

"I was sure that if you turned me down…Jesus would be waiting for me."

All the time Gabriela is speaking our eyes are locked together. She blinks, and a tear trickles down her cheek. Bending down, I kiss the tear away, whispering, "Thank you, Lord, for giving us another chance!"

For a long moment we remain with our arms intertwined, unable to speak, aware of the presence of a heavenly host, their wings moving in silent applause.

I pull back. "What about your family and friends? You told me they'd reject you if you married me."

Reaching under her pillow, she pulls out a slim red Bible. "I grabbed this up when they came to take me to the hospital. Since we talked yesterday I've been devouring it. Last night I was reading the book of

Ruth. My sweet Andee, Ruth's promise to her mother-in-law is my promise to you:

> Where you go, I will go, and where you stay I will stay.
> Your people will be my people, and your God my God.
> Where you die I will die, and there I will be buried. May the Lord deal with me, be it ever so severely, if anything but death separates you and me.

Our tears mingle as we embrace.

After a moment she continues: "Andee, I drifted away from the God who rescued me when I was crazed with grief from the loss of my little son. I'm so ashamed…I've asked him to forgive me and promised things are going to be different from now on. But I'm going to need your help. Will you pray for me…for us? Right now?

Dropping to my knees beside her bed I take her outstretched hand and pour out my heart to the loving, patient God who brought us together and has been patient with us when, again and again, we thwarted his plans.

CHAPTER 40

▼

"THEY SHALL BE ONE FLESH"

When my prayer is finished, Gabriela squeezes my hand and whispers, "Amen!"

As I get to my feet she yawns. "I feel great! And sleepy. What time is it?"

"Can you believe it? Almost twelve. I'll bet the nurse is waiting outside the door to fuss at me for overstaying my limit."

"They'll be bringing my lunch. Afterward, I'm sure I'll sleep for hours. Love, see if you can find my hotel key."

I pull out a drawer. "Here it is."

"You look like you need rest. Go to my hotel and use my suite. You'll love it, it overlooks the Danube. When you come back bring me some clothes, because I'll be leaving here tomorrow."

"Think so? So soon?"

"I'm sure of it, here feel my forehead." She reaches out for my hand. "See? my fever's gone. With your jet lag, I'll bet you feel worse than I do."

"All right, I'll go to the hotel, but I'll be back to spend the night with you."

Fifteen minutes later my taxi is crossing a bridge separating Pest, the flat side of the city from Buda, the hilly side. The banks of the river are covered with new snow, as are the groves of green firs adorning the hillsides. Five minutes later we turn from the avenue onto a less-traveled side street. Here the snow and ice have not been broken by traffic, and I hold my breath as the driver struggles to control the taxi. The wheels spin and the vehicle slips and slides from one side of the street to the other, in constant peril of falling into the ditch.

Hotel Rózsadomb, perched atop a low hill overlooking the Danube, has the dignity and enchantment of a medieval castle. Its mammoth lobby, warmed by a ring of thumping radiators, is adorned with inviting red leather sofas. When I show the clerk Gabriela's key his boyish face lights up. "And how is the charming lady?"

"Much better, thank you."

"When she fell ill we were devastated. We've been calling the hospital every day. Last night when we learned that she had passed the crisis we toasted the good news."

He pauses, staring at my ring finger. "May I inquire, Mr. Kelly, if you are a member of the family?"

"I'm her fiancé. We plan to be married as soon as she's released from the hospital."

He reaches over the desk and pumps my hand. "Congratulations! Would you like to have your wedding here in the Rószadomb? We'll be happy to place our facilities at your disposal."

"Really? Sounds great. Tell me, how does a foreigner go about getting married in your country?"

He speaks into the interphone, and a moment later a smiling young woman in a dark business suit extends her hand: "Mr. Kelly, I'm the hostess, and I'll be happy to secure the necessary documents for your wedding."

Half an hour later I lie soaking in a warm bath, celebrating all the miracles falling like rain from heaven. By the time I flop into the bed I'm giddy from exhaustion, barely able to set the alarm before dropping off into a dreamless sleep....

I'm surprised at how early the sun has set, it's barely five o'clock and already the street lights are on. I pinch myself to make sure I'm not dreaming. Less than seven hours ago I was hurrying through these same streets, not knowing if Gabriela was alive or dead, and now we're living the first day of the rest of our lives together! Not even the jet lag, still looped about my shoulders like a heavy backpack, is able to dim my elation. I want to shout out my joy to all the weary-faced people on the sidewalk heading for home after a day's work. Could there be anybody else in this dark city as deliriously happy as I? As the taxi nears the hospital, my fingers caress a tiny velvet box in my coat pocket. I hope Gabriela will like the one-carat solitaire I chose. I suspect I could have bought it for half the price in Houston. But after what's happened today, I'd have paid double what they asked and not complained. Thank goodness for credit cards!

The taxi brakes and I grab up the pretty light-blue suit bag I found in Gabriela's room. Walking toward the hospital I pray she'll be pleased with the flowered blouse and gypsy skirt I chose from her overflowing closets.

Remembering how I felt when I opened the door to her suite, my body goes warm all over: the faint fragrance of her perfume made my skin prickle. As I fumbled through the array of expensive frocks the old misgiving assailed me: was I making a mistake, marrying a woman accustomed to such luxury? Then I reminded myself that Gabriela's wealth was nothing more than a footnote to a relationship ordained by God, and my uneasiness evaporated. Sure, I had little to offer her materially, but I was giving her something infinitely more valuable, a love that had already survived time and disaster.

As I pass the nurses' station a young woman signals to me, smiling. Talking rapidly in that baffling tongue of the Magyars she places a folder on the desk, opens it and points first to the name, Gabriela Mancini, then to a physician's signature.

Now in English: "Doctor say okay to…leave tomorrow."

I float to Gabriela's room.

As soon as I enter she throws back the covers and swings her feet off the bed. "Help me to stand, I want you to hold me!"

I drop the suit bag on a chair and very gently pull her to her feet…and for the first time she is really in my arms! We stand for a long while whispering sweet, intimate caresses and I know why it was impossible for me to fall in love with anyone else those long, desperate months.

Finally she kisses me gently and settles back on the bed. Easing into a chair, I take her hand and we sit smiling at each other, our eyes misty.

"Tomorrow at nine you're going to take me to my hotel, she tells me in a firm voice. "Meanwhile, I don't want you out of my sight for an instant. I'm still not sure this is really happening."

I can't wait another minute! Reaching into my pocket I take my treasure and slip it on her finger. The words seem to come without thought: "I give you this diamond, my sweet love, to remind us that a million years ago, when this gorgeous stone was just a grain of sand, God had already decreed that Andrew and Gabriela would become one flesh."

She brings the ring to her lips. "May I say a prayer now, Andee?"

Her prayer echoes the thoughts of my heart:"Dear Father, forgive me for ever doubting that Andrés and I could be one. We're so different, but you made us for one another. Thank you for giving me so much love for him, a love I had decided I could never feel again."

By midnight Gabriela is winding down, like a clock on a spent battery. We agree it's time to rest. She turns off the bedside lamp and immediately falls asleep. Lying on a cot the foot of her bed, I'm not ready for sleep. I get up and stand for a long moment studying Gabriela's face in the dim light reflected from the street below. So many times in these lonely months I've closed my eyes and tried to remember her face: the porcelain skin, the exquisite nose, that tiny mole, like an exclamation point beside her lips. Those lips are smiling now. Is she dreaming of me? Dear God, is it a sin to love someone so much?

Of course not! Like she said in her prayer, God gave me this love. Now I understand the waiting, the frustration, the heartbreak. God tempered our love with the fire of suffering so that nothing can ever destroy it!

Gabriela's eyes open, then close. Beneath the sheet her slim body, buffeted by illness, looks delicate and vulnerable.

I shiver. The day Gabriela first told me of her life-changing encounter with God I knew in my heart I was falling in love with an exceptional woman. Later, when she confessed she was too afraid of change to lay hold upon happiness, I wondered if I had been mistaken.

Now I know I wasn't mistaken. Last night on this bed a miracle happened: heaven's door opened for a moment, she took a step toward it, then turned and walked back to me.

The next day we arrive at the Hotel Rószadomb in the bright noon sunlight. The hospital had wanted to bring Gabriela in an ambulance, but she adamantly refused. They finally agreed to a taxi when I promised I'd personally carry her to her room. We sweep through the lobby to the applause of the staff and the stares of the guests. Upstairs the bell boy opens the door to her suite and I carry my bride across the threshold. Finally! We're all alone in our personal Eden!

An hour before our appointment with Hungary's equivalent of the Justice of the Peace, I remember my promise to call Margaret. The announcement of my wedding provokes such a squeal I drop the telephone. Beside me, Gabriela laughs and claps her hands. Next I call Rebeca, and she repeats over and over, "I knew it! I knew it!"

In a handsome suite glutted with red roses and white carnations, at exactly 7:12 P.M., Andrew Kelly and Gabriela Mancini are pronounced husband and wife. With child-like excitement Gabi suggests we go down to the dining room for a wedding dinner.

"Absolutely not!" I tell her. I'd noticed how glad she was to sit down after the vows. So, in what is now *our* suite, we enjoy a meal prepared in our honor by the chef.

We go to bed early. Lying in my arms she whispers, "Andee, I'll be happy to give myself to you right now, but I'm still not strong. Would it better to wait? I'd hate for it to be a disappointment."

I kiss her tenderly. "Loving you a disappointment? Impossible! But we've waited for years, so why not wait a little longer for the perfect moment? We'll know when that moment arrives."

In the following days we dedicate ourselves to enjoying an unplanned leisurely honeymoon. We spend the first morning in the thermal baths steaming away the last traces of jet lag and fever. Then we drive to a tiny pastry shop called *Ruszwurm* and gorge on crisp *turo-staka* cheese Danish and *tejeskave*, Budapest's café con leche. We smile back at the gilded angels adorning the bright walls. And we talk! We relive the frustrations of the past two years, event by event, not blaming each other, just letting our love wash away memories of hurt, sadness, and anger.

The next day Gabriela feels strong enough to stroll from our hotel to the National Art Gallery and visit Dante's doomed lovers, Paola and Francesca. That night, to our surprise, we're so charged with energy we're ready to enjoy a Beethoven concert presented by the Budapest Philharmonic. Halfway through the concert the orchestra plays Claire de Lune. As always when I hear that melody, tears fall. I smile when Gabriela leans close and whispers in my ear, "*Mi amor*, may I borrow your handkerchief?"

At breakfast on day three Gabriela tells me she wants to explore the Castle district. We spend hours strolling the narrow streets, poking into quaint shops, peering through lace-curtained windows. Twice we restore our spirits with thick black expresso. As noon approaches we hail a taxi and cross the Danube to a restaurant that specializes in *fogas*, snowy white fish from lake Balaton.

When are we going to run out of things to talk about? I wonder. But it doesn't happen. I laugh with her about the exasperating snooping of the *monjas* in her *preparatoria* and she giggles when I describe childhood escapades with my Louisiana Cajun cousins.

We exchange the latest about our children: one morning a couple of months ago, she tells me, Angelica appeared with bruised forearms and a black eye. She refused to talk about it, but Cuauhtémoc has not come back since. As for Hector, after their confrontation he decided to move in with his father. She sees him a couple of times a month and is worried about the surliness clinging to him like sticky mucilage.

Gabriela is pleased she'll get to meet Margaret at our stopover in Houston on the way back. And she's fascinated by my description of Victoria's formidable character.

"When will I meet her, Andrés? You know, for years I've dreamed of opening a store in the States. Do you think she might be interested in working with me on it?"

That night, wrapped in warm wool blankets, we sit on our balcony sipping tea and watching the lights of boat traffic on the Danube. Our communication is languid and intimate, the conversation of two people who've been in love for centuries.

When talk lags she murmurs, "Andee, how do you feel?"

"Great!"

"Not too tired?" Was there something special in her voice?

"Too tired for what?" Can she see my smile in the half-light?

Getting up, she lays the blanket aside. "Don't run off, I'll be back."

She returns smelling of bubble bath and cologne, dressed in the exquisite lingerie she purchased on our first foray into town.

"Wow! But be careful, it's cold out here!" Jumping up, I wrap her in a blanket, hugging her tight, biting her ear, her perfume sending my head into a spin.

I murmur gruffly, "Now it's my turn."

I find my pajamas and hurry to the shower. Gabriela has placed her Bible by the sink, opened to the Song of Solomon, underlined in sun glow red liner pencil:

> My lover has gone down
>> to his garden
> to the bed of spices,
> to browse in the gardens
>> and to gather lilies.
> I am my lover's and my lover is mine;
>> he browses among the lilies.

Later, Gabriela lies asleep, breathing evenly at my side. I'm sleepy, but I'm not ready for sleep. I want to celebrate this night, engrave on my soul forever each delectable, incredible second. Pulling on my robe I tiptoe out to the balcony. The air is crisp and cold, and in the quiet silver current of the Danube I see the reflection of the full moon. A shiver runs Through me. Is it the cold air…or this icy, cascading joy?

My heart sings! Here I am, at an age when illusions of the perfect love are supposed to have evaporated. Yet tonight I have experienced an ecstasy I never dreamed possible.

Going into the bathroom I pick up Gabriela's Bible, and leafing through the Song of Solomon, find the passage I'm looking for. I outline the sentences with the her liner pencil:

> How delightful is your love,
>> my sister, my bride!
> How much more pleasing is
>> your love than wine,
> and the fragrance of your perfume
>> than any spice.
> For love is as strong as death.
> It burns like a blazing fire,
>> like a mighty flame.

Many waters cannot quench love,
>   nor can the floods drown it.

Placing the open Bible on her bedside table I crawl into bed beside her and drift off into the most peaceful sleep I've known since the loss of my first love.

CHAPTER 41

▼

REMEMBERING MOISÉS DREAM

"Dr. Kelly, I need your help!…(sob)…should I leave my husband?"

Isabel Buenaventura, a plump, petite young woman, sits at the edge of her seat, dabbing at her sad brown eyes with a delicate lace handkerchief. Her oval face, pleasantly pretty, is framed by short, fine black hair, freshly shampooed and blow-dried. Knowing who she is, I try not to stare. She looks like a middle-class housewife who's spent the morning in the beauty parlor.

But looks can be deceiving!

The day she called my office a video cassette clicked on in my mind, taking me back to nearly five years ago. It's after midnight. I'm in my living room, pacing back and forth, unable to sleep. The phone rings. Moisés is calling from Mexico City, his voice excited: "Andrés, yesterday God gave me a vision…of you walking through the front door of *Los Pinos*."

That vision brought me to Mexico! It's been a long time since I've thought about it.

Today I must think about it. Isabel Buenaventura's husband is one of the most powerful men in Mexico. And he sits behind a desk in Los-Pinos, next door to *el Señor Presidente de la República*.

Is the blessed parenthesis of the past two years about to come to an end? Gabriela and I laugh now at our tortured fears about our "irreconcilable differences". It didn't take us long to discover that our veneer of differences concealed a remarkable unity of mind and heart about the things that matter: God...integrity...roller coasters.

Returning from Budapest Gabriela made *mi casa su casa*. To Gabi, changing to my modest apartment must have been like moving from the Ritz to a Motel 6. But the miracle of her resurrection from the dead had produced a second miracle: we both came to understand how insignificant material differences are when two people are in love and both are committed to giving God first place in their marriage.

Three weeks later our church had a special service to celebrate our wedding. Gabriela and I walked down the aisle, Carlos preached a sermon on marriage, we repeated our vows and Anastacia prayed a beautiful prayer of dedication. After we had cut the cake, I baptized Gabriela in Anastacia's swimming pool. When I raised her out of the water Anastacia shouted "*Aleluya!*" and Gabriela reached up and pulled me under, white shirt, tie and all. We surfaced gasping, laughing. Anastacia and Carlos jumped in beside us, and then, one by one, the entire congregation followed, whooping and shouting and praising the Lord! Only Mercedes maintained her dignity. From the poolside, her patent leather shoes soaked from the splashing water, she shook her finger and yelled, "*Hermanos*, remember Paul said we should do everything decently and in order!"

Mercedes went for towels just as Carlos shouted from the middle of the pool: "Quiet, everybody! Anastacia has an announcement."

Anastacia, bobbing in the deep water to keep her balance, declared, waving her arms excitedly, "The Lord just told Carlos and me we should follow the example of Andrés and Gabriela. We're getting married next Saturday, and you're all invited!"

A few months later, after a Tuesday night Bible study, I informed the congregation it was time make a decision. Our Sunday crowds were overflowing Mercedes' party room. What would we do? Rent another building? Purchase property?

Gabriela signaled me. She looked especially beautiful tonight, maybe because she'd arrived minutes before from a New York buying trip and I was aching to take her into my arms.

She came forward and stood beside me at the podium, looping her arm into mine. "I haven't had time to talk to Andrés about this. I hope he'll forgive me." She turned and offered me her cheek for a quick peck, then continued.

"As some of you know, since I moved in with Doctór Andrés my daughter has lived alone in my big house in Lomas de Chapultepec. Just before I left on my trip she informed me she'd decided to share an apartment with one of her colleagues at the architectural firm where she works. Every time I had a spare moment during the week I was away I mulled over what I should do with my home."

She brushes away a tear. "I love that house very much. It was deeded to my father by my grandfather, then my father passed it on to me. But I don't ever want to move back, too many bad things have happened there.

"Now I'm sure what God wants me to do. I'd love for it to be the headquarters for our church. Would you accept it?"

The next morning at breakfast, for the first time since our marriage, I found the courage to bring up a fearsome subject. The bats in the attic at Gabriela's house: we must get rid of them before our congregation moved in!

Without a word, Gabriela got up from the table, took off her apron and hurried from the room. My heart stopped. She was angry! All the hurt and frustration of the last time we'd tried to do something about that curse came crashing down upon me. I shot a prayer arrow up to heaven.

She reappeared with a broom, a mop and a bucket. "Andrés, I'm ready to face the devil himself. Let's go clean out that attic right now!"

A surprise awaited us. We climbed the long stairway to the attic, she turned the key in the lock, I pushed the door open and...nothing. The bats had flown!

We stared at each other, mouths open. At last Gabriela threw her arms around me and said, "I know what happened. Quetzacóatl knew he didn't have a chance, so he retired his army from the field before the battle began!"

After sweeping and mopping the attic, we called up the gardener to haul away the trash. He was the only help remaining, Angelica had dismissed the maids when she moved out.

Hand in hand, we went downstairs to survey the parlor.

"My living room is at least as large as Mercedes' party room, don't you think? Gabriela said. "If we remove the wall separating it from the dining room we ought to have space for another year's growth. And there are plenty of rooms upstairs for the children's classes."

"But what about your furniture?" I asked.

"No problem, I'll just give it away or sell it." She frowned. "But not my heirlooms. The dining room furniture, for example." Running her hand over the thick mahogany table, she mused, "Grandfather had this made in the Yucatan and shipped by boat to Vera Cruz. I couldn't bear giving it up."

"And your clothes? You've filled our spare bedroom closet just with the stuff you brought from Budapest."

Coming over, she takes my hands in hers. "Andrés, I've been waiting to tell you something. Something that may upset you. I don't want your answer until you've had at least an hour to think about it. Promise?"

Kissing her forehead, I complain, "Hey, that's not fair! What have you got up your sleeve?"

"Promise?" She's smiling, but I can see the anxiety in her eyes.

I shrug. "Okay, you win. Now tell me what I've let myself in for."

She pulls out a dining room chair. "Here, sit down. I want to look you in the eye while I tell you about it. I'm really excited and I hope you will be too."

She sits facing me, our knees touching, and taking my hands again, eyes shining, she says, "The day before I left on my New York trip I visited a fantastic new high-rise in Polanco. You've seen it, it overlooks Chapultepec Park and it's only five minutes from your office. Guess what, one of their two penthouses is still for sale."

"What? Now look…"

"Remember, you promised!" Checking her watch, she pushes back her chair. "I had a reason for asking for a one-hour truce: yesterday, from the airport, I called a sales representative. We have an appointment with her in exactly half an hour."

In her new Chrysler we drove through Chapultepec Park toward Polanco. Half a mile away Gabriela pointed ahead and exclaimed: "Look, you can see it from here!"

Watching that soaring round copper-colored high rise under construction, I'd asked myself more than once how much they'd had to pay for permission to build a skyscraper on the edge of Chapultepec Park. It had never crossed my mind to wonder how it might be live in such a place.

With the pretty young saleswoman we zipped up thirty-two floors in less than thirty-two seconds and the elevator doors whispered open to an anteroom elegant in off-white understatement.

"Come with me," our hostess said, bubbling with excitement "your penthouse is waiting. I know you're going to fall in love with it."

Five hundred square meters of gleaming parquet floor. A master bedroom spacious enough for a game of racquet ball. A pink bathroom with a huge round Jacuzzi. Closets everywhere! Enough to hold everything Gabriela had accumulated in fifteen years of gleaning fashion shows in New York, Paris and London. The broad picture windows in the living room took my breath away: to the south a panorama of

Chapultepec Park's green forests and rowing lakes, and to the east a bird's-eye view of downtown.

We stepped out on the balcony. "Look!" the saleswoman exclaimed. Last night's rains had pushed aside the dark brown curtain of smog, leaving a breathtaking view of Popocatépetl and Itzlacihuatl.

Afterward, as the elevator descended, I could feel Gabriela's eyes on my face. I checked my watch. Our pact still had ten minutes to go.

Downstairs in the foyer the young woman said, "Now if you would like to accompany me to the office, I can prepare the papers."

Biting her lip, Gabriela asked, "What time do your offices close?"

Our hostess answered, too eagerly, I thought. "Mrs.Kelly, take your time. I'll be there until you call."

"Time's up!" I said moments later as we drove through Chapultepec toward Reforma.

"Please, Andrés, five minutes more," Gabriela pleaded, pulling over under a shady oak. She switched off the motor and turned toward me.

"*Mi amor*, I love your apartment, but you know, don't you, that it's time to move?"

"You think so?" I wanted to be grouchy, but how could I? More than six months had passed since our return from Budapest, and not once had she complained about having to live in my cramped, dowdy quarters.

"Darling, how many times have we talked about inviting your daughters and grandchildren to come and spend time with us, but decided we didn't have enough space?"

A low blow! As I'd expected, Margaret and Gabriela had become almost obsessive friends, our phone bills were outrageous. Little Jeff, five now, had fallen in love with his new grandmother. And I had a hard time not feeling jealous when, every time they met us at the airport, two-year-old Gretchen reached out to Gabriela instead of to me.

We'd already spent several overnights with Margaret and her family. Houston was a convenient stopover on Gabriela's buying trips to

Europe and New York, a weapon she used shamelessly to convince me to accompany her!

As for Victoria, she'd spent a weekend with us at Margaret's, but had been ill-tempered and uncommunicative. Every time I called her she complained about exhaustion from the eighty-hour weeks her law firm expected of her.

Then everything changed. Late one Thursday night in our New York hotel room I impulsively dialed her number. When she answered I could tell I'd awakened her. I was about to apologize, when Gabriela took the phone from my hand.

"Victoria, why don't you fly up and spend the weekend with us here in New York?"

"But *we're* inviting *you*. Please, let us pay your ticket and hotel. And you'll be my guest at a style show."

She hung up, without returning the phone to me. Smiling, she said. "Your daughter accepted my invitation!"

To my surprise, Victoria turned out to be an exuberant, good-natured guest. They went to the style show together, I managed to get good tickets for the theater and Sunday we took the ferry to the Statue of Liberty.

That night it was very late when Gabriela returned to our room and crawled into bed beside me. "What on earth have you two women been talking about?" I grumbled.

She mumbled contentedly into my chest: "I think I've about convinced your daughter to open a *Modas Mancini* in Houston."

In the ensuing months, ignoring my skepticism, Gabriela and Victoria moved ahead with plans for opening a *Mancini's* branch in The Woodlands, a wealthy young Houston suburb. Victoria had resigned from her position at the law office and was dedicating eighty hours a week to the enterprise....

Gabriela turned the ignition and punched in the air conditioner. The afternoon rains would be falling in another hour, but right now the bright sun was bringing the thin Mexico City air to a slow simmer.

She reached over and hugged my arm. "Please, Andee, don't be angry. Believe me, we can afford it."

I touched her face. How could I be angry with this incredible woman? Might as well admit it, in business matters Gabriela had her doctorate and I hadn't yet graduated from kindergarten!

Gabriela continued: "You know, Andrés, in the six months we've been married we've never talked about my money."

I squeezed her hand. "I like the way you're content for us to live like an ordinary middle class couple. Except for those outlandish phone bills!"

She smiled. "There's something I haven't told you, *mi amor*. Because of his suspicions about my ex-husband, my father set up a trust in my name. It matured a few months before we married. I've tapped it for my project with Victoria."

"I hope you're right about my daughter. I'm not so sure she's going to be such a great business executive."

Gabriela shrugs. "Don't you worry about Victoria. She's brilliant. And hardworking. And in spite of her hard head, she's letting me teach her. Mark my word, within a couple of years she'll be grossing more than I am here in my Mexico City store."

She pauses. "But starting up the Woodlands store will put only a small nick in my trust. Please, Andrés, let me buy our condominium. It's a good investment, and five years from now, if we want, we can sell it for twice what we paid for it."

I've decided I'm not going to give up without a struggle! "What if I tell you I love my humble little apartment?"

"Keep it, we'll use it as a guest house. And when you get tired of me you can take off and spend a few days there."

The same week we moved to the penthouse our congregation occupied Gabriela's villa.

Carlos and I began taking turns at the Bible studies, with Anastacia filling in quite often. She and Carlos were taking night courses at Trinity Seminary and I wasn't sure which of the two was the better preacher.

A few months later, soon after Gabriela and I returned from the inauguration of Victoria's *Modas Macini* in the Woodlands, Mercedes dropped a bombshell:

"Doctór Andrés, I called Rebeca and had her make an appointment for Isabel Buenaventura. You'll be seeing her tomorrow."

"Buenaventura. The name sounds familiar."

She smiled. "It should, her husband Benjamin is in President Justo Gonzales' cabinet. He's our Secretary of Commerce."

"And...and his wife is coming to see me? How did this happen?"

"It's a long story. Remember, I told you I attended the *Universidad Anahuac* after leaving the theater. That's where I met Isabel. Of course I was fifteen years older than her when we both entered as freshmen. In my very first Sociology class I sat next to her. I could feel her eyes on me. Finally she slipped me a note: 'I think I know you.'

She invited me to lunch. Told me about the first time she saw me on stage: on her twelfth birthday her mother took her to the theater where I was playing the part of a heartbroken princess. She fell in love with me. Never missed one of my plays after that.

"We were friends for all of our university career. When she married the ugliest, most brilliant of our graduates I was the maid of honor. They left almost immediately for Harvard Business School where Benjamin had a scholarship for doctoral studies. Then we lost touch until about five years ago when she appeared at one of Anastacia's plays. By then her husband was on the fast track in national politics. A year ago she called again and invited me to lunch. She'd become very lonely. Her husband was so involved in his job he had little time left for family. A couple of weeks ago when she told me she was considering a divorce I recommended she talk with you."

The day Isabel Buenaventura walked into my office, I suspected: this was the end of our idyllic parenthesis. That today was the beginning of the final battle with Quetzalcóatl.

CHAPTER 42

▼

THE MAN FROM
LosPinos

"Divorce your husband, *Señora*? Such a radical solution?"

She's sitting on the edge of her chair, nervous fingers twisting a white lace handkerchief. "I've decided it's time to face the facts. For fifteen years I've been telling myself things were going to get better, but they never do."

"Fifteen years. That's a long time to be in an unhappy marriage."

Sighing, she settles back in her chair. "I guess Mercedes has told you she and I met at the university. Benjamin was a classmate. We started going together when we were freshmen. In our junior year he asked me to marry him." For the first time she brightens. "None of the other girls would give him a second look. He was short, very dark..." she frowns..."and they said, homely. But I always thought he was handsome. And besides, he was the most intelligent boy in our class." She pauses. "I guess you've seen pictures of him in the paper?"

Embarrassed, I confess I'm not sure what her husband looks like. Outside of the President and Mexico City's Mayor I don't keep up with Mexico's politicians.

She takes a small black and white snapshot from her billfold and hands it to me. "You need to see his picture if you're going to understand what I'm about to tell you."

I study the photo. "His name is Benjamin," she tells me, "but since university days his friends have called him 'Benito.' Can you see why?"

I chuckle, nodding. "Benito Juárez!"

"Looks a lot like him, doesn't he?"

"Could be his twin brother!" I'm impressed. Her husband has the same deep bronzed skin, intense dark eyes, and straight black hair as the man some historians describe as Mexico's Abraham Lincoln.

"He should be proud," I tell her, returning the snapshot, "Benito Juarez was one of Mexico's greatest Presidents. At least, that's *my* opinion."

"You know, he was President of Mexico at the same time Abraham Lincoln was President of your country."

"And they were a lot alike," I say, warming to the subject. "Both started out as obscure country lawyers. Because of their unpolished appearance people tended to underestimate them. Both had brilliant minds, a deep love of country and were absolutely incorruptible. And they both spent their lives fighting their countries' oppressors."

She nods her head vigorously. "Mercedes told me you're a student of Mexico's history. I can see she was right."

"And what about your 'Benito', *Sra.* Isabel, does he have the same admirable qualities as his namesake?"

Another spirited nod. "That's what attracted me to him!" The corners of her mouth droop: "And now, that's why I've about decided I can't stay with him any longer."

I lean forward. "I don't understand."

"You've heard about the massacre in the *Plaza de las Tres Culturas?*"

"Of course." (How could I ever forget Moisés' heart-wrenching story of the government's slaughter of Mexico's youth on the eve of the 1968 Olymplics!)

"Benito was there with his older brother. He was only fifteen at the time, but something happened to him that day that changed his life forever. He told me about it five years later, and the horror was still in his eyes as he described running for his life, hearing the guns popping and the screams of his comrades as they fell wounded."

My heart skips a beat, remembering another young man fleeing the slaughter that day. Did their paths cross, maybe, for an instant? Did Benjamin glimpse Moisés, see in his face a mirror of his own terror?

"He never saw his brother again. And he made himself a promise: he'd see to it that nothing like that ever happened again! He'd get a good education, claw his way into politics and find some way to change his country."

Fascinated, I ask, "Does he still feel the same way?"

She sits for a long moment studying her finely manicured hands. At last she says, very quietly, "Doctór Kelly, you're an American. I don't know how much you've learned about our problems here in Mexico."

I choose my words carefully. "Enough to know it must be tough being the wife of a government official."

She hides her face for a moment in her handkerchief, then, wiping her eyes, continues: "The same ex-classmates who thought I was crazy to marry Benito are jealous of me now. They think I'm having a great time as the wife of a cabinet member. They don't know how lonely it is!

"Ever since I first met him, I've known Benito is a man obsessed. At Harvard he studied day and night, seven days a week. By the time we returned to Mexico one of his boyhood friends was rising in national politics. He latched on to Benito and three years ago when he became President appointed him Secretary of Commerce.

"Now it's worse than ever. On good days he's gone just fifteen hours. Other days he sleeps in his office. It's been months since we made love. Our children hardly know him."

"Have you tried talking to him?"

"Of course." She glares at me. "But he's never listened to me before, so why should he now?

"You asked me if he still has his dream. I guess he does, only he's so angry I don't know what he's thinking." She sighs. "He's always been an angry man, but for over a year now he seems to have lost control. When I try to get him to tell me why, it only makes him more irritable. Maybe *you* can find out what's wrong."

I drum the desk with my fingers, wondering if she's wasting her time. "Do you think he might talk with me?"

Her chin comes up. "He's got to! He'll tell me he's too busy, but I've decided I'm going to give him an ultimatum: either he convinces you there's hope for our marriage, or I'll file for divorce."

I smile. "Sometimes a good threat works wonders."

"There's only one problem. Benito doesn't like Americans."

I resist the temptation to push back my chair and stand to my feet. "Then shouldn't you be talking to somebody else?"

Very carefully she rearranges her long flowered skirt. When she looks up, her eyes are hopeful. "Dr. Kelly, I don't know what's happened to my friend Mercedes and her daughter but I'm impressed by what I see. And Carlos! I want my husband to love me he like Carlos loves Anastacia! That's why I've come to you. I'm hoping maybe something of what you people have will rub off on him."

"Bad news, Doctór, he's canceled!" Rebeca's voice on the interphone is indignant.

"Not again!"

"Do you want me to tell his secretary you're no longer available?"

"No, no…he's going to be the one who gives up, not I!"

This is the third time Benjamin Buenaventura has canceled an appointment at the last moment. Each time, a courier has arrived later with a check for the consultation and a short note of apology from Buenaventuras's secretary.

"Rebeca, bring a couple of coffees. Let's chat a while."

When she walks in a minute later Rebeca's grin tells me she's pleased at my invitation. I take a cup from her hand and lean back in my chair, stretching my arms. "Guess I'd better take advantage of every opportunity to spend time with you. In a little more than a month I'll no longer have you around."

"So you're going to fire me when I get married?"

"No, but from what you tell me, that husband you're acquiring is very *macho*. Every day when he leaves for work he's going to lock the door and take the key with him!"

My voice is bantering, but I'm concerned. When Rebecca has a ring on her finger, what's going to happen to that special smile she's always had for me?

As she reaches for the sugar her fingertips brush my hand. "Doctór, Edgar knows how important my work is to me. Whether he likes it or not, I'm going to stay on…at least until a baby comes."

I'm surprised at the relief washing over me. This is the first time we've talked about what Rebeca might do after she marries. We've avoided the subject ever since she asked me to do her wedding ceremony.

I've kidded Rebeca about being an expert at "courtship evangelism." Half a dozen times in the four years she's worked for me she's met a boy at school, brought him to church, got him converted, then dropped him.

But it didn't turn out that way with Edgar. After graduation from the university she began working the night shift at *Petroleos Mexicanos*. Within a month she introduced me to her newest conquest, a handsome young man she had met at work. I never saw him again. After a while I stopped asking when he was going start going to church with her.

"But Rebeca, do you think you'll be able to continue with two jobs after you're married?"

"No, Doctór, but it wasn't hard to decide which one I want to keep."

Our fingers touch again as she hands me the spoon, the light caress of dear friends. What would I do without Rebeca at my side?

"Rebeca, you haven't told me how much you're making at *Petroleos*. Tell you what, if you stay with me I'll match it."

She shrugs. "You don't have to do that. Don't you know I'm staying on because I enjoy working with you?"

Making a face, she adds: "Even though you haven't been able to forgive me."

Ouch! When Rebeca asked me to do the ceremony for her marriage to a non-believer I reached for my Bible and read her Paul's warning that Christians shouldn't be "unequally yoked together with unbelievers." Her eyes flashed and she warned me not preach at her. We had our first real fight since she'd come to work with me. The argument continued for weeks. At last I realized I wasn't going to change her mind, and dropped the subject. There's been a subtle chill between us ever since.

Time to end it! I put down my cup.

"Rebeca, I'm still not convinced Edgar is God's man for you, but I'm no longer angry with you." Her eyes told me she wasn't convinced, so I added: "I keep reminding myself that God works all things together for good to those who love Him."

A little voice whispered in my heart, "Even when we disobey Him?"

The phone rings. Rebeca answers, and her hand over the phone, says, "*Señor* Buenaventura is on the phone. Must be calling from his automobile. Says he can be here in twenty minutes if you'll see him."

I look at my watch. "Who's scheduled for twelve?"

"Her name is Carla Montejo. She's new."

"Call her and and reschedule." What arrogance, calling at the last minute! Hope I'm not making a mistake, I've never done anything like this before. But of course I never had a patient like Benjamin Buenaventura before...

By 12:25 I'm at the point of leaving for an early lunch. The buzzer sounds, and Rebeca, advises me *Se;or Buenaventura* has arrived. I stand to meet him.

"Doctór Kelly, it is very kind of you to receive me on such short notice." He looks like Benito Juarez, all right, but at least ten years older than the photo his wife showed me. Quite thin, shoulders erect and stiff, large round head topped by a thick shock of unruly jet-black hair, he's dressed in an expensive black Gucci suit, white shirt and dark tie.

I extend my hand. "Have a seat, *Sr.* Buenaventura, it's a pleasure to meet you."

As he sits, he glances at his watch. "As you know, *Maestro*, I am here because of the insistence of my wife."

As always when I'm meeting a new patient, I try to get the feel of him. Benito is easy to read, fidgeting, seated tautly at the very center of the chair, a tiny muscle quivering at the base of his thick dark-bearded jaw. I imagine touching his button and seeing him spring out of his chair and land in a corner of the room. It's obvious he's angry about being pressured to make this visit. What's worse, he doesn't like gringos! How can I reach him? I ask myself. Well, I'm not going to fawn over him!

Consciously relaxing, I say slowly, "I want to make something very clear, *Señor*. It's imperative to me that a person come of his own volition. I'm not in the habit of employing emotional blackmail to get people in my office."

Sitting back, he takes out a cigarette. I decide to say nothing about my no-smoking rule, maybe a few puffs will help to defuse this ticking time bomb!

"My own volition?" He runs a hand through his stiff black hair. "I'm sure you know about my wife's threat." Inhaling deeply, he shrugs, "but she's right, I've been treating her abominably." His eyes dart to his watch again.

"*Sr.* Buenaventura, thirty minutes remain of the fifty I set aside for you. Do you have thirty minutes available?"

He stubs out his cigarette on the sole of his shoe and says, more to himself than to me: "*Dios mío*, what's wrong with me? I'm about to lose my family!"

I wait. I can't remember anyone ever leaving my office before their time was up. Even if a man is not interested in saving his marriage, he's usually pleased if someone is willing to listen while he explains why it's impossible to keep on living with the woman he married. I wonder where Benito Buenaventura stands. I decide to test the waters:

"Your wife seemed to be very anxious to find healing for your marriage. Do you feel the same way?"

His brow furrowed, he massages the back of his neck. Fully half a minute passes before he answers, measuring his words, "I...I guess I do. Let me make something clear: Isabel's a good woman, and I'm not here to blame her for our problems."

"I see. Tell me, *Sr.* Buenaventura, why do you suppose she's about decided to give up?"

"She says I don't spend enough time with her. And she's right, of course.

"Then I suppose you'd like for us to talk about what you might do to find more time for her."

He taps out a cigarette from the package and lights it. "That's the problem, Doctór. Right now I see no possibility of any change in my schedule."

We sit in a silence for a moment. At last he sighs, blows a cumulous cloud toward the ceiling and grunts, "All right, let's have the lecture!"

I chuckle. "Is that why you came, *Sr.* Buenaventura, to...receive a lecture?"

"Isn't that what this is all about? You tell me my wife's conditions for staying with me, I tell you I can't meet those conditions, and then you give me a lecture and I give you a check."

Leaning forward, I wait until his eyes meet mine. "*Sr.* Buenaventura, that's not the way I work."

"Then how do you work?"

"My first priority is to get to know my clients. I don't have the right to lecture anybody until I'm able to feel what they're feeling."

He makes a face. "That could take a long time."

"Yes, it could...how long have you and *Sra.* Isabel been married?"

"Nineteen years."

"Would you be willing to invest nineteen hours to save a relationship that's lasted nineteen years?"

For the first time he smiles. "And if I say no? Is that when the lecture comes?"

I smile back. "Well, I don't claim to be perfect."

I'm pleased when he laughs. Now I know. This is not an arrogant egotist, but a human tortured by some passion I don't yet comprehend. I can feel a spark kindling between us.

"Look, Doctór, I'm going to be honest with you. I'm here because I love my wife and don't want to lose her. But I'm afraid you're wasting your time. I know of no way I'm going to be able to give her the attention she wants from me. I guess that's why many of my colleagues in government have opted for lovers rather than wives. Maybe the kindest thing you can do for to Isabel is to tell her there's no hope and she might as well divorce me and look for somebody who's not married to his work!"

Good! Now he's letting me know how he feels. Time for a proposition he may be willing to accept. "Look, *Sr.* Buenaventura..."

"My name is Benjamin."

"Thank you, Benjamin. And my name is Andrew. As I was about to say, Isabel tells me I'm going to have to convince her to stay with you."

He makes a face. "And I'm going to have to convince you it's worth her while?"

"I suppose you could put it that way."

"And how long is she willing to wait?"

"She didn't say."

"So, as long as I'm seeing you, she'll hold off on the divorce."

"Probably."

He puffs on his cigarette and blows a cloud of smoke right at me. "That's noble of both of you, but ¡*Qué diablos*! What's the use of putting off the inevitable?"

Determined not to lose my cool, I wave away the smoke with both hands. "Benjamin, if you really thought divorce was inevitable, you wouldn't have come today!"

Head down, he studies the bright end of his cigarette. Just before it reaches his fingers, he drops the cigarette into an empty coffee cup, and looks up. "You know, I guess you're right. He takes a deep breath. "O.K., you win. Where do we start?"

I sit back in my chair, again willing myself to relax. "We still have fifteen minutes. I'm going to ask you to do something for me: tell me about the most important thing that ever happened to you. In your entire life."

Closing his eyes he turns his face toward the ceiling. What will he talk about? Meeting Isabel? Receiving the doctorate from Harvard? His appointment to the Cabinet by the President?

At last he begins. "I was fifteen at the time. My brother was nineteen. We were just ten days away from the beginning of the Olympics in Mexico City and I was trying to convince him to let me go with him to a rally in La Plaza de las Tres Culturas I'll never forget that day, as long as I live...."

CHAPTER 43

▼

BENJAMIN TELLS HIS STORY

"Walk through the door!" Did I hear her correctly? I press the phone to my ear.

"What? Gelda, what are you talking about?…What door?"

"I don't know, Andrés. I'm just repeating the words the Spirit whispered in my ear a few minutes ago when I was reading Revelation. Remember John's letter to the church in Philadelphia? Christ says, 'See I have set before you an open door and no one can shut it.' As I read those words the Spirit said to me, 'Tell Andrés to walk through the door!'"

"I don't understand."

"Neither do I. I was hoping you might know what it meant. Oh well. Guess we'll just have to wait."

I hang up, shaking my head, and buzz Rebeca. "Rebeca, pull my file on Benjamin Buenaventura, please. I've only got a few minutes before he arrives.…

"Sr. Buenaventura…"

"The name is Benjamin, remember?" I'm pleased to see the suggestion of a smile lighting his dark face.

Smiling, I say, "Have a seat, Benjamin." (Dare I? Yes!)

"Or would you prefer I call you 'Benito'?"

Taking a chair across from me, he measures me with those intense black eyes. "So! Isabel told you?" He pauses. "Doctór Andrés, how much do you know about Benito Juarez?"

"Enough to admire him immensely!" I pick up the interphone. "Rebeca, bring us some coffee, please." Turning my attention back to my visitor, I say, "You know, Benjamin, I can't imagine the courage it must have taken for Juarez to face the armies of France with just a handful of poorly armed volunteers."

"Then you can understand why I feel unworthy of such an illustrious name!"

"Thank you, Rebeca." She sets the tray on my desk and retires.

I hand him a cup. "As I remember, Benito Juarez was a Zapotec Indian, wasn't he?"

"That's right," Benjamin answers, sipping his coffee, "just like me. He practiced law in his home state of Oaxaca until he was elected governor. In 1859 he became President, but fate seemed against him. France invaded Mexico, deposed him and installed Maximillian as dictator. I guess you know a lot of books have been written about Emperor Maximilliano and his Queen Carlota."

"I've read several."

"For five desperate years Juarez waged war, as you mentioned, with just a handful of guerrillas. Finally France decided Emperor Maximillian's kingdom had become too expensive, and gave up."

"I'm not sure I approve of what happened next, Benjamin. I mean Juarez standing Maxilillian before a firing squad. Wouldn't it have been simpler just to expel him from the country?"

Frowning, Buenaventura drains his cup and returns it to my desk. "Those were desperate times, Doctór. Juarez must have felt like he had to tell the world, 'Don't underestimate me, I'm in charge!'"

"And he was, wasn't he? He reinstated the Reform Laws he'd enacted before France's invasion, separating Church and State. And stripped the Church of the wealth and the lands it had held for centuries. I read somewhere that by that time the hierarchy owned eighty per cent of Mexico's real estate."

Getting up from his seat, Benito Buenaventura steps over to the window and stands looking down at the traffic. His back still to me, he says, "I guess I need to tell you the rest of the story about my nickname."

"I wish you would. I've been wondering ever since we ran out of time on your last visit."

Turning, he massages his temples with his fingers, as if trying to erase painful memories. "I don't think I mentioned that the day of the massacre we were celebrating the centenary of Benito Juarez' revolution. It was exciting to be young in those days. Such dreams! We were ten days away from the beginning of the Olympics. The government had constructed a huge stadium on the freeway, near Xochimilco, for the event. The eyes of the world would be fixed on our country. It seemed like the perfect time to call our corrupt leaders to account!"

"And install a communist government?"

He stops pacing, and looking out the window again, says, "That's what the students wanted."

"So…the rally was a declaration of war?"

"Not exactly. We were convinced the government would give in to our demands when they saw how united we were."

"But instead, they answered with bullets."

Returning to his seat, Benjamin leans toward me, his voice deep, solemn: "Tell me, Andrés…do you believe in destiny?"

"You bet I do!"

He nods. "I thought so. I'm going to tell you what happened that night after I escaped from *La Plaza de las Tres Culturas*. Maybe you can help me clear my mind. I've got to make a decision."

He settles back in his chair. "As soon as the bullets began flying I took off running. Soon I found myself downtown. Soldiers were everywhere, plucking kids off the street like scattered chicks. I still don't understand how they missed me! I turned right on Avenida Juarez and headed for Chapultepec Park.

"When I got there I threw myself on the ground in the shadow of a big eucalyptus tree, gasping for breath, waiting for the sudden shock of a rifle poking me in the back. After a long while I eased myself up, not daring to believe I'd escaped.

"I was surprised to see I was still clutching a pamphlet someone had thrust in my hands just before the shooting began.

Fingers trembling, I spread it out on the ground. "Big red letters blazed in the dim street light: *Libertad! Centenario de Benito Juarez*. I panicked. If a soldier came upon me at this instant...!

"I ripped it up and dug a hole in the ground and buried it.

Suddenly it hit me: my brother! I'd never see him again! I put my head between my knees and cried my heart out.

"At last, exhausted, I sat up. Idly, I picked up a scrap of paper from the ground. Only a name was left: 'Benito Juarez.'"

He pauses. "I've never told this to anyone. Maybe I shouldn't tell you, you're going to say I'm crazy."

I'm silent, waiting for him to continue.

Unwilling to look me in the eye, he drops his face into his hands. I strain to hear what he's mumbling through his fingers: "I...felt a hand on my shoulder...and heard my mother's voice calling my name: 'Benito,...Benito.' That was all, nothing more."

Reaching into his coat pocket he takes out a pack of Marlboros. "Well, what do you think, have I lost my mind?" "I say softly, "No, *Licenciado*, I don't think you've lost your mind. But I am confused. You say your mother called you 'Benito'? How could that be? Your wife told me you got that name in the University."

Lighting his cigarette, he inhales deeply. "That's how Isabel remembers it. I guess only my father would remember the truth: that my mother started calling me Benito when I was very small. You've noticed the way we Mexicans use *ito*, haven't you? Abuelito, papito, hijito. It's a diminutive, and mamá used it because I was the smallest of her three sons. But only my mother. Everybody else called me Benjamin, the name my father had given me."

He grinds out his cigarette. "After…after I heard my mother's voice I sat there for a long time, shivering, remembering what happened the day she died. I was six, and was standing with my father and two older brothers beside her bed, all of us crying. She told everybody else to leave the room. Then, taking my hand, she told me: 'Benito, soon after you were born, the doctor told me the bad news: your heart was failing and you were going to die. After he left I lay there praying, begging God to spare you. And God spoke to me! He told me not to worry, he had special plans for you.' She pulled me close, kissed me on the cheek, and whispered, 'God told me that one day you'd be another Benito Juarez.' Reaching up, she wiped a tear from her cheek. 'Now you know the real reason why I've always called you Benito.'"

I feel goose bumps prickling my arms. "Wow! Incredible!" We sit in silence for a long moment. At last I say, "And after your mother died nobody else used that name?"

"Nobody. And as the years passed my mother's dying words faded from my mind."

"Until that night."

He nods. "What do you think, Doctór, was it just my imagination?"

I shake my head. "I doubt it. And anyway, what matters is what happened afterward. How that experience affected your life."

He tries to steady his hand as he lights another cigarette. "You're right. When I arrived home next morning my family welcomed me like someone returned from the dead. After all the shouting was over I climbed the stairs to my room. For some reason, I wasn't sure why, I was dying to look in the mirror. I opened the door, stepped up to the dresser, and for the first time in my life, really saw who I was.

"I cried with joy. You see, for the last three or four years I'd hated myself. Instead of growing taller like all my friends, I seemed to be stuck with this stunted body. And my skin kept getting darker. My father had made a joke of it, he said I was a throwback to the Zapotec ancestors on my mother's side."

"But now, staring at myself in the mirror, I knew: these last three years, all the time I was hating the way I looked, fate was shaping me for my destiny."

"But people still didn't call you 'Benito'?"

"No, they called me other names, ugly names: *indio, negrito, chaparrito*. But I didn't mind, I had a secret! I began reading every book about Benito Juarez I could lay my hands on. And I decided I'd be a lawyer, just like my hero.

"I studied my head off in the preparatory, and made top grades. The *Universidad de Anahuac* gave me a full scholarship." He smiles, blowing a smoke ring toward the ceiling. "I was an oddity among all the light-skinned sons of the rich in that expensive school.

"Then one day it happened. In a history class the prof was lecturing on Benito Juarez. Suddenly he stopped and stared at me, as if seeing me for the first time. He called me up before the class. '*Damas y Caballeros*, he said, 'I've been discoursing on the great Liberator. It gives me pleasure to present him to you in person. Meet *Don* Benito Juarez.'

"The class burst out laughing. But the teacher picked up a book, opened it, and showed them a full page portrait of Benito Juarez. I can still see their eyes as they stared, first at the picture, then at me, their mouths falling open.

"From that day on, everyone called me 'Benito'."

Benito pauses. "Am I wasting your time? We're supposed to be talking about my marriage."

"But when we talk about you, Benjamin, we *are* talking about your marriage.

I take a deep breath, trying to gather my thoughts. "You said you've got to make a decision. Want to talk about it?"

He consults his watch. "How much time do we have?"

"Ten minutes."

"That's not enough. Next time...."

After he's gone I sit staring out the window, only vaguely aware of the rumble of traffic below, wondering about the decision he's facing. "Benito Juarez in the flesh," I repeat out loud, smiling "How strange!"

I jump. Gelda's phone call a while ago! She said: "Walk through the door."

I'm remembering another call, a call from Moisés, late one night nearly five years ago: "Doctór, I had a dream. I saw you walking through the front door of *Los pinos*." Getting up, my heart thumping, I begin pacing back and forth.

That call brought me to Mexico! Is the door about to open?

We're seated at our dining room table, sipping our after dinner coffee, admiring the lights of the city spread out like a magic carpet below.

"I still can't get over the coincidence!" Gabriela tells me.

"When Isabel told me today you'd had lunch together she left me speechless."

"Did she tell you how it happened?"

"Only that she'd met you at *Modas Mancini*."

"I'm sure this isn't the first time she's shopped in my store. It's a popular spot for government wives, you know. But I hadn't met her before, I seldom wait on customers. This morning I looked up from my desk and saw her standing by a rack of dresses. I figured she was waiting for someone to help her. We started talking, and she mentioned she had a busy afternoon ahead. That among other things she had an appointment with her therapist. I said, 'How interesting. My husband is a therapist.' When I mentioned your name she dropped the dress she was about to try on. Suddenly I knew who she was: the Isabel Buenaventura we've been praying for."

"I'm surprised you were able to accept her invitation to lunch on such short notice," I say with a chuckle.

Laughing, she reaches for my hand. "I surprised myself. I'm behind in my preparations for that buying trip to New York next week, so I'd brought along a sandwich to eat at my desk. But when she invited me, I just went."

"I forgive you."

María de Jesús, the cook refills our cups. As she clears the table we chat about the weather. I've noticed some people act as if maids were robots, talking about the most intimate things at meals. Gabriela and I have agreed we're not going to make that mistake.

María returns to the kitchen. Gabriela adds, "Isabel told me Mercedes has been inviting her to our Bible study. Said she'd try to come next Tuesday night."

I was impressed by the change in Isabel when she entered my office this afternoon. Last time she seemed to be strangling on the sad, depressing words coming out of her mouth. But today she walked in with her chin up and a smile on her face, and began talking before she sat down.

She told me about her lunch with Gabriela. I waited for a moment, to see if she and her husband had commented on their visits with me.

At last she said, "You're going to be surprised what Benito said about you!"

"Oh? So you've talked?"

She shakes her head. "Not really, but at least I got him to say *something*. After his first visit I was afraid to ask how it had gone, he'd been so angry about my demanding he see you. I was pleased when he made a second appointment, it meant he'd be coming this time because he wanted to.

"As usual, he got home after midnight. I was waiting up with a snack. He had nothing more for me than a peck on the cheek, but he didn't seem as angry as usual.

"Just before we went to sleep, I got up the nerve to ask him how your meeting had gone. He just grunted. But when I kept insisting he said, 'He's not bad for a gringo. Now go to sleep, woman!'"

"Was that good?"

"Fantastic! My husband's a cynic about Americans. I'm sure he was prepared to despise you. What did you do to him, Doctór?"

I smile. "Nothing. We got along great. He's not bad for an Indian!"

She laughs. "I'm going to tell him what you said!"

"If you do it will be the end of a very short friendship!"

We explore her childhood. She's the youngest daughter of a typical upper middle-class family. Her parents got along well and she felt loved by both of them. Until she met Benjamin she'd never had a steady boyfriend. I decide there's no hidden agenda we'll need to explore.

She stands to leave. "Doctór, it was a pleasure meeting your wife."

"How nice of you to ask her to lunch."

With her hand on the door, she turns back and says, "She invited me to your Tuesday night Bible study. Think I'll accept." Smiling, she slips out the door.

CHAPTER 44

▼

A FATEFUL DECISION

"Do you really think he'll come?"

Perched on the edge of the love seat, fidgeting, twisting her hands, Isabel is behaving more like a jittery bride than a wounded veteran of nineteen years of marriage.

I check my watch. "He's only ten minutes late. He'll be here, he always calls when he can't make it."

This is a crucial meeting. I've asked Benjamin and Isabel to meet together with me. I'm always careful to utilize the dynamics of both apartness and togetherness in marriage counseling. People in conflict have a hard time being authentic when they're together, so I spend time alone with each of them. On the other hand, I can't make a realistic assessment of the chances for healing until I observe them together. Are they capable of listening to each other? Is each willing to accept his own share of fault? Do they respect each other? Are they disciplined enough to work at saving their marriage?

The intercom buzzes. *Sr.* Buenaventura has arrived."

"Send him in."

Benjamin enters, shakes my hand, and instead of sitting beside Isabel on the love seat, takes the empty chair. Did they have breakfast together this morning? I doubt it. But at least they're together now!

"This morning," I tell them, "I want to see how you communicate. I'll listen as you dialogue, and with your permission I'll be interrupting from time to time."

"What do you want us to talk about?" Isabel asks, her voice a nervous squeak. "We don't have much practice."

"Don't worry, I'll help you. Now, I want you to sit facing each other."

Benjamin moves his chair opposite his wife's, and I take my place beside them. They haven't exchanged a word since he entered.

"Closer, please, I want your knees touching. Now each of you will have the opportunity to make three statements. First, I want you to mention two things you like about your marriage. That earns you the right to bring up one thing you wish could be changed. Who'd like to begin?"

"*Damas primero,*" Benito says, still avoiding his wife's eyes. I can see he's anxious to get this over with.

"Well," Isabel begins, "I'm very proud of my husband, he's the most intelligent man I know."

"No, Isabel, don't talk to me, talk to Benjamin. And look at him, not at me."

She blushes. "Benito, you know that's what first attracted me to you. You always seemed to have the right answer in class."

"*Gracias.*"

"Benjamin, look your wife in the eye."

"And...let me see...you're a good man. I trust you, Benito." Her voice catches, "in spite of all our problems, I've never worried about you being unfaithful.

"But Benito, why have you shut me out of your life? I feel like I don't know you." Her face crumbling, she reaches for a Kleenex. "You haven't been an easy man to live with, *mi amor*, but I've put up with it, because I was proud of what you were doing. At Harvard I didn't complain when you worked day and night because I knew getting your doctorate was important to you. When President Gonzales took you into his cabinet, I was so happy for you. But in the last couple of years you've changed. You act like you don't care for anything. The *patria*. Your dreams. Me…The children. Please, tell me what's happened!"

His jaw set, Benjamin looks at his watch, then at me, his face getting redder with each tick of the wall clock.

But Isabel hasn't finished. "And Benito, for over a year now you've stopped taking me to your dinners and cocktail parties. Why?" Leaning toward him, she places her hands on his knees. "Are you ashamed of me?"

His eyes flash. "No! I'm not ashamed of you!"

"Then why don't you ever take me with you?"

Benjamin looks at his watch again. "Now. Is it my turn, *Doctór*?"

I must be careful. This man is ready to bolt, and if he does, he'll never return.

I say, squeezing the emotion out of my voice, "Benjamin, this is *supposed* to be a dialogue. Don't you want to answer Isabel's question?"

Still not looking at his wife, Benjamin growls, "Look, woman, I warned you when I took this job there'd be things I couldn't discuss with you."

"But *mi amor*, I'm not talking about state secrets. Why won't you tell me what's wrong?" The last words are a wail of anguish. Benjamin's head jerks up, eyes wide with surprise. Isabel has broken an unspoken agreement! These two people are committed to being polite, to never raising their voices, even as they witness the slow, inexorable strangulation of their marriage.

He speaks curtly, the veins standing out on his neck, "*Mujer*, I don't want you associating with those people I work with. They're *una cochinada*!"

A pigpen? What's he's talking about? His dark face has turned the color of a spoiled beet, and his hands are clenching the arms of the chair so tightly I expect to hear it splinter.

"I don't understand, Benito, you work with the cream of our society, the richest, most cultured people in the country!"

He's yelling now: "'The cream of our society?' Look, *mujer*, why are you such a fool? Don't you know what's going on?"

Benito gets to his feet, and I'm afraid he's going to throw open the door and rush out. Please God, don't let it happen!

Isabel is sobbing, struggling to catch her breath. At last she dries her eyes and says coldly, "Well, Benito, even hearing you say I'm a fool is better than banging my head against the wall of silence you've built between us."

He stops pacing and glares at her, fists clinched. I wait, willing myself not to speak, knowing that at this moment everything hangs in the balance: their marriage, Moisés' vision…what else? I imagine angels leaning over the parapets of the heavenlies, holding their breath.

The clicking of the hands of the wall clock echoes through the room…Gelda, I hope you're on your knees right now…and you, Anastacia and Mercedes!

Reaching up, Benjamin yanks open his shirt collar and a button rockets across the room, landing somewhere near my desk. He opens his mouth, shuts it, swallows so hard his Adam's apple bobbles. Is he going to pull the cork on what's bothering him, or shut it up inside forever?

At last he comes back to his seat, sits down hard, sighs and says, his voice calm now. "Isabel, forgive me for calling you a fool. I'm the fool, thinking I could make a difference…" His voice trails off.

She says softly, "What are you talking about, Benito, I still don't understand."

"Don't you remember? I told you about it before we married. How I found out in the Plaza de las Tres Culturas that the people running this country would do anything, even kill their own people, before they'd give up their power."

She reaches out and tenderly takes his hand. "But Benito, you decided you were going to change all that. That's why you studied to be a lawyer, why you worked so hard for your doctorate. And now you have the opportunity."

I see a mask falling over Benjamin's face. He turns to me. "Well, Doctór, now you see where the problem is with our marriage. It's me, not my wife."

He looks at his watch. "Our time is about up. Do I have your permission to say something to Isabel?"

"Of course, Benjamin."

He turns back to her. "Isabel, You've been a good wife. You have every right to leave me."

He stands, straightens his tie and steps through the door. The door clicks shut.

We sit without speaking for several long minutes. Isabel's eyes are dry, but her face is somber.

At last she says. "I must go, it's time for your next appointment."

"They can wait, Isabel."

She takes a deep, shuddering breath. "It's all over, isn't it?"

"What do you mean?"

"He's going to leave me."

"No, he's not going to leave you, didn't you hear what he said? But he gave *you* permission to leave *him*. Will you?"

"No, but…"

"But you're going to let him keep thinking you might?"

The corners of her lips turn down in a cheerless smile. "I'm going to keep reminding him of my promise: I'll stay with him as long as you tell me I should."

"After what happened Tuesday night, you know what I'm going to tell you, don't you?"

Last Tuesday night Isabel shared with the Bible study group that, with the help of Mercedes and Anastacia, she had invited Christ into her heart. Afterward, hugging her, I knew that her conversion was another piece in this jigsaw puzzle of God's battle plan for the defeat of Quetzalcóatl....

"I don't know why you're discouraged, Benjamin, there have been a lot of changes these first four years of the President's *sexenio*. He's jailed half a dozen corrupt bosses of *Petroleos Mexicanos*, the economy has improved and for the first time I can remember people are talking about the future with optimism.

After two weeks I had about decided I'd never see Benjamin again. Then yesterday his secretary called, and Rebeca juggled today's agenda so she could plug him in. When he walked in fifteen minutes ago we picked up where we'd left off, as if nothing had happened.

Benjamin doesn't answer at once. At last he says, "Andrés, do I still have your promise of absolute confidence?"

"Of course."

He moves to the edge of his seat, his face intense: "When I first joined the government I was optimistic. President Justo Gonzales was a man I'd known since we were kids. We had the same dreams for our beloved *patria*. But now I'm disillusioned. You're right, he has made some changes. But they're mostly cosmetic. Everything's the same!" He sinks back into his chair.

I know now why Benjamin returned. It's not so much because he's worried about his marriage falling apart but because he's found a confessor! Here's a man dying to talk to someone, but whom can he trust? He doesn't dare confess how he feels to any of his colleagues. Andrew Kelly, on the other hand, is trained to listen without judging. And committed to not spilling the beans! He continues. "Somebody said 'Power corrupts, and absolute power corrupts absolutely.' He was right. It's the same old story, time after time. Our Presidents begin their *sexenios* as messiahs, and finish them as pariahs. They start with the dream of changing everything, and end up being changed themselves, transformed into men without a conscience."

"And this President?"

Glancing over his shoulder, he mutters. "Just wait! When this *sexenio* ends, the scandal he leaves behind will make the Presidents that preceded him look like saints by comparison."

Pouring a glass of water, he takes a quick gulp and says, "But let me come to the *real* reason I'm here."

"Not to talk about your marriage?"

He snorts. "No, not about my marriage." Reaching for a cigarette, he growls, "Well, maybe it *is* about my marriage. I'm going crazy over a decision I've got to make. Once I get that out of the way maybe my marriage will have a chance."

I wait as he lights up, blows out a dark rolling cloud and watches it drift toward the ceiling. When he says nothing I ask, "Do you want to tell me about it?"

His black, haunted eyes glare at me. "Look, you told me you believe in destiny. But how can a man recognize destiny when it knocks at his door? How can he be sure?"

"That's a tough one, Benjamin. But I still don't know what you're talking about."

"I'm talking about the person destined to be the next *primer mandatario*. You know how we elect presidents, don't you? The President in power can't succeed himself, but he does have the privilege of naming his successor. A couple of years before the end of his term he decides who he wants to take his place. Then he begins lining up the support of the army, the industrialists, the unions, the *campesinos*. With that kind of backing, the election of his man is assured."

I take a deep breath. "Are you that man, Benjamin?"

Savagely, he grinds out his cigarette. "If I want it."

My heart skips a beat. The doors of *Los Pinos* are cracking open! "And you're having trouble deciding?"

"Can't you guess why they want me for their candidate? Our party has a critical image problem. The opposition accuses the PRI of being hopelessly corrupt. But look at me:" He makes a face, "Benito Juarez in the flesh!"

I try to smile. "And who would dare accuse Benito Juarez of being corrupt!"

"It makes me want to throw up!"

"But Benito, I'd vote for you. You *are* incorruptible."

"Am I really? And especially if I accept their offer! They just want to use me, to saddle me with a system that's rotten to the core!"

"Then change the system!"

"Impossible!" Springing to his feet, he stands over me, fists clenched. "Don't you understand what I'm trying to tell you? After four years of watching my good friend in *Los Pinos* slowly lose his conscience, just like his predecessors, what right have I to think I'd be any different?"

It's time to be assertive! "Benjamin, sit down, please, let's try to analyze the problem."

He complies.

"Do you agree that Mexico's only hope is a leader who can cure the country's obsession with self-destruction?"

Nodding, he tells me, "Look at our history. We've never lacked dreamers. What nobler man ever lived than the priest José María Morelos y Pavón, the Father of our country? He had all the intelligence and integrity of your George Washington. In 1812 he led the Mexico in a revolution against Spain. But a few years after gaining our independence the country slipped into anarchy. Then there was Benito Juarez, my hero. What a let-down after he died: fifty years of dictatorship under Porfirio Diaz. In 1911 another bloody revolution toppled Diaz. When the Revolution was over, our leaders told us socialism was going to make Mexico a paradise. What a sick joke!"

"It almost looks like Mexico is under a curse, doesn't it?"

He retrieves the smoldering butt of his cigarette and puffs it back into life. "A curse?" he repeats thoughtfully. "Maybe that's the best word to describe our addiction to disaster."

I reach over and tap him on the knee. "But what if destiny has chosen you to undo this curse?"

He chuckles grimly. "I guess you're going to tell me how to do it?"

I feel my skin prickling. I want to get up, lay a hand on his shoulder and say, "Yes, Benjamin, I *can* tell you!" And lead him to faith in the all-powerful Son of God.

But is he ready? I'm afraid…so afraid my head is spinning.

"Absolutely not!"

"But it's our only hope!"

In the throne room of Quetzalcóatl Thanatos struts back and forth, arching his long red neck, his black wings raised as if for flight.

Quetzalcóatl uncoils to his full length, bringing his rancid mouth to within inches of the curved black beak of his visitor: "It is not for you to decide if there is hope. That is in the authority of the Prince."

"Is the Prince blind? Doesn't he know what's going on in Bethlehem? They're grooming the white horse!"

"What white horse?"

"The horse that will be spurred into battle against the Prince by the man that simpering Apostle John calls Faithful and True. Can't the Prince see what's happening?"

"Blasphemy!" Quetzalcóatl roars, writhing in anger, "Have you still not learned, Thanatos? That mouth of yours is going to be your doom."

"But I must speak! That's why I insisted on this audience with you, oh mighty Serpent. Unless we take drastic measures calamity is inevitable!"

There is no love lost between Quetzalcóatl and Thanotos. Eons ago when the Prince was choosing his sovereigns for the kingdoms of the world, Thanotos was a candidate for ruler over Mesoamerica. But wary of the rebellious spirit of the angel of death the Prince gave the nod to a demon he could count on to follow his orders without question. Even so, Thanatos has

*always had his sinister eyes on Quetzalcóatl's throne. He keeps telling him-
self that one day the Prince will realize he made a mistake.*

*He continues: "But why are we giving up? Why are you letting this
bogus Benito Juarez drift into the presidency without a fight?"*

*"Thanatos, I've given you the word from the Prince. Benjamin
Buenaventura's life is beyond our authority!"*

*"But he's wrong," Thanatos protests. "The Prince himself gave me the
right to impose the sentence of death in my province. Before his campaign is
over, this Buenaventura is bound to visit my territory. That will be my
chance. I want you to work up a diversion to occupy El's angels and I'll…"*

"Absolutely forbidden."

*"But why? Never before has the Prince abrogated my rights in my prov-
ince!"*

*"Why? Look, comrade, you know as well as I the great paradox of our
cosmic battle. Our Prince can only act within the permissive will of El. On
the day of the Celestial Schism they made a list of men who would be
untouchable in the generation of the Great Tribulation. The name of Benjamin Buenaventura is on that list."*

*"Then strike it off!" Thanatos emits a war cry so fierce he silences for a
moment the mournful wails wafting up from Genenna, and with one swift
flap of his powerful wings sweeps past the thousand steps leading up to the
Temple of Quetzalcóatl and slips through the gap in its apex.*

*A student from India, busy sketching the Pyramid of the Sun, is startled
by a huge black shadow that for an instant darkens the entire pyramid.
When he turns his eyes to the cloudless sky he sees nothing.*

CHAPTER 45

▼

THE UNTHINKABLE

"¡Viva Mexico!"

As one voice, fifty thousand people respond to the cry of the next President of Mexico: "¡Viva México!"

The headline in the newspaper they left outside of our hotel room door this morning was a bold affirmation: *Benito Buenaventura Will Be Elected President One Month From Today*. Here in Benjamin's home town the vote is sure to be unanimous.

This is his first trip to Oaxaca since the beginning of the presidential campaign. The downtown streets are criss-crossed with bright banners proclaiming "*Bienvenido,* Benito." Frenzied commentators saturate the radio and television. Each puts his own spin on the electrifying campaign of *Don* Benito.

Gabriela and I arrived here at the soccer stadium an hour before the program was to begin, but even so we had a hard time finding seats. Advertisements on the stadium walls for Corona Beer, Pepsi and *Llantas* Goodrich have been covered by streamers welcoming the native son.

"¡*Bravo!*" the crowd thunders.

He's been speaking for an hour, and still the people around us lean forward, waving their colorful red, green and white Mexican flags, shouting their "*bravos*" for the next President of the *patria*.

For such a small man, the volume of Benitos's voice is astonishing. I've read about the evangelist Whitefield addressing crowds of fifteen thousand before the invention of the sound system. But Benito outdoes Whitefield. If the loudspeakers should fail I suspect he could continue his speech without any of the fifty thousand gathered here missing a word.

But it's not only the stentorian voice that makes him a spellbinder. He reminds me of a well-known black preacher in Houston who always sets my pulse to pounding because of the way he hammers words together. Benito communicates the passion of deep conviction. At most political rallies *campesinos* and *obreros* are trucked in by the thousands to cheer bombastic speeches crafted to stir the emotions and put the mind to sleep. Not so with Benito! Listen to him: "I will not be elected by names on tombstones! And if you want to vote for another candidate I'm going to see to it you have that right. I've asked the United Nations to send as many observers as they can."

"*Bravo!*"

"Once I'm elected our legislature will no longer rubber-stamp what the President wishes.

The legislative and the judicial branches of our government will be free to act independently on matters important to the people."

"*Bravo!*"

"I promise you I will not enrich myself while in office. Independent auditors will make public my financial status when I begin my *sexenio* and when I leave. I will demand the same from all of my people."

"*Bravo!*"

The crowd loves him! But we worry about Benito. We've heard that many of the old guard have sworn they'll never allow him to take office.

Gabriela and I are determined to be optimistic. God has chosen Benito Buenaventura to bring in a new Mexico! So God will protect him. We took off three days to drive here over the mountains, just to be near him. Hearing him now, feeling the excitement of the crowd, it was worth it.

Three years have passed since the first time Benjamin Buenaventura sat in my office. I still have to pinch myself when I think of the things that have happened since then....

After he told me they'd tapped him for the presidency, I did a lot of praying. What had I gotten myself into? But when he returned for our next session I was surprised at how confident I felt. The night before, in our Bible study, Anastacia had given a word of prophecy: the Lord's hand was upon Isabel's husband. Benito Buenaventura would become a follower of His Son. Earlier in the day Gelda had called to tell me the same thing....

"Shall we take up where we left off last time?" I ask Benito.

"*De acuerdo.*"

"You told me you're at a crossroads: since you were a kid you've had a dream. Now the dream is at your fingertips, but you've lost heart. Is that right?"

"Yes! What's the use? There's just too much corruption at the top."

"But wasn't it that very corruption provoked your dream?"

He's silent for a long moment, his eyes almost closed. At last he says, "You're right."

"Then what's happened to your dream?"

"I guess I grew up."

"But you were so sure you had the answer."

He makes a face. "Marxism. It was a beautiful vision, but Fidel Castro is the only one left unwilling to admit man is too evil to make this world a paradise."

Breathing a prayer, I reach for my Bible:

There is none who does good, no, not one.
Their throat is an open tomb,
With their tongues they have practiced deceit.
The poison of asps is under their lips....
Their feet are swift to shed blood,
Destruction and misery are in their ways...."

He mutters. "A good description of the human animal! The Bible? I nod. He grunts. "Christianity. Another failed illusion!"

"I haven't heard you say it failed for your mother. She's the one who first gave you your dream, and she was sure she got it from her God."

His face turns an angry red. "Look, Andrés, would you deny that three centuries under the thumb of the Church was the worst thing that ever happened to Mexico?"

"Absolutely not."

He eyes me suspiciously. "So you agree that Marx was right? That religion is the opium of the masses?"

"Even if I do, what has that got to do with your mother's faith?"

He frowns at me, squinting his eyes. "What are you talking about?

"Marx was repulsed by religion married to politics. So are you. So am I. So was Christ. Don't tell me, Benjamin, that you're unaware Christ was murdered by religious people."

Benjamin's face is working, as if he suspects he's being led into a trap. "But you are a religious man."

"Please, Benjamin, don't lump me with the people who killed Jesus. And raped Mexico. I reject that kind of religion just as much as Jesus did. And as you do."

"But Jesus founded a religion."

"Did he? Not once did Jesus say he came to found a religion."

"Then why did he come?"

"To make men free. He told the religionists of his day, "If you abide in my word...you shall know the truth and the truth shall make you free."

He throws up his hands. "So! He invites men to come to him for freedom, but his people enslave entire nations."

"Not *his* people. Religious people."

Brow furrowed, Benjamin growls, "What does that mean?"

I pause. "I guess I'm saying I'd like for you to know the Jesus I know."

"Look, Andrés, when I came to you I knew you were a religious..." he shrugs "...a believer. So I expected that sooner or later you'd try to convince me. But believe me, I'm not interested."

(I should back off now. But I can't!)

"Benjamin, I'm going to ask you the question you asked me some time ago."

"What's that?"

"Do you believe in destiny?"

"I..." he runs nervous fingers through his thick black hair, "right now, I don't know. I did once, but I guess I'm about to decide I was wrong."

"And if you decide you were wrong, that means you've decided life has no purpose."

"I guess you're right." He tugs at his chin. "Who was the German philosopher that said life is nothing more than a question mark squeezed in between two nothings?"

I reach over and tap his knee. "Benito, you don't believe that garbage, you couldn't survive with such a philosophy. Tell me I'm wrong!"

He shrugs. "Of course you're not wrong! Why the devil do you think I came to you?"

I press on. "In your heart you know life has a purpose, and that there has to be a Someone who gives it purpose."

He lets out a long sigh. "Look, Andrés, I..."

I decide I've said enough for now. I say softly, "Our time is up. But I'd like to leave you an assignment."

He looks at his watch. "Well, I guess so, if you think it'll do any good."

"I think it will. I want you to read Jesus' words about the difference between religion and an authentic faith."

He shrugs. "I can't. I don't have a Bible."

"No problem, I'll lend you my New Testament. It'll fit in your inside coat pocket." I wink. "That way nobody will know."

For the first time he smiles.

I jot on the front page of the Testament: "Read Matthew, chapters 13 and 25, and John, chapters 3 and 8."

After he's gone I sit trying to evaluate our session. "You almost persuade me to become a Christian." How did Paul feel after his interview with King Agrippa? Did he ask himself if he should have pressed Agrippa harder? Paul never had another opportunity. Will I have another chance with Benjamin?

It's been a week since I've seen Benito Buenaventura. He sits down, takes the New Testament out of his inside coat pocket and drops it on the coffee table. "Doctór Kelly, I thank you for what you've done for Isabel and me."

(I'm uneasy. Why is he calling me "Doctór?") "Thanks, Benjamin, but we've barely begun."

He takes a crumpled sheet of paper from his pocket and spreads it on the table. "Last night I couldn't sleep, so I spent a while trying to sum up what I've learned since we began talking: "Number one, *I'm* the problem in our marriage. Until I overcome my obsessiveness I'm not fit to live with Isabel...or with any other woman, for that matter."

"Number two, my obsession is that I'm the only one who can solve Mexico's problems."

"Number three, I must decide what to do about that obsession, if I'm going to take control of my life."

Sounds like Benjamin has decided this will be his last meeting with me!

"Benjamin, you *are* obsessive, but that's not necessarily bad. To be obsessed with a fantasy is neurosis. To be obsessed with the truth is the key to greatness."

"I've come to a decision."

(uh—oh!) "And…?"

"I *am* going to take control of my life. I'm going to drop out of politics, move back to Oaxaca with my family and take up the practice of law again."

"And what about this destiny you've talked about?"

"Andrés, you're a therapist. Isn't it your job to help me understand that a man of forty has no business letting himself fall the victim to the foolish dreams of his adolescence?

I pick up the New Testament. "I see you did read this book."

"What do you mean?" He reaches for a cigarette. (By now I've learned that when Benjamin is unsure of himself he lights up.)

"You read the words of Jesus and they shook you. You realized the only way you can find the courage to follow your destiny is to seek Christ's help. But you're not ready for that."

Rising, he walks to the window, the unlit cigarette still in his hand. His back to me, he grumbles, "Andrés, there you go again, getting inside my head."

"So what turned you off? I thought you'd like Jesus' warning about who's going to heaven and who's going to hell."

He takes out his lighter, gets his cigarette going, and blows a smoke screen between us. "*Hombre*, what an eye-opener! Our priests say if you don't belong to the church you're going to hell. Your Jesus says people who refuse to help the hungry, the naked, the ill, the prisoners are the ones going to hell. You're right, I liked that!"

"And what about his 'woes' against the religious leaders?"

He chuckles. "I read it so many times, I memorized it: 'Woe to you scribes and Pharisees, hypocrites! For you devour widows' houses, and for a pretense make long prayers…. Blind guides who strain out a gnat and swallow a camel…you cleanse the outside of the cup and dish but inside they are full of extortion and self-indulgence.' You're right, I like it!"

"So do you understand now why I said Jesus didn't come to start a new religion?"

He strides over to the table, crushes out his cigarette and, as if someone has pushed him, falls into a chair. "But what he said to Nicodemus: 'you must be born again.' That's ridiculous!"

I say with conviction: "You're right, Benjamin, it *is* ridiculous. Beyond human understanding. That was Nicodemus' complaint, too."

He growls, "Then what makes you think I'd want to follow a person who spouts such foolishness?"

"Because you believe life has purpose, Benjamin. And because you know by now you can never fulfill that purpose alone. Paul was like you, he believed in destiny. So he chose Jesus. I hope you'll follow his example, not the example of that weak Nicodemus."

He grunts. "So you want me to follow the example of Paul. Look what happened to Paul: he got his head chopped off!"

I'm getting angry. God has chosen this man just as surely as he chose Saul of Tarsus. And he's about to turn away! I get up from my seat, go over to him and place my hands on his shoulders. Looking him in the eye I say, "All right, Benjamin, go on back to Oaxaca and start your practice. I'm sure you'll get rich. But one day you'll hate yourself for not having the guts to follow your destiny!"

He pushes away my hands and stands to his feet. Checking his watch, he says quietly, "Doctór, I regret having to leave early, but I have another engagement. I'll be in touch."

Without shaking my hand he turns and stalks out. Something tells me I'll never see him again in this office. I whisper a prayer, "Oh Lord, go with him. Don't turn him loose!"

Down below Benjamin has completed his speech, and now a crowd has gathered before the platform. Isabel stands beside him, smiling.

After every speech he invites people to come forward for dialogue. He introduced this innovation a few months ago, and Gabriela and I don't like it. It's as an open door to anybody who might want to harm him.

We remain in our seats, listening, praying.

I'm remembering the day I picked up my phone and heard the excited voice of Carlos: "Andrés, can I come over? I've got something to tell you that will blow you away!"

"Can't you tell me over the phone?"

"It's too important. And besides, I want to see your face."

"Right now I have a patient waiting, but I'll expect you in exactly fifty minutes." I hang up, get on the interphone and tell Rebeca to cancel my following appointment....

I greet Carlos with an abrazo. He has turned out to be a brilliant businessman. The consulting firm he founded four years ago has branches now in five cities. More important, Carlos has become my strong right arm. I still teach the Tuesday night Bible study, but he preaches Sundays. He's also the Administrator of a congregation that has grown to more than a thousand.

Releasing me from the *abrazo* he says, "Guess who I spent two hours with this morning?"

"I have no idea. Who?"

"Benjamin Buenaventura."

"No!" Three months have passed since Benito walked out of my office, and I haven't heard a word from him. How in the world—"

"Remember my plans for an *Asociación de Asistencia Privada?*"

"Of course. Since you told us about your project for helping needy families Gabriela and I have been praying for it every day."

"You may recall I mentioned these associations must be approved by a committee of the Federal Government. I had a meeting with the committee this morning."

"Don't tell me Buenaventura is a member of the committee!"

"No, but he drops in on their meetings occasionally. As Secretary of Commerce he's been after Mexican industry to take more interest in the needs of the poor. He's the one that persuaded Congress to pass laws for chartering these *Asociaciones.*"

"And he was there this morning when you presented your petition?"

Carlos smiles. "Yes. What do you think, was it a coincidence? He dropped in after the proceedings had begun. I should have recognized him, but I was too absorbed in my presentation."

"And how did it go?"

"Pretty rough at first. Few people in the business world are interested in sharing their profits with the less fortunate. I could see right away the committee suspected I planned to use the association as a ploy to avoid taxes.

"Were you able to convince them they were wrong?"

"I'd thought a lot about it and decided I was going to be completely open about the reason I'm doing it."

"What did you tell them?"

"That I wanted to set up an *Asociación de Asistencia Privada* because I'm a follower of Jesus Christ."

"Wow!" I shake my head. "What did they say?"

"As soon as I got the words out of my mouth the Chairman closed his folder and pushed back his chair. He reminded me the government prohibits religions from mixing in this type of organization, and scolded me for wasting their time."

"I can guess what you said next."

"I told him religion would have no participation in my Association. The guy looked at me like I was an idiot: 'But you just told us it would!'"

I kept trying to get them to understand the distinction between a religious organization and an individual motivated by Christian principles.

"After ten minutes or so one of the men said, his face very red, '*Don* Carlos I don't know if you're devious or just dense. The only way you'll get a charter is by guaranteeing your association will have nothing to do with your religion.'

"That's when Benito Buenaventura bellowed, in that incredible pipe organ voice, "Gentlemen, this man is not dense, you are! Can't you understand the difference between a personal faith and belonging to a religion?"

I jump to my feet and give him a high-five. "So Benjamin did believe me after all!"

"Just wait, Andrés, and you'll see how much he believed you. He came over to the table and stood behind me with a hand on my shoulder. And he gave them a lecture on the difference between belonging to a religion and having a personal commitment to Jesus of Nazareth. He quoted Jesus' words about helping the hungry, the ill, people in prison, and his condemnation of the religious hierarchy of his day for oppressing the poor."

"Incredible! It must have set them back on their heels!"

"I thought their eyes would pop out of their heads. He finished saying something like this: 'Señores, you may not agree with *Don* Carlos about his faith. I'm not sure I do. But don't penalize this man for taking seriously the words of Jesus Christ. All through our country's history the poor and ignorant have been victimized in the name of religion. We've had precious few men who, because of their faith, feel compelled to help people in need."

"Did he change their minds?"

"They sat there gaping for a moment. Then an attractive young woman stood up and stuck out her hand. 'Carlos, you must forgive us for being skeptical. I guess we haven't met a man like you before.'

"She moved my application be approved...and there wasn't a dissenting vote."

"*Magnífico!*" I jump up and give Carlos another *abrazo*.

Grinning, he gently pushes me away. "Wait a minute, I haven't gotten to the best part yet!

"By this time I knew who our visitor was. As the members of the committee drifted away one by one I took my time gathering up my papers. Buenaventura had gone back to his chair and was sitting there, fidgeting. I picked up my attaché case, walked over to him and held out my hand.

"Carlos,' he said, 'if you have a minute I'd like to talk with you.'

"Of course. Delighted!" Pulling up a chair I sat facing him. I was surprised when he reached inside his coat and pulled out a New Testament.

"'At the recommendation of a man I respect I've been reading the Bible. The teachings of Jesus fascinate me. I've been imagining what would happen to the *patria* if people would take them to heart.'

"Reaching down, he opened his brief case, removed a book and dropped it into my lap. 'Two days ago, browsing through a book store I came upon this biography of Mahatma Ghandi. What a man! Practically alone he changed the history of his country. Late last night I was trying to finish the book when I came upon a quote that startled me. Ghandi wrote: 'Jesus Christ was the greatest teacher that ever lived. I would have become a Christian long ago…if ever I had met one!'

"'Shaken, I lay down the book. I heard myself saying, 'I too would become a Christian…if I ever met a man who truly followed Jesus' teachings.'"

Carlos stops, choking out the words, "Then, Andrés, Benito just sat staring at me for a long time, like he was trying to get up the courage to say something. I waited, wondering what was going to happen. Finally, he broke the silence: 'This morning, Carlos, I have met the man Ghandi was looking for. Will you tell me how to become a follower of Jesus Christ?'"

We've agreed with Benjamin it wouldn't be wise for him to attend our church. Benito and Carlos meet each Monday morning in Carlos' office for Bible study and prayer.

Gabriela takes my arm. "Andee, we'd better start down. Looks like Benito has finished his dialogue with the people."

Dozens of the curious have pushed up on the platform and are crowding around the candidate. Every time I see this happening I get nervous. Benjamin has so many enemies! I don't know how many people know about his conversion, but he's got the entire country country buzzing about his urgent call for a moral and ethical renewal, and the old guard is outraged.

"Pow! pow! pow! pow!

A loud scream pierces the sudden stillness in the stadium.

Somebody has set off a string of firecrackers!

.... Oh no, those weren't firecrackers, they were gun shots! People are milling about, pushing and shoving and yelling.

Just below us an Indian woman in native dress, her copper face frozen in a mask of horror. Cries out:

"*Dios mío, Dios mío*, they killed *Don* Benito!"

Groaning. I grab Gabriela's arm and we start downstairs, toward the platform. Halfway down we halt, afraid of being crushed by the crowd I hear just overhead, like the echo of a distant thunder, a coursed, vulgar chuckle.

I look up...*I* see nothing.

A thick black feather, the width of my palm, flutters down and lands at my feet.

CHAPTER 46

▼

ECLIPSE FOR QUETZALCÓATL

"Assasin! Down with the PRI!"

From his balcony overlooking the Zocalo President Justo Gonzales is delivering a eulogy.

Or trying to.

The TV newsman puts at half a million the crowd gathered for Benito Buenaventura's memorial service. Of these, only a handful accept the official version of a lone assassin. The rest are convinced that Benito was murdered by the old guard of his own party. He was much too radical, their jobs were in danger, so they acted to save themselves....

The President continues: "*Don* Benito was my dearest friend, God's gift to the *Patria*, a bright star lighting the pathway to a new future. All of his *compatriotas* in the government are crushed by this cruel deed of a heartless assassin. We will not rest until..."

His words are drowned out by an ear-splitting chorus of shrill whistles, the Mexican version of a Bronx cheer.

The President pauses, his face pale, and takes a step backward. Below, a company of soldiers ringing the balcony lower their rifles to "ready".

Gabriela and I are watching the ceremony from our living room, seated together on the sofa, hands tightly clasped. We had no desire to go to the Zocalo today, it's much too dangerous.

Anyway, yesterday we attended a much more meaningful ceremony, a private service in a small funeral chapel. Only the family and a few close friends were invited. At the family's insistence a priest said mass. Then Carlos gave a brief meditation and prayed. Afterward they took the body away to be cremated....

That night the phone rings as we're sipping our after-dinner coffee. "You know who that is," Gabriela says.

"Margaret again!".

I go into the living room, pick up the receiver and settle into an easy chair. Since the assassination Margaret has called every day insisting Gabriela and I come spend a while with them. She's worried. The Houston Chronicle is headlining rumors of an eminent revolution. The stock market dropped 15% the day after the assassination and since then has crashed another 30%.

Foreign investment that had been pouring into the country is being withdrawn. The big companies are laying off people by the thousands. Banks are calling in loans on houses and automobiles.

We talk for a while, then I say, "Thanks for calling, Darling, we're thinking about it." I cradle the phone.

"Andee, if you want go, I'll go with you." Gabriela is kneeling beside my chair, her arms around me, her head on my shoulder.

"Why did God let it happen?" I say dumbly. I don't know why I keep asking that question. I realize know there's no answer.

Gabriela kisses my cheek. "*Mi Amor*, you've got to stop torturing yourself, you're going to make yourself sick!"

This anguish of soul, it frightens me! I was so sure: the meshing of my destiny with Benito Buenaventura's was the last piece of a curious jigsaw puzzle that began with Mary's tragic accident.

I shiver. Quetzalcóatl has won after all!

I haven't shared with Gabriela the nightmare that jolted me awake just before dawn. Quetzalcóatl slipped into our bedroom, wound his scaly tail around my body and brought his face inches from my own. His fiery tongue was lashing my cheeks, his poisonous breath sickening me. I sat up suddenly, startled by sound of his mocking laughter.

I pull her sweet face to mine and kiss her warm lips. "Sweetheart, please don't worry about me. As long as I have you I won't go crazy. But I'm so confused."

I'm talking to her in Spanish. I've learned I need to communicate in her native tongue when I want attain that special intimacy of soul communing with soul. Gabriela's quite fluent in English, but when she prays, or when she expresses deep feeling, she always does it in her birth language.

Cradling her, I look out over the balcony of our penthouse, upon the dark, restless metropolis I've come to love. In the last months, seeing the miracle of Benjamin's acceptance by the people, knowing the integrity of his heart, the brilliance of his mind, his incredible energy and his commitment to Christ, I had persuaded myself his *sexenio* would usher in a golden age for this troubled country I now call my own.

I groan: "It doesn't make sense. Before Benito was born, God had already chose him to lead his country. God brought me to Mexico to introduce Benito to Christ. He even shaped Benito in the image of the statesman Mexicans most honor, so they'd fall in love with him and follow him.

"And now God's man is dead. God's enemies have won." I rest my cheek against hers. "This is insane!" I whisper hoarsely, "utterly insane!"

She kisses me behind the ear. "Dear, some day we'll know the answer. Until then we must accept God's inscrutable wisdom." Taking my face in her hands, her face very close to mine, she whispers, "Andee, my love, we're not supposed to understand the ways of God. But one thing we know: God brought us together, you and I, to love each other as long as we live. Isn't that enough?"

Her lips caress my mouth, my eyes, my throat. I know that in a moment I'll take her into my arms, and carry her to our bed. But I feel guilty, as if I've lost the right to celebrate our love.

It had all come together! I'd discovered why I was born. Gabriela, Mexico, Benito Buenaventura and Andrew Kelly were all a part of an exquisite pattern woven by God's own hand. Now the pattern has been shattered.

I wrap myself in my wife's warm body, trying to drive out the chill that has invaded the marrow of my bones. I'm tormented by the most awful fear possible: that maybe, after all, God is not in control....

"Fool! Maniac! Usurper!"

In the darkness of their stone hut on Popocatépetl, a thousand feet below the snow line, Don Crisóstomo and his family hear the words as a rumble of thunder. How could they know they've been awakened by the angry voice of The Prince of This World?

"But Master, I warned Thanotos, I forbade him!" On the snow-crowned peak of the dark mountain, a blinding flash of lightening, a split-second million-watt spotlight, illumines a stark drama: the Feathered Serpent is lying prone at the feet of his Lord. By his side, in snow piled high at the slippery edge of the volcano's menacing depths, Thanotos huddles like an ailing vulture, shivering, his black wings drooping.

Millenniums have passed since the last time Quetzalcóatl was face to face with his Master. It has not been necessary. Always their communication has been instantaneous, from awful brain to awful brain. Not being omnipotent, The Prince has preferred to remain in that mysterious abode he claimed when El cast him out of heaven, plotting the final destruction of the Lamb and his kingdom, basking in the adulation of his subservient host of demons. Quetzalcóatl has always felt like an extension of his Lord, a cell of his body. Their communication has never been in words. Always Quetzalcóatl has been instantly, instinctively aware of the intentions of the potentate to whom he has dedicated his life, and has always obeyed, nurtured by his Lord's approval.

But now, the nearness of his Lord terrifies him.

He dares not look at Lucifer, he only senses that awful presence, the bizarre blend of splendid beauty and stomach-turning ugliness that constitutes this son of the morning who dared to defy Elohim. Lightening flashes constantly, as if nature herself were struggling to identify, to quantify this one who said "I will exalt my throne above the stars of heaven."

Thanotos says nothing. What can he say? At his side sprawls the mighty angel that The Prince placed over him That Day. For an instant he relishes the fall from favor of the being who has humiliated him for so long. Then he shudders, remembering that his own fate is joined to that of his overlord.

But he must speak! With great effort he raises his head, weakly shakes wings laden with the snow of the frigid mountaintop and croaks, "Oh my Lord, have mercy. I did it for you. Benito Buenaventura was about to destroy the kingdom that you and your humble servants had labored for millenniums to establish!"

The face of the Prince is a dreadful, consuming fire. The mountain trembles at the thunder of his voice: "You were informed that Benito Buenaventura was exempt from the sentence of death. Who authorized emergency measures to save my kingdom? Do you understand, ingrate, that you have upset the equilibrium of powers established here on earth the day of our glorious revolution?"

"Forgive me, Oh, Lord, I did it out of passion for your Majesty's Kingdom!"

"You idiot! You have placed my Kingdom in eminent danger. In my battle with El for control of the earth we both fight to win, but we battle according to the rules established at the beginning. I've been granted the right to place in bondage the defective beings created in his image, as many

as I can convince them to trust me. On the other hand, they have the right to break that bondage by invoking the blood of the Lamb.

"Since Eden El has trumpeted the eventual triumph of the Lamb. I have challenged him on every hand, and have won more battles than I've lost, thanks to the weakness of that defective being created in his image. But now I must pay the penalty for your transgression of the rules."

Painfully, Quetzalcóatl raises his head and asks, already intuiting the answer: "And what is that penalty, Oh Majesty?"

"You both will be sent away at once to Gehenna, to await with the others already there the Battle of Armageddon."

The Feathered Serpent moans, "But what of my territory, oh Master?"

"Your people will do the best they can without your direction."

"But oh, my Lord, there will be anarchy!"

"Enough of this!" The Prince raises his arms and lightening streaks from his fingertips, ripping open the rocky seal of the volcano. "Let it be done!"

At the thunder of his voice ten thousand demons, whirling and gibbering like bats gone mad churn up from the guts of Popo. Buzzing around Thanatos and the Feathered serpent, they wrap them in golden chains as fine as cobwebs, around and around, around and around, until all that can be seen are the beady, hateful eyes of Thanatos and the black flicking tongue of Quetzalcóatl.

"Take them below!" The Prince roars, and ten thousand demons enfold the felons in their black wings and bear them downward, screaming now.

Don Crisóstomo and his family, feeling the rumbling of the mountain, rush from their hut. "Look!" cries the wife, pointing to the peak. Fire is gushing from the mouth of the volcano. Suddenly a bright tongue of flame breaks away and flashes upward like a soaring comet, emitting a shrill cry. In response, the flame flowing from Popo writhes like a giant red serpent, and ten thousand voices, some tenor, some bass, some soprano, some alto, echo the cry of the soaring comet. The music is deafening, ominous, terrifying.

...Hours later, side by side on their petites, Crisóstomo and his woman whisper together, still trying to decide what to make of the dreadful scene they have witnessed tonight. At last he says, "In two hours the sun rises and I must go to the milpa. Let's get some sleep, woman."

She gloats, "I'm glad this is market day. I can't wait to tell the women what we saw and heard."

Don Crisóstomo pushes himself up on one elbow, and his big hooked nose touching the nose of his wife, mutters sternly, "Don't you dare tell them, they'll say we've lost our minds!"

EPILOGUE

▼

"This is crazy, *mi amor*, we should be at home with the doors locked and the windows shut tight!"

I turn and grin at her. "You're absolutely right, Gabriela, shall we turn around?"

Moving closer to me, she hugs my arm and leans over to bite my ear. "Don't you dare! This is a day to celebrate! As long as the windshield wipers work we'll make it."

At 12:47 this afternoon the city was rocked by a 5.9 earth tremor. Thirty seconds later the ground quivered again, this time to the rumble of a distant explosion. Soon, smoke and fire billowed up from Popotactéptl, fifty miles away. The sooty ashes began falling an hour later.

At eight o'clock they're still falling, coating the streets, the trees, the buildings. There's not much traffic. People are afraid, I guess. The seismologists are warning that the ashes being borne in from our millenniums-old volcano could turn at any moment into flaming cinders capable of converting the city into a roaring inferno.

So I suppose everyone's at home glued to their televisions, not only worrying about the ashes, but following that strange bright cloud Popo belched out seven hours ago. They tells us it's traveling eastward at the speed of sound. When we left the house it was far out over the Atlantic.

But as for my wife and me, we have other things on our minds....

"*Feliz aniversario!*"

Feliz aniversario!" Our glasses clink and my love and I smile across the tiny candle-lit table....

The years have been kind to Gabriela. But the laugh lines at the corners of her eyes are a bit deeper now and there's a hint of gray in her dark hair. As usual she's dressed in understated elegance: white wool, a string of pears at her throat and the turquoise ear rings I bought for her on our last trip to London.

...And no, it's not my imagination! She's lovelier than the first time she sat across from me at this table so long ago.

Last night when we sat down to dinner I found a faded scrap of paper by my plate.

"What's this?" I asked, holding it up for examination.

"A surprise, *mi amor*. It's something I ran across a few weeks ago. I decided to wait and serve it for dinner on the eve of our anniversary." Gabriela giggles.

Hm-m-m. Looks like...is it a check from a restaurant?"

"Yes, but from *what* restaurant?"

"*El Tab*...Oh, I know, *El Tablillo!*"

"That's right. And what's the date?"

"Let's see, it's so faded I can barely make it out." My mouth fell open. "Don't tell me!"

"Yes, it's the check from the very first time we ate there. Remember? I'd just picked you up at the airport and..."

"...and I was already in love. Of course I knew love at first sight was a ridiculous idea. Besides," I reached for her hand, "a man of flesh and blood dares not fall in love with an angel! Say, where did you find this?"

There are tears in her eyes. "Rummaging around in my old armoire. As soon as I saw it I remembered what had happened. That night in my bedroom, after our meal in *El Tablillo,* I took the check out of my purse and threw it in the waste basket. Then, on impulse, I retrieved it and placed it in the top drawer of my beloved armoire." Smiling, she squeezes my hand: "You know, it was love at first sight for me too!"

So tonight we're back at *El Tablillo*, celebrating the anniversary of a miracle.

"You know, my darling," she sets down her glass and reaches out to touch my cheek, "God sent you to me, to fill that horrid void in my heart."

I kiss her hand. "And dumb me! I tried to deny my heart and simply treat you as a patient."

"That was the beginning of two and a half bittersweet years, wasn't it?"

"Yes. They were sweet because, however much we tried to deny it, we both knew God had brought us together."

Her lips tighten. "But they were bitter because our love seemed to be under a curse."

And it was! Satan was determined to keep us apart."

She smiles. "But God's blessing turned out to be more powerful than Satan's curse!"

"*Sus ensaladas, César Señores.*" The smiling waiter places our salads before us.

Our hands clasped, I pray: "Lord, thank you. It was not good for me to be alone, so you brought this beautiful person into my life. Truly, she is now bone of my bones and flesh of my flesh.".

And Gabriela prays: "Yes, Lord, thank you for this good man you gave me! You were so patient with me. And now you have truly made us one flesh!"

"Gabi," I say, reaching for my fork, "speaking of blessing and cursing, I'm going to share something with you. I've been thinking about it a lot lately. I hope you won't think I'm losing my mind."

She blinks at me. "Try me!"

"The death of Benjamin Buenaventura. Could it have been, somehow, an atonement for Mexico's past?"

Taking a bite of her salad, she says thoughtfully. "I...I'm not sure I understand what you're saying. Are you talking about the things that have happened since Benito's death?"

"Yes. Isn't it ironic? The people who killed Benito wanted to destroy his dreams. But instead, they seem to have opened the door for his dreams to be fulfilled!"

"The death of Benito, turned out to be the birth of a new Mexico." I whisper, unwilling that anyone else should hear, "Kind of like what happened when they killed Jesus, don't you think?"

"Wow!" Gabriela puts down her fork, her eyes big. "I'm remembering the sermon Carlos preached several Sundays ago. About Peter's Sermon at Pentecost." Reaching into her purse, she pulls out a little New Testament.... "Here it is: 'Jesus of Nazareth, a man attested by God to you...you have taken by lawless hands, have crucified, and put to death; whom God has raised up....'"

Closing the Testament, she leans over the table and takes both my hands. "I think you're right. It's happened again! God's enemies thought they had rid the world of God's chosen messenger. But God fooled them: he raised Benito from the dead!"

"And guess what? God not only raised Benito, it looks like he buried somebody!"

"Quetzalcóatl!" Now it's Gabriela that whispers.

"Since Benito's death, not a word from him!"

"*Mi amor*, what do you think happened? Did something take place in the heavenlies that we know nothing about?"

"I'm sure of it! What's been happening here on earth is proof of it." I take my last bite of salad. "The curse on Mexico seems to have been lifted. Record crops, the lowest rate of unemployment in decades, crime is down...."

"And the rest of the world is taking notice. It was great to see our President addressing the U. S. Congress last week, wasn't it?" Gabriela takes a sip of her wine. "And the topic they assigned him: what can the United States learn from Mexico's remarkable recovery?"

"And the way people are turning to Christ!" I gulp down the rest of my Coke. "Look what's happening to our Sunday morning service! We had to move it to the largest convention hall at the María Isabel Sheraton!"

"And we still turn folks away." Giggling like a five-year-old Gabriela hits my hand with a high-five. "God *is* pouring out his blessings on *mi querido Mexico*! Isn't it strange? Before, everything Mexico did seemed to come out bad. Now it's just the opposite!"

The smiling waiter places our steaks before us. "*Felicidades Señores!*"

Like two lovers surprised in their own private world, we jump and look up at him.

"Pardon me, *Señores*, but I can see you're very happy!"

"It's our anniversary," I tell him.

He takes a bottle of champagne from his cart and sets it on the table. "That's what the manager thought. Compliments of the house!"

"And our compliments to the manager," I say, taking a bite of my steak, "the food's delicious."

We eat in contented silence for a few minutes. Then, patting her lips with her napkin, Gabriela says, "You know, when Benito died it seemed like the end of the world. Then, slowly, things began to change. And who would have thought it would be because of Martin Brambilla!"

"I still remember the first time I saw Brambilla on T.V. The PRI was presenting him as their replacement for Benito."

Replacement? Imagine a fox trying to take the place of a lion! Tall, thin, scholarly. Horn-rimmed glasses. He read from a manuscript in a dry, professorial voice. His promise to fulfill Benito's pledge of a new Mexico sounded ridiculous.

"You know," Gabriela says, finishing off her baked potato, "his election was a fluke. The other parties had been so sure they didn't stand a chance against Benito Buenaventura, they'd fielded even less promising candidates."

"And what about that awful scandal after he took office! Just like Benito had warned me, it turned out that his boss, Justo Gonzalez, had stolen more money than any other President in history."

…The day after Brambilla's inauguration a comic opera played out on television. Half a dozen big black Lincolns crammed with *policia judicial* speeding down the airport runway trying to intercept the ex-President's private jet before it took off, and the plane zooming into the air a dozen yards ahead of the police.

Gabriela takes a last bite of her steak. "Remember? Within a week after Justo Gonzales' escape to Madrid the panic began."

"How could I forget! We dreaded turning on the news. First the market crash. Then a drastic devaluation of the peso. The price of everything doubled and tripled. Factories began shutting down and soon people were selling off their furniture to buy food to put on the table."

"I'll never forget look on Isabel's face that night she showed up at our door. With my backing she had opened a branch of *Modas Mancini* in Lomas de Chapultepec. Invested most of her insurance money. But now she was going to have to close the store. The few people who still had money were no longer interested in expensive fashions."

"For the next three years even you struggled to keep your store open."

Smiling, Gabriela claps her hands. "Three cheers for your stubborn little daughter Victoria! The profits from her store in the Woodlands kept my business here in Mexico afloat during those impossible years."

"I confess my error, *mi amor*. I was wrong to think Victoria couldn't pull it off. The store has turned out to be a gold mine."

When the waiter arrives with our cheesecake we're talking about how Mexico closed out the Twentieth Century and moved into the new millennium:

Gradually, almost imperceptibly, the mood of the country began to change. Though Martin Brambilla wasn't much of a politician, people soon learned he was a man of intelligence and integrity. After he'd paid off the crushing foreign debt capital began flowing back into the country. The President allowed the PAN Party to elect a governor in the state of Chihuahua and the PRD a mayor for Mexico City.

"I'll never forget the night Brambilla gave his first "State of the Union" address, one year after his inauguration." Gabriela says, smiling. "That was the night he revealed the reason he was different. What a sensation!"

"As Brambilla spoke, I could feel the depression that had clung to me for over a year melting away. At last I understood!"

"We sat there with our mouths agape when he told us what happened six months before Benito was assassinated. One night Benito called in Martin, his school chum, and bared his heart. About how he had given his life to God. About his premonition of an early death."

Gabriela lays down her fork, shaking her head in wonder. "My heart stopped for a moment when Brambilla put aside his script, took off his horn-rimmed glasses, and looking straight into the camera, said 'When I was elected your President, I knew I had an obligation to my dear friend Martin...and to his God, to do for this country what Martin would have done."

They were quiet for a long moment, remembering.

"Know what," I say, "I knew the economy had turned around the night you came home and couldn't eat dinner, you were so excited by the visit of a group of French investors."

Laughing, Gabriela finishes off her dessert. "It took them all afternoon to convince me they were truly interested in financing the reopening of our Modas Mancini store in Lomas de *Chapultepec*."

"And now Isabel is the world's happiest businesswoman."

Gabriela's eyes are shining. "After me. Oh, Andrés, I'm so thankful for the happiness you brought me!"

I reach for her hand. "And what about me? Loved by the most fantastic woman in the world! And you know, I'm thankful for something else: the love I feel for your country. Like Ruth said, 'your people have become my people.'"

Gabriela blinks back tears. "And your God has become my God!"

Later, when we start for home in Gabriela's car, I activate the windshield washers. We didn't recognize it when the valet brought it around. The charcoal blue Cadillac was glistening when we took it out of the garage a three hours ago, but now it's filthy. Popo is still raining ashes.

Gabriela calls to me from the bathroom: "Please, Andee, could you mute the TV?"

Lying in bed, I press the "mute" button on the remote control. "Sorry, I just want to see the latest on Popo...oh, oh! They're talking about that crazy cloud!" I hit the mute again to bring back the sound:

"Damas y Caballeros, here it is, a baffling phenomenon that has meteorologists worldwide shaking their heads. When Popo blew at noon today it spewed great balls of flame into the air. Every fire station in Mexico City was put on alert. Until now, *gracias a Dios*, we've been spared. Instead...well, see for yourself: this was the scene in Veracruz at 3:32 this afternoon:

The camera is focused on the beach, where the surf glows weirdly, as if the fires of hell had broken through to earth. Then the camera pans the sky, fixing on a thick, glowing cloud. It flows swiftly, majestically eastward.

The announcer continues: "Scientists estimate this celestial river of red-hot ash to be ten kilometers wide and twenty-five long!

"Oh, I just got word! We're going to hear from our correspondent live in Rome."

"Gabi! Come quick!"

She rushes in and flops on the bed. "*Dios mío!*"

From St. Peter's the camera is recording the passage of the same immense, glowing cloud that illumined Veracruz earlier in the day. It seems to slow over the Vatican, painting the dome of the great cathedral a ghastly red.

The announcer continues: "Observation planes have been following this strange cloud since it blew out of Popo twelve hours ago. It has been moving steadily eastward at jet speed, boiling like a cauldron, constantly changing form, not dissipated by the prevailing winds, as was expected. The pilots that took the risk of flying close to the cloud were startled by a blackout of their guidance systems."

He pauses. "And ladies and gentleman, there's something else." He looks at the co-anchor seated beside him, as if asking permission to continue. The man shrugs, wiping the perspiration from his brow with a rumpled white handkerchief.

"Well, here it is, you decide for yourself: the pilots report receiving on their radios the sounds of...*honest this is how they described it*: a shrill, discordant chorus of wails and shrieks!"

The camera pans the studio. The stunning blonde who will give the weather report after the next commercial stands immobile beside her map, biting her lip. A tear trickles down her cheek, mussing her mascara. Off-camera, an engineer, obviously appalled at the announcer's breach of common sense, buries his face in his hands.

After a long pause the co-anchor asks: "Tell us, Rodrigo, where is this...this ridiculous cloud headed?"

"Right now it seems dead on course for Israel."

"Please, Andee, enough of that!" Crawling closer to me, Gabriela takes the remote from my hand. Turning off the TV, she snuggles close.

I hug her to my chest and click the T.V. back on. "Well, my love, what do you..."

She puts a sweet-smelling hand over my mouth. "Andee, don't you dare ask me what I think! We had such a wonderful dinner, I'm not going to let you spoil it with the ugly problems of this world...." She clicks off the T.V. again.

"Andee, wakeup!"

Gabriela is leaning over her husband, shaking him by the shoulders.

Groaning, he pushes himself on one elbow. "Woman," he grumbles, "It's two A.M. What's the matter?"

"Did you hear it, Andee, did you hear it?"

"Hear what? He turns on the bedside lamp. Gabriel's hands are covering her mouth, her eyes huge. Andrew is not sure if she's giggling or sobbing.

"That noise! It woke me up! It sounded like..."

Suddenly, the earsplitting blast of a trumpet, so loud the bedside lamp vibrates.

Andrew tumbles out of bed and onto the floor, pulling Gabriela with him, and another blast pierces the air, so shrill he wants to stop his ears, yet so glorious he wants to find the trumpeter, embrace him and shout hosannas!

Gabriela is on her knees, hands clasped, eyes raised to heaven.

Andrew grabs her hand. "The balcony! Let's go to him! Let's..."

Now Gabriela is on her feet, pulling Andrew. "Yes, yes! Run, mi amor, run."

Just as Andrew throws open the sliding glass door the trumpet peals again. The sound comes from light years away, yet so close it embraces them, suffuses their minds, their souls, their trembling bodies.

From thirty stories up they can see lights flickering on all over the city, like fireflies suddenly awaking. So! Others have heard the sound of the trumpet! In the street below a police car roars to life and pulls away from the curb, burning rubber, siren screaming.

All at once a brilliant flash arcs from east to west, blinding them. In the afterglow they watch speechless as the sky becomes an enormous Christmas tree adorned with ten thousand points of light drawing closer, ever closer, borne on waves of celestial music, part symphony, part halleluya chorus.

Gabriela and Andrew are clinging together, cheeks touching, tears flowing like rain. Andrew can feel the beating of his love's heart in ecstatic harmony with his own.

"The lights!" she whispers, "the beautiful lights! They look like...can it be?..."

Two of the lights glide toward them...now they can see: Yes! Glory to God! Angels!

Wrapped suddenly in gossamer wings Andrew and his love are lifted upward...upward...upward...

0-595-26966-4